Praise for
THE JER1CH0 DECEPT10N

"*The Jericho Deception* spins out a brilliant premise into a ripping good novel, brimming with excitement, imagination, vivid settings, and personable characters"
—Douglas Preston, #1 Bestselling Author of *The Monster of Florence*

"This one pushes the envelope to the edge and beyond, captivating with plausibility and imagination. A gritty thriller."
—Steve Berry, *NYT* Bestselling Author of *The King's Deception*

"Chock full of fascinating insider detail, *The Jericho Deception* by Jeffrey Small is a thrilling roller-coaster ride into the beauty and darkness of the human mind. With muscular prose and a high quotient of believability, you'll be riveted watching scientists, politicians, and spies vie for control of the Logos machine. Send out for food. You won't want to stop reading."
—Gayle Lynds, *NYT* bestselling author of *The Book of Spies*

"A blisteringly original, wondrously structured descent into a literal and figurative hell. Jeffrey Small's stellar tale of murder, treachery and international daring-do breathes new life into the moribund religious thriller genre as it blends science seamlessly with superstition. A high-tech *Da Vinci Code* on steroids, only better written."
—Jon Land, bestselling author of *Pandora's Temple*

THE JER1CHO DECEPT1ON

Also by Jeffrey Small:

The Breath of God, a Novel of Suspense

THE JER1CHO DECEPT1ON

JEFFREY SMALL

WEST HILLS PRESS
ATLANTA • SAN FRANCISCO

PUBLISHED BY WEST HILLS PRESS (www.WestHillsPress.com)
A division of Hundreds of Heads Books, LLC

Image © Igor Kovalchuk/123rf.com
Author Photograph is by Kelsey Edwards

All of the characters and events in this book are fictitious, and any resemblance to actual persons, living or dead, is purely coincidental.

ISBN-13: 978-1-933512-44-0

Printed in U.S.A.
10 9 8 7 6 5 4 3 2 1

For Alison and Ella,
You Inspire Me.

PART I

"*I am a Hindu, I am a Moslem, I am a Jew, I am a Christian, I am a Buddhist!*"

Mahatma Gandhi

"*I am a deeply religious non-believer.*"

Albert Einstein

PROLOGUE

The rider had no way of knowing that a simple fall from his horse would change the course of history.

For now, all he could focus on was the mission ahead. He adjusted the leather bag hanging from his shoulder. The mass of the parchment letters inside was insignificant, but the importance of the contents weighed heavily on him. The letters, signed by the High Priest himself, contained the names of those he would arrest and bring back in a fortnight. The rider knew the fate that awaited these unsuspecting men and women; he had made similar treks before. The lucky ones would die quickly, their flesh torn from their limbs by the ravenous animals kept for this purpose. The others would languish in a dark, dank cellar awaiting more gruesome tortures.

The rider shifted on the horse. He was sweating underneath his cloak, especially where the bag bumped against his body in time with the horse's stride. The sun had nearly reached its zenith, and the flat beige desert provided only an occasional thorny bush or limestone rock outcropping for shade. He squinted against the glare, wiped the sweat from his forehead, and massaged his temples.

At least summer is months away.

He kicked his horse with the heel of his sandal. The animal the council had provided him ambled forward as if it knew of the terrible task ahead. Heat radiated from its damp brown coat, and the bony creature looked like it hadn't eaten well in months—in contrast to the powerful steeds of the three Roman legionnaires in front of him. The legionnaires, two in their mid-twenties and the third barely a teen, joked with each other, passing a wine sack between them.

Pagans, he thought, but necessary to carry out his mission. He glanced at the long swords sheathed to their saddles. Men like these had to be watched carefully. For them, killing was a sport. At least he was a Roman citizen, and he had rights. *But out in the desert no one would know if I simply disappeared.* He shook his head to clear it. They would arrive in Damascus soon.

His first stop would be to eat. After two days of only bread and wine, his mouth watered in anticipation of the juicy leg of lamb he would buy. Then his mission would begin. The closer they got to their destination, the more jovial the legionnaires became. The rider, however, didn't relish the job he was sent to do. He was in the right, of course. The High Priest had made it very clear that this cult must be stamped out.

They don't have to die, he thought. *It's their choice.* They were stubborn. Not one had renounced his or her ways.

A sudden glint of sunlight off the armor chest plate attached to the rear of the saddle in front of him flashed into his eyes. A shot of pain pierced through to the base of his skull. He snapped his eyes closed and massaged his neck.

Not again. Not now, please, he prayed.

The headaches had pestered him for the past year at the most inconvenient times. Usually he retired to his room, lying in the darkness for hours until they passed. For the past two months, this thorn in his flesh had occurred more frequently, especially since the council had charged him with ridding the land of the cult.

When he opened his eyes, he saw that the steeds ahead of him had distanced themselves. He kicked his horse, bringing him to a trot. When he caught up, the youngest of the three Romans turned and stared.

"You don't look well," Marcus said in an educated Greek. He held up the depleted wine sack. "A drink, maybe?"

The rider shook his head, which was a mistake because the pain spread from the base of his skull to his temples. He brought the sleeve of his tunic to his face and wiped his eyes. He sensed this one would be worse than the others. When he dropped his arm, he noticed that Marcus was still staring at him, a curious expression on his stubble-covered face. That's when he noticed the taste. *Copper*—as if he'd placed a coin on his tongue to clean it, which was an unusual thought, he realized, because he'd never done such a thing. But he could think of no other description for the metallic flavor.

He almost said something to Marcus when he noticed the light again. As the legionnaire's horse walked along the compacted sand, the sun reflecting off the armor danced in his vision. But this time it didn't exacerbate his headache. To his surprise, the pain, which moments earlier had thundered through his skull, dissipated. He watched with interest as the light radiated outward from the armor, eclipsing the legionnaire and the desert around him. A moment later he could see nothing but the light.

He wasn't sure what caused him to fall from his horse. The light seemed to lift him from his saddle and deposit him on the coarse earth. He felt no pain.

"Paulos!" Marcus called to him. The words came from a great distance. "Paulos, are you hurt?"

The rider knew he should respond, but another voice eclipsed the legionnaire's. This voice, however, didn't come from the other Romans. It spoke to him from a different place. He had never heard this voice before, but at the same time it was familiar, as if it had been with him all along.

He listened. Then he understood.

His mission, his life, his very identity—none of it mattered anymore. The wonder of the revelation spread through his body like a drink of hot cider on a winter day. The answer had been within him from the beginning. He had just never listened. He had misunderstood the cult—they had been right all along.

CHAPTER 1

YALE-NEW HAVEN HOSPITAL
PRESENT DAY

"Do you smell something, Doctor? Like honey?"

Dr. Ethan Lightman placed a hand on his patient's shoulder. Bedside manner wasn't one of his strengths, but he made an effort. "Liz, just relax. You're in the early phase of the seizure."

He suspected that she was experiencing the first stages of an SPS, a simple partial seizure, which could affect a patient's senses—smell, touch, sight, hearing, taste—but not their consciousness. *Good*, he thought. *It's beginning.*

"I'm scared." Her eyes were wide and her pupils dilated. "I haven't been off my Phenytoin for over two years." She tugged at the handmade quilt that covered her on the narrow hospital bed. The IV line attached to her arm swung above her body. "And I told you what happened then."

He nodded. He knew his patient well: Elizabeth Clarkson, a thirty-six-year-old woman whose curly black hair and freckled face gave away her Irish descent. She looked like a younger version of Ethan's mother, who had passed on her dark hair and fair complexion to him. During their initial interview, he'd learned that Liz had been on epileptic management drugs since she was seventeen. The unpredictability of her seizures made holding down a job difficult. She now worked at a flower shop part-time. But her misfortune, he hoped, might solve the mystery that had consumed the past five years of his life. Her seizures were special.

"That's why we have you in the hospital." He gestured to the nurse with the silver hair tied in a bun on top of her head who was arranging instruments on the stainless steel table on the opposite side of the bed. "Judith has some nice drugs for you if the experience becomes too intense."

"That's right, Sweetie"—Judith touched her arm—"I'll take good care of you."

The fifteen-by-twenty-foot space was larger than the standard private hospital room because it was set up for longitudinal studies. Liz had lived there for two weeks, undergoing LTVM—long-term video monitoring, a protocol used on patients with difficult cases of epilepsy. She was continuously monitored by video and by EEG, electroencephalography. Although the room had the sterile smell of antiseptic, and the clean but scuffed white linoleum tiles left no doubt as to the hospital setting, they'd let her hang a swath of multicolored silk in an Indian design over one wall, which, along with the pictures of her three cats on the bedside table, helped to soften the room.

She smiled at him. "Are you sure you're old enough to be a doctor?" Her blue eyes dropped down the length of his body. He felt his face and neck flush.

Ethan knew he looked younger than his thirty-two years. Although he was nearly six-four, he was lanky. At times, usually inopportune ones, he tripped over his own size thirteen shoes. He had a runner's build—though he didn't run. His high school track coach had begged him to try out for the team, but after a few practices, both knew he wasn't meant to be an athlete.

"Old enough," he said, returning her smile. He suspected it looked awkward. He pulled his penlight from the breast pocket of his lab coat to keep himself focused.

"At least you don't think I'm crazy. I mean, the things I used to see during my spells."

He didn't think she was crazy. On the contrary, he was determined to understand the etiology, the causation, of her visions. During her early twenties, Liz had been active in her church. In addition to working as the minister's administrative assistant, she'd led an adult Sunday school class, a Tuesday morning Bible study, and a prayer group. However, after she'd revealed the details about her special experiences to the minister, he had asked her to leave. The things she saw were not natural, he'd explained, and he feared that the devil might be at work in her mind.

Ethan checked the connections of the nineteen wires attached to her scalp; they joined in a single bundle below the bed and then ran along the floor until they terminated at a computer monitoring station. The computer recorded the electrical signals originating from Liz's brain—her EEG—and had sent a text message to his cell phone fifteen minutes earlier, as soon as it detected unusual sharp-slow waves.

He hoped this time he would get the data he needed. He felt the tension in his shoulders as he bent to examine the dilation of her pupils with his penlight. He and his mentor, Professor Elijah Schiff, needed a breakthrough. They weren't there to cure Liz of her epilepsy. Her condition was under control with the medication that he'd stopped when she entered the study.

If I could just capture an EEG of one of her episodes, then maybe . . . He let the thought trail off.

Ethan and Elijah had hit a dead end, and they were running out of time. They had exhausted their grant several months earlier. While Elijah was out canvassing the nonprofit community for more money, Ethan was working harder than he had in his life, trying to demonstrate progress—trying to prove that their idea wasn't just a pipe dream. In his gut, he felt they were close to making one of the greatest breakthroughs in modern psychology. But not everyone believed that their theory was plausible. In fact, most of their colleagues ridiculed the idea.

"Dr. Lightman!" an urgent voice from the back of the room interrupted his thoughts.

He'd almost forgotten about Christian Sligh, the second-year grad student sitting at the small wooden desk overflowing with computer equipment. The bundle of electrodes attached to Liz's scalp terminated into ten differential amplifiers, which boosted the slight electrical signal coming from her brain activity. These signals were picked up and analyzed by the computer workstation, which filtered out extraneous signals, such as any electrodermal response—spontaneous electrical impulses across the skin caused by a fluctuation in emotion—or the EMG signals produced when muscles contract. Ethan only cared about capturing the electrical signals produced by her brain.

Chris stared at three twenty-inch LCD monitors. With his shaggy blond hair, he appeared more like a surfer from Malibu than a psych graduate from Notre Dame. The flip-flops and shorts enhanced the surfer image, but his wool sweater was a concession to the cold New Haven rain they'd experienced that fall. Ethan didn't know what he would do without his grad student. Chris had a knack for wading through the bureaucracy of the various university approvals their study required. Ethan didn't have the patience for paperwork; he was too busy spending late nights working on the project itself.

The faint beeping of equipment echoed in the background. "I'm getting some interictal activity in the temporal lobes," Chris said.

Ethan turned to Liz. She stared at the ceiling without blinking. Judith reached for her arm to place a blood pressure cuff on it. He touched the nurse's shoulder, shaking his head. He didn't want any external stimuli to influence the patient's experience or disrupt the EEG. Judith withdrew the BP cuff with an annoyed look.

Liz gazed at the ceiling with an expression that exuded relaxed concentration. He guessed that the seizure was spreading: *probably evolving from an SPS to a CPS, a complex partial seizure.* He wondered if it was still primarily located in the left temporal lobe. He was torn between observing at her side and joining Chris at the computer screens. But the EEG was being recorded, and he would spend the night studying it.

"Doctor," Judith said in a voice just above a whisper, "hasn't it been long enough?" She held a syringe in her hand. Her brow was furrowed.

He shook his head. He'd explained the protocol to her several times before, but she'd grown close to the patient over the past weeks. Next time, he would rotate the caregivers.

Liz's voice caused both of them to break their stare-off and look down at her. "It's beautiful."

He was uncertain what to do. Did he engage her in conversation or let the experience play itself out? Sensing Judith's restlessness, he asked, "What do you see?"

"Beautiful." Her voice had a distance to it.

"Uh, Doctor," Chris called from behind him, "the seizures are originating in the left temporal lobe."

I was right, Ethan thought.

"But they're spreading quickly!"

At that moment, Liz's body went rigid. Her legs and arms stiffened as if she was being hit by a sudden jolt of electricity. Her hands arched upward on the quilt, each of her finger joints locked out.

"It's time, Doctor," Judith said. She moved the syringe toward the IV.

"A minute more." The most important data would be from the early stage of the seizure, when it was isolated to the temporal lobe, but he needed a complete picture. Too much was at stake.

Then Liz's eyes rolled back in her head, and her body began to convulse. Her chest heaved while her arms and legs shook as if being shocked by a rhythmic electrical pulse.

"She's going myoclonic!" He lunged for her shoulders.

"Doctor!" Judith screamed.

Ethan knew he was losing control of the situation. Judith jammed a roll of gauze into her mouth—*quick thinking*, he realized, but he should have asked for it earlier.

"Now!" he instructed the nurse while he struggled to control Liz's shaking arms. "One gram of Phenytoin, two of Ativan." Normally he would have doubled the Ativan dose on a seizure this strong, but he wanted to control it without sending her into unconsciousness. He needed her clear memory of the experience.

Within ninety seconds of Judith administering the antiepileptic and anti-convulsant meds, the myoclonic jerking ceased. Ethan released the patient's arms. Judith wiped Liz's forehead with a cloth while gently removing the gauze from her mouth. The nurse didn't look at him.

He realized that his own hairline was also damp with perspiration. Taking a step back from the bed, he wiped his eyes on the sleeve of his white lab coat. His heart was pounding, and he was breathing deeply. He recognized the signs: his own sympathetic nervous system was engaged in a fight-or-flight response.

Liz's eyes opened as if she was awakening from a nap. "Try not to move," Ethan said. "The seizure is over now. We've given you some medication that might make you feel a little groggy."

He stepped to the bed, bent over her, and placed two fingers on her neck. Her pulse was coming down. He wished his would do the same. He focused on her expression, curious as to what she'd remember in the post-ictal state. Many patients had complete amnesia, but the rare ones with her condition recalled every detail. Those details often changed their lives forever.

While he waited for Judith to give her a few ice chips, he grabbed his black notebook from the leather satchel he'd left near the room's entrance, pulled a chair over to the bed, and opened the notebook.

"Liz, if you're feeling up it," he asked, "can you describe what happened?"

She turned to him, locking her eyes onto his.

"Infinity."

She smiled a dreamlike smile, as if to say anything else would be inexact.

CHAPTER 2

MALL OF EMIRATES
DUBAI

Mousa bin Ibrahim Al-Mohammad shifted the backpack from his left shoulder to his right. He was sweating underneath his heavy coat. At least the air conditioning in the mall provided some relief from the October heat wave Dubai was experiencing. He walked across the polished marble floor, passed the gleaming brass columns of the Middle East's second largest mall, and paused at the window of the Harvey Nichols store. Amira, his eight-year-old daughter, pressed her nose against the glass. The mannequins were dressed in crisp linen pants and bright polo shirts, as if they were enjoying at day at the yacht club. He wished he was dressed similarly, rather than in the jeans, pullover, and heavy coat he was wearing. He shifted the backpack again.

Turning back in the direction he was heading, Mousa almost ran into another man hurrying by who was dressed as inappropriately as he was, and similarly sweating. "Pardon me," he said to the man.

Without breaking his stride, the man turned his head and nodded. "As-salaam alaykum."

The man was about Mousa's height, just under two meters, and had a similar olive complexion and short dark hair. He was younger than Mousa by a few years—late twenties or early thirties—but unlike Mousa, who was clean-shaven, this man had a week's growth of beard. *Jordanian like me*, Mousa thought.

"Wa alaykum as-salaam," Mousa replied.

A grin crept across the other man's face as he continued his journey in the direction of the food court. Mousa noticed that they carried the same backpack in a different color. The man's was blue and his was red.

"Baba, may I have a cocoa, please?"

Mousa smiled at his daughter. "Don't you want to get on the slopes before they get too crowded?"

He pointed to the giant glass windows to their right. Beyond the windows lay a sight that still astounded him, even though this was the third time he had seen it. In the middle of this shopping mecca in the center of a desert country on the edge of the Persian Gulf was an indoor ski slope over eighty meters high. The chairlift wound up to the left past where he could see. A wooden play structure with several tubing runs, one of his daughter's favorite activities, occupied the lower section of the slope closest to the windows. The main ski slope lay just beyond, complete with real snow and fake evergreen trees. Nothing like this existed in Amman, their home. He made it a point to stop here whenever he had a conference in Dubai. He looked forward to the cold air inside; then he would appreciate his extra layers of clothes.

Traveling to Dubai was like exploring another world. Whereas Amman blended aspects of a modern city with its ancient heritage, Dubai looked as if it had sprung out of the desert overnight. Even New York, where he had been two years earlier, paled in comparison to the hundreds of skyscrapers rising from the red sand and piercing the cloudless blue sky. While he was proud to see a fellow Arab country achieve this level of success, something about the conspicuous display of wealth disturbed him. He thought of the Egyptian laborers, also fellow Arabs, who were bused into the city's construction sites each day from communal living quarters he didn't even want to imagine.

He also thought of his own country and the burden of the thousands of Palestinian refugees his government struggled to accommodate. At King Hussein Hospital, where he was an orthopedic surgeon, he often saw Palestinian patients whose limbs had been blown off by land mines. These people had been displaced from their rightful land by the Israelis, certainly, but what had his Arab brothers done to help besides complain about Israel in the media?

Taking in the opulence of the mall—Dolce & Gabbana, Escada, Tiffany, Versace, not to mention the ski resort he was going to—he knew that much more could be done among his own people.

Amira, his princess, tugged on his sleeve. "Baba!"

He gazed down at her. With her sharp nose, angular jaw and cheekbones, and wide eyes, she looked noble. *Like the queen,* he thought, and like his wife, Bashirah, who had stayed behind in Amman with their newborn son.

"What if we ski first, and then I'll get you an extra large cocoa?"

She put a little finger to her lips, thought for a minute, and then asked, "With cream?"

"Extra cream." He grinned.

"Good. We ski first then." She took his hand and skipped beside him as they headed toward the entrance.

Fifteen minutes later, they sat together on the chairlift as it approached the top of the slope. He placed a hand on his daughter's head. She was bouncing in the seat. "Do you remember from last year?"

"I liked France," she nodded. "But indoors, Baba! This is really neat."

Mousa clicked his skis together, shaking off the bit of snow that had stuck when he boarded the lift. He wished he had more opportunities to ski. He tried to schedule at least one medical conference a year somewhere cold. Last year, he'd taken his wife and daughter to the Alps.

As they began to descend the slope, he stayed a couple of meters behind Amira. He cut slow arcs in the grainy snow as his daughter headed straight down, her ski tips pointed toward each other in a snowplow position.

The explosion hit without warning.

Just below and to the right, the glass windows separating the ski slope from the interior of the mall, the same windows where he and his daughter had been standing minutes earlier, imploded in an orange ball of fire. He watched the shards of glass shred the clothes and skin of a Saudi family of four skiing just fifteen meters below them. Before his brain had a chance to register the horror of the sight, the pressure of the blast's concussion hit him like a solid wall of heat. He felt his right eardrum rupture. He rocked backward but somehow managed to stay on his skis.

Amira's hands flew to her head. His daughter's ski tips crossed, and she tumbled forward. Her body appeared to fall in slow motion toward the fire and glass raining on the snow before them. Fear cinched Mousa's heart.

He shifted his weight to the outside of his right ski, cut across the snow, and focused on pointing his body straight downhill. Bending at the waist, he picked up speed. He was almost parallel to his daughter, whose descent on her stomach was slowing. He thought he could hear her scream, but it was hard to discern anything with his ruptured eardrum and the explosions booming from the mall.

The moment he passed her, he carved his skis to the left. His plan was to arrest her fall by stopping in front of her. Then the ground underneath him buckled upward, as if an earthquake had struck the ski slope. He toppled over.

The manmade snow wasn't as soft as the powder he'd skied on in the Alps. He hit hard on his side, his left leg twisting underneath him. He felt something pop in his knee and knew instantly it was his ACL—he'd performed many reconstructions of this ligament on Jordan's top football players. He ignored the searing pain that shot through his leg and forced his body to roll over as his momentum carried him down the slope. He had to reach his daughter.

There!

Amira was beside him, a wide-eyed expression of terror on her face. He shot out a hand, grabbed her fluffy pink jacket, and dug the heel of his ski boot on his good leg into the snow. They stopped about midway down the slope. He pulled his daughter to him. Her head fell into his chest. He felt her press against the small travel version of the Qur'an he kept in his pocket.

Allah, please let my daughter be okay, he pleaded.

He shouted over the screams of the wounded skiers around them, "Amira, where are you hurt?"

Her lips quivered. "Baba, what happened?"

"Are you injured?" He tried to push himself upright, but his left leg collapsed underneath him. He shifted his weight and rose to his right knee instead. He ran his hands along her body, carefully palpating her limbs, feeling for any sign of injury.

"I'm okay, I think," she whimpered.

For the first time since the explosion occurred, Mousa allowed himself to take a breath. *What happened?* Surveying the destruction around them, the horror of the tragedy came to him. The mall had been bombed.

As soon as the realization struck him that the explosion was most likely deliberate, another more disturbing thought occurred. *The smell.* Not just fire and smoke, but the sickly sweet aroma of burning plastic. All that remained of the plate glass windows between the slope and the shops of the mall were a few jagged shards thrusting out of the twisted metal frame. He could see none of the shops, nor the food court where they might have been enjoying their cocoa. Gray smoke billowed from the mall into the ski area. The smoke glowed orange where a fire raged somewhere behind it. If they didn't leave quickly, they would die. As if to accentuate the point, the eerie sound of protesting metal came from above his head.

He knew that an emergency exit to the outside must be located somewhere at the bottom of the slope. He scanned the area around him. The formerly pristine snow was littered with bodies and debris. Some of the skiers, faces contorted in agony, held onto limbs leaking bright red blood onto the white snow. Others lay quiet, dead. A moment of indecision struck him. He was doctor, and these people needed help.

"Baba?"

He gazed into the dark eyes of his daughter, who clung to his side. Then a loud groaning noise pulled his attention upwards. The ski lift was swaying back and forth. The metal poles holding the cables aloft slowly bent over toward them.

He made his decision. He sat back onto the snow and pulled his daughter onto his lap. With the screeching of the metal becoming louder and the stench of the smoke bringing tears to his eyes, he pushed off, watching below to make sure they avoided the glass that had peppered the slope.

As they picked up speed on their controlled slide, a loud pop echoed through the resort. The lights went out, and they were plunged into darkness.

CHAPTER 3

SHEFFIELD-STERLING-STRATHCONA HALL, YALE UNIVERSITY

---

ive years' work. The breakthrough no one thinks is possible.

F Dr. Ethan Lightman gazed at the machine in the center of the room: *the Logos.* It offered so many possibilities, and yet he was balancing on a narrow ledge. He had to produce results—and fast. He swiveled his chair around to his desk, the wheels creaking against the well-worn strips of maple flooring. He'd worked for the past ten hours in the expansive room that doubled as his lab and office in Sheffield-Sterling-Strathcona Hall, known by everyone at Yale as SSS. The gothic cathedral at the intersection of Grove and Prospect Streets housed Yale's Psychology Department. All of the lights in the lab were off except for his Tiffany desk lamp and the blue glow from his laptop. The hallways were silent.

Ethan ran his fingers through his hair. *I should leave and come back in the morning.* The last thing he'd eaten was a Snickers bar, and that was five hours ago. But he sensed that he was close. He focused on the lines of code displayed on his monitor.

The data he'd collected from Liz's EEG during her seizure was rich with potential, particularly when combined with the results from a study he'd worked on as a young medical doctor writing his PhD dissertation in the field of neuropsychiatry. He clicked a window that brought up a color image of the two hemispheres of the brain of one of the subjects from the earlier study. He thought back to the small group of Buddhist monks and Catholic nuns who had been quite willing, even curious, to be injected with radioactive dye so that he could scan their brains using SPECT and fMRI analysis. Since Liz's seizure the previous day, he'd studied the spikes and troughs of her EEG until he was dizzy. His dilemma now: how to combine Liz's data with the earlier brain scans so he could program the machine in the center of the room? He knew he could make it work; he just wasn't sure yet how he would do it. His colleagues in the psych department delighted in predicting that the Logos would do nothing. He would prove them wrong. He had to: his shot at tenure depended on it.

Massaging his temples, he reclined in the chair whose frayed fabric seat cushion had seen several generations of Yale professors come and go. An untenured assistant professor, Ethan needed to produce results or he'd find himself teaching at some small college in a town he'd never heard of before. But it wasn't only his career that drove his search for answers; he longed to understand what had happened to him *that day*. He pushed the memory away. *Ancient history*, he thought. He was a research scientist, and right now he needed to focus on the task before him.

He massaged his temples again. *Not now*, he thought. He took a moment to inventory himself. *No tunnel vision, no nausea.* Those were the usual symptoms that indicated a migraine was beginning. If one developed, he wouldn't be able to work for the next twenty-four hours. He opened the top drawer of his desk and removed a yellow prescription bottle. He popped the Topiramate into his mouth and washed it down with a swig of water from a half-full bottle. He was first prescribed the drug when he was thirteen. He needed it most frequently when he was under stress.

He glanced at the desk to his right. While his workspace was always immaculately organized, Professor Elijah Schiff's had stacks of psychology journals and notebooks filled with his illegible scrawl strewn about. Five years earlier, when Ethan became his research assistant, he'd tried to organize the senior professor, but the attempts hadn't lasted long. Elijah had his own system. He also possessed the most brilliant mind Ethan had ever encountered. After his father's sudden death from pancreatic cancer when he was a junior in high school, Ethan had been without a male mentor until Elijah took him under his wing. The senior professor had also been his main source of comfort after the horrible accident that had taken Natalie, his fiancée, three years earlier. He shook his head to clear the memory.

Just then his eye caught a Post-it note stuck to the cover of one of the journals. Elijah was fond of leaving bits of wisdom for his students on these notes, and he still considered Ethan one of his students. Ethan peeled the yellow note off of the magazine and stared at the mixture of cursive and print: "Truth cannot be known, only approximated."

He slapped the note back on the magazine. *If truth can't be known, then what are we doing here?* He and Elijah shared the same professional interests and goals, but they approached their project from two different perspectives. Maybe that was why they worked well together.

Suddenly, he had a flash of inspiration that caused him to start, as if a glass of cold water had been poured over his head. *The wavelength, not the amplitude, of the EEG is the key*, he realized, *and it has to be applied asynchronously to the left and right temporal lobes.*

The idea was like a spark that had smoldered within him and suddenly ignited with a breath of air. As he returned to his computer, he was grateful the headache was keeping itself at bay. His fingers flew across the keys as he rewrote a portion of the code. Then he reran the simulation analysis. He wiped his palms on his khakis while he stared at the three open windows on his laptop. One contained the script of the code he'd been writing, the second a graph showing the electrical impulses the Logos would create in a subject's brain, and the third a series of ones and zeroes—binary code—that was the computer's translation of his programming.

When the analysis was complete, he studied the results. Was the answer to the past five years of research really that simple? He swiveled his chair and stared at the machine. Now all they had to do was to test it.

He thought back to Liz's vision. "What do you mean by infinity?" he'd asked her.

"Words are inadequate, trivial," she'd said. "It's something that must be experienced."

"Can you try?"

She'd put a finger to her lips for a moment, shrugged, and said, "God."

CHAPTER 4

DUBAI

A s his daughter played in the white sand on the edge of the blue-green Persian Gulf, Mousa sat on a beach lounge chair by the Royal Mirage Hotel. He rewrapped the Ace bandage around his knee, pulling it tighter and crisscrossing the joint to add stability. He didn't need an MRI to know that the ligament that normally did that job was ruptured. He tugged his linen pants leg down over the wrap. It fit, barely. He'd picked up an elaborately carved cane in the hotel's gift shop, much fancier than he needed, but it would allow him to walk well enough until he returned to Amman. He thought about which one of his colleagues would do the surgery to repair his ACL. *Too bad I can't operate on myself,* he thought.

Their flight left in four hours, and it was time to head back inside the hotel to clean up, but he decided to give Amira a few more minutes to play. She was chatting to herself as she built a sand castle, miraculously uninjured from the bombing that had killed countless others the previous day.

Alhamdulillah, Mousa mouthed for the hundredth time that day. *Praise Allah.* The emergency lights above the ski slope had kicked on a few seconds after the main power went out. Mousa had somehow navigated down the slope on his back, maneuvering past the dead and dying in the bloody and blackened snow, frantic to get Amira out before the entire building ignited in flames. When they reached the metal fire door at the bottom of the slope, he put a hand on his daughter's bony shoulder to steady his balance as he stood. He hopped on his good leg to the door as Amira clung to his waist. The cries of his fellow skiers called to him to do his duty: to help. He was a doctor, after all. But the groaning sound of metal twisting against its will overpowered the voices. And what use would he be if he couldn't even steady himself?

He and Amira had managed to wobble out onto a side street and into the harsh sunlight. He led her away from the exterior of the mall in case the walls failed. In the time it took to reach the intersection with the main street, police and fire trucks screamed up to the building. He'd paused, breathing deeply and resting his leg. People and smoke poured out the main doors to the mall.

How could this happen? he'd wondered, paralyzed by the shock of the past few minutes. Then an image popped into his head, one that was almost as disturbing as the injured people he'd passed on the ski slope: the other Jordanian he'd seen in the mall, the one with the backpack.

Mousa surveyed the police cars screeching to a halt in the street around them. He had to get Amira far away. The ambulances were arriving, and he rationalized that they wouldn't need one more doctor, especially one who was lame and accompanied by a child. If he stayed, the police would ask him questions. A quiet voice in his head told him that he had a duty to tell them about the Jordanian, but he also knew how things worked. A louder voice said that it was better not to get involved. He had a greater duty to the little girl beside him.

Now that he sat on the peaceful beach out of danger, his daughter safe and himself with only a burst right eardrum and a bum knee, he felt guilty. Maybe he should have remained and helped. But he'd been afraid. Terrified, if he was honest with himself. More for Amira's safety than his own, of course, but he'd also heard rumors of where men were taken after a terrorist attack. He shook off a chill even though the sun warmed his skin. Within a few hours they would be back in Amman with his wife and new son.

As he looked up across the flat waters of the Persian Gulf, he noticed how the city looked manufactured, the same thought he'd had the previous day in the mall. The beach was groomed by a crew with rakes every morning and was off limits to the local population. He and Amira were the only Arab-looking people on the beach; only guests at one of the expensive hotels bordering the Gulf were allowed access. Three German tourists strolled ankle-deep in the water. Bellies, pink from overexposure to the sun, extended over their too-small bikinis. Just offshore he saw more high-rise buildings than he could count, thousands of condos recently constructed on a manmade island in the shape of a palm tree.

The display of wealth around him reminded him of the news reports that morning. The story about the bombing played worldwide. The UAE was supposed to be an example of a peaceful, safe Muslim state that had put aside politics and religious fanaticism in the name of capitalism. But that was exactly why terrorists had targeted the city.

An Internet press release from an unknown terrorist group had declared a jihad against any Muslim state or organization that had turned its back on the teachings of the Prophet and had embraced Western capitalism and the lust for material items. The actions of fanatical Muslim terrorists over the past two decades pained him. Their exploitation of his religion—a faith centered on prayer, charity, and justice—in the name of terrorism was a dismaying phenomenon he'd seen develop since his childhood. In the seventies and eighties, when terrorism in the Middle East began to rise, its proponents had been motivated by politics. He recalled hearing Yasser Arafat, founder of the PLO, quip that "fighting wars over religion is like arguing about who has the best imaginary friend." But the previous day's bombing was even more troubling: now they were pitting Arab against Arab.

The irony was that Mohammad had been known during his day not just as a Prophet of Allah, but as a great statesman—a ruler who had united the Arab world and brought an economic prosperity that had not been seen before and would last for centuries. Mousa shook his head. The problem in his fellow Arab countries was not rampant religious fanaticism itself; it was poverty, a lack of opportunity for young men, and illiteracy. Discontentment bred anger, and those who couldn't read and think for themselves were easily led astray. The billions invested in the construction on the fake island before him was one example of the wasted resources of countries that concentrated their vast oil wealth to benefit the few. *Simple economics*, he thought.

"Baba, come play with me."

He pushed himself out of his chair and hobbled to her side. "Just for a minute, dear, and then it is time to go home."

"I miss Ummi."

He thought of Bashirah's silky curls, her warm embrace, and the mischievous twinkle in her eye. "I miss your mum too, Princess."

While he searched the signs for directions to the departure gates, Mousa kept an eye on Amira, who pulled her small pink suitcase behind her. He wished he could take her hand, but he pulled his own suitcase in one and used the other to bear down on his cane.

Dubai International Airport was like the rest of the country: new, shiny, and large. The main terminal was a giant stainless steel and glass tube designed with a nod to an aircraft fuselage. Palm trees grew down two rows the entire length of the tube. Mousa noted that many of the same posh clothing and jewelry stores that were in the Mall of the Emirates had outlets here too. He shuddered at the memory.

When they reached customs, the muscles in his chest tensed. Military men dressed in black and carrying machine guns paced around the passengers who waited in front of a line of desks at passport control. Mousa had never seen so much security at the airport before. Their taxi had been stopped three hundred meters before the building while a bomb-sniffing German Shepherd circled the car. He looked down at his daughter in order to tear his gaze from the eyes of a security guard who was staring at him.

"Let's wait in this line, sweetheart." He stopped behind two American businessmen. While Amira chattered to a stuffed puppy she had pulled from her backpack, he glanced at the backlit advertisements on the wall to the left of the customs agents. He had no reason to feel guilty, but the way the military men studied each passenger was unnerving. The bright ads drew his attention: each was for a different high-end condominium in the city. One declared that anyone who bought a property would be given a free Bentley; another promised that buyers would be entered into a lottery whose grand prizes included a year's use of a private jet and an island off the coast of Africa.

"Next!"

The customs agent in front of them waved impatiently. Mousa approached the desk, pulled his and Amira's passports from the inside pocket of his tan blazer, and handed them over. The man was dressed like all the other customs agents, wearing a white robe that reached to his ankles, sandals, and a red-and-white-checkered headdress. The agent was well fed, but not obese, and had a darker complexion than Mousa. He took the passports without smiling. With the practiced movement of countless repetitions, he opened each to the first page and studied the pictures. First, he scrutinized Amira and then swiped the bar code on her passport through the scanner on the computer. Next, the agent opened his and held it up so that he could compare the photograph with Mousa's face. He never knew what he was supposed to do in that moment: did he smile, look bored, make a small joke?

He stayed quiet and looked passively ahead. The agent studied him for a few seconds longer than he was used to, and the tension began to creep back into his chest again, restricting his breathing. After the trauma of the previous day, he assured himself that his anxiety was natural. He pushed back the twinges of guilt he still felt for leaving the mall without speaking to the police or helping with the injured. His first duty was to his daughter. Allah understood that.

Finally, the man seemed to be satisfied. He swiped the passport through the computer, but he didn't hand it back to Mousa. Instead, he stared at the monitor, his bushy brow furrowed. Then he keyed in a command and looked up.

"Network slow today. It will just take a moment." He smiled. Mousa thought the smile seemed forced.

An unmarked white door behind the customs desks opened, and three military officers hurried out. They were dressed similarly to the others patrolling the terminal: black cargo pants, thick-soled black boots, black turtlenecks, and black bulletproof vests. The lead officer had a pistol on his belt; the two behind him carried submachine guns. Following the three men was a woman dressed in a traditional black burqa with a scarf over her hair, but her face was uncovered and she wore a subtle shade of lipstick.

The men split up and strode around the desks. Then they converged on Mousa and Amira. The other travelers waiting in line stepped back. The tightness he'd felt in his chest cinched in like a python trying to squeeze the air from his lungs.

"May I help you?" He tried to keep his voice relaxed.

The lead officer rested a hand on the butt of his pistol and asked, "You are Mousa bin Ibrahim Al-Mohammad?"

"I am *Doctor* Al-Mohammad." His voice came out weaker than he wanted, even with the emphasis on *Doctor*. He had done nothing wrong, but the determined look in the officer's eyes concerned him. Before Mousa could process what happened next, the officer standing to his left grabbed his arms, jerked them behind his back, and tightened a plastic handcuff tie around his wrists until it dug into his skin. His cane rattled to the ground.

"What are you doing?"

"Come with us, please," the lead officer said.

"Baba! Don't leave!"

His heart lurched. He turned his head to see Amira staring at him with terror on her face for the second day in a row.

"My daughter—" He struggled against the men who pushed him forward. "Please, let her come with me."

"She will be taken care of." The officer nodded to the woman in the burqa who bent to Amira's level and put a hand on her shoulder.

"It's okay, Princess," Mousa tried to sound comforting in spite of the surging fear in his gut. "Just a misunderstanding. This will only take a minute, I'm sure."

"No!" she pleaded. "Let my Baba go!" The tears streaming down her face tore at him.

He hesitated again but was shoved from behind. His weight fell on his injured knee and he stumbled, but the men on either side of him grabbed his arms and dragged him toward the white door. The first officer opened the door, which led into a narrow hallway. The last sounds he heard before the metal door slammed behind him were his daughter's screams.

CHAPTER 5

SSS, YALE UNIVERSITY

A s the memory of Liz's mystical vision echoed through his mind, Ethan packed his laptop into his satchel. He was tired, and the dark silence of the building reminded him that once again he'd worked too late.

"Dr. Lightman, explain yourself."

Ethan jumped in his chair. He swiveled to see Samuel Houston, Chair of Yale's Human Research Protection Program—the HRPP—standing in the doorway. Houston was in his late fifties, a few years younger than Elijah, wiry thin, and mostly bald with a ring of salt and pepper hair around the crown of his head.

"Explain what?" He tried to keep the tension out of his voice. He didn't have much contact with Houston, and that was by design. He let Elijah handle the temperamental chair. A former researcher and psych professor himself, Houston was now a full-time administrator whose job was to oversee human experimentation at Yale. When he took his position four years earlier, he had moved from being a peer to being a thorn in the side of his former colleagues.

Houston removed the wire glasses that teetered on the tip of his nose and stabbed them in Ethan's direction. "I should have terminated your research when your funding dried up a few months ago, but Elijah persuaded me to give you two more time. After what happened yesterday, I'm making an executive decision: your time is up."

"But the data we collected . . . I just—"

"Your treatment of your patient, *Doctor*, was out of line."

My treatment of Liz?

"You've let your ambitions for this project cloud your professional judgment." His voice was larger than his slight frame seemed capable of.

"How dare you question—" Ethan took a breath and fought the urge to lash out at the administrator. In his role as Chair of the HRPP, Houston had the power to close down a lab, to prevent a researcher from receiving funding, and to keep a professor from achieving tenure.

He tried again in a calmer tone. "All of the protocols were followed to the letter. My patient gave the necessary consents to stop her medication. She volunteered to have a seizure so we could conduct the EEG testing."

He glanced toward the far corner of the room to Chris Sligh's desk, bare but for a thick file folder. The grad student conducted preliminary patient interviews and obtained the necessary consents before they began any experiments. Ethan knew how paranoid the university was about liability. Since the cutting-edge but controversial experiments conducted there in the 1960s by Stanley Milgram, the administration was especially sensitive to human psychological testing.

In a now infamous study, Milgram had devised an experiment to see how far people would go in deference to authority. His subjects were falsely told that the experiment they volunteered for was about the effects of punishment on recall and learning, through the administration of electrical shocks that the subjects would give when a confederate answered a question incorrectly. Although the experiment showed how powerful authority could be in determining behavior, it also created a firestorm of controversy over the intense stress and anxiety the subjects suffered as they went ahead shocking people against their better judgment.

But that was fifty years ago, Ethan thought. Houston was overly cautious, worried about a past that was no longer relevant.

"My information is that you withheld medication when the seizure spread, putting the patient in danger of injuring herself."

Judith. He'd worried the nurse might be a problem. Neither she nor Houston understood the true nature of his work.

"If you review the patient's chart, and you are welcome to watch the video as well, you'll see the protocols were followed exactly as approved by the institutional review board." Ethan's colleagues who had reviewed his proposed experiment and then reported to Houston's committee had been skeptical that the Logos would ever work, but they had approved the research. "We had to allow the seizure to proceed along its natural course to capture all of the relevant EEG data. Liz agreed to this protocol precisely."

"I will review *everything*." Houston enunciated each syllable. "We aren't the Yale of Stanley Milgram anymore. My responsibility"—he stretched his body to its most erect posture—"is to shut down any project that doesn't smell right. It's not just the university's reputation that's on the line; half-a-billion dollars in federal grants is contingent on us upholding the highest ethical standards." He leaned in close to Ethan. "From the beginning, this nonsense you and Elijah have concocted hasn't smelled right to me."

Ethan forced a smile. "My grad assistant, Chris, will email you the files in the morning."

Houston surveyed the lab, his eyes lingering on the two-foot-square metal box in the center before returning to Ethan. "So, does this machine"— he gestured to the Logos with a dismissive wave of his spectacles—"do anything yet?"

"Just before you walked in, I may have figured out what was wrong with our programming. You see, I combined the data from Liz's EEG with—"

"Doctor," Houston sighed, "every time I come here to question you or Elijah about this failing project, you're on the verge of some major new progress, and yet the only thing you seem to do well"—he made a show of looking around the room again—"is take up valuable real estate in one of our larger labs."

Ethan felt his face flush as he tried to formulate a response that wouldn't aggravate his superior, but he wasn't as smooth as he wished. The perfect comeback always seemed to form in his brain a minute too late to be effective. He had the same problem speaking with women. Feeling his heart rate and breathing increase, he reminded himself that he was experiencing a typical sympathetic nervous system response to stress. He'd discovered during medical school that naming the biological basis for his response to anxiety helped to calm the nervousness he often felt under pressure.

"We got it!" boomed a Brooklyn accent from the lab's open doorway.

Startled for the second time that night, Ethan turned to see his mentor, Elijah Schiff, bound into the room. His eyes sparked with excitement below his thick, white, unkempt hair. His khaki pants sported a coffee stain on one knee, while a striped tie whose advanced age was betrayed by the frayed strings of silk around its edges hung around the open collar of his blue oxford shirt. He held up several sheets of paper crumpled in his hands.

Ethan wondered what had brought Elijah back to the office at this hour, and he figured he'd be none too pleased to see Houston here. But when Elijah met Houston's glare, he seemed unfazed, as if he'd expected him to be there.

"What is it you *got*?" Houston asked.

"Funding." The elder professor's smile revealed crooked teeth that his working-class family had never had the money to fix.

"You're serious?" Ethan asked.

When their first grant started to run low, Elijah had tried to get re-funded by the original foundation but had been told that the foundation's priorities had changed toward projects "with more concrete medical benefits." Elijah had suspected that the continued failure of the Logos to produce any results in their test subjects had more to do with the rejection than did any changing priorities. The other foundations the senior professor approached had dismissed them out of hand, questioning whether the topic of their study was an appropriate one for psychiatry or, as one foundation director put it, "better off left to the Theology Department."

"And where did this last-minute funding come from?" Houston stuffed his hands in his pockets.

Although Elijah was close to retirement age, Ethan had noticed how his mentor made Houston uncomfortable. Maybe it was because Elijah refused to participate in the game that was university politics, or maybe it was just because the professor was so much smarter.

Elijah waved a hand. "A new foundation based in Dallas—last-ditch try, really. I met today with an old classmate of mine from Harvard who's the Executive Director."

Ethan didn't remember Elijah mentioning a classmate.

"Which foundation?" Houston asked.

"The NAF: Neurological Advancement Foundation."

"Never heard of it."

Elijah shrugged. "Until recently, me neither."

"How much are we talking about?"

Elijah's smile widened. "Two hundred fifty thousand for the next eighteen months."

Houston's eyebrows shot upward, while Ethan's jaw dropped. Such an amount was huge for a psychology study. *How does he do it?* Ethan wondered.

"The foundation was set up by a Texas software tycoon whose teenage son committed suicide." He paced over to his desk and dropped the papers in the midst of his journals. "Schizophrenia. He claimed he heard the voices of saints—they were a strong Catholic family, you see."

The perfect funding source, Ethan thought. "So this tycoon is interested in the psychological basis of religious experiences?"

"How convenient," Houston said.

"Imagine for a moment"—Elijah pulled out his desk chair and sat, reclining so far back that Ethan worried he might tip over—"that certain individuals have the ability to sense that which most of us cannot see." He picked up a ballpoint pen from his desk and began to twirl it between his fingers. "Life is something more than mere matter made of molecules. What is it that animates life itself? I'm not talking about a God who molds us like a sculptor making figurines from clay or a God who acts on the world like a puppeteer manipulating the strings of a marionette. What if God is more intimate to life itself? If physicists can study the Big Bang by examining the background microwave radiation left in the universe from that event, maybe we can hear the echo of God that is inside of us."

"Unanswerable questions," the dean huffed. "We are concerned with scientific inquiry here that can be demonstrated empirically."

Ethan hated to admit it, but Houston had a point. His own interest in the Logos Project had always been from a different angle than Elijah's. He cleared his throat. "Religion is one of the most powerful motivators of humankind. Over ninety percent of the world's population believes in God. If we can unlock the biological basis—the neurological and biochemical processes—that leads to these beliefs, we will have accomplished a feat no scientist has ever accomplished."

Houston sighed. "That's a very big *if*. After five years of university resources, all you have to show for this"—he pointed to the machine in the center of the room—"is, well, nothing."

Elijah said, "Samuel, I'm not sure it's productive for us to revisit this discussion. We just need more time to figure out the right programming. Now that we have our funding, you shouldn't be concerned. Ethan's work with temporal lobe epileptics who experience hyperreligiosity holds great promise. The Logos will work, and the results will be spectacular."

The professor's words reminded Ethan of his earlier breakthrough, but he bit his tongue while Houston turned to leave.

"Don't screw this up," Houston said, casting a final wary glance at the machine. "New funding or not, I will shut this program down if I hear so much as a hiccup."

Once he was out the door and out of earshot, Ethan turned to his mentor. For the first time, he noticed the strain behind the excitement in Elijah's eyes. "We're going to need to show results now more than ever, aren't we?" he asked.

"How did your programming go?"

Now it was Ethan's turn to smile. "I think I did it."

CHAPTER 6

CIA HEADQUARTERS
LANGLEY, VIRGINIA

"**W**hen do I see something for my $20 million?" demanded Casey Richards, Deputy Director of SAD, the Special Activities Division of the CIA's National Clandestine Services. He spoke into the phone on his desk on the sixth floor of the New Headquarters Building at the CIA's 258-acre campus in Langley, Virginia. While he waited for the delay as his words bounced off the satellite and then rerouted through the scrambler, he massaged the top of his scalp with his free hand. He'd started to lose his hair in his early thirties when he was still a field spook. When he became a desk jockey ten years ago at the age of forty-five, he'd finally shaved it.

He eyed the bulge created by the pack of Marlboros in the pocket of his suit jacket, which hung on the back of his door. He longed for the old days when he could smoke in the office. Since joining the Company in the eighties after serving a stint in Army intelligence, technological advances had fundamentally changed the business. *Not all changes were good*, he thought.

"I'm just as anxious as you, but Project Jericho has only been online for eight months," the refined baritone voice replied. "PSYOPS aren't an exact science."

Richards propped his feet on the unopened packing box next to his large oak desk. He'd moved into the office four months ago from the OHB, the Original Headquarters Building. He preferred the larger windows and contemporary steel and glass structure of the NHB, but he found it ironic that they referred to a twenty-year-old building as "new."

He'd been promoted from being the head of the CIA's Counterterrorism Center to the position that oversaw all of the Agency's clandestine activities when his predecessor left for a quadruple bypass. He'd only had time to unpack the essentials—his files. The walls and his desk were still bare of any personal mementos. He was always struck by how modest in size and plain in design most government offices were compared to the Hollywood portrayal. But that was fine by Richards. He didn't care about the perks that the political appointees he reported to valued so much. His job was to ensure his country's security, not his own.

"Right now"—he raised his voice—"I've got the White House, the DNI, and that bozo in Homeland Security riding my ass."

"Dubai?"

"That bombing could change the dynamics of the region."

"How were we to know about a target that doesn't even pertain to us?"

"The NSA claims they've been warning the Intelligence Directorate for months about increased chatter. But there's always chatter. Damn it, I need to show that we're doing something now."

Over the previous few years, the various Islamic terrorist groups had been relatively quiet as they nursed their wounds from a decade of pressure from the US military. That had changed two days ago with the bombing in Dubai. Now that the UAE, one of the most stable, and certainly most capitalistic, of the Arab countries had been hit, the Agency was picking up rumblings in Turkey. None of the secular Muslim states were considered safe from attack anymore.

Since the end of the Cold War, the CIA had struggled with its mission and its methods. He knew firsthand that combating Islamic extremism was not as easy as the talking heads on TV thought it was. Failures had occurred on many levels prior to 9/11: lack of focus, too high a reliance on technology rather than HUMINT, marginalizing the few analysts who warned of the dangers. The US had become complacent with being the sole surviving superpower for having won the Cold War. Human intelligence was more difficult when one's adversary was driven not by politics but by religion. As a motivating force, religion was more powerful than lust, greed, or ego. Men were not just willing to die for their religion, they were enthusiastic about becoming martyrs.

"I told you in the beginning I needed more leeway with Jericho," the man on the phone said.

Richards usually wouldn't have tolerated such insubordination, but the man was an off-the-books subcontractor, not an official employee. He had also devised the most creative plan to combat the difficulties they faced that Richards had ever heard.

"This isn't the 1960s anymore."

"Unfortunate indeed."

"Look, I spoke with the director this morning. You have the go-ahead to ramp up Jericho. Just bring me some results."

Richards's oversight of Project Jericho, one of the boldest and potentially most explosive—if, God forbid, it was ever made public—covert operations undertaken in the post-Cold War era, was the key reason he'd been tapped for the role of Deputy Director. His career, not to mention the potential for peace in the Middle East, hinged on the success of the project this man had first pitched to him several years ago. Prior to 9/11, the man never would have gotten a meeting with Richards. The sort of operation he was proposing hadn't been attempted in almost four decades, which was exactly why Richards thought it just might work.

"I may have a surprise for you too."

Richards cringed. Surprises were rarely a good thing in intelligence.

"We may have a new technique that will revolutionize our work."

"Tell me."

"It's better if you don't know all of the details now."

Knowing the man's checkered reputation and questionable ethics, he could only imagine what he had planned. Richards had reviewed the file of the experiments the man had overseen early in his career. Even as a CIA covert-ops veteran, he'd been shocked by some of what he'd seen. But if anything, the man was a patriot.

Anyways, all aspects of Jericho took place far away from American soil, with no discoverable links to the American government or the CIA.

Richards didn't ask for elaboration.

CHAPTER 7

SSS, YALE UNIVERSITY

"How do we know what is reality?"

Ethan gazed at his students from behind the podium on the stage of Lecture Hall 114, two floors below his lab. The auditorium reminded Ethan of a medieval castle: twenty-foot-long burgundy curtains hung over leaded glass windows; the wood ceiling was decorated with a faded blue and gold coat of arms; Art Deco steel pendant lights were suspended over the theater-style seats. Most of the blue cushions were filled with undergraduates.

Several students looked at him expectantly, as if the question he'd posed was meant to be rhetorical. The others, dressed in sweats and jeans, were taking notes on their laptops—at least that's what he liked to believe. He suspected they were checking their Facebook pages, messaging each other, or playing a game. Although his class, Abnormal Psychology, or Psych for Psychos as the students referred to it, was one of the more popular lectures on campus, students today had shorter attention spans than when he was in school. His class was required for all psych majors, but many others took it as well, based on his reputation as an engaging teacher. As uncomfortable as he was in one-on-one conversations with people he didn't know well, especially women, he enjoyed lecturing, even excelled at it. When he stood in front of his students, he felt as if a veil dropped from him and released his tongue.

He clicked the laptop on the lectern and a slide was projected onto the twenty-five-foot by fifteen-foot screen behind him. The class sat up straighter. The simple black-and-white drawing had their attention.

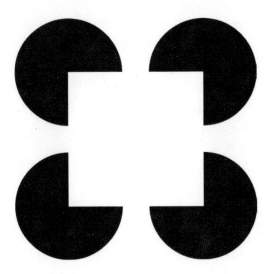

"What do you see here?"

Two dozen hands shot up. He pointed to a brunette with glasses and pigtails in the sixth row. "A square."

He nodded in understanding, but not in agreement. "Let's take a survey here. How many of you see the white square in the middle as what stands out most in the drawing?" Two thirds of the class raised their hands. "Now look at just the black areas. What do you see?"

This time he called on a woman from the front row. Her chestnut-colored hair was streaked with blond highlights, and it flowed around her face and shoulders in waves of loose curls. Her pale complexion, uncovered by makeup, was accented only by a small diamond stud in her nose. He noted that she wore only black, from her sweater to her shiny boots. With over four hundred students attending his lecture, he rarely got to know anyone's names, but his visual memory was close to eidetic; he recognized each and every student who showed up for class. She was always one of the first to arrive, and she took notes every day with a pen in a notebook, paying close attention to his words. She also often had her hand in the air, usually to challenge him on some point.

"The drawing is just four partial circles," she said. "Our brains are only extrapolating the square in the empty space—it's an illusion. We're imagining something that doesn't actually exist."

She held his gaze confidently, and he found himself smiling at her.

"Illusory contours," he said. "The lines of the square do not exist." He broke eye contact and looked across the room at the rest of the class. "An Italian psychologist named Kanizsa developed this optical illusion to show how our brains take input from our five senses and then combine those sensations with our previous knowledge, experiences, and expectations in order to construct the view of reality we expect to find."

"Are you saying our realities are relative?" the woman in black called out. "That our brains are just making guesses?"

This one is sharp, he thought. Her round blue eyes held a spark that drew him in as he nodded his head. He stepped from behind the lectern and answered her question with another, one of his favorite Socratic teaching techniques. "How does any individual know that an experience they are having is real or imagined?"

A voice called out from the rear, "Physical evidence."

He turned his attention to the new voice, a male in jeans and an oversized Yale sweatshirt. "If I were to put you under hypnosis and then prick a finger on each hand with a needle, causing them to bleed, I could make a hypnotic suggestion to you that your left hand was being immersed in cold water. Even though in reality both hands were at room temperature, your left finger would stop bleeding, while the right would continue to flow."

A murmur went up among the class.

"The complexity of the brain is what makes abnormal psychology, the subject of this class in case anyone wandered into the wrong room"—he elicited a few laughs—"such a fascinating and difficult field. The line between normal and abnormal, between reality and fantasy, is not a bright one. Why are religious leaders' hearing God's voice any different from schizophrenics having visions?"

He returned to the lectern and clicked the laptop. The slide changed to an image of Caravaggio's painting *The Conversion of St. Paul*. The Apostle Paul had been riding his horse along the dusty road to Damascus, Syria on his way to arrest early members of the Christian sect when he was struck by a powerful vision of Jesus. The painting that now riveted the students' attention depicted Paul lying on his back after falling from his horse. His hands covered his eyes, his body spotlighted by a light from above.

After three seconds, the slides cycled through other religious images: Bernini's sculpture *The Ecstasy of Santa Teresa* from the Santa Maria della Vittoria church in Rome; a photograph of the Mormon Tabernacle in Salt Lake City, taken as the sun rose above the church spires; and finally a section of Michelangelo's Sistine Chapel fresco containing a red-robed and white-bearded Ezekiel—the Old Testament prophet famous for his graphic visions.

With this generation raised on constant visual stimuli, Ethan knew that the best way to capture their interest was to play to their need for multisensory input. As he scanned the students engrossed by the slides, he noticed an unfamiliar face in the first row of the balcony staring at the front of the room from behind iridescent orange sunglasses. A feeling of unease crept up Ethan's spine.

At first glance, the man appeared to be a jock—football or hockey—judging by his size, the dark blue sweats on his legs, and the gray sweatshirt embroidered with a giant blue Y in the center. He perched like a statue in his chair with a military-erect posture that leaned forward as if he were waiting with anticipation for the rest of the lecture. Then Ethan noticed that the man wasn't the typical large athlete. His bulk strained the fabric on his sweatshirt; his trapezius muscles bulged out of the neckline, almost reaching his ears, while his pectorals distorted the shape of the embroidered Y on his chest, threatening to pull it apart like a wishbone.

Steroids, Ethan thought. He'd never seen such extreme muscle hypertrophy outside of the movies. *Who is he?* The Yale athletic department didn't tolerate juicing. Although the sunglasses made it difficult to know for sure, he appeared older than the undergrads in the room, and he was tan, unusual for a New Haven fall.

A realization deepened his sense of unease: *muscleman is not a student.* Before he could ponder what the man was doing in his class, he sensed the anticipatory silence from his audience. He shifted his gaze to the students who were waiting for him to continue.

"During medical school, I learned how an uncommon but not rare form of epilepsy that originates in the temporal lobe of the brain produces intense religious visions in the sufferers."

An African American man in the middle raised his hand. "So if we see someone thrashing around on the ground from a seizure they could be speaking to God?"

"Probably not. A grand mal seizure such as you described affects the whole brain—it's like the entire electrical system short circuits, causing neurons to misfire and create the seizure."

"Like the electricity in my dorm room last weekend when we plugged in the extra amps for the party?"

He laughed along with the students. "Something like that. But a grand mal seizure usually causes unconsciousness and amnesia. With other seizures that are limited to certain areas of the brain, such as the ones that cause hyperreligiosity, the sufferer may have no idea that they're having a seizure. They may see a strange light, smell something unusual, hear a voice, or have a full-fledged vision while remaining conscious."

The woman in the front row spoke again. "So, Professor, are you claiming" —she pointed to the image on the screen, which had cycled back to Caravaggio's painting—"that St. Paul was knocked from his horse by an epileptic event that also caused his vision of Christ, and"—she paused as the slides transitioned—"that the Spanish mystic St. Teresa de Ávila, Joseph Smith—the founder of Mormonism—and the Prophet Ezekiel also each suffered from temporal lobe epilepsy that led to their religious visions?"

She is sharp, he thought again. "Look at the other symptoms these figures had: flashes of light, strange sounds or smells, their obliviousness to the world around them—all classic symptoms of epilepsy. Is it more likely that an imbalance in the electrical firings of neurons in the brain, which we can record today with modern equipment, caused their visions, or that a supernatural deity spoke to these people from heaven?"

The anticipation of the test of his Logos Project later that afternoon flashed through his mind.

"In the ages during which these figures lived, people had no concept of modern medicine or psychiatry. What we might call an *abnormal* event today—a vision caused by epilepsy or schizophrenia—might have been interpreted as either a demonic possession or an oracle from God."

"But if that's true," she continued, "then the basis for these religions—Christianity, Mormonism, Judaism—so influenced by these visions would be called into question."

He let her last comment sink into the other students. As he paused, a memory from his own past intruded on his thoughts, but he pushed it away as he'd done many times before. "A question we can leave to the theologians."

He glanced at the clock on his monitor: 11:50. He closed his laptop, cutting the video feed to the screen. "Next week's assignment is posted on the website. Enjoy the discussions in your groups."

He looked for Chris Sligh as he descended the steps from the stage. They needed to go over a few details before the experiment, but he didn't see his grad assistant in his usual seat. When he landed on the main floor, students encircled him, peppering him with questions about the lecture. He did his best to answer them while he walked, making his way to the rear of the hall. His mind was already spinning through the possibilities of what might happen that afternoon. When he reached the steps that descended from the balcony, he glanced at the students filing down. The unease he'd felt earlier crawled from his spine to the back of his neck. The muscleman with the orange glasses had disappeared.

CHAPTER 8

DUBAI INTERNATIONAL AIRPORT

A mira's screams tore at Mousa's heart.

"Please, what is going on here?" His voice came out sounding more desperate than he wanted. The three security officers who dragged him along the white hallway said nothing.

"My daughter, you don't understand what we've been through. She needs me." He knew that he was pleading, but he couldn't help himself. Questions spun in his head like a desert sandstorm picking up debris: where were these men taking him, and who was the woman who had his daughter?

When they reached the end of the hallway, the men stopped at a door marked "Secure Area" in both Arabic and English. The lead officer, the one who had spoken to him at the customs desk, produced an ID card with a magnetic stripe. Mousa took a breath, rested his weight on his good right leg, and evaluated the situation. The two other officers glanced at him warily. Each grasped one of his arms just above the elbow. In their other hands, they held submachine guns.

He turned his attention to the officer working the electronic lock. *The door must lead into the airport security room*, he thought. *I'm going to be interrogated.* He had only a moment to gather his wits and calm himself. The officers had made a mistake. Maybe his name was similar to someone on their watch list. Or could something have been wrong with his visa? If he calmly explained who he was—a respected Jordanian surgeon—they would have to listen. He might have to wait while they checked out his story, but many people at the

King Hussein Hospital in Amman could confirm his identity and legitimacy. With his hands bound behind his back, he couldn't see his watch, but he estimated that his flight wouldn't depart for another two hours. If he remained calm and professional, maybe the security men would clear everything up in time for them to return home that afternoon.

As the lead officer opened the door, Mousa reminded himself not to antagonize the men during the questioning. Regardless of his innocence, he surmised that the security forces in the UAE were like those in Jordan—not to be trifled with.

A wall of hot, dry air rushed into the air-conditioned hallway and dismantled his resolve to stay calm. The door didn't lead to an interrogation room. It led outside.

"Where are you taking me?" he demanded.

The black-clad men shoved him into the naked sun.

"I haven't done anything!" he screamed. "You've made a mistake."

Then he noticed the vehicle. Parked on the tarmac just in front of the sidewalk sat a gray, late-model van. It had no markings, and he noted with a growing sense of dread that its windows were blacked out. The lead officer hurried to the van and slid open the side door, revealing a stripped out interior with a metal floor. The only seats were the driver's and the front passenger's. Mousa stopped, forcing his feet in front of him. He leaned backward against the pressure on his arms.

"I am a respected doctor in Amman." He attempted to use his most authoritative, professional voice, the one he used to navigate cumbersome hospital bureaucracy. "I demand to speak to your superiors! You have made a career-threatening mistake here."

He couldn't allow these men to remove him from the airport grounds. If they did, he knew that the odds of seeing his family again were slim.

As the words left his mouth, the man to his left swung his submachine gun. Mousa caught only a blur of its movement before the blow struck him in the solar plexus, sucking out his breath. His legs buckled. He would have doubled over in pain, but the men held him aloft. The desert sun became blurry as his diaphragm spasmed in a failed attempt to draw a breath.

The men shoved him into the van. When he landed on the scuffed aluminum floor, a screw in the floorboard cut a gash along his cheek. The men jumped in around him and slammed the door. One jerked his head up by his hair, bringing tears to his eyes. The officer then pulled a black sleep mask, the type the airlines gave out in first class on overseas flights, over his eyes.

In short gasps, Mousa's breath returned. The air tasted of oil and sweat. Once he recovered his faculties, he opened his mouth to yell again. This time he resisted. The officers had a plan, and telling him anything was not part of that plan. As the adrenaline coursing through his body dissipated, the indignation over his arrest and the frantic urge to be released was replaced by a new emotion: fear. The sudden realization that something more serious than a faulty visa was behind his arrest opened a pit of darkness in his gut.

Before his mind could race through the possible permutations of his predicament, the van stopped. They'd traveled less than five minutes. He heard the door slide open, letting in a deafening noise along with the hot desert wind. This time he didn't resist as the men lifted him outside. Although he could only see darkness behind the mask, he felt the sun beat down on his blazer. The moment he realized the source of the rhythmic thumping, he instinctively ducked his head to avoid the rotors of the helicopter. He'd been on call at the hospital when the Life Flight chopper brought critically injured patients to the landing pad on the roof. He tried to swallow but found that his mouth had gone dry.

The men shoved him forward. His thighs hit metal, sending a jolt of pain from his injured knee through his body. Hands seized him under his shoulders and lifted him. His leg protested when he collapsed onto a ribbed metal surface.

Shock replaced the fear of a moment ago. He felt detached from the events, as if he were in the middle of a surrealistic dream. Just a few minutes earlier, he'd been standing in the airport with his daughter as they waited to leave for home.

The bass thumping of the rotors increased in frequency. His stomach lurched as the floor moved upward and forward at the same time. The helicopter was lifting off, taking him somewhere. Somewhere away from his home. Somewhere away from Amira.

CHAPTER 9

CAPLAB, YALE UNIVERSITY

"**M**ay I help you?" a female voice crackled over the intercom in the basement hallway.

"Dr. Ethan Lightman. I'm here for CapLab."

Although he visited Yale-New Haven Hospital weekly, he'd never paid attention to the three-story building down the block whose small windows and ribbed concrete exterior gave away its 1960s heritage.

"Be right there, Professor," the voice replied.

The only marking on the door before him was the suite number: 108. No signage revealed its true purpose: CapLab, Yale's capuchin monkey research laboratory. Because of animal rights protests at other primate labs around the country, Yale kept the location of its research facilities secret.

After his lecture that morning, he'd found Christian Sligh in their office. His graduate assistant had given him the tightly guarded directions to CapLab and then left to make sure that the experiment would be ready when Ethan arrived. Chris had taken the Logos with him.

Ethan heard the lock click on the other side of the door. When it opened, a familiar face greeted him.

"Hi, Professor." The young woman stuck out a petite hand with manicured nails but no polish, just as she wore no makeup. "I'm Rachel Riley."

The student from the front row of his lecture class stood before him. Her chestnut hair was pulled into a tight ponytail, her wide blue eyes staring at him with the same intensity as during his lectures. Her handshake was stronger than her delicate fingers would have suggested.

"You're one of my students."

He towered over her—*can't be more than five-two*, he thought—but she carried herself with an energy that seemed befitting someone of much larger stature. She held his gaze.

"Grad student—first year." She spun around, started down the hallway, and stopped at an unmarked door at the end. "Evolutionary Biology."

Even though his legs were considerably longer than hers, he had to hurry to catch up. "So what are you doing in my undergrad course?"

"Thought Psych for Psychos might give me some perspective on my research here." She flashed a smile that lit up her face. "And, I heard you were a decent teacher."

He felt his neck flush, but before he could look away, she turned to the wall and punched a code on a keypad. When the electronic lock beeped, she opened the door and motioned for him to enter. His first impression upon stepping into the room was that it looked more like a dorm than a lab. Jackets and book bags were piled on top of a couch that looked as if it had been purchased at a thrift store. Starbucks cups crowded the surface of a wood-laminate coffee table.

"What's up, Prof?" Chris waved to him from his seat at the desk against the wall to the right. Ethan's laptop was open on the desk.

"We ready?"

"The Logos is programmed and warming up now." Chris flipped his head, flinging blond hair from his eyes. "Rachel's been quite helpful in organizing the apes." His eyes lingered on her.

"All hominids are apes, including you." She jabbed a finger in Chris's direction. "Ape is too imprecise a term. These are capuchins, monkeys." Her tone was firm, but from the crinkles around her eyes, Ethan suspected her displeasure was feigned.

"You work here?" Ethan asked her.

"Since freshman year. I was an undergrad here too. One of the reasons I came to Yale was CapLab. I took a gap year after high school—well, two actually—working at an animal preserve in Kenya. I'm the head tech now. I help Professor Sanchez with her research."

"Where is Laura?"

Ethan respected Laura Sanchez, a fellow psychology faculty member who'd just received tenure last year. Her determination and enthusiasm had been the driving force behind establishing CapLab as one of the leading primate research centers in the nation. She'd also been helpful when he and Elijah had approached her about testing the Logos in her lab.

"Atlanta. Conference at Yerkes. I've been instructed to assist you guys with anything you need." She cast her eyes down the length of his body for a moment so brief that he wasn't sure that it had happened.

Did she just check me out? As a young faculty member, he'd experienced female students flirting with him before, but he'd never pursued that dangerous path, even though he'd known others—even much older professors—who had done so. *Not my type anyway*, he told himself. The memory of Natalie's tall body, jet-black hair, and olive complexion popped into his head, bringing with it the familiar pang of regret in the depths of his stomach.

A touch to his arm brought his attention back to the woman standing before him. Her hand rested on his upper arm; it was warm.

"You've had your TB tests, right? We can't risk an infection that would wipe out our whole population."

"We both have," Chris rose from the chair.

"Yes, both negative," Ethan confirmed.

"So, can we go in now?" Chris gestured to the plate glass window that took up most of the wall to their left.

With his attention focused on Rachel, Ethan had failed to notice the giant window when he entered, though it was the focal point of the room. Tree branches swayed on the other side, giving the impression that he was looking outdoors—an impossibility since they were in the basement of the building. Closer inspection revealed a chain-link fence and a concrete floor covered in wood shavings that defined a large room on the other side of the window. The tree branches were bare and several ropes connected them to the ceiling and to each other. A dozen small brown monkeys played in various parts of the room-sized cage. Some groomed each other; others climbed on the branches or swung from the ropes; a few chewed on chunks of fruit before tossing the rinds to the floor.

"Do you have the paperwork showing the negative results?"

"Here." Chris picked up a manila folder from the desk and handed it to her. Ethan once again appreciated how well his graduate assistant handled the myriad regulations their research required.

"Not trying to be a pain." She flipped open the folder. "I don't want the IACUC coming down on my ass because the protocols weren't followed. Just last month we were cited because one of the monkeys was underweight. They refused to listen to us. We provide them more than enough food. He was just a lower ranking member of the community." She tossed the folder on the desk. "Bureaucrats. Last year, they actually changed the locks on the office doors because they said it was too messy in here!"

Ethan chuckled. The IACUC, the Institutional Animal Care Use Committee, was just as difficult as Samuel Houston's Human Research Protection Program Committee with its IRBs. Each of these committees saw it as their jobs to bust the researchers before the feds did. In addition to the university's committees, they had to deal with inspections by government agencies like the USDA and AAALAC—the Association for Assessment and Accreditation of Laboratory Animal Care. The acronyms drove him crazy.

"Tell me about it. I'm struggling with the HRPP right now."

"You work with Sam Houston?"

"Not sure I would say 'work with'—more like try to avoid at all costs." She laughed at his half-joke. Talking to the attractive yet earnest grad student felt unusually easy to him. "You know Houston?"

She glanced away from him toward her desk. Her voice dropped. "Let's just say that we've had our run-ins too."

From the change in her tone he guessed that whatever had happened with the administrator wasn't something she wanted to discuss. He could relate. He followed her gaze to the desk. Two items caught his attention: a dog-eared paperback by Walt Whitman and a chunk of quartz the size of a softball.

"A Whitman fan?"

"*Adore* him." She enunciated each syllable. "His idea that an ineffable power enlivens nature speaks to me. Like the Native American view that everything has a consciousness—humans, eagles, mountains, rivers—and that consciousness is what links all of us together."

The emptiness in his gut returned. Natalie had loved Whitman too, but for different reasons. She'd admired his use of language in describing nature. For the second time since he'd entered the office, he forced the memory of his deceased fiancée from his mind.

Chris snorted. "You're telling me this rock has consciousness." He picked up the translucent stone and held it up to the light.

"First off, it's a crystal—quartz. Second, I don't mean a consciousness like the awareness that we have, but a certain force—an energy of existence. And third, many wise people believe that the unique molecular structure of crystals can hold this energy and that it can even provide healing powers."

Ethan resisted the urge to roll his eyes. He put the whole New Age crystal theory, as well as Whitman's pantheistic musings, on the same plane as Wiccan magic, ESP, and angels causing miracles. The human mind's ability to imagine a pattern or an unseen force behind a series of unrelated but coincidental events was well documented. In his class, he demonstrated this principle by projecting a photograph of clouds in the sky. He would then ask the students to play the childhood game of *what do you see*? After they shouted out their divergent, and often hilarious, answers, he pointed out that each of their own proclivities influenced their interpretations of this random display of nature. The human brain doesn't like ambiguity, he explained. Our minds have evolved to make assumptions about our surroundings and to draw conclusions from incomplete information. The same neural processes that allowed a hunter in the savannah to make a quick decision about which animal to pursue or to avoid also cause some people to see the Virgin Mary in a cloud or a corn field.

"Shall we get started?" he asked. He glanced at the evolutionary biologist in front of him and wondered how she reconciled her spiritual views with her studies. But he had more important work to attend to than engaging in a philosophical discussion with two grad students.

"Sure. Once your assistant stops touching my stuff." Rachel took the quartz from Chris's hand and replaced it in the desk.

She shot a sideways glance at both men before leading them through a metal door next to the large window. They entered another fluorescent-lit hallway whose vinyl tile floor and bare white walls were similar to the one that led to the office. At the end of the hall, they entered through another metal door into an anteroom with a bench along one side and hooks above it. The opposite wall held a row of lockers, and across from where they entered was yet another door. Rachel turned a lock on the door they had just entered.

Ethan glanced between the two doors. "You have an air-lock system here?"

She laughed. "It's not quite a spaceship." She nodded to the second door. "But that leads to the monkey room. We need the multiple layers of security because they're smart. We've had some close calls with escape attempts."

She opened a locker and from it pulled out two sets of blue surgical scrubs, shoe covers, masks, and eye shields, which she handed to the men. For herself, she pulled out a set of scrubs in tie-dye.

"Why the scrubs?" Chris asked. "The experiment is noninvasive."

Ethan wondered the same thing. It was one of the conditions for conducting the tests at CapLab; this was a psychological research lab, not a medical one. When he first approached Dr. Sanchez about testing the Logos on the monkeys, he had to assure her that no surgical techniques or drugs would be used. The Logos would only send weak magnetic pulses aimed at the capuchins' skulls.

"It's to protect the monkeys from human diseases," she said as she slipped her scrubs over her clothes, "but sometimes they bite and throw feces."

Ethan pulled the strap of his surgical mask over his head. The last thing he wanted was a mouthful of monkey poop.

"They bite?" Chris asked.

"In the nineties"—she bent over to slip on her shoe covers—"a researcher at Yerkes was bitten by a macaque and died from encephalitis."

She opened the last door into the monkey room. They were greeted by loud vocalizations from the capuchins and the distinctive smell of a zoo. The room was approximately thirty feet square. Two-thirds of it was enclosed by the chain-link fence. At the far end was the large window that opened onto the office, but from this side he could only see a reflection of the room they were in; the window was a one-way mirror. Sitting on a metal cart with wheels just outside the cage was the Logos.

The brains and the mechanics of the Logos were contained in a black metal box the size of a large stereo receiver. The box had several dials to adjust the power and frequency of the electromagnetic pulses it generated, but it also had a serial port into which Chris had loaded Ethan's proprietary algorithm from his laptop that morning. His programming, rather than the dials, would determine the exact protocol by which the machine would generate its outputs. Extending off of the box was a metal articulated arm that telescoped out three feet. On the end of the arm were what appeared to be headphones—the kind that covered one's ears—although these were wider and ended in three-inch plastic disks rather than plush cushions.

The Logos was designed to be placed on either side of a subject's head without touching it. Instead of speakers, the disks contained solenoids, tightly wound loops of wire that would produce variable magnetic pulses when an electrical current was passed through them. Today, the solenoids were suspended above a rectangular wire tunnel that branched off of the main cage by a few feet. The tunnel was large enough for a single monkey to crawl through. At the end of the tunnel was a wire box with a small hole and a U-shaped foam attachment on top.

Ethan felt the anticipation building within him. The past five years working with Elijah, the scorn from their colleagues, their financial difficulties—once they made the Logos work, the long nights and early mornings would be worth it. *If it works*, he thought. The first dozen tests had failed, no matter how they'd tweaked the programming. Then he'd had the epiphany to base the algorithm on the EEG of epileptics who experienced hyperreligiosity. That was six months ago.

Elijah had leapt out of his desk chair when he'd made the suggestion. Receiving the approval of his mentor meant more to Ethan than all of the snide comments his friends in the department made. However, Elijah had insisted on the extra safety test on a non-human primate: "Just to make sure we don't induce a full-fledged seizure." Ethan didn't think that was possible with the care he'd taken in programming the algorithm. He was anxious to get to the human phase, to get answers to his most pressing questions. They were scheduled to begin human testing next week, if the tests today proved the machine safe.

The screeching from the monkeys grew louder as Rachel walked to the fencing. A capuchin leaped from a branch to the cage by Rachel's face. "Hey, Anakin," she cooed.

The monkey—one of the younger ones, judging by its small size—pressed its back up to the wire. Rachel reached in two fingers and scratched it.

"You aren't seeing this. Strictly against the rules."

"The monkey's name is Anakin?" Chris asked.

"That one"—she pointed to a larger one with graying hair—"is Obi Wan. Over there we have Luke, Lea, and the black one is Darth."

"*Star Wars*?" Ethan asked. Although he rarely went to the movies anymore, he'd grown up on *Star Wars*. He'd seen all of the movies multiple times.

"Makes it easier to remember the names."

Well, little Anakin, he thought, *I hope you don't have a grand mal on me here.* This was their last chance. He and Elijah were out of ideas, and even with their new grant, Houston wouldn't tolerate many more failures. But in his heart he knew the Logos would work. He hadn't wasted the past five years chasing a phantom dream.

"Are we ready?" Chris asked from behind the Logos.

Rachel glanced from the two men to the black box by the cage. When she'd asked Chris about the machine earlier, he'd been evasive, and Professor Sanchez hadn't given her much before hurrying to catch her flight to Atlanta. Professor Ethan Lightman might be brilliant, *and attractive*, she admitted to herself, but she was nervous about putting her babies at risk.

Ever since she was a young girl, she'd had a way with animals. She'd thought that she could feel what they were thinking. Plus, they were appreciative of being taken care of, unlike her two younger brothers. Rachel had been the one responsible for feeding and cleaning up after them. Her dad was rarely home. He worked late nights and weekends, and when he was physically present, he was emotionally distant. *And Mom*— She pushed away the memories. Rather than make their own meals, her brothers would complain if she made PB&Js or chicken fingers two nights in a row. On the other hand, Commander, her fluffy terrier mix, and Flotsam and Jetsam, her hamsters—and even Tiggie, her parakeet—were always happy to see her. After making sure her brothers had what they needed, she would shut herself in her room with her pets.

She put her hands on her hips and said, "We can begin once you tell me what this machine is going to do to my capuchins."

"I can assure you there is no danger to the monkeys," Ethan said.

That's not an answer, she thought. Standing beside the wire tunnel that led from the cage to the Logos, she folded her arms like a sentry guarding the entrance of a castle.

"I'm sorry, but didn't Professor Sanchez sign off on this?"

"Well, when she's not here, they're my responsibility." Just because he was a professor, not to mention tall and sexy, didn't mean she would be intimidated.

He sighed. "The Logos"—he pointed to the metal box on the stand—"generates a series of electrical pulses whose amplitude, wavelength, and frequency are determined by an algorithm I designed. The pulses travel along these wires"—he gestured to the black wires that coiled around the metal arm—"to the two solenoids here, which convert the electrical pulses into magnetic ones." He pointed to the plastic discs. "We direct these magnetic pulses predominantly toward the left temporal lobe of the subject's brain. It's really just a modification of a Transcranial Magnetic Stimulation protocol." He shrugged as if the procedure were no big deal.

"You're going to microwave my monkeys' brains?"

Chris jumped in. "Hospitals use TMS technology all the time. The FDA has approved it for the treatment of depression."

She frowned. "I know that neurons are like tiny electrical circuits, firing small charges across their synapses, but you're telling me that these circuits can be influenced by magnetic fields from outside the skull?

Ethan nodded. "Studies have shown that TMS can be more effective on depression than medication, with no side effects."

"But my monkeys aren't depressed."

"Of course not." Chris smiled. "We've just tweaked the programming of the machine for our experiment."

"For what purpose?"

She caught the men exchanging a glance.

"Because you know the monkeys so well," Ethan explained, "we want you to observe them to see if you notice any behavior changes during the test. Although we didn't design the experiment as a double blind one, we didn't want to tell you too much and risk coloring your report to us afterward."

She held his gaze. *He's telling the truth*, she thought, *but he's nervous*. His hands were clasped behind his back. From the tension in his shoulders, she could tell that he was trying not to fidget. *Well, Laura did authorize the tests.* Professor Sanchez was the only one who cared about the monkeys more than she did.

She dropped her arms, walked over to a mini-fridge in the corner of the room, and removed a bowl with sliced green apples and oranges, a small vial of clear liquid, and a syringe.

"Ketamine," she said, answering the men's curious looks. "In case you're wrong about your machine." Ketamine was a tranquilizer that would immediately paralyze the monkey. The forms they had to fill out to get it were endless because the drug was often abused by ravers who referred to it as Special K.

She pulled a chunk of orange from the bowl. "We can only test one at a time. How many are we going to run?"

"Three, please."

She held up the slice so that the monkeys could see it. Anakin, who was still the closest to her, began to chatter. She slid open a mesh door that closed off the wire tunnel from the main cage. Anakin leaped toward the tunnel, but just before he entered Obi Wan swung down from a higher branch and pushed him out of the way.

"Wow, aggressive," Chris said.

"Not at all, just hierarchical." She closed the tunnel door after Obi Wan entered and held the orange where he could see it as he scooted toward the wire box at the end. "Food, toys, and attention are divvied up according to the hierarchy of the group. Typically the older and larger males eat first and get the most." She looked up at Ethan, who was at least a foot taller than her, and grinned. "Fortunately, some of us have evolved beyond those instincts."

When the monkey poked his head up through the small hole in the top of the box, she gave him the orange while snapping the foam collar around his neck, securing him in the position. The first time she'd done this for other experiments, she and the monkeys were nervous, but now it was routine. Ethan nodded to Chris, who lowered the headset so that the two black solenoids were positioned on either side of Obi Wan's head. Eating his orange, Obi Wan paid no attention. Chris then stepped behind the Logos. When the graduate student hit a switch, a low hum emerged from the metal box. Rachel felt her pulse increase in time with the vibration. She hoped she was making the right decision by allowing them to proceed with their tests.

Ethan's heart pounded against his sternum as if it were knocking on a heavy door. He had to remind himself to breathe. *All of our work*, he thought. If a monkey had a seizure, their project was over. He pushed the thought from his head, but then another more disturbing one intruded: *What if the machine didn't work at all?*

Elijah's theory about the nature of mystical experiences was controversial, and their colleagues looked on them with skepticism at best. If the machine worked, they would be vindicated. But then, what if their peers were right?

Scientists had learned more about the brain in the past two decades than in all of prior history. They now had pills that could affect one's emotions, and others that could stop schizophrenic hallucinations. Experiments demonstrated that electrodes planted deep in the brain could trigger memories of certain smells or tastes; other electrodes could induce orgasm. With all of these advances, the one area that had never been conquered was the control of one's thoughts and beliefs. What better way to attempt this, Elijah had first theorized years ago, than through religion—one of the most powerful belief systems of the human mind?

Inevitably, Ethan's thoughts drifted down a path he'd tried to repress for years—the secret that had plagued him since he was a child, the answers that he'd sought for two decades.

Suddenly, Obi Wan dropped the orange from his mouth. Ethan felt his breath catch. He waited for any sign that might suggest the monkey was about to begin convulsing from a generalized tonic-clonic seizure. Rachel, who stood beside him, stiffened.

"He's okay," Chris said.

Ethan wondered whether the grad student believed his comment or was expressing his hope. He bent forward to stare more closely. The monkey's eyes appeared to be tracking something that none of them could see. His arms hung by his sides inside the wire box, but his body didn't slouch—he appeared relaxed. Ethan even imagined that Obi Wan looked thoughtful.

Rachel exhaled. "Yes, he is okay."

A strange thought occurred to him. They'd come here to test that the magnetic pulses from the Logos didn't cause a seizure in the animals. Could it be that something else was happening—something he wouldn't have thought possible in a non-human primate?

He turned to Rachel, who stared at Obi Wan with her head cocked. "Monkeys, they don't—" He struggled with how to phrase his question. "Do monkeys have mystical experiences?"

"I think all living organisms have the capacity to experience the deeper dimension that is the creative energy of existence." Her eyes locked onto his. "Don't you?"

CHAPTER 10

UNDISCLOSED PRISON FACILITY
UNITED ARAB EMIRATES

*W*here am I?

Mousa had asked the same question countless times—for how many days, he was no longer sure. The helicopter ride from the airport had taken an hour or two. Then he'd been shoved in a van and driven to a prison where he was strip-searched, given a blue cotton jumpsuit to wear, and tossed in a rancid cell. The brief hope he'd held at the airport for a quick resolution to whatever misunderstanding had brought him this trouble had vanished. He'd been neither asked nor told anything since he arrived. When he questioned the guard who probed his naked body, the only answer he received was a stinging slap across the head.

How was he supposed to clear his name if he didn't know what he had to clear it from? They had his ID: his passport, credit cards, and hospital pass. Maybe they would realize their mistake on their own. The empty feeling in his gut indicated that this was unlikely.

The terror he'd felt at the airport still coursed through his veins. His body had been pumping cortisol, the stress hormone, since he'd been taken captive. He guessed his blood pressure was a steady twenty points higher than usual. The lack of sleep made his exhaustion worse. American hip hop music blared from a speaker in his cell's ceiling at random intervals, which, along with the bare halogen light bulb in the ceiling of his two-by-three-meter concrete cell, made sleeping all but impossible. On his first day, he'd made the mistake of unscrewing the bulb. Not only had he burned his fingers, he'd earned a beating from two guards who'd burst into his cell. His jaw still hurt, but he was too tired to care.

The clanging of metal against metal brought clarity to his mind. The door to his cell slid open. He shrank into the corner of his narrow cot. The two guards who had beaten him earlier marched inside. Dressed in black from their boots to the berets on their heads, their complexions were equally dark. One was tall, trim, and clean-shaven, while the other was shorter, solid, with several days' worth of stubble. Each held a baton.

Without speaking, the short one pulled him off the cot, flipped him around, and snapped handcuffs on his wrists. Then the guard pulled a black hood over his head. The fear of suffocating under the fabric, which smelled of sweat and vomit, was so overpowering that he had to force himself to take shallow breaths through his teeth.

They led him out of his cell to the right; twenty-four paces, he counted. Then they turned right again, at which point he sensed they had entered another room. He had no feel for the prison's size or layout. The door to his cell was solid steel, with only a sliding opening at the bottom big enough for his captors to shove through a plate with a single boiled potato or some cold rice, which they did once a day. The rap music prevented him from hearing anything outside his cell.

The guards uncuffed him, pushed him into a hard wooden chair, and then reattached the handcuffs behind the back of the chair. His shoulders burned from the strain. When they yanked the hood from his head, he inhaled deeply. After his eyes adjusted to a light that was even brighter than the one in his cell, he saw that the room was several times larger than his own, but it had the same dull gray concrete walls. The guards stationed themselves beside the single door. His chair sat at one end of a metal table in the center of the room; across from him was a second, empty chair.

I'm in an interrogation room, he thought.

He turned his head to the right. Against the wall was a large wooden trunk with a padlock securing it. He tried not to think what the trunk might contain.

Then he rotated his head further. The chasm in his gut grew deeper when he saw the metal chains hanging from bolts in the ceiling. The concrete floor underneath the chains was stained with dark blotches.

Then a spark of hope flickered through him: maybe this was the opportunity he'd waited for—the chance to explain himself, to clear his name. As the thought occurred, the door opened and a man entered. In contrast to the military black of the guards, he wore a charcoal suit, blue shirt, and striped red tie. His mustache was as groomed as his slicked-back hair.

Mousa felt the tension in his body ease. This man looked like he was here to help: a lawyer, a government official perhaps. He set a laptop and a manila file of papers on the table.

"Mousa bin Ibrahim Al-Mohammad?" The man smiled at him. He spoke in a cultured Arabic.

"Yes, that's me." He was surprised how rough his voice sounded.

The man opened the folder on the table and scanned through several pages. Mousa saw his picture in the corner of one of the pages.

"You are a doctor, an orthopedic surgeon at King Hussein Hospital in Amman, Jordan?"

"Yes, yes, I am." He exhaled deeply as he nodded. The fog in his head began to clear. Finally, someone knew who he was.

The mustached man looked at him with a curious but friendly expression. Then he realized the man had not introduced himself. Before he could ask his name, role, or any of the other questions that began to flood into his mind, the man pulled a large color photograph from the folder and placed it on the table.

"Who is this?" His tone was cordial, but firm.

Mousa squinted at the photo. His glasses had disappeared at some point during his abduction. The man in the photo looked vaguely familiar but was not someone he knew personally. He appeared to be around thirty years old with short hair and the dark stubble of a beard. He wasn't looking at the camera.

"No idea." He shrugged.

The mustached man's unblinking gaze urged him to study the picture again. Mousa bent as close as the handcuffs would allow and studied the blurry features. The man appeared to be Jordanian. A feeling of unease began to spread across his skin like a cold wind, causing the hairs on his body to stand on end. He remembered where he had seen the man before: *the Mall of the Emirates, before the bombing.* With the upheaval in his own life, he had forgotten about the suspicious man with the backpack with whom he'd spoken before he took Amira on the ski slope.

He looked up at the man in the suit, who was smiling as if he knew that Mousa recognized the person in the photograph. He now had an inkling of why he was there.

He took a breath, straightened, and stared the man directly in the eye. "My daughter and I were in the Mall of the Emirates during the explosion. I may have seen him there, but I don't know him. When we escaped, I wanted to get her out of the area quickly, so we returned to our hotel."

He told the truth, but he omitted his suspicions about the man's involvement in the bombing. His guilt at not going to the police after they escaped the mall returned. How could he explain now why he didn't do so?

The mustached man nodded, but Mousa wasn't sure if he was nodding in agreement or in understanding of something else.

"What is his name?" He tapped on the picture with his finger.

"His name? I told you, I don't know him."

"He is Jordanian, like you."

"Yes, I'm Jordanian."

This isn't going well, he thought. His questioner's smile had vanished, along with his friendly demeanor. Then he pulled a second photograph out of the folder: a picture of Mousa and Amira in the mall.

"What was in the red backpack?"

The red backpack?

"My daughter and I went to the mall to ski, and I brought our ski clothes in the backpack." He was worried that his explanation didn't sound convincing. He was telling the truth, but his nerves seemed to be controlling his voice. He knew that if he could convince this man of his innocence, of the truth, then surely the man would file his report and release him to return to his family. The thought of his family brought a pang of longing deep in his core again. *Amira. Where is she?* Had they contacted his wife to come and get her, or was she being held by strangers somewhere too? *God willing, they wouldn't harm a child,* he prayed silently.

"You do not know this man?" His interrogator opened up the laptop as he spoke.

"Correct. I can't even say if the man in this photograph is who I saw in the mall."

The interrogator pressed a key on the laptop, and a video began to play on the screen. The streaming numbers in the corner of the video displaying the date and the time indicated that the video was from a security camera. The quality of the recording from the mall was surprisingly crisp. After a few seconds of random shoppers passing by, he and Amira came into the frame. They walked hand in hand as she tugged on his arm. Seeing his daughter was painful yet strengthening. He had to get out of this place, *wherever this is*, to find her. Then he saw the other man, the one in the picture. The other Jordanian carried a backpack identical to his but in blue rather than red.

As the two men passed each other on the video, Mousa clearly saw himself nod to the suspected terrorist. Although there was no sound to the video, he watched both of their lips move as they spoke to each other before heading off in opposite directions.

He felt the back of his neck flush hot as his predicament became clear: the arrest at the airport, the imprisonment, the days without sleep before the interrogation. The UAE government thought he was part of the plot to bomb the mall. The man who he had recognized as a fellow Jordanian, the man he had greeted, was the terrorist.

He looked up from the laptop to the interrogator. He felt as if a heavy weight had settled in his stomach, pressing him down into the hard wood of the chair. The pain had returned to his shoulders and the handcuffs bit into his wrists. *How do I explain the mistake?* His walking past the terrorist was an unfortunate, random occurrence. He had recognized a countryman and said hello. The expression on his interrogator's face was as businesslike as his dark suit. Mousa knew that the mustached man would never believe the explanation.

He wouldn't have either.

CHAPTER 11

SSS, YALE UNIVERSITY

Professor Elijah Schiff was nervous.

He didn't say so, but Ethan could tell that his mentor was preoccupied. He scurried about their lab, straightening the piles of journals teetering on the edge of his desk and stuffing overflowing folders into the file cabinet, then muttered to himself as he turned toward the Logos, which Chris had moved back into the lab. The machine sat behind a leather reclining chair they had picked up at Goodwill; the solenoids were positioned over the headrest. Elijah pulled a white handkerchief from the inside pocket of his tweed jacket and began to dust the machine and then the recliner. Ethan watched the nervous energy from his desk chair. He was just as apprehensive, but he pushed it inside and maintained a calm and composed exterior.

He focused his attention outside the leaded glass of the gothic bay window in front of their desks. The lights of the cars backed up on Grove Street two stories below sparkled through the gray mist of the chilly New Haven afternoon. At any minute, the head of the Neurological Advancement Foundation—the group that had thrown them their final financial lifeline, without which their project would be terminated—was due in their office.

Although Elijah had described the funding to Samuel Houston as a done deal, the reality was less clear. Elijah had signed the paperwork that Chris had helped prepare, but the foundation hadn't returned their signed copy of the contract. The NAF wanted to inspect the lab first. Ethan wiped his palms on the thighs of his khakis and then straightened his striped blue tie.

"Don't worry," he said. "I have faith in your ability to close the deal." His words were more to comfort himself than Elijah.

"Ah, my friend, faith is a state of mind, not a belief."

Ethan smiled at the Zen-like response he was accustomed to hearing from the elder professor.

"Is Chris joining us?" Elijah asked.

"He's over at CapLab, picking up the final report from the tech who helped us observe the capuchins' behavior."

The image of Rachel's smile flashed through his mind.

"Before we move to human testing," Elijah said, "I'd like to study that report in detail."

Ethan suppressed a sigh. His mentor was brilliant, but he was overly cautious. The monkey tests two days earlier had gone well. Only one, Anakin, had even been agitated by the strange contraption humming near his head. Ethan was anxious now to test his programming on a person. Then they might have something more impressive to show the NAF than a quiet machine hovering over an empty chair in the center of the room.

The door to the lab opened. A distinguished man in a navy pinstriped three-piece suit, with a yellow tie and matching pocket square, strode into the room. Ethan stood.

"Elijah!" the man boomed in a baritone voice with a hint of a New England boarding school accent.

The man gripped Elijah's hand in both of his and pumped it up and down. "So good to be working together again. It's been how long?"

"Over four decades." Elijah returned the man's smile, but to Ethan it looked forced. He'd never seen Elijah under this kind of stress before. He knew the two men had been in graduate school together in the sixties, but it was a time Elijah never discussed. He wondered what history these men shared.

"And you must be Professor Lightman." He gripped Ethan's hand. "Dr. Allen Wolfe, but please call me Allen." From the inside pocket of his jacket he produced a business card which identified him as the Executive Director of the Neurological Advancement Foundation.

"Likewise. Ethan."

The foundation director had a full head of silver hair swept back in a wave across his head. Wolfe was tall—not quite up to Ethan's six-four, but close. He glanced at the Dallas address on the business card before putting it in his pocket.

"You flew in from Texas?"

Wolfe shook his head. "Been in DC the past two days. Working with our Congressional lobbying firm. I'm sure I don't need to tell you that funding for mental illness research sorely lags behind that of physical ailments." He looked each of them in the eye as he spoke, confident but relaxed at the same time.

"That very issue has threatened to shut down our study."

He felt Elijah shoot him a glance as soon as the words came from his mouth. The senior professor was the one who handled the grant proposals, and for good reason. Sometimes he spoke too directly, as if the inner censor between his thoughts and his mouth was a step behind his tongue. He knew better than to reveal the desperate nature of their financial condition, but something in the way Wolfe nodded his head in agreement gave him comfort that this man understood their plight and genuinely wanted to help.

"Well, I hope"—Wolfe paced over to the Logos as he spoke—"we can do our small part to fill in the research gaps that others have overlooked." His erect but fluid posture communicated the same refined ease as his speech.

When Wolfe reached the machine, he bent over and touched the solenoid headset. He was delicate yet curious at the same time, as if he were examining an antique automobile at a car show.

"So this is it. Have you finished the primate safety tests?"

"We get the final report back this afternoon." Ethan was surprised that the head of the foundation was conversant in the protocols of the experiment. "But the tests appeared to be successful. I watched all of them."

Elijah cleared his throat. "Yes, Allen, we didn't expect to have any problems, but we might want to run a few more rounds with the primates just to be sure."

Wolfe turned to face the two professors. The grin on his face, golden from the Texas sun, revealed straight, white teeth. He reminded Ethan of a classic Hollywood star from the movies his father used to watch.

"You always were the cautious one, Elijah. I see nothing has changed in all these years." The director's fingers drummed on the leather of the recliner. "Certainly we want to ensure that all necessary safety protocols are followed, but you need to understand that the NAF works differently from other foundations. Our principal benefactor made his billions through decisive action and taking risks. Now that he's dedicating himself to philanthropy, he wants to bring the same spirit of entrepreneurialism to the staid and slow-moving world of academic research."

A man of action, Ethan thought. The more he heard about the NAF, the more he realized what a perfect fit they would be.

Wolfe continued, "Your work is exactly the kind of bold genius we're looking for. I haven't seen this kind of thinking since our grad school days, Elijah. You have certainly outdone yourself."

Elijah gazed at the ground, fidgeting. Ethan had never seen his mentor awkward before. Usually Elijah was the passionate salesman about their vision. He wondered again about the history between the two men at Harvard.

"So this software tycoon, does he have a name?" Elijah asked.

"He prefers to remain anonymous. I've really given you too much information already. A foundation with a three-hundred-million-dollar endowment receives many requests for its funds. The last thing he wants is to be lobbied personally."

"Hmmf," Elijah grunted.

Wolfe walked around to the rear of the machine. "So this really works?"

"We think it does," Ethan said. "We'll know as soon as we start our human trials."

Elijah nodded. "Ethan has devised a new software algorithm that's a significant advancement from our earlier versions."

"Yes, Dr. Lightman's involvement in this project, particularly his work with epileptics and hyperreligiosity, sealed the deal for us. But as I said, we are concerned with results, not theory. We aren't afraid to put out money as long as the projects are moving along."

Wolfe reached into his jacket, produced a white envelope, and handed it to Elijah. "This contains a check for two hundred and fifty thousand, as well as our signed agreement, all as we discussed."

Ethan struggled to keep his jaw from dropping. Project funding never happened like this. They usually submitted detailed draw requests on a quarterly basis. Allen Wolfe had just given them an amount that would sustain them for over a year and half. He thought of the rejections they'd received from countless other foundations, the roadblocks put in front of them by Sam Houston's HRPP, the skepticism of their colleagues. All of that was in the past. He and Elijah would revolutionize the field of psychology and the study of religious experiences at the same time. His mind jumped to his tenure hearings, which would come up next year.

Then one small thought intruded on his euphoria: *the Logos needs to work*. He pushed the thought aside. Of course it did, and their human trials next week would prove that.

"Your project here"—Wolfe swept his arm through the air above the Logos—"is as important as anything done by Freud or Jung. Now let's get the ball rolling, shall we?"

Ethan couldn't suppress what had to be a ridiculous-looking grin. Allen Wolfe was the first person who really understood their work. Then he glanced at Elijah. His mentor was twirling the envelope with the check, a curious expression on his face—as if contemplating whether he should keep it or give it back. Whatever reservations Elijah had, he was the one who had approached Wolfe's foundation first. So why was he acting so strangely?

CHAPTER 12

UNDISCLOSED PRISON FACILITY
UNITED ARAB EMIRATES

The screams at night were the worst.

The previous day the rap music had stopped. Mousa had been thankful at first, thinking he could finally sleep. Lack of sleep was causing him to hallucinate. Then the screams started. Judging from the voices, all in Arabic, begging alternately either to be spared or to be killed, Mousa guessed that five new prisoners had been brought in. He wondered if that was how his own screams had sounded during his torture.

As he lay in his cell on a thin mattress that reeked of urine, Mousa palpated his hands over his body, checking his injuries. He had no broken bones, yet. Most of his skin, however, was bruised gruesome shades of purple and green. His right shoulder had been dislocated, which he'd fixed himself by leaning over the porcelain sink in his cell and jerking downward while twisting his arm with his left hand. Putting the shoulder back in place had been just as painful as when it had dislocated: he'd been hung from the ceiling in the interrogation room by chains wrapped around his wrists.

He examined the skin on his wrists: still shredded. Even worse were the burn marks on his nipples from where the electrodes had been attached. The knee with the torn ACL from the mall's ski slope was still swollen, but he could put weight on it now. He could walk, maybe even run in a straight line if he had to, but any twisting or sideways pressure would cause it to slip out of place.

But running was the last thing on his mind. He doubted he would ever run again. He was going to die in this cell. During the interrogation sessions with the mustached man, he had prayed to Allah for death more than once. As a doctor, he had treated terrible injuries—a broken leg where the tibia jutted through the skin was one he particularly remembered—but he had never before experienced true physical pain himself. During the beatings that both preceded and followed the daily interrogation sessions, the mustached man never touched him. He let the two guards handle that. But he always watched. He watched as if he enjoyed it, like he was looking at pornography.

Worse than the physical pain, the hunger, or the lack of sleep was the psychological torture of not knowing what had happened to Amira. When he'd asked the mustached man about his daughter, his interrogator had laughed, telling him that he would never live to see her again. He was going to die in the prison never knowing the fate of his beloved child, never again feeling the embrace of his beautiful wife, never seeing his newborn son grow into a man.

Despite his repeated denials and his giving the interrogator all of his personal information about his medical practice in Amman, the man refused to believe that he was not connected to the plot to blow up the mall.

"You Jordanians are jealous of our prosperity, no?" the mustached man had taunted him before his last brutal session, one that involved whipping the bottoms of his feet until they were bloody and then beating him with hoses until he slipped into unconsciousness.

That session had been a couple days earlier, as best as he could tell. Since then, he'd heard nothing but the disembodied screams of his fellow prisoners. As guilty as the thought made him feel, he was thankful that the guards had turned their attention on others. His tormentors had given him an unexpected rest. Maybe they were afraid they would kill him too soon, or maybe it was because during the last session, he'd finally given in. Weeping, he'd told them that he would admit to anything they wanted. He would sign any piece of paper they put in front of him.

As he lay on the stained mattress, which had neither sheet nor blanket, his eyes wandered around the tiny cell. The gray concrete walls were cracked and chipped in some places, stained with blood and excrement in others. He looked to the bucket in the far corner that acted as his toilet. The only way he had to empty it out was into the porcelain sink attached to the wall opposite the door, the same sink that also was his only source of drinking water. He imagined that the sink at one time had been white. One advantage of having his nose broken during an interrogation was that he could no longer smell the stench of the prison—it reeked of death.

He glanced to the wall above his sink. High up was a window. Only six square inches, with rusty iron bars crossing the opening, it was his only connection to the outside world and the only source of fresh air in the fetid cell. From the pale light filtering in, he guessed that it was dawn, time for the *salat al-fagr*—his morning prayer. He grunted as he rolled off the cot onto the floor and crawled toward the sink. The three-meter-long chain attached to a metal collar around his ankle dragged behind him. Using the sink, he pulled himself to his feet and then washed his hands and face. He ran his wet fingers through his hair and then shuffled to the center of the concrete floor. His injured knee and bruised body made getting into the proper position difficult, but he did the best he could to face the window, kneel, and then touch his forehead to the ground.

When he finished reciting his prayers, he opened his eyes but remained sitting on the floor, too spent to move. A single word popped into his head: *Islam*. The name of his faith also carried a crucial meaning: true peace through surrender.

Haven't I surrendered, Allah?

He had given up hope that he would ever see his family again. The only reality left to him in the wretched cell was the Beloved One, the Source of his very existence. *Yet where is my peace?*

Then a tiny movement caught his eye. *Something on the wall by the bucket.* Maybe he was having another hallucination. But then he saw it clearly.

He crawled to the corner of the room, training his eyes on the insect, a black beetle with a yellow stripe down its back. The bug explored its surroundings, feeling with hair-like antennae along the cracks in the concrete. It seemed content, going about its life, oblivious of the larger meaning of its surroundings. Mousa reached out and placed his palm up on the wall next to the insect. The bug stopped when it reached his thumb, testing the skin with its antennae. The tiny creature crawled onto his hand, tickling him. He brought it close to his face and stared at it. The bug seemed to stare back. All of a sudden, he was transported out of his cell.

He was on a hill in Gilead, a couple of hours' drive north from his home in Amman. The sun warmed his face and a soft wind blew the grass like waves in the ocean. The hills around him undulated out to the mountains on the horizon. White limestone rocks and boulders dotted the grass. He sat on a blanket, eating a handful of green almonds. Laughter filled his ears. Amira rolled on the grass, giggling uncontrollably, as Bashirah tickled her and laughed just as hard. Out of the corner of his eye, he spotted a bug, a large black ant, crawling across the blanket, heading for the plate of bread and cheese. He flicked it off of the blanket. The memory faded.

Although he grasped for the images, willing them to reappear, all he saw was the insect crawling across his palm. He rose on shaky legs, careful not to disturb the bug. Bracing his free hand on the sink for support, he rose onto his toes and extended his hand toward the window. He stretched farther, ignoring the aching in his bruised rib cage and the soreness from his shoulder dislocation. He couldn't quite reach the window, but the bug got the idea. Maybe it smelled the fresh air or saw the light. It scurried off of his hand onto the wall.

The screeching sound of metal against metal echoed through his cell. He threw himself onto his mattress. Someone was pulling back the heavy bolt locking his cell door. If they caught him reaching for the window, they might think he was testing it for an escape attempt. Who knew what brutality they would inflict upon him then? He didn't know if he could survive another session.

As the door rolled back on its track, he waited for the mustached face of his tormentor or the two guards who carried out the torture with enthusiasm. Instead, four new men entered his cell. Dressed in all-black commando gear, they looked similar to the officers who had arrested him at the airport, but with one terrifying difference: these men wore ski masks covering their heads and faces. A deep nausea rolled through his gut. He had to focus so that he wouldn't lose control of his bowels. He knew what was coming.

His interrogator had realized that he'd extracted all he would get, and today was the day he'd told him about: his execution. After the torture, death would come as a relief. He almost wished for it, but then the image of the wide, terrified eyes of his daughter at the airport came to him. He thought of his wife's radiant smile, and the innocent expression of his baby boy, who would grow up without a father. As much pain as he was in, he didn't want to give up.

When the man closest to him spoke, shock replaced the fear.

"Down on the floor!" the man commanded, *in English.*

He recognized the accent as American. Since he'd been taken captive, he'd heard nothing but Arabic. He complied with the order. Lying on his stomach, he waited for the inevitable stomp of a boot in his back, but it never came.

Instead the man said, "Don't move."

He kneeled on Mousa's back, which was uncomfortable but not painful. The man brought his hands around and handcuffed them with a plastic tie. One of the others bent over and unlocked the shackle around his left ankle. Then they attached leg irons, which meant only one thing: they were taking him somewhere. Were his captors using the Americans to carry out the execution, or did they have a new level of torture designed for him?

With his left cheek pressed against the cool, hard concrete, he could only make out the movements of the men with his right eye. Their actions were coordinated, more practiced and efficient than the brutal handling he'd received from his fellow Arabs. Their uniforms were devoid of markings, and they communicated with each other using nods and hand gestures rather than speech. After the man finished with the leg irons, he approached Mousa's head. Mousa saw that he was carrying a black sack in his hand, about the size of an extra-large bag of rice. The man kneeling on his back shifted his weight and then lifted Mousa's upper torso off the ground.

Just before they pulled the bag over his head, he noticed a movement high up on the wall. The beetle had reached the edge of the window. He watched as it crested the edge of the sill and disappeared through the iron bars into the light of freedom.

Then his world went dark.

CHAPTER 13

SSS, YALE UNIVERSITY

"**S**o then, I'm not crazy, am I?"

A woman in her mid-fifties, wearing simple black cotton pants and a black turtleneck, reclined in the green leather chair underneath the Logos. Her head was shaved, the stubble on top a silver gray. Her robes hung on the brass coat stand by the door.

"If only we were all as sane as you, Sister Terri," Elijah said from his stool beside the Logos. He wore a white lab coat over a black T-shirt with red lettering declaring THE SPARK OF GOD LIES WITHIN ALL OF US. THE BESHT.

Ethan glanced over Elijah's shoulder at Terri's file. The elder professor scribbled a note in a script legible only to him. He'd just finished reviewing the results of the Minnesota Multiphasic Personality Inventory that Terri had taken an hour earlier. Their protocol dictated that their subjects show no signs of a psychological condition that could be adversely affected by the experiment. Also, none could have a history of epilepsy. Although the monkey tests had gone well, they didn't want to risk setting off an epileptic episode in someone preconditioned to it. His eyes fixed on the one cautionary note, written in red ink under the section titled "Other Medical History."

"How are you feeling today, Terri?" Ethan asked.

Her forest green eyes locked onto his with a directness that, had it come from anyone else, would have made him uncomfortable.

"What you mean to ask is how is my cancer progressing?"

He nodded.

"Finished the final round of chemo five weeks ago. The treatments slowed the cancer but didn't eradicate it from my lungs or spine."

Her matter-of-fact delivery seemed incongruous with the information she revealed. He'd last seen Terri almost a year earlier, when they'd tested an earlier version of the Logos with lackluster results. Reviewing her medical history then, he'd felt a deep fear for the nun with the irreverent sense of humor. The cancer that had begun three years earlier in her breasts had metastasized throughout her body. He and Elijah had discussed whether her medical condition should disqualify her from this stage of the experiment, but she'd lobbied to be included. She'd been one of Elijah's subjects five years ago in the experiments in which he'd first begun to develop his theory of a God part of the brain. Terri insisted that although her body may be suffering, her mind was clear.

"Ironic, isn't it? Over thirty years ago I took a vow of chastity when I entered the order. I never needed my breasts for their original biological function, to nurse a child"—she waved her free hand across her flat chest, where both breasts had been surgically removed—"yet they will be the cause of my death."

"I'm so sorry, Terri."

What did one say to comfort the dying? He tried to push away the thought that this gentle woman had limited time left. *Why does tragedy have to strike the best of us?* He thought of Natalie.

"We all shall die. That is God's design for us."

He forced a smile, and said, "We shall all die, yes, but I'm not sure God has anything to do with that."

What he didn't add was that a God who would allow good people to suffer was either not as omnipotent as was claimed, or was cruel and capricious. *Or more likely*, he thought, *doesn't exist at all. Nothing more than a created image of the human subconscious, a projected desire for a father figure, as Freud argued.* But he wasn't there to challenge this woman's deep faith. Instead, he wanted to understand it. He glanced to the metal arm that held the solenoids that would soon be positioned near Terri's head. *A God*, he thought, *created by electrical impulses firing in the temporal lobes of the brain.* Then her warm hand alighted on his arm.

"What do you believe in, Ethan?"

He felt his neck redden. He was a medical doctor, a Yale professor, but the question caught him off guard. He was the one who was supposed to be asking the questions, not his patients or his research subjects. But Sister Terri was different. He sensed that Elijah was waiting for his answer as eagerly as she was.

What do I believe?

"I believe in the scientific method."

"So you place your faith in science?"

"Faith? I'm not sure that faith has anything to do with science. I believe in what I can measure and verify: in experimentation and objective observation."

"Yes, a popular misconception of faith." She turned her penetrating gaze from Ethan to Elijah. They shared a look he interpreted as meaning they understood something he didn't.

She continued, "Faith does not ask us to turn off our minds or our powers of perception. Faith is not the belief in the impossible. God gave us our powers of reason, and so we should use them."

He cocked his head. "Then what is faith, if not belief in the absence of proof, or worse, belief in the face of disproof?"

His mind scrolled through the scientific problems of religious faith: the creation stories, the descriptions of the cosmos as comprised of realms of heaven and hells populated by divine and semi-divine beings, the miracles attributed to divine powers—all things impossible according to the theories and evidence provided by modern science, an understanding absent in the cultures from which these religious myths developed.

"What if we defined faith as trust rather than as belief?"

"I trust what I can measure, what I can see."

"As do I, which is why we are here today. Isn't it? You are interested in measuring something special that I can see."

"Even scientists like us," Elijah added, "need faith. We trust those scientists who came before us; we have faith in their theories and the results of their experiments."

"But religion is different." Ethan turned. "If I disagree with a previous theory, then I'm free to perform new experiments and either validate or invalidate those theories. As scientists, we can break new ground."

Sister Terri smiled broadly. "My experience is the same. I don't read scripture as either a history or a science text. Instead, I trust in the lives of those before me who had revelatory experiences of the divine. But I understand that these people lived two and three millennia ago in a different age with a different understanding of the mechanics of the world. I use their experiences as the starting point for my own spiritual practice. I seek my own revelation of God."

"Which brings us to the Logos!" Elijah jumped up from his stool.

"It does," Terri said, "but remember that the mind isn't the only way we perceive. We understand through the heart too." She touched her chest.

"The heart?" Ethan asked.

"Through love."

Love? He tried not to grimace. How does one measure love? Love was ephemeral, changing, impermanent. Intellectual truths were lasting. The memory of Natalie's death arose again. Love could not be relied upon.

The door to the lab opened, saving him from voicing his thoughts. Christian Sligh, wearing a striped rugby shirt with a blue and white Yale scarf tied around his neck and white knee-length shorts, strode in from the rainy weather looking like an out-of-place J. Crew ad.

"Chris, where have you—" He stopped mid-question when he saw Rachel Riley standing next to him.

Rachel shook off a dripping black raincoat that matched her shiny black boots, and gave Ethan a very pleased wink.

"Sorry, Prof." Chris flicked his head, moving the damp blond locks out of his eyes. "Didn't Elijah tell you? He asked me to pick up Rachel from CapLab."

Ethan shot at look at Elijah, who had moved to the door and offered to take Rachel's coat. He'd only wanted the three of them present.

"Guess I forgot." The senior professor shrugged. "Since Rachel observed the Logos in the context of the capuchins, I wanted to get her perspective on our first human trial."

Ethan was torn. As precarious as their relationship was with Houston's committee, they couldn't afford to have any negativity get back to him if the test didn't go well. On the other hand, he felt an unexpected excitement at sharing the groundbreaking experiment with such an insightful student. He turned his gaze toward her, and they locked eyes. When she smiled at him, he imagined she could hear the debate waging inside his head. He nodded. "Okay then, shall we get started?"

Rachel's heeled boots clicked across the wood floor until she stopped on the opposite side of the Logos from Ethan, extending her hand to Sister Terri.

"Hi, I'm Rachel. Chris was telling me that you're a nun?"

"Franciscan, since I was nineteen." Terri took her hand in both of hers. "I'm Terri."

"Rachel helps out at the capuchin lab where we tested the Logos last week," Ethan said.

"You guys were so cryptic then. I know this machine has something to do with testing spiritual states or something in the brain, but what exactly are you doing?"

Elijah walked to her side with a bounce in his step. He reached across Terri and lifted her medical file from the table. Flipping back pages, he turned to a series of colored images.

"Five years ago, when Ethan was a new MD working on his PhD, he and I conducted a study in which we used SPECT imaging to scan the brains of five Franciscan nuns from Terri's convent and five Tibetan Buddhist monks. Each of these subjects engaged in either deep contemplative prayer or meditation during the scanning process. The nuns' prayers consisted of repeating a short verse of the Bible and contemplating the image of Christ, while the monks focused only on the in and out of their breathing."

"And Terri was one of the nuns?"

"She was." Elijah pointed to one of the brain scans. "This area here?"

"The orangey color?"

"That's Terri's left temporal lobe. Although the monks' and nuns' religious doctrines were different, we discovered that the neurological activity in their brains during their spiritual practices was essentially the same." He pointed to a darker section on the image. "Most areas of the brain that are active during conscious activity are quiet, but the temporal areas here"—he pointed again to the orange section—"are lit up with a type of activity that we don't see during baseline measurements in either wakefulness or sleep."

"So even though the nuns are focused on God and the monks on their breath, they are having the same religious experiences?"

"This is what fascinated me. Their respective interpretations of their experiences were different. The Buddhist monks believed the world and themselves to be impermanent and in a constant state of flux. The purpose of meditation for them was to achieve Nirvana, a state of Absolute Reality that is the absence of desire and suffering. The nuns, on the other hand, saw their mystical prayer as leading to a communion with God."

She nodded. "So while their religious beliefs were different, they were having similar experiences from a neurological standpoint."

"Exactly. Their descriptions of the subjective feelings and emotions that resulted from their spiritual practices—feelings of cosmic unity, a subjugation of the individual self to a larger reality—are common descriptions of mystical experiences that exist in every world religion."

"So the Logos"—Rachel pointed toward the metal arm suspended over the chair—"measures these spiritual experiences?"

Ethan couldn't suppress a grin. "No, Elijah's insight was that if a common neurological mechanism in the human brain seemed to account for religious experiences, then maybe we could induce such experiences in others."

Her eyes widened. "You mean to *cause* someone to experience God?"

"I wondered," Elijah added, "whether we might be able to induce, if not a belief in God, then at least the experience of what such a belief or connection with the divine might feel like."

"You can do that?"

Ethan nodded. "Psychologists in the 1960s inserted electrodes into the areas of the brain that produce emotional responses. When they sent electrical impulses through the electrodes, their subjects felt pain, happiness, and pleasure, depending on which area they stimulated."

Chris, who was still standing behind Elijah and Rachel, spoke. "The professors are being too modest. The Logos isn't just about showing that there is a God part of the brain, just as there are parts related to smell, taste, and touch. If the experiment works, they'll be the first ones to change thoughts and experiences in a directed and purposeful way."

"What about hallucinogenic drugs?" Rachel asked. "Don't they control our thoughts through specific neurological pathways?"

Ethan tilted his head, impressed. "True, but they're crude. When taking mescaline or psilocybin, you don't know what kind of vision you may have: will it be sacred or profane, religious or alien? We think we have tuned the Logos to produce a uniquely religious experience of the divine."

"But you aren't inserting any electrodes into the brain."

"My first desire," Elijah said, "was to do this in a noninvasive way." He touched the arm of the Logos. "I hoped that by stimulating the areas of the temporal lobes that were active on the brain scans from the nuns and monks that we might induce some kind of mystical experience. We took a TMS machine and played with the settings and experimented with magnetic stimulation in the left temporal areas."

"By tuning the magnetic pulses in a particular way," Ethan added, "we hoped to cause the neurons to fire in a predetermined pattern—a pattern we thought would produce a religious vision."

"Seems like something out of science fiction movie, shooting a beam into someone's head to affect their thoughts," she said.

"Indeed." Elijah laughed. "But the technology has been around for many years. Our problem was that we never understood how the brain takes these electrical signals and turns them into thoughts. Our early testing of the Logos was too blunt. We didn't understand how to program it." He nodded at Ethan. "The breakthrough came from the brightest student I have had in my many years here. Ethan theorized that by recording EEGs from epileptic patients who experienced hyperreligiosity, we could capture the specific neurological electrical patterns that led to their corresponding religious visions."

"So"—she looked between the two men—"that's why you wanted to test the machine on my monkeys with your new algorithm—to make sure that the magnetic currents you'll induce in Sister Terri's brain will cause a religious experience but not an epileptic seizure?"

"You got it." Ethan grinned.

Rachel returned his smile, her eyes lingering on his for a few seconds before she looked down at Terri. "But, Sister, why are you here? I mean, using a machine to induce a sacred experience?"

Terri patted her arm. "Anyone can have a mystical experience, dear, even"— she pointed at Ethan—"Mr. Skeptical here, but some people are just more receptive to it than others."

"Like how some people have a natural ear for music or an artist has an eye for color?"

The nun nodded. "Whether it's because of my decades of practice, my genetic makeup, or a combination, I am one of those people blessed with the ability to connect with my divine center."

She tugged on the bottom of her turtleneck, smoothing the wrinkles. "Just think of the possibilities if this machine actually works. An astronomer uses a telescope to explore the universe, to see back in time to the earliest moments of creation. How could I turn down the opportunity to do the same for the mind?"

Elijah put his hand on Terri's shoulder. "We wanted to test the Logos first on someone accustomed to having mystical experiences. Terri can compare the effects of the Logos with what she sees in her spiritual practice."

Rachel looked between the men. "So you've created a God Machine!"

"God Machine." Elijah laughed. "That's catchy."

She turned to Ethan. "In class you taught us about Freud's critique of religion as a mass delusion: God is caused by neurological misfirings of the brain." Her eyes seemed to pierce his. "Don't you know how threatening your work would be to most of the world's population if you prove that belief in God can be produced by a machine?"

Elijah raised a hand. "Whoa, slow down a minute, Ms. Riley." He pointed to the image of the brain scan he still held. "This section of the brain at the rear, above the cerebellum, is known as the visual cortex. Electrical impulses from the optic nerve that originates at the back of the eye are processed here. If I scanned your brain when you were looking at a particular color—red, for example—one area of your visual cortex would light up. Does that disprove that the color red exists as an independent reality? Just because an electro-chemical reaction causes you to perceive the color?"

She shook her head. "Definitely not."

"Why isn't it the same for God? If people had real experiences of the divine, we would expect to see corresponding neurochemical and electrical changes in the brain. We are simply locating these areas."

"Now, Elijah," Ethan said. He knew better than to get entangled in this disagreement yet again, but he couldn't let his mentor's assertions stand un-challenged. "Just because an area in the brain is tuned to believe in God or to have certain mystical experiences, does not mean that God exists. I can think of several evolutionary reasons for these brain developments: to give comfort and strength in the face of adversity; to provide group cohesion. We don't believe that a schizophrenic who has hallucinations of voices or visions is ex-periencing reality, so why do we afford religion some special status?"

Sister Terri sighed from the chair. He realized he'd just insulted her faith. He was usually careful about revealing his own misgivings about religion out-side of academia. She reached out and took his hand. The personal contact made him uncomfortable, but her touch was warm.

"Maybe, Dear, because even with all of its shortcomings, with the tragedies that have been committed in its name, religion opens us up to a depth of our very existence, the very ground of our being, that we need to live a fulfilled life."

He stared down at the nun. As she had demonstrated in their previous meetings, she had a way of making her faith sound so meaningful and reason-able, yet he still struggled with understanding it.

"That's so poetic," Rachel said, saving him from having to respond. "But what I'm still not getting is"—she paused to run her fingers through her hair—"why, if the nuns' and monks' mystical experiences originate from the same brain activity, are their religions so different?"

"Such insightful questions!" Elijah said as he walked to his desk, opened a drawer, and pulled out a four-inch-tall glass pyramid. He held it up so that the light streaming in from the window passed through the glass, casting a color spectrum on the wood floor.

"A prism?" Rachel asked.

"Imagine for a moment that the divine, by whatever name we may call it—God, Allah, Yahweh, Nirvana—is like the electromagnetic spectrum, like the sunlight that passes into the prism. As finite creatures, we cannot see the light in its full spectrum. Humans, for example, only see a small portion of this spectrum that we call visual light. Now imagine how we view our lives through each of our own lenses: prisms shaped by who we are, where we come from, the languages we speak, the time we live in, and what we are taught to believe." He pointed to the rainbow of colors dancing across the floor. "So you might look at the light through your prism and see blue while I see yellow through mine. We might argue about what the true nature of light is—blue or yellow—maybe even come to blows over the disagreement. Each of us would be right, but our visions would also be incomplete. Blue and yellow are not the same, but both are part of the spectrum that is light."

"Or," Rachel said, turning to Ethan, a mischievous glimmer in her eye, "some might not open their eyes in the first place, so they'd never see the light."

Elijah chuckled. "The word *mystical* comes from the Greek *mystos*, which means 'that which is hidden from ordinary sight.'"

Ethan massaged his temples, chastising himself for allowing the discussion to go down this road. Was he starting to develop a headache?

"Enough philosophy!" Elijah clapped his hands. "It's time."

He placed the prism on the desk, walked to the head of the recliner, and lowered the arm so that the solenoids were positioned on each side of Terri's head.

Ethan slipped a Topiramate from his pants pocket and swallowed the pill, just in case a migraine developed. Then he moved to the rear of the machine and clicked on the red power button. The Logos began to vibrate and hum at a low frequency. *Will it work?* he wondered. In minutes they would know the result of the past five years of their efforts. He looked up. Rachel was holding Sister Terri's hand. The nun appeared as calm as she always was.

"Are we ready?" he asked.

Elijah grinned at him like a child waiting to open his birthday gifts. "Let's make history."

"Terri?"

She winked at him and then closed her eyes.

He rotated a green knob. The humming grew louder. The dials indicating the frequency and amplitude of the electrical pulses flickered in response to the programming he'd uploaded. He felt his pulse beating in his ears in time to the pulses from the Logos.

"Okay, Terri, just relax," he said, wishing he could follow his own advice. "Here we go."

CHAPTER 14

THE MONASTERY
ASWAN, EGYPT

The Bishop hurried down the cloistered hallway of the Monastery, wondering whether the email had come through yet. He pushed the sleeve of his silver robe from his wrist and glanced at his watch, a thin gold Patek Philippe. *Six thirty in the evening.* The wait was the worst part.

He tugged at the collar around his neck. He should be used to it by now, but his neck felt swollen and hot. The collar was restricting his air, and the scent of incense that he usually found pleasant threatened to overwhelm him. The candelabras along the right wall danced shadows against the sand-like texture of the Venetian plaster; their gray smoke stained the barrel-vaulted ceiling. He wondered whether the candle flames were sucking too much oxygen out of the air.

He thought of the difficulty he'd gone through to build this monastery. He glanced to his right again. Every fifteen feet, spaced between the candelabras, were heavy oak doors set within stone arches—twenty in all in this cloister, and two other cloisters extended off the central core ahead of him, like spokes from a hub. The Monastery could house sixty monks, and that didn't count the separate living quarters for his staff of priests and assistants. Currently he was at half-capacity, but his benefactors wanted to see the facility full.

The Bishop looked to his watch again. He wasn't normally the type who worried. He was the one others came to for answers. But his situation had changed recently. He was under pressure now.

Continuing down the cloister, he stopped in front of a stained glass scene that extended the twelve feet from floor to ceiling along the length of the wall. Each of the three cloisters contained similar windows. He had commissioned the work himself. Construction of the Monastery had taken three years and millions of dollars, even with the cheap Egyptian labor. Building such a large project in secrecy in the remote desert on the outskirts of Aswan had complicated the plans. But as was the case with everything he did, he'd been meticulous about every detail of its completion. He admired the stained glass; although it appeared to be lit from a sunny afternoon, the glass wasn't really a window. They were twenty feet underground.

The vibrant colors were backlit by LED lights. The scene of this window depicted Jesus on the cross. Mary was weeping at his feet, while in the distance the apostles ripped at their clothes in despair. A Roman guard had just finished piercing Jesus's side with a spear, and the blood glowed crimson. Getting the expression on Jesus's face just right had held up installation for weeks. His eyes were full of hope, not suffering. Although his skin had an olive Mediterranean complexion, his eyes were emerald green, and like the Mona Lisa, they followed you as you walked down the cloister. The Bishop knew that the work had a profound effect on the monks. He'd watched them pass by it in reverence, as if the image itself had a power. He didn't try to persuade them otherwise.

He closed his eyes and inhaled the dusty cave aroma, the scent mixed with incense and candles. Gradually, he became aware of the music. Low and melodic, the chanting of monks echoed throughout the stone hallway. Another of his favorite details: the music was not coming from his monks, who were in their rooms resting or studying. Instead it came from speakers hidden along the walls. It had the effect of creating an atmosphere conducive to faith, and he felt the tension in his shoulders relax. He opened his eyes and looked into the emerald eyes that seemed to read his mind. He needed to be patient. His efforts would pay off. He had faith in his convictions.

Feeling better, he walked over to the oak door opposite the stained glass. He had to bend over to peer through the six-inch opening in the door, crisscrossed with hand-hammered iron. The monk's cell was identical to all others:

fifteen-by-ten feet, it held a cot for sleeping, a desk for studying, and a wash-basin for cleaning. This particular room belonged to Brother Youssef, a twenty-four-year-old from Pakistan who had been one of the first monks to arrive just over a year ago. He lay on his cot staring at the ceiling, immobile but for the occasional blinking of his wide eyes. Father Dawkins sat by the bed on the simple wooden chair he'd pulled from the desk. He read to Youssef in Arabic from the Bible open on his lap. Nicholas Dawkins was one of the more advanced priests. Broad-shouldered with close-cropped hair, he'd also been part of the project from the beginning. Although he was American, Dawkins had extensive training in both Arabic and Farsi.

With the soft background music, the Bishop couldn't hear what passage they were reading, and even if he could, he didn't speak Arabic. *Probably Revelation*, he guessed. He'd designed the educational program at the Monastery to have maximal effect on the new monks. Faith was a tricky business. That was why he was so anxious to receive the email he'd been expecting. The new chapel was almost completed. The sacred space would dramatically speed up the journey for his monks, making his job much easier. Youssef would be the first of the monks to experience the chapel.

The rapid fall of leather dress shoes on the limestone floor echoed behind him. He turned his head. Another of his priests, dressed in a flowing black ankle-length cassock, hurried toward him. The Bishop noticed that his white collar was unbuttoned, revealing a thick neck that bulged with veins the size of cords. He infused his low baritone voice with authority when he spoke to the young priest.

"Brother, have you looked in the mirror?"

The priest, newly arrived from the States via Kuwait, fumbled at the unfamiliar collar with hands that seemed more attuned to moving heavy objects than fastening tiny buttons.

"Sorry, Sir, I've been looking for you. You had a call from the home office."

The Bishop felt the heat begin to creep back into his neck. If there was anyone less patient than he, it was his benefactor. He forced an exhale. He couldn't show concern in front of his fellow priests.

"I will call them back once I have something concrete to say."

He turned and walked to the cell next to Youssef's. While he peered into the window, he asked the priest waiting behind him, "What's the status on the chapel?"

"Final cleanup today, Sir. There's a fair amount of construction dust. It'll be ready for the monks as soon as we get the final specs on the cathedra."

The cathedra, he thought. The monks' final induction would take place there. They would approach the marble altar, which he'd imported from Italy. He would give the Eucharist while the monks knelt at his feet. Then they would partake in the final ceremony—a ceremony that would certainly meet with the strong disapproval of the Roman Catholic Church if anyone from its ranks were to witness it firsthand. He would rise from the cathedra, the bishop's throne, and trade places with the monk, who would take a seat in the chair carved from mahogany and gilded in bronze. He would explain that they were all equal in the eyes of God. Next, he would ask the monk if he was ready to receive the Holy Spirit.

Then everything would change.

"We shall be ready soon, my son." He nodded at the young priest, who had finally managed to put himself together. Then he moved to the next door.

Bending slightly, he gazed through the door's iron-crossed window at their newest monk, a Jordanian who had arrived four days earlier. *Mousa*, he remembered from the file: a doctor who had been at the wrong place at the wrong time. Mousa had been unconscious since his arrival, healing from his ordeal. He looked peaceful, lying atop his cot in a simple cotton T-shirt. An IV bag hung from a pole beside the bed. In a few days they would begin to taper off the drugs. When Mousa woke, he would be given his brown monk's robes. The doctor's training would begin then.

CHAPTER 15

SSS, YALE UNIVERSITY

Ethan stuffed his hands deep into his pockets to prevent them from shaking. The humming of the machine changed frequency as the electrical pulses alternated in the solenoids. He felt the low vibration of the Logos in his bones.

The overhead fluorescents in the lab dimmed, causing his heart to lurch. He cut his eyes over to Elijah and then Chris. The Logos changed tune again as it cycled to a higher frequency. The lights came back to full power. *Strange*, he thought. The machine didn't draw much power.

He studied his subject. Sister Terri's eyes were closed, her breathing normal. A tightness crept into his chest. She had the same relaxed demeanor she'd displayed during the first test, when nothing had happened. If the Logos refused to produce any results this time, he was at a loss as to what to do. Their detractors in the department would be proved right. Maybe they really were trying to do the impossible.

Then her eyes popped open. He resisted the urge to ask how she was feeling. He didn't want to influence the test by giving her any stimuli other than what the Logos delivered. He noticed that she wasn't blinking, nor was there any change to her dilated pupils. She inhaled deeply.

"I smell honey," she whispered before closing her eyes again.

It's starting, he thought, his own breath quickening. Pleasant smells and sounds often accompanied hyperreligiosity. As if on cue, the corners of her mouth turned up in a half-smile.

"Church bells!" Her voice was stronger. "So beautiful."

He wiped his palms on his khakis and then nodded at Chris, who was similarly transfixed by the nun. His student opened a spiral notebook and began scribbling his observations. The Logos changed tones again, cycling through another frequency. This time her breath caught in her lungs halfway through an inhalation. Other than the low hum of the machine, the room was silent. The urge to reach out to her, to ask her to describe her feelings, was overpowering, and he guessed from Elijah's anxious expression that he felt the same way.

Another ninety seconds passed, and then the vibration from the Logos cut off. He'd set the program for three minutes, more of an arbitrary choice than anything scientific. Religious visions could last from a few seconds to an hour or more. For the first test, he'd wanted to err on the conservative side.

Terri's eyes blinked open as if she were awakening from a restful sleep. Her face beamed. If Ethan hadn't known that cancer was close to defeating her, he would have thought she was in the prime of her life.

"Santa Teresa." She seemed to be talking to someone else, not those around her in the room.

Ethan recalled that the name was the one she'd chosen upon taking her vows: it came not from the tireless advocate in Calcutta who dedicated her life to helping the poor, but from Teresa de Ávila, the sixteenth-century Spanish nun renowned for her spiritual visions who was also the subject of one of the slides he'd shown his class. Although Terri had never had such vivid visions as Saint Teresa, she was regarded in the convent for her dedication to her daily prayer and worship practice. Ethan noticed that tears now streamed from her eyes.

"Before, I thought I understood," she said, "but now I know there is no understanding. Only an experience of His love."

Ethan debated whether he should ask questions or let the experience play out. He decided on the latter and waited in silence for her to continue. But instead of speaking, she stared at the ceiling. After several minutes passed, he glanced to Elijah with raised eyebrows. His mentor shrugged as if to say he was also unsure how to proceed, but the excitement in the senior professor's eyes was clear. Elijah reached over Terri and swung the solenoid headset up and away.

As if on cue, Terri blinked several times and sat up. The distant look on her face vanished. She turned her piercing gaze on the two professors and smiled.

Elijah cleared his throat and asked, "Can you describe it?"

"Words are not adequate." She shook her head. "The Holy Spirit entered me like a breath of pure light and energy—the breath of God."

She swung her legs over the side of the chair. "I've had glimpses of this light in the past, during my deepest prayers, like a candle flame at the end of a deep cave. This spark of reality, this taste of God's power, hinted to me that His essence runs through us all. But today . . . this was different." Her smile grew. "That tiny spark was a blinding light!"

Ethan could hardly believe what he was hearing. Elijah wore a grin as large as the one he felt plastered across his own face.

She reached out her hand and took Elijah's. "Thank you. You have given me a gift. You have opened my eyes to a depth of reality I could only suspect was present before. Today I experienced that reality for myself."

After all the years of work, the frustration of failed experiments, the loss of their funding, and the near closing of the project, they had done it. Ethan felt the weight of expectation drop from his body like a heavy coat he'd shrugged off his shoulders. He felt a lightness to his breathing he hadn't experienced in years. Then a buzzing noise caught his attention.

"Sorry," Rachel said, lunging for her bag on the floor by the stool where she'd sat transfixed by the scene. She removed her cell phone. He felt a tug of annoyance. He should have made clear to everyone the obvious point that all cell phones should be turned off during the experiment. Then he noticed that just as Rachel was checking her phone, Chris, who was standing behind the Logos, was bent over his as well, typing with both thumbs. He knew that students had active social lives, but they were in the middle of one of the biggest moments in psychological history. Couldn't their plans wait?

"Oh no," Rachel said, still scrolling through a message on her phone.

"What is it?" Elijah asked.

"A problem at CapLab. I just got a text from one of the monkey janitors."

The technicians and students who worked in the capuchin lab referred to the hourly employees who cleaned the cages and fed the monkeys as the monkey janitors. Despite the unglamorous title, Ethan knew how respected they were by the research students and vets alike. These employees spent so much time on a daily basis with the monkeys that they often knew the animals better than anyone else.

"Is it serious?" Elijah asked. The smile had disappeared from his face.

"It's Anakin, one of the capuchins we tested the Logos on." She caught Ethan's eye. The elation he'd experienced moments before drained from his body, replaced with a void of uncertainty.

"And?"

"He's not right."

CHAPTER 16

THE MONASTERY
ASWAN, EGYPT

The sounds came to Mousa first.

The world around him was dark, but he heard music. As the volume inside his head increased, he realized that the sound wasn't exactly music, but voices chanting. He was tempted to drift back into the darkness of unconsciousness, carried by the chant like a raft floating on the sea, but then another voice intruded into his thoughts.

As the new voice became clearer, he realized that it spoke in English; it sounded American, and it was reading to him. He attempted to open his eyes, but his lids were heavy as if they'd been taped shut. The urge to return to sleep was overpowering; he resisted by focusing on the words.

"And . . . no one shall come to the Father except through me."

He willed his eyes to open. The light hit him like a board across the forehead. He snapped them closed. Inhaling sharply, he tried again, cracking his eyelids into slits so that only a little light came through. As his pupils constricted, he opened them fully. The light came from a wrought-iron chandelier with six candles around a hand-hammered ring suspended from the ceiling by a rusty chain. As his eyes adjusted to his surroundings, the fog in his mind began to clear.

The voice that had been reading to him stopped. Smiling at him from a wooden chair was a blond-haired, blue-eyed priest.

"You're awake now," said the man, who appeared young enough to have just graduated from seminary. He wore a black robe that gathered at his ankles; a white-banded collar peeked above the robe's lapel.

Mousa tried to push himself upright, but he only succeeded in raising his body an inch or two. He grunted and collapsed on his pillow.

The priest placed a hand on his arm. "Give your body some time. You've been asleep for a week."

A week! The words shifted his mind into a higher gear. He tried to remember where he was and how he'd gotten there. He opened his mouth to speak, but his tongue was swollen and tasted of cotton.

"What . . . where . . . ?" His voice was hoarse. He tried to swallow and start again, but his mouth was too dry to accomplish even that simple task.

The priest lifted a glass from the desk and held it to his lips. "Drink slowly. Just enough to wet your mouth."

The water tasted like nectar. He gulped down more than he should have, and he started to cough. The priest replaced the glass on the desk by the bed. "When you arrived here, you were very sick. The monastery doctor gave you some medicine to help you rest and sleep it off."

Sleep it off for a week? That didn't seem right. Even in his hazy state of mind, he couldn't recall a single patient he'd ever treated who had slept for a week, unless they'd been in a coma. Why couldn't he remember what had happened to him? He knew that comas could be induced in a variety of ways: head trauma, extreme fever, powerful drugs.

He evaluated his symptoms. A quick glance at his body, covered by a single sheet, didn't reveal any bandages or other sign of trauma. His fogginess, the amnesia, and the difficulty moving were not surprising considering how long he'd been unconscious. He wiggled his fingers and was relieved that they moved. He lifted his right arm, which also responded. An IV needle was stuck into the back of his hand and wrapped with tape. He followed the clear hose to the head of his bed, where a half-filled clear bag was suspended on a pole. *Saline and sucrose*, he guessed.

He glanced about the room. It contained a single twin bed, a small desk, and the chair the priest sat on. The floor was stone and the walls and ceiling were plaster. The young priest continued to grin at him, patiently waiting for him to orient himself. Then another thought struck the doctor. *What's a Christian priest doing by my bedside rather than a nurse or a doctor?*

"Where am I?" He'd found his voice.

"St. John of the Cross Monastery."

"Not a hospital?"

"One of my brothers is a doctor, and he has seen to your care."

The priest hadn't answered his question.

"You were brought here for your safety, so that you could recover before you return to your family in Jordan."

The mention of his family went through his body like an electric shock. Using all of the strength he could muster, he pushed himself into a sitting position. As soon as he was upright, the blood began to drain from his head, and the room began to go dark again. He felt the priest's hands steadying his body.

"Careful there, Mousa! Don't get me in trouble by falling out of your bed on my watch."

The memories flooded into his mind like grains of rice pouring out of an upended sack. *The white limestone buildings of his neighborhood in Amman, the rolling green hills of the countryside dotted with pink-flowering almond trees, the laughing faces of his wife, his daughter, and his newborn son.* The thought of Amira brought back a new set of memories, but these were not so pleasant. He felt the blood rush back into his head as he recalled the explosion in the Dubai mall, the arrest at the airport as Amira screamed for him, and his imprisonment and torture.

Almost unconsciously, he rotated his right arm, the one that had been dislocated. *Only a little tender*, he realized. He palpated his sides with his fingertips. The bruising must have healed, because he couldn't find any damage from the abuse he'd suffered at the hands of the brutal guards. Then he turned his attention to the young man in the robes beside him. His eyes narrowed and his voice came out stronger than he would have expected.

"What has happened to me? Where is my daughter?"

The priest seemed taken aback by the force of his words—his smile vanished. Mousa guessed that people rarely raised their voices in monasteries.

"Well . . . my understanding is that you were a prisoner in Dubai after a bombing in which you were accused of playing a role."

His final memory came to him. He'd been dragged out of his cell, certain that he was being taken to his execution. The military men who had taken him were Americans, like the priest, but he could remember nothing else.

"You had been treated horrifically. You arrived here unconscious and badly bruised. That is why you were allowed to rest until you healed. And your daughter"—the smile returned to the priest's face—"she was returned to your wife in Jordan after your detainment at the airport. She is fine."

Mousa bowed his head while tears ran down his face. Amira's fate had been the one hope that kept him going. He wiped his eyes on the sleeve of the white cotton galabeya they must have dressed him in.

"Thank you. But how"—he gestured to the room—"did I end up in a monastery?"

"Two years ago"—the priest rose from his chair—"the Bishop, our abbot, had a dream that the brotherhood should be doing more to reach out to those in our community." He began to pace the room. "In the three centuries after the death of our Lord Jesus Christ, much of the doctrine of the early Church was formed in monasteries just like this one in the Egyptian desert. We refer to our spiritual ancestors as the Desert Fathers."

He paused by the desk, fiddling with the wood surface before moving back to Mousa's side. "We try to live by the edicts of Jesus—caring for our fellow men, our neighbors who are in need, even if, like the Good Samaritan, they are not of the same culture and religion as us. We opened the doors of the monastery to political prisoners so that we could help them recover and reenter society as healthy individuals."

The thought that his ordeal might be over flooded Mousa like a warm ocean wave. The knowledge that both he and his family were now safe brought an unexpected feeling of being tired again. He lay back on the bed, resisting the weight of his eyelids.

"I'll be going home now?"

"Soon. Soon, my friend." The priest patted his shoulder. When he did so, Mousa noticed that the clear tubing of his IV fell from the man's hand. As he drifted off to sleep again, he thought he noticed something odd, but maybe his mind was just playing tricks on him. He was so sleepy.

He must have imagined the syringe in the priest's hand.

CHAPTER 17

YALE UNIVERSITY

Elijah knew that he'd been desperate. He pulled his cell phone a few inches from his ear as his Harvard classmate continued to pontificate. His other hand held an umbrella that wasn't doing its job of keeping out the mist of cold rain that had kept others inside that evening. He was walking toward his office. He'd only passed one other person so far, a large athlete rummaging through his gym bag on the previous block. With the clouds blocking moon and stars, the only illumination came from the buzzing streetlights, which cast a faint yellow glow on the gothic architecture, reminding him of a scene from a Dickens novel.

He shifted the phone to his other ear, switching hands with the umbrella as Allen Wolfe continued to speak without letting him get a word in. Funding issues had threatened for months to shut down their project. So when he'd received the out-of-the-blue call from Wolfe, he'd grasped at his offer like a man overboard grabbing for the flotation ring thrown to him by the only person who'd seen him fall.

He'd rarely heard from his former friend over the decades since they'd been in grad school together. As postdocs they'd shared exciting psychological research, digging deeper into the understanding of the mind than anyone had before. But as the purpose behind their research shifted and the nature of the experiments grew darker, Elijah had distanced himself, while Wolfe had taken up the slack with relish. When the government finally shut down the project in 1969, they'd gone their separate ways. Elijah stayed in academia, while

Wolfe entered private practice. How he had ended up heading the NAF, a foundation Elijah had never heard of, was unclear. But when Wolfe called saying he'd heard about their funding problems and wanted to help, Elijah hadn't asked the questions he should have.

"It's just a monkey." Wolfe's voice came through the cell phone clearly despite the splashing made by passing cars. "It didn't have an epileptic fit, right?"

"Something else has happened that Rachel, the lab tech, can't explain. She's looking into it now."

"But the other monkeys are fine?"

"A single complication can reveal a flaw in our programming of the Logos."

The contract he'd signed with the NAF was unusual. On the positive side, he'd received the two-hundred-and-fifty-thousand-dollar check up front. On the other hand, Wolfe had demanded more oversight and immediate reporting of their work than was typical. He'd explained that the foundation's benefactor was generous with his money, but that he expected results. Truth was, Elijah had had second thoughts as soon as he took the money. Maybe by revealing the new concerns with the capuchins, he could slow down the process.

"So what exactly is the monkey doing?" Wolfe sighed.

"He was one of the smaller, more reserved capuchins, but now he's become aggressive, taking food from the larger, higher-ranking monkeys."

"You want to delay further testing because you're worried about the social standing of a monkey!"

"It's not that simple. Rachel believes that Anakin has become unstable emotionally and mentally. I need to understand if he had an adverse reaction to the Logos and why."

"It's just an animal!"

He recalled hearing a similar tone decades ago in Wolfe's voice. His former colleague was always the one willing to push ahead in the more controversial experiments, regardless of the consequences, in order to "see where it would lead." That morning, he'd encountered a similar frustration from his younger partner too.

"That's Ethan's thought as well," he admitted.

"At least one of you has some sense. Wasn't he the one who came up with the protocol for the machine in the first place?"

"He was, but I'm concerned he's gotten so close to the project that he's lost his perspective."

Since Ethan had been his graduate student, Elijah had admired the power of his mind to see problems from different perspectives. His work ethic was legendary in the department, especially following the tragic death of his fiancée. Elijah knew all too well how hard he had taken her death; he'd been the only one Ethan had confided in about the exact events of that night. But in his zeal for progress, Ethan could also be insensitive to the nuances of the research process. The problems he had with the university oversight committees were indicative of his lack of finesse with bureaucracy, which was necessary in a large research institution.

For that matter, Elijah thought, *I lost my own perspective when I agreed to take Wolfe's money.* From the day years earlier when he'd published a paper postulating that the brain contained a God area, just as there were parts that processed vision and smell, he'd dreamed of unlocking the code to human mystical experience. Now that he was a year away from retiring, he wanted to see his work completed. *But not at the expense of repeating the mistakes we made forty years ago*, he told himself as he half-listened to Wolfe rant on about the need for immediate results. Ethan hadn't even been alive then. His concept about the direction these projects might take was naïve. Elijah's last two conversations with Wolfe had reinforced his concerns. He'd resisted asking the question he should have posed when presented with the offer: *What is the true source of the foundation's funding?*

"Look, Allen," he said, stopping in front of the SSS building to fish for his keys. It was after nine and the building was locked. "We need to put the project on hold to study the Logos more."

"But why not run a few more human tests? Especially after your spectacular success with the nun."

Spectacular success? Elijah had mentioned to him only that they were encouraged by the test, but it was still too early to tell. He'd intentionally played down the results. So how did Wolfe get "spectacular success" from "too early to tell"? Then a disturbing thought occurred to him. Wolfe thought highly of Ethan. Could the young professor be talking to the foundation director behind his back? *No*, he assured himself, *that isn't Ethan's style.* He inserted the key into the heavy wood door at the top of the stone stairs of the SSS building.

When he turned to enter the building, he noticed that the athlete he'd passed earlier was across the street, bent over tying his shoes. At least he thought it was the same student he'd seen earlier, judging by his tremendous size. *With only a light shell on, he's got to be cold*, Elijah thought as he shook out his umbrella. Then he refocused on the unpleasant task of his call.

"Look, I appreciate all you have done for us, but maybe this isn't the right fit."

"You want to pull out of our agreement?"

"Maybe I was hasty in accepting your offer."

"Have you checked with Ethan about this?"

"I am the one with ultimate responsibility. He'll be disappointed, but we'll find a way to make it work." He sighed. "I'll have to report my concerns to our Institutional Review Board."

"Don't do anything rash." Wolfe's voice was measured, calmer than Elijah would have expected. "If that committee thinks you have a problem, they'll file forms with the FDA. Spooking the government serves neither of our purposes."

"We have procedures we have to follow for the safety of our subjects. I'll have the university lawyers get back to you on how we can unravel this relationship."

He hung up the phone and let the heavy door close behind him. Proceeding up the gothic staircase, he walked with a new spring in his step, as if a weight had been lifted from his shoulders. As happy as he'd been to get the funding, his former colleague and the Texas foundation rubbed him the wrong way.

This new hiccup would worry Ethan, but they had proven the concept of the Logos. Now they just had to work out the kinks. First, they would investigate what had so disturbed the monkey. Although he hated to admit it, he was sure the problem had been caused by the Logos. His intuition was usually accurate. They'd missed something important—something fundamental that was right in front of them. But he was confident that they would correct the problem. Getting new funding would be easier then. He would just be more careful. If Allen Wolfe was working with the group Elijah suspected he was, he was the last person he wanted to be involved with again.

CHAPTER 18

SSS, YALE UNIVERSITY

Elijah scrolled through the website. Other than the blue glow of the laptop's LCD screen, the only other light on in the lab was the lamp on his cluttered desk. He knew that Ethan tried his best to organize him, but he felt that if his life was too regimented, he would lose the creative spark that had driven him all of these years. He'd never been one of those professors who was happy to sit back after receiving tenure and teach the same class for twenty-five years. His work infused his soul.

"Ah, there it is," he said to himself. He clicked on the link on the university's website.

Ethan would take the news about their latest setback hard. His former student, now colleague, was like a son to him. He was proud to see how he'd matured into one of the department's most popular lecturers. He felt confident about Ethan's chances for tenure next year. Three years earlier, after the tragedy with his fiancée, he'd worried he might lose his brightest pupil, but Ethan had worked through his sorrow. Elijah had tried to comfort him with words about the larger meaning of life and death, but Ethan, like many of their colleagues, held more of a biological than a spiritual worldview. Unlike the others in the department, however, Ethan had been fascinated from the beginning about what made spiritual people the way they were.

They shared a belief that the human mind was hardwired for belief in God. Ethan, however, saw this hardwiring as a leftover evolutionary mechanism, while the ability of the human mind to transcend ordinary consciousness and enter into mystical states had fascinated Elijah from a young age, when he'd listened to the stories of the Hebrew prophets' experiences with the mysteriousness of the divine. For him, something more than coincidence, more than an evolutionary blip, explained why each of the world's religions contained mystical traditions. He believed that an ultimate and absolute reality existed in the universe, and that this reality was what people called God. Because this reality was beyond human comprehension and language, the only way to speak of it was through metaphor and symbols. The problems occurred when people began to believe that the symbols were the reality. Thus, various religions claimed to be the absolute truth, rather than being different expressions of the infinite.

He turned his chair and glanced at the machine sitting in the dark. The Logos held the potential to unlock the God-consciousness within the human mind, to give the elusive mystical experience to the common person who did not have the will or inclination to dedicate his or her life to prayer, meditation, chanting, fasting, and the other disciplines that brought about such experiences. *The Logos could transform the way we view reality*, he thought.

He turned back to his desk, removed the top Post-it note from the thick yellow pad, and smiled when he read the words he'd written a few days earlier: *Faith is NOT believing in the unbelievable but trusting in the unseen*. He leaned to his left and stuck it on Ethan's immaculately clean desk. Then he glanced at the computer screen and scribbled on the next blank yellow square. Ethan would understand once he confided in him about the dark history he shared with Allen Wolfe. Then he clicked his web browser back to his email. Next would come the unpleasant part: emailing Sam Houston about the hiccup in their plans.

The creaking of the door caused him to jump in his seat.

When he swiveled his chair, he expected to find either Ethan, who often worked late since Natalie's death, or one of the janitors. Instead, a man dressed in athletic sweats, who was almost as broad as the doorway, blocked the lab's entrance.

"May I help you?" Elijah asked. Then he recognized the man as the athlete he'd seen on the street earlier, but something about his appearance caused a shiver to run up the back of his neck. He straightened in his seat as the man strode into the room.

"Professor Elijah Schiff?" He barked out the name as if doing a roll call.

"Are you a student?"

The man paused when he reached the Logos. He surveyed the machine. Then he reached out and squeezed the arm of the chair, as if testing a melon for ripeness. Elijah realized what about the man's appearance was puzzling. *His face.* He wore mirrored orange sunglasses that clung to his wide cheekbones, but seeing a kid these days with the pretension to wear sunglasses at night wasn't odd; it was the deeply tanned, verging on burnt, complexion of the man's face itself. Thanksgiving break wasn't for another two weeks, and his classmates were all pasty from the gray New Haven fall, yet this man looked as if he'd just stepped off a tropical beach. He was also the largest person Elijah had ever seen, like something from a superhero comic. His neck appeared as if it had been woven together by thick chunks of rope, while the veins on his forearms stood out like cords stretched across a generous cut of steak.

"Elijah Schiff?" he repeated, now just a few feet from the professor's chair.

Elijah felt a lump form in his throat. His intuition told him something was wrong. Then he noticed the blond crew cut and the erect posture of the man. He didn't walk with the bored sloppiness of a student. He moved with a military precision. Elijah thought about his conversation with Wolfe and the concerns he'd only tonight come to terms with.

Then an idea came to him.

"Yes, that's me," he replied with a steady voice and a forced smile. "But can you give me a minute?" He reached into his pocket. "My phone's vibrating."

The bluff seemed to work. The man stopped four feet from him, cocking his head to the side.

"Hello, this is Professor Schiff."

While nodding his head as if listening to the other person, he searched with his thumb for the numbers 911. To disguise his actions, he stood as he was dialing, pushing himself from his chair. But with his focus on the monster of a man, he pushed backward on his chair at too great an angle. The chair rolled away from him. With his weight moving forward, he lost his balance.

He flailed his arms in a vain attempt to right himself, but in doing so his cell phone flew from his hand. He cringed as he heard it hit the hardwood floor and splinter. He, however, didn't hit the ground. A calloused hand shot out and cinched around his upper arm so tightly that he felt pins and needles in his hand.

"Sorry about that," he said, both embarrassed at his clumsiness and concerned about his cell phone.

He gathered his feet underneath him and stood upright. His nose was inches from the man's inflated chest. The thick fingers still encircled his arm. Then he noticed the man's free hand. He felt the breath suck from his chest as if it had been vacuumed out.

Dangling from the man's palm was a white, plastic-covered clothesline about an eighth of an inch in diameter and several feet long.

CHAPTER 19

KOFFEE, NEW HAVEN

"Look, Rachel, I really could use your help here." Ethan's voice was quiet but firm as he leaned across the circular iron table at Koffee, the café at the corner of Audubon and Whitney, a five-minute walk from his office. At seven thirty in the morning, only two other early risers occupied a nearby table.

He was concerned that Elijah might do something rash. His mentor wanted to inform the Texas foundation that they were having complications. *But jumping to that conclusion is premature*, he thought. His programming of the Logos had worked just as they'd hoped with Sister Terri. Elijah was being overly cautious, and Rachel's position that one of the monkeys was having psychiatric issues wasn't helping.

"I'm not sure what you want me to say." She shrugged her shoulders. "Are you asking me to lie to Professor Schiff?"

"Certainly not." He toyed with the edge of the folded-up *Yale Herald* newspaper. "We don't know if anything is wrong with Anakin, much less whether any change he *may* have undergone is a result of the Logos."

She leaned across the table so that her face was close to his. He couldn't help but notice the flowery fragrance of the hair that framed her face in loose curls. She jabbed a finger into his paper.

"I know my monkeys. They live in strict hierarchical groups. Anakin was docile, even submissive to the others. Suddenly he's displaying dominance behavior that's totally out of character."

He suppressed a sigh at the thought that the future of his research could be determined by one monkey taking grapes from another.

"Professor Sanchez returns from her study at Yerkes next week. Maybe we should get her opinion before—"

"You want to delay further capuchin testing too?"

"Professor, I'm not trying to be difficult here." She ran her fingers through her hair. "The capuchins aren't just animals to me. They're family. CapLab's restriction on invasive medical research was one of the reasons I came to Yale." Her voice softened. "They certainly act more like a family than the one I had growing up."

As frustrated as he felt, he couldn't help but be drawn to the passion she radiated when she spoke about her work. Involuntarily, his eyes dropped down her torso. Her cream turtleneck clung to her curves, just as her black pencil skirt clung to her stocking-covered thighs. Catching himself, he darted his gaze back to her face. She flashed a knowing grin, revealing small but perfect teeth behind full lips. He felt his neck flush. He chastised himself for even allowing his mind to go down that road. She was a grad student, and now she was also another speed bump in the progress of his study.

"You had a challenging home life?" He changed the subject since he wasn't getting anywhere with his pleas not to slow his research.

"Dad was distant physically and emotionally. He worked such long hours that we only saw him on Sundays, and then we weren't allowed to be too noisy until he finished the *Times* crossword puzzle." She glanced down at the *Herald*. "Mom was an alcoholic. I can't count the times my two younger brothers and I carried her to bed when we came home from school and found her passed out at the kitchen table with an empty bottle of vodka rolling around on the floor."

"I'm sorry." He shifted in his chair. "That must have been difficult." Just as with Terri, he struggled with what to say whenever someone revealed personal information, especially when the other person was female.

He'd never been smooth with the opposite sex. His friends always prodded him to approach girls, assuring him that his tall frame and mass of dark hair worked in his favor, but in his mind he only saw the lanky, awkward kid who was more comfortable discussing *Star Trek: Next Generation* than whatever it was girls liked to talk about. In junior high his classmates had nicknamed him SB, stick bug, because that was what he'd looked like. Even after he'd filled out during his last two years of college, he hadn't been able to shake the image from his mind.

"Yeah, well, the first chance I had to escape home I did. Wanted to get as far away as I could."

"That's why you went to Africa?"

"Kenya changed my life." The spark returned to her eyes. "I'd always loved animals, but working with them in their natural state, not to mention in the cradle of civilization, fueled my interest in both animal behavior and evolutionary biology."

He nodded. "Working in the field can often be more educational than the classroom."

"It was more than that." She reached out and rested a hand on his forearm. "Spending days in the savannah, I felt a connection to nature that I'd never experienced growing up in an urban environment. When I sat in the grass with my camera and notebook, I could literally feel an energy to life that seemed to radiate around me." Her grip on his arm tightened. "I sensed that I was also part of that same energy."

"You're starting to sound like Whitman." He laughed.

"When I discovered him in frosh English, I was moved by how he put into words the feelings I had there."

He noticed that her hand still rested on his arm. He enjoyed the touch but simultaneously felt guilty about doing so. He moved his hand to his lap. "When you returned to the States, were things different with your parents?"

"They got divorced while I was away—really the best thing for both of them. Mom found AA, which probably saved her life. She's been sober for almost five years now. After watching her miserable marriage, I told myself that I would never depend on a man to take care of me or to make me happy."

"And your dad?"

"Our relationship improved, but we still have our rocky moments. He'll never be the warm, comforting father whose lap I wished I could curl up in when I was a little girl. But as I've gotten older, I've seen how we share some of the same interests." She leaned across the table, closer to him. "But enough about me. What about your family?"

"I'm an only child, and my father passed away during my junior year in high school." The memory of his dad, a math teacher, spending hours helping him with his homework—usually by giving him more challenging problems to do—caused his chest to constrict. "Pancreatic cancer."

"Wow, losing your father as a teenager, just as you were starting to explore who you really were, must have been so hard on you."

The compassion and understanding in her tone eased the tension in his chest. He had come to terms with his father's passing many years ago, but he still missed him. Natalie's death, on the other hand—he pushed that memory back into the box in which it belonged.

"Mom coped by joining a new church where she became born again. Dragged me with her *every* Sunday. We argued a lot then. The fundamentalist preacher was rampantly superstitious and unscientific. He railed against everything from evolution to homosexuality."

"Religion doesn't have to be intolerant and exclusive, you know."

"That's what Elijah says."

She laughed. "He's a smart man. You should listen to him."

Her laugh, like her touch, seemed to pierce through his exterior, warming his core like the espresso he'd just finished. In spite of the frosty start to their conversation, talking with Rachel was unexpectedly easy. He hadn't spoken to anyone about his parents since . . . Natalie.

This time the memory burst through the box in his mind and struck him like a blast of cold air upon opening a door on a winter morning. Suddenly he realized that he'd asked Rachel to meet him in the same coffee shop where he'd first met Natalie six years earlier.

He had stopped into the café after leaving SSS, where he'd interviewed with Elijah for his application to the PhD program. When he'd turned from the counter with his large double espresso filled to the rim of the ceramic mug, Natalie had been standing in line behind him. Tall and slender, with shimmering black hair and smoky eyes, she flashed a smile that struck him like a car's high beams.

Momentarily blinded, he tripped over his size thirteen feet and splashed his coffee all over her fleece hoodie. In his attempt to recover his balance, he knocked into the table beside him, spilling the two drinks sitting on it. He was mortified. He tried to apologize to the people at the table and then to the beautiful woman he'd just soaked with coffee, but the words came out as a jumble of nonsense.

He'd cringed in anticipation of the angry words that he expected to spill from the exotic beauty's mouth. Instead, she looked down at her fleece and then back up at him and started to laugh—a warm, infectious laugh that caused him to take in the carnage he'd created in the coffee shop and begin to laugh himself. They started dating that afternoon and rarely spent a day apart for the next three years—until the accident. She was a student at the Drama School, hoping to become a playwright, and was like no other girl he'd dated before. Natalie was alive and a little dangerous. Many nights they would stay up into the early morning talking. Somehow, she was able to draw out of him his deepest secrets, concerns, and worries. He even told her about the incident that had happened when he was a teen. She was the only one he'd ever confided in regarding his true motivation behind his professional interests. He felt safe opening himself to her. Sex with her had been creative, intense, fulfilling—and on more than one occasion they were almost caught in a compromising situation in a public place on campus.

They had been planning to marry the following spring when the accident occurred. As intense as his love for her was, his depression the weeks after her death was deeper. On some mornings he'd wondered how he could make it to the end of the day. Sleep at night came only courtesy of Ambien. Then he'd started the SSRI medication. As his serotonin levels increased, he'd returned to work with a renewed focus on his research rather than the tragedy. He'd chastised himself for becoming vulnerable and allowing himself to be hurt. Unlike love, science could be controlled.

"Professor?" Rachel's voice brought him back from the memory.

He smiled. "Sorry. I took a vacation in my mind for a moment." Part of him was tempted to share the memory that was so much more painful than his father's passing. The urge surprised him. He didn't really know this woman, and he was not a sharer.

"No worries. My dad does that too."

"So now I remind you of your father?" It occurred to him that he hadn't asked what her father did that had made him so unavailable when she was younger.

She made a point of looking him up and down. "In some ways, but don't worry"—she winked—"I'm not searching for a father figure."

"Good. I don't think I'd make a very good one." He laughed again and then glanced at his watch. As much as he'd enjoyed his time with the attractive grad student, Elijah was waiting for them in their lab. His stomach began to knot in anticipation of what his mentor might say.

Ethan dug into his pocket, searching underneath his wallet for his keys. Rachel waited beside him outside the door to the Neuropsychology Lab on the third floor of SSS. He noticed the hum when he inserted the key into the lock. He cocked his head to listen. Other than the hum, the building was quiet. They had passed only one of his colleagues on the walk down the hallway. The noise seemed to be coming from his lab.

Could it be?

He turned the key. It moved freely. The door was already unlocked. Pushing it open, his eyes widened at the sight in the center of the room.

"Elijah?"

His mentor lay semi-reclined in the green vinyl chair of the Logos. His eyes were closed and the solenoids were placed above his head. The hum he'd heard outside the lab was the machine vibrating as it cycled through its various frequencies of electromagnetic pulses. But the noises coming from the machine were louder than during their usual tests.

"Elijah!" he shouted over the machine as he hurried to the center of the room.

The elder professor was unresponsive. His mind raced. *Did he come in early to test the machine on himself? Did he of all people choose to violate our protocols?* But something struck him as odd. The machine wasn't acting the way it should have with his programming. He reached out to shake his friend out of his trance. That's when he noticed Elijah's pallid complexion.

"Oh my God," Rachel cried.

He felt his blood jump from his chest to his head, as if his heart had kicked into overdrive. He searched for a pulse in the carotid artery on his neck. Elijah's skin was cold and firm to the touch. Even as he probed his fingers next to Elijah's trachea, he knew he wouldn't find a heartbeat. He pulled back Elijah's eyelid, exposing a fixed, glassy pupil.

"Call 911!" he shouted.

He grabbed the metal lever on the side of the chair and wrenched it downward. The chair flattened so that Elijah was prone at the level of Ethan's waist. He knocked the arm of the Logos out of his way. The sound of the metal bouncing on the wood floor hardly registered with him. With the heel of his right hand, he pressed Elijah's forehead backward while pinching his nose with his thumb and index fingers; with his left hand, he pulled the professor's gray, stubble-covered chin up and outwards. He delivered two forceful breaths, watching out of the corner of his eye as the professor's chest expanded with each breath. Then he began chest compressions.

"Come on, Elijah!" he begged.

But he knew his efforts would be in vain. The sharp compressions made Elijah's body jerk, and the remnants of the breaths he'd given him fluttered out of his lips, but Ethan's medical training told him that it was an illusion of life. Nothing he could do would bring his mentor back. In spite of this knowledge, he continued the CPR.

"Why, Elijah? Why?" He spoke quietly to his friend as he continued to pump away on his chest, as if his sheer willpower could work magic. The recliner squeaked in time to his compressions.

He heard Rachel frantically explaining their emergency to the operator, yelling over the continued hum of the Logos. He tried to think of the possibilities of what had happened, but his thoughts came in slow motion, like they were trudging through a bog on their way to his consciousness. *Did he have a heart attack or a stroke while testing the machine?* The blue tint to his lips suggested that oxygen deprivation of the brain had been involved in the cause of death. The calm way in which his body was lying in the chair suggested that unconsciousness had come quickly and unexpectedly. *But why would Elijah test the machine on himself, and why is the Logos acting so strangely?*

The doctor within him told him to stop. But he couldn't force himself to give up on his friend. He had lost his fiancée three years ago and his dad years before that; how could he lose Elijah now? When he paused the compressions to give another two breaths, something caught his attention that he hadn't noticed earlier.

Tilting the professor's chin upwards, he saw a thin red welt across his neck. He traced a finger along its path. The possibility of a more disturbing cause of death began to circle his mind.

He felt a hand on his shoulder. "The paramedics will be here in five minutes."

He nodded, unable to speak the words that went through his head. An ambulance wouldn't matter now. He stumbled back from the recliner.

"Why are you stopping? You're a doctor! You can save him, right?"

He shook his head. "He's been dead for hours." The words sounded so clinical coming from his mouth, as if another doctor was delivering the news.

"But—"

He swallowed back the burning in his throat and turned to Rachel, but he was unable to prevent the tears that began to stream down his face.

"Oh, God." She threw her arms around his neck.

He held her tight. *Why, Elijah?* He buried his face in her hair, finding some comfort in the embrace of this woman he'd only just gotten to know. Then her body began to shake as she started to cry.

After several minutes, the vibration from the Logos box and the rattling of the arm against the floor pierced through the fog of confusion and sadness in his mind. He couldn't think properly. He gently moved her hands from his neck, walked behind the recliner, and jerked the power cord from the wall. A wave of silence washed over the room.

CHAPTER 20

SSS, YALE UNIVERSITY

"**W**hen will the autopsy take place?" Ethan looked up from his office chair at the New Haven police officer, one of several crowded into the lab.

"Weekend's coming up." The officer, a thirty-something African American male with close-cropped hair, tore off a piece of paper from a white spiral pad and handed him a phone number. "Call the coroner's office Monday."

The officer flipped back several pages and reviewed the notes he'd taken over the past two hours. The crime scene investigators had arrived an hour earlier. They had photographed the scene and were now zipping Elijah into a black body bag. Rachel stood by his chair and squeezed his arm.

"Now, Doctor," the officer said, "I want to make sure I have this correct. You noticed this welt on Professor Schiff's neck some time after you began CPR?"

Ethan dropped his head and ran his fingers through his hair. If he weren't so drained, he would have yelled at the officer. How many times did he have to answer the same questions? Although the officer spoke in a cooperative tone, Ethan had the feeling that he was trying to twist his account around, as if to insinuate that he had played some role in his friend's death. He was grateful to feel Rachel's touch. Her eyes were red and puffy, but they were dry now, and her gaze was strong. He was comforted having her by his side.

"That's exactly what I said. Will the coroner be examining that as a potential cause of death?"

"We will be looking into all the possibilities. Now, again, just so I'm clear. This machine of yours"—he turned a page in his notebook—"this Logos was running when you entered the office?"

"You could hear it from the hallway it was so loud," Rachel said.

"Was it normal for you to run experiments on yourselves, with no one else present?" The officer peered over his notebook at him.

"I've already answered that." He started to rise. He didn't like either the officer's tone or the direction in which the questioning was heading. Rachel's hand on his arm tightened. He sat back in the chair and released the breath he'd been holding. "Elijah never would have done that."

Then a thought occurred to him. "Wait a minute!"

He jumped from his chair, causing both the officer and Rachel to flinch. He hurried to the Logos. Everything about Elijah's death was wrong: his presence alone in the chair, the red welts on his neck, *the way the machine had been running.*

Ethan knew one thing with certainty: Elijah had been murdered.

"Over here," he called.

The officer approached the Logos as if the peripherals on his belt weighed him down. Ethan pointed to the controls on the back of the metal box. A faint layer of powder covered the box where a technician had just finished dusting for fingerprints. Ethan and Rachel had given prints to the technician so that theirs would be distinguished from any unknown persons.

"The Logos isn't set up properly." He tapped on the empty Ethernet jack. "It's just a reconditioned TMS machine." Noting the blank look on the officer's face, he elaborated, "A medical device used to treat depression by sending magnetic impulses to the brain. We developed a proprietary programming for our experiments that is delivered from my laptop into this jack here. These dials"—he gestured to the dials on the machine underneath the square LED display—"also control the machine. They are all turned up to the maximum level. None of these settings are consistent with our work."

"Is it possible—"

Ethan shook his head, anticipating the question. "The machine in its original configuration is FDA-approved. Even at these high settings, it could never be fatal. The electromagnetic fields it generates are much too small for that."

"You're saying the machine couldn't have killed him, in your medical opinion?"

The last phrase rubbed him the wrong way. *It isn't opinion*, he thought. "What I'm saying is that Elijah was murdered."

"Who would want to kill the professor?

"No one." He cast his eyes to the floor. The words came out softly. "Elijah was the gentlest man I've ever known."

The officer closed his notebook and nodded to two of his colleagues, who stood by the door.

"We'll be in touch, Dr. Lightman." He handed him a business card. "In the meantime, please call if you think of anything else, no matter how insignificant."

"Certainly, I . . . Wait! What are they doing?" The two other officers had coiled the power cord on top of the Logos and were lifting it off of the cart.

"Your machine is evidence in our investigation. We'll need to take it with us."

"But it's one of a kind! I already told you it couldn't have caused his death."

"It will be returned, eventually."

"You don't understand. This project was the culmination of Elijah's lifetime of research."

"Well, it's not going to continue until after this investigation."

As the officers carried both Elijah's body and his most important work out the door of the lab, Ethan felt as if they were taking his life with them too.

PART II

"Those who can make you believe absurdities can make you commit atrocities."

Voltaire

"Faith, being belief that isn't based on evidence, is the principal vice of any religion."

Richard Dawkins

CHAPTER 21

CIA HEADQUARTERS
LANGLEY, VA

Deputy Director Casey Richards cracked his knuckles as he surveyed the room and its three other occupants. The anticipation of the first test of Project Jericho weighed on him heavier than any black op he'd overseen in his career. Jericho was the most ambitious and riskiest covert action the Agency had conducted since the events leading up to the Cuban Missile Crisis fifty years earlier.

The windowless operations room on the sixth floor in the center of the CIA's NHB, New Headquarters Building, was like its bigger brother in the OHB, only smaller. Behind a sentry-guarded, card-accessed metal door, the ops room was soundproofed and isolated from any electronic eavesdropping through its construction as a floating room within a room. Three fifty-inch flat-panel monitors hung on the wall underneath a row of LED clocks displaying the time in various zones across the world. The four desks in the center of the room each contained two workstations. He preferred the use of this smaller ops room to monitor the most sensitive operations. The fewer people who were exposed to these off-the-books actions, the more he could maintain operational security and deniability; plus, the room was just down the hall from his office.

One of the two technicians in the room, a late-thirties woman with black cat-eye glasses and dark hair tied in a neat bun on top of her head, keyed in a command at her workstation. One of the flat panels came to life, switching from the blue CIA logo to a satellite picture of a mountainous region.

Alternating patches of evergreen trees weaved between brown patches of dirt and rocks. The technician entered another command and the picture zoomed in to reveal a village of tin and wood shacks dotting the foot of one of the mountains. The resolution from the satellites never ceased to impress him. He could count the sheep and goats grazing in the wood pens behind the huts.

The second technician, a new but thoroughly vetted recruit in his late-twenties, who held a PhD from MIT and spoke fluent Arabic, Farsi, and Pashto—the result of a Pakistani father and Egyptian mother, both doctors and US citizens—held his hands on either side of the Bose headphones on his ears, his eyes focused somewhere beyond the room.

"Shouldn't they have arrived by now?" asked the silver-haired man standing beside him.

Richards turned to face the doctor. They had become friends fifteen years earlier after his son's attempted suicide. The doctor had saved his son's life, though with the various medications his son took he sometimes found it hard to recognize the boy he had raised.

"It's only been two hours. The road's pretty rough."

He suspected that the impatient and imperious tone the doctor had taken masked an apprehension that the mission might fail. Both of their careers were riding on this. The doctor was the mastermind behind Project Jericho. In two years, Richards had already pumped twenty million dollars from one of his discretionary accounts into a program that had no paper trail—a program that had the potential to destroy both of their careers and bring down a popular president who had no idea of its existence. More troubling was the devastation that public knowledge of Jericho would have on US relations with the Arab world. They were risking an all-out religious war in the Middle East, a confrontation in which the US would be isolated from any sympathetic nations.

The potential payoff, however, was just as grand. The arrogant doctor had a concept as brilliant as it was dangerous; a concept that had the potential to bring a lasting and stable peace to a region that had been seized by religious warfare for thousands of years. Richards understood that being the world's only superpower meant making those types of difficult decisions.

After the closing of Guantanamo several years earlier, the prisoners who had been swept up in the US War on Terror who could be tried in court had been relocated to federal penitentiaries. Suspected terrorists on whom they didn't have enough evidence to try in a US court were hustled to secret locations across the world, delivered into the hands of cooperative nations who were generously compensated for their trouble. The question remained, however, about what should be the ultimate fate of these men. Richards had anticipated this issue. He'd known that many of these terrorists would eventually be released. They needed a way to reintegrate the men into society. The doctor had crystallized a plan and then implemented the project now known as Jericho.

"Sir, they're coming into range now," the female tech said.

"Where's the drone?"

"Overhead now. I'm bringing it online." She tapped a button on her console. "Transferring control from the USS Ronald Reagan to my terminal."

A second monitor flickered on, displaying a beat-up flatbed truck moving down a dirt road and trailing a cloud of dust behind it. Three men sat in the cargo area. Unlike the first stationary satellite picture of the area, this one occasionally blurred or degenerated into digital pixels. The live feed came from a MQ-1 Predator drone that was flying high enough overhead that it could be neither heard nor seen from the ground.

"Any audio yet?"

The tech with the headphones said, "Nothing distinct from the truck. Do you want to hear?"

When Richards nodded, the tech rotated a dial. He and the doctor both jumped as the roar of an engine blared from the B&W studio speakers mounted in the corners of the room.

"Sorry!" The tech twisted the volume knob, reducing the noise to a hum.

No one spoke for the next twenty minutes as they watched the monitors. Then the woman broke the silence. "Here we go!"

His breath quickened. As many of these operations as he'd witnessed, he'd never gotten over the rush, nor the fear, that something could go horribly wrong. In addition to worrying about the loss of the lives of his operatives, he also had to worry about exposure. The image of the truck appeared on the first monitor as it drove into the middle of the small village.

"Youssef was one of our very first subjects," the doctor said. "We've been working with him for eighteen months, and we just tested the new protocol on him before he left our care." The doctor beamed. "Spectacular, really!"

Richards recalled the file on the twenty-four-year-old Pakistani they had picked up two years earlier in an Afghan border village controlled by the Taliban. After a thorough bombing, a SEAL team went in to pick up the pieces. They found him battered and dirty but alive. What Richards remembered the most about his photograph were the eyes. The hatred in the dark eyes behind the mass of straggly black hair seemed to jump out of the picture as if it were in 3D.

With his patchy beard, Youssef was no more than a boy. He'd grown up in the slums of Islamabad, illiterate, with no hope of finding anything other than menial labor. His prospects of finding a bride were near impossible. With the radical group hiding in the mountains of Pakistan, he'd found a brotherhood and meaning to his life he'd never known before. In their leader, he'd found the father figure missing from his own life. The terrorist leader had unfortunately been away from the camp during the bombing. Combating the fanaticism born of such life experiences had confounded the US for years. Until Jericho.

"How did you get him back into Pakistan?" the doctor asked. "Will his former comrades suspect anything?"

"He was released with a larger group of non-violent prisoners. We issued a press release stating that we'd concluded that these men were not threats, and that we didn't have cause to hold them. As to whether his former associates believe it, we shall see in a minute."

"He'll be convincing. He's a different man now."

"He won't forget the code?"

"His conditioning was complete. If he finds the leader of his old terrorist cell in this village, he'll let us know."

"He has no suspicion of what awaits him then?"

The doctor shook his head. "During an induced sleep, we drilled a hole in one of his molars. After a week of complaining about the pain, we took him to our dentist, who replaced the molar with the tooth you provided us. He has no idea we're listening or that he's working for us. He's doing what he is doing because he believes it."

The rumble from the engine ceased. Both monitors now depicted the same image: the truck stopping in front of a hut in the village. A man emerged from the hut wearing a fur hat and a bulky coat. When the three men jumped off the bed of the truck, the new man embraced Youssef. Voices speaking Pashto came over the speakers.

The tech with the headphones closed his eyes and translated: "God willing, you have been returned to us, Brother!"

Brother? Richards glanced at the doctor. Had Youssef just returned to his family? If so, they'd wasted over a hundred thousand dollars on this operation.

The doctor pointed to the screen. The new man began to frisk Youssef. He relaxed. Family members didn't frisk each other. He was thankful that he hadn't gone with the original concept of the mission: strapping a bomb onto Youssef before sending him back into his terrorist cell. He never would have made it to the cell's leader. Plus, as confident in Jericho as the doctor was, Richards wasn't sure the protocol would work as well as he claimed.

"How I dreamed of this day!" the tech translated Youssef as saying. "Abadi?"

"He's waiting for you now. He has many questions about what the Americans know."

Richards straightened in his chair. The jackpot he'd been waiting for! Under intense interrogation, Youssef had revealed that he was the personal assistant to Abadi-Jabbar Mohammad, one of the leading Al Qaeda operatives hiding in the mountains on the Pakistani side of the border with Afghanistan. Unfortunately, Abadi-Jabbar constantly moved around. Nothing that Youssef had supplied them had led them to the terrorist leader—until now.

He watched the two men enter the small wood building whose tin roof reflected the bright sun. He realized he was holding his breath, but he knew that telling himself to relax would be useless.

A new voice came through the speakers—scratchy and weather-beaten. Richards wished that they had a voiceprint to match Abadi-Jabbar, but he was smart enough to avoid using cell phones. They were reliant on Youssef's identification.

"Ah, Youssef! Come here," the tech translated. "How have you been?"

Youssef's reply seemed out of context, both in its ebullient tone and the final two words in clear English.

"Abadi-Jabbar, I must tell you how my life has been saved by Jesus Christ."

Both techs and the doctor turned to Richards. *That was it.* The code they had been waiting for. He could hardly believe what he'd heard. The doctor had done it. To Youssef, this was not a code, but a sincere belief.

"Execute," he said to the female tech.

She nodded and turned back to her console. Seconds later a bright light flashed on the screen. Richards watched as a thin trail of smoke traced like a pencil line across the image. The Predator carried two AGM-114 Hellfire Missiles. *Now,* he thought, *it has only one.*

The terrorist leader's voice sounded confused even before the translator said, "What are you saying to—"

A loud static pop echoed from the speakers and then the audio cut off. The shack containing Youssef and Abadi-Jabbar disappeared in a cloud of splinters, smoke, and fire. The three men waiting outside were incinerated as well.

For a full minute, the operations room remained silent as they watched the ball of dust expand outward from the shack. As the smoke settled, Richards saw that the two closest huts were also consumed by fire. Villagers raced from the surrounding structures, some holding children in their arms, others half-dressed, looking over their shoulders in bewilderment at the destruction that had unexpectedly occurred on a calm, sunny day. He wondered who had been in the other two houses. Then he heard the sound of slow clapping from beside him.

"Now that was something." The doctor grinned broadly.

CHAPTER 22

SSS, YALE UNIVERSITY

Ethan peeled back the yellow police tape that crisscrossed the entrance to his darkened office and let himself in for the first time since Elijah's death five days ago. He walked across the empty floor, not bothering to turn on the overhead lights. He couldn't deal with the harshness of the fluorescent bulbs highlighting the empty space in the center of the room where the Logos had been.

The thought that he would never again see his mentor made the office feel even emptier. The autopsy had revealed that his friend had been killed by strangulation. The police had concluded that Elijah's death was a robbery turned violent. They'd found his wallet down the street in a trash bin, minus the cash and credit cards, and his laptop was missing. Other details of that night, however, unnerved Ethan. *Why would a robber have gone to the trouble of putting him in the machine?* Also, Elijah had been acting strangely the past few days about their research. Certainly these events could be related.

He dropped into his chair and flicked on the desk lamp. The soft yellow light, which he usually found comforting on quiet nights alone in the gothic building, cast sharp, black shadows from the neat stack of textbooks and journals on his desk.

Without his research to work on, he wasn't sure of the purpose of being there. Samuel Houston had revoked the committee's approval for the Logos project. The thought that Elijah's culminating work would never be finished, that his own questions from years ago would never be answered, opened up a gulf of despair within him. He wasn't even lecturing. Houston had suggested he take a couple of weeks off from his teaching duties to "allow himself time to heal." One of the grad students was filling in for him. He hadn't argued; he knew that the time off was not a request. With nothing to focus on, his mind occupied itself by replaying the scene of discovering Elijah's body in the recliner over and over. Each time, he relived the shock and the fear as if it were happening again.

He reached out and adjusted the Tiffany lampshade so that the shadows falling across the desk would appear less dagger-like. He removed his laptop from his satchel, along with a stack of unpaid bills. He was meticulous about paying everything the day it arrived, but with his life upside down he'd fallen behind.

After logging in to his bank account, he began keying in the amounts for the e-checks. As much as he relished the details with his academic work, money matters were a hassle to him. He could make three times his salary in the private sector, but wealth had never been a motivating factor for him.

How's that possible?

He stared at the box in the bottom right corner of the page: his account balance. His balance usually hovered around three thousand dollars. Now it read over twenty-four thousand. *Another bank screw-up?* They'd done strange things with his account in the past, usually to his detriment—like double mailing online payments. He knew what he'd spend his day tomorrow doing: wasting hours on the phone sorting through their mistake. As he scrolled back through his list of transactions, searching for the source of the excess funds, he saw something out of the corner of his eye.

A yellow Post-it note had been stuck on top of a nearby stack of journal articles. He hadn't noticed it the previous week in the aftermath of discovering Elijah's body.

He peeled the note from the journal and tilted it toward the desk lamp. His breath caught in his throat when he recognized the scribbled handwriting. *Elijah.* But this note didn't contain one of his mentor's reflections. He scrunched up his brow. The series of letters and numbers appeared to be some sort of code. He flipped the square paper over, but the other side was blank. He stared again at the writing.

HV5822 L91 L44 1985, 214.

What is this?

He racked his brain for what Elijah might have meant. *Not a phone number or address; maybe an account?* He thought about the excess money he'd just discovered, and an uneasy feeling began to spread through his gut. *But bank accounts don't have letters in them,* he told himself. Something about the code looked familiar, but he couldn't place it. His mind had been operating in slow motion since the murder. He'd been finding it hard to concentrate, and not having his work to think about had only made his thoughts foggier.

He'd spent his newly found spare time working out at Payne Whitney Gym, especially on the indoor rock climbing wall, which had proved to be a great all-over body exercise. As a teenager he'd gone to a summer camp in the mountains of Virginia, where he'd learned to climb. Although his long, skinny limbs had seemed to get in his way during school sports, he'd found that his lanky body and high strength-to-weight ratio made him a natural climber. Finally, he'd discovered a sport he could do better than the bulky jocks who taunted him at school. He'd climbed a few times with friends in college, but as his workload increased in graduate school he'd given up the sport. His discovery three days earlier of the indoor climbing wall in the gym had seemed fortuitous. The burning sensation in his forearms and legs after an hour's climb had helped to clear his mind.

He stared at the code again. The familiarity of the letters and numbers nagged at him. He pulled his cell phone from his pocket. The screen showed two missed calls from Samuel Houston, which he'd ignored. He needed a break from dealing with the Yale bureaucracy. He scrolled to the speed dial menu. He'd left a message for Chris to call him but hadn't heard back yet. His graduate student had left town right after the test with Terri to return to his family in Ohio, where he was dealing with his father's cancer. Having experienced the same challenge himself, Ethan hadn't wanted to burden his student with the news of Elijah's death, but then he'd relented and called. Now he selected the number after Elijah's, which he hadn't had the nerve to delete yet.

"How was your climb?" Rachel's voice came on after the first ring. They had spoken every day since the death that had traumatized them both. The outspoken grad student had been more of a comfort than his colleagues, all of whom were supportive but also awkward around him.

"I needed it. I'm at the office now."

"I told you not to go back there yet."

"Didn't know where else to go."

He glanced out the leaded-glass window into another misty evening. Even before the tragedy with Elijah, he'd preferred the quiet of late nights and early mornings in the lab. At ten thirty on a weeknight, the streets were quiet. He saw just a single student out for an evening jog. Obscured by the fog and only dimly lit by the yellow streetlamp, the student—*some kind of athlete*, Ethan thought because of his size—shortened his stride, came to a stop, and then bent over to tie his shoelace on the sidewalk.

"I found something strange." He held up the Post-it note.

"In the lab?"

"A note Elijah left. Some sort of code."

"Can you decipher it?"

"It looks familiar, but my brain has been kind of fuzzy."

He knew it was time to wean himself from his nightly Ambien. More than a week or two of use would result in his developing a dependence on it. He hadn't slept well after Natalie's death either.

"What does it say?"

"I told you, I can't figure it out."

"No, the code, what is it?"

"Oh, sorry." He wiped his brow with the back of his hand that held his phone and then squinted his eyes. "HV5822 L91 L44 1985, 214"

He heard her writing as he read the code. She was silent for about fifteen seconds. Just before he was going to ask if she was still there, he heard her laugh. He couldn't help but smile. Even though he didn't know why she was laughing, her laugh was contagious.

"What?"

"You are tired, aren't you?"

"You know what Elijah meant?"

"I'm heading out the door. I'll be there in fifteen."

"You don't have to come here. Just tell me—"

"I'm grabbing my bike now."

Before he could protest further, she clicked off. He studied the note, frustrated that he couldn't place what seemed so familiar yet was just out of reach. He felt conflicted about Rachel hurrying over to help him late at night. While he welcomed how understanding the insightful and attractive woman had been over the past few days, she was still a grad student and he a professor. He couldn't allow himself to develop feelings toward her. He glanced back out the window; the jogger was gone.

Rachel bounded through his lab door, flushed from her ride, hair damp from the mist.

"That was fast," Ethan said, unable to suppress a grin. In spite of his caution, he was happy to see her.

"Guess I needed the exercise too."

She dropped her helmet and jacket by the door and pulled Elijah's desk chair next to his. When she sat, their knees touched.

"Okay, show me this *code*."

He handed her the Post-it note. She glanced at it for a few seconds and then returned it to him, smiling. "Yep, just as I thought."

When she explained its meaning, he slapped the note onto the desk. "Of course! How did I not see that?"

"You're exhausted."

He rubbed his eyes and then massaged his temples. He knew that in response to the stress he'd been under his adrenal gland had been producing copious amounts of the hormone cortisol, which allowed him to work longer hours and continue to function, but the downside was that his body was starting to wear down.

"Yeah, I know."

She leaned in toward him and put her hands on his knees. "Look, you just lost your mentor, a man who had become a father figure to you. It's okay to grieve."

Her eyes seemed to be searching his, as if she were trying to communicate something more than her words were saying. But he had never been good at reading people in that way.

"I've been thinking lately—" he began.

She threw her arms in the air. "Thinking! You can't think or analyze your way out of this situation, Ethan. Sometimes you need to feel your way to the truth."

"That's what Elijah told me after Natalie died."

"Who's Natalie?"

"She was my fiancée."

"The woman you were engaged to died?"

He felt his breath catch in his chest. He hadn't spoken about Natalie's death to anyone other than Elijah in years, but something in the way she stared at him, patiently waiting, caused him to open up that compartment in his mind. The story began to spill out. His words seemed to flow from him like a river winding its way through a valley without obstruction.

"A drunk driver? My God, that's horrible."

"The funeral was surreal. I still remember the texture of the mahogany wood of her coffin: cold and slick. The scent of flowers seemed to burn my nose. To this day I still can't stand the smell of lilies. Then I had to smile and nod at the platitudes of those who came to pay their respects." He shuddered at the memories he'd tried to keep safe in their dark home in his mind.

She took his hand. "I can't imagine what you've been through. First your father, then Natalie, and now Elijah: you've had those closest to you suddenly taken away." Her fingers interlaced with his. "And worse, you were helpless to do anything about it."

"But I did have control with Natalie." He swallowed hard. His throat had tightened, constricting his air. "I was driving the car that night. If my reactions had been faster, I might have been able to swerve out of the way when the other driver came into our lane. I might have saved her." He swallowed again. "She died and I barely received a scratch."

Her fingers tightened around his. "You can't do this to yourself. In our interconnected lives, any control we think we have is only an illusion. You'll never find peace if you play the *what-if* game. There will always be more *ifs*."

He knew she was right. But then, there was still one piece to the story he had omitted; a fact he would keep locked away forever. He gazed at their hands, resting on his knee. Her skin was smooth and warm. As painful as talking about Natalie's death was, he was surprised to realize that he felt some easing of the tension he'd been carrying in his chest.

"I wish I knew how to stop that," he said.

"When I was in Kenya, one of the park rangers I worked with pointed out to me how the animals had an advantage over us in a strange way. Evolution has blessed us with minds that can reason and learn, but our minds also cause us to worry, to replay the past in an endless loop, and to project an infinite number of troubling futures. But the animals don't have these concerns; they live in the present."

"But my mind is my greatest asset. It's how I make my living."

"True, but are you in control of your mind, or is it in control of you?"

He'd never thought in those terms before. He'd always assumed that he was in control, but then he'd never really examined what *he* meant. He, Ethan Lightman, was a neuropsychologist at Yale studying the innermost workings of the human brain, but was he just his mind—his thoughts and conscious awareness—or was there something more? He thought again of Elijah and the Logos. Might their machine address this question?

Her eyes were still searching his. He smiled and released her hand. Somehow their roles had reversed. He was older, and he was the professor. Yet this student had challenged him to look at his life in a different way. He was feeling an inkling of a connection to her that he hadn't felt in years, but that was as far as it would go. He glanced at his watch. He had just enough time.

"Thanks for listening to me ramble on, but the library closes in thirty minutes." He peeled the yellow note from his desk—the one containing the code that Rachel had deciphered as a call number for a book in Sterling Memorial Library.

"Always happy to give unsolicited advice to a professor." She winked as if to acknowledge the role reversal that had just taken place. Strangely, he didn't feel uncomfortable with what had happened. "Can I come with you? I'd love to know what book Elijah was planning to check out."

"Sure, I could use the company." He told himself that her opinion might be valuable in case the book had something to do with the mystery of Elijah's death. But the truth was that he enjoyed having her around, even though he knew their conversations had already become too personal.

As they hurried out of his lab, he shifted his attention to what might be waiting for them in the dark stacks of Sterling Memorial Library. Elijah had sent him a message from the grave. He had to find out what this book might reveal.

CHAPTER 23

THE MONASTERY

Something was wrong with the monk walking toward Mousa. He had just rounded the bend at the far end of the cloistered hall. The man was dressed in a brown cassock, just as he was; and like him, he was also accompanied by a young priest. The priest's white collar seemed too small for his wide neck, and his short dark hair was matted with sweat from the effort of half-carrying the frantic monk.

When the two men reached him, he saw in the candlelit darkness that the monk struggling in the priest's arms was also an Arab, like the other monks he'd seen in the monastery. His pupils were dilated, and they darted back and forth as his mouth produced a series of unintelligible grunts and whimpers.

"Hello, Brothers," the approaching priest said through clenched teeth.

He found it strange that no one in the monastery addressed each other by name: it was "Brother" this and "Father" that. Still, the treatment he'd received from the American clergy was better than what he'd received from his own kind in the UAE prison. Soon, they promised, he would be well enough to go home to his family. In the meantime, all he had to do was humor their good-hearted but persistent attempts to convert him to their faith.

"He's very ill," the priest continued. "Going to the infirmary."

The two priests exchanged concerned glances. He thought that he detected a slight shrug coming from his own companion. Then the deranged man caught his eye. For a brief moment the monk's eyes locked onto his. The voice that came from him spoke in a high-pitched Arabic that communicated pure fear.

"I've seen him! Satan! Allah has sent me a vision of Hell!"

Before he could respond, the man's eyes glazed over, and he returned to his babbling as the priest ushered him down the hall. During a rotation in a psychiatric ward as a resident, Mousa had seen a patient who had experienced a psychotic break with reality. This man's symptoms were quite similar. Then, as now, he was surprised by the real terror such an experience had the power to induce. He then recalled the horrors of the secret prison and the tortures he had endured. Maybe this man had endured worse. *Allah, praise these priests for helping,* he prayed. But he suspected that the monk's condition was more than they could handle here. He needed to be in a psychiatric hospital.

The young blond priest he'd met a few days ago spoke as if reading his thoughts. "He has suffered greatly. He may be beyond our care here. God's plans for us are a mystery."

"You believe that God plays with our lives as a chess master moves pieces around a game board?" The words came from his mouth before he had a chance to censor them.

He'd tried to keep his faith to himself during his stay at the monastery. How long had he been there? He wasn't sure anymore. They never went outside, and he always felt tired. He couldn't recall ever sleeping so much in his life. During the days (or nights, he wasn't ever certain) when the various priests sat with him in his room, reading from the Bible and talking to him about their faith, he politely listened and occasionally nodded in agreement. He thought it best not to offend the men who were nursing him back to health. Anyway, he was already familiar with many of the stories they told him, since the Qur'an told many of the same tales.

"Just because we cannot understand God's plan does not mean He doesn't have one, Brother. Just look at the incredible design that is the universe we live in. How could there not be a plan?"

He weighed his response. Ever since he had taken up an interest in science as a young man—before he'd even thought of becoming a doctor—he'd begun to question the meaning of Allah. If Allah could just tinker with the world at will, then what meaning did the scientific laws have? Everything in his world, from televisions to airplanes, worked without exception because of fixed, unchanging scientific principles, not divine intervention. On the other hand, if Allah was only a creator deity who formed the universe and the laws behind it, but then left it to run itself, then why even believe in such a remote God? When he was seventeen and had finally gathered up the nerve to express his questions to his physics teacher, his teacher had given him a book of writings by the seventeenth-century scholar Mulla Sadra. That book had changed his spiritual life.

Mousa chose his words carefully. "Maybe our problem is in thinking about God as supernatural being."

The young priest cocked his head. "But how else does God have meaning? How else can we account for existence?"

"What if, Father"—he found it strange to address a man two decades his junior as *Father*, but he respected their customs—"we see God not as an all-powerful, Zeus-like figure, but as something greater than *a* being? What if God is the essential source of being itself?"

The priest scrunched up his brow. "I'm not sure I see how that works."

How did he explain what was impossible to explain? What was beyond words, beyond symbols, beyond understanding? Then he recalled an explanation his physics teacher had used after young Mousa had returned from reading Mulla Sadra filled with questions.

"Take snowflakes."

"Huh?"

Mousa knew the metaphor was imperfect, as all such talk of Allah must be, but he tried to explain. "Think of each of us as a snowflake. Each snowflake is a unique individual with its own distinct, crystallized structure."

The young priest thought for a minute and then said, "So you see God as the cloud that produces the snowflakes?"

He shook his head. "What if God is more like the water that makes up the snowflake? The water is not only responsible for the existence of the snowflake, it also links each individual snowflake with every other snowflake—each is unique, yet each shares its essence in an eternal connection with the others."

The priest was silent as they approached the end of the hallway, where a pair of carved wooden doors with heavy iron hardware was set into the wall.

Mousa had seen these doors numerous times on his way to the dining hall, whose entrance they'd just passed on his left. He knew that the doors led to the chapel, but he had never been inside it before. He turned to the priest, who rested his hand on the large iron ring that acted as a handle. Had he gone too far in explaining his understanding of Allah? The priest seemed to be contemplating his words, his eyes now fixed on the door before them. Then, with a slight shake of his head, the priest turned to him.

"Today is a special day, Brother Mousa." The priest smiled. "You are about to meet the Bishop."

He turned the handle, and the heavy door swung open without a creak or groan. The intense light that poured forth from the chapel rocked Mousa backward, blinding him.

CHAPTER 24

STERLING MEMORIAL LIBRARY
YALE UNIVERSITY

Ethan and Rachel climbed the stone steps of what appeared to be a tenth-century gothic cathedral. The imposing façade before them was actually the early twentieth-century Sterling Memorial Library, whose fifteen levels of stacks held over four million books.

Ethan pulled the iron ring on the heavy wood door, revealing a second, smaller glass door inside. They were the only ones entering at this late hour; weary students filed out past them. The heels from Rachel's shiny black boots echoed in the cavernous and quiet hall. Stone buttresses rose from the floor, holding up arches far above their heads. The ceiling was carved from thick wood beams, while the stained glass windows in the side walls added to the cathedral atmosphere. Directly ahead of them, where the altar should be, was the main circulation desk. Ethan's eyes caught the painting above the desk: a woman holding a book. The flat dimensions and rich gold and red colors reminded him of a pre-Renaissance painting. To his left was the main reading room with its arched windows, barrel vaulted ceiling, and walls lined with shelves of reference books. At almost any other time of day the long tables in the room would have been filled with students clicking away on their laptops, but now they were empty. He pulled the slip of yellow paper with Elijah's writing on it from his pocket and approached the middle-aged woman with short mousey-brown hair and thick black eyebrows who was stacking books on a trolley behind the desk.

"Excuse me, can you tell me where to find this book?"

The woman peered from behind round wire glasses, looking him up and down. "Faculty?"

"Professor Ethan Lightman, Psychology." He nodded to Rachel. "Ms. Riley here is one of my graduate students."

"If you leave this with me"—she took the note from his fingers—"I can pull the book from the stacks in the morning and have it delivered to your department by lunch."

He stuffed his hands in his pockets and shifted from one foot to the other. "I hate to ask, but I really need this tonight."

"Well, the stacks are open. You're welcome to go up there yourself." She glanced at the paper again. "HV—that's political science. Third floor mezzanine."

"Thank you," he said, taking back the note.

"You need to hurry. Library closes at eleven forty-five."

Turning to his right, he removed his wallet from his front pocket and approached another desk, this one smaller and lower. He held his Yale ID out to a man in a blue rent-a-cop shirt with a head of wispy gray hair. His attention on a magazine, the guard barely glanced at either his or Rachel's IDs before raising a wooden arm that led to a bank of elevators.

When Ethan bent over to push the elevator button, Rachel whispered in his ear, "I bet if anyone walked up confidently and flashed a credit card, that guy would let them pass."

He laughed. "Half the time, my ID is backward."

When they stepped onto the terrazzo of the third floor two minutes later, a chill crawled over his skin. In their rush to arrive before the library closed, he'd forgotten to grab his jacket on the way out of his office. The night had been cool, not cold, but now that he was still, he was shivering.

"Why is Sterling so spooky at night?" Her voice echoed off the brick-lined hallway.

"I think it was purposely designed to intimidate the students." He smiled, but he also felt the unease that the deserted gothic library engendered that close to midnight.

He led her down the hall, turned right, and opened a low wooden door, inviting her to enter the stacks first. Twenty-five rows of metal shelves on either side of a narrow walkway stretched before them. The ceiling above their heads was also metal; it served as the floor of the mezzanine, their destination. The rows of shelves were ensconced in shadow. Switches at the end of each row controlled fluorescent lights, but at this hour they were off. As they continued down the narrow aisle, he breathed in the aroma of old books.

A squeaking sound pierced the silence in the darkness ahead of them.

"What was that?" she whispered.

He froze in place and tilted his head to the side. Not hearing anything further, he shrugged and resumed his quest down the aisle. When he reached the metal staircase leading up to the mezzanine, he paused again and looked back from where they came. The aisle was still empty. His imagination was messing with him. He started up the stairs.

That's when the figure appeared before him.

He jumped backward, causing Rachel to let out a startled gasp. The student descending the steps two at a time in front of him abruptly halted his descent.

"Hey!" The voice came not from the male who stared at them with the shocked expression of someone who thought he was alone, but from behind him, where a mass of disheveled blond hair appeared over his shoulder.

Regaining his composure, the male student said, "What's up, Professor?"

"Late-night studying?" His pulse recovered from the surprise encounter as he recognized the student from a lecture he'd given the prior year.

"Yeah, that's right." A grin spread across the student's face. Then he seemed to notice Rachel, and his grin widened.

The woman behind him glanced away as she passed them, her cheeks and neck glowing red. Her hands were tucking her navy blouse into her long wool skirt. Sex in the stacks was somewhat of an unspoken tradition. Natalie had even convinced him to experiment there on more than one occasion.

"The library is about to close," he called after them.

"We're just leaving." The student's voice held a hint of relief. "Thanks, Prof."

"Busted," Rachel said under her breath after they reached the top of the stairs. He suppressed a laugh.

Five minutes later, they sat next to each other in a study carrel—a metal desk attached to the wall at the end a row of books. The clanking of radiators echoed around them. The window to their right looked down onto a retail intersection of New Haven streets. Neon lights proclaiming the "Hip Hop, Metal, Dance, Rock, Funk" of Toad's Place, a popular nightclub, lit up the foggy evening. Just beyond that, he could make out the four spires of the other campus building designed to look like a cathedral, Payne Whitney Gymnasium, where he had been rock climbing earlier.

"Are you going to open it?" she asked.

He turned his attention to the leather-bound book he'd just selected from the shelf by the carrel. Its call number matched the number Elijah had left. He sat up straight in the wooden chair while Rachel leaned in close beside him. He enjoyed feeling the warmth from her body. He flipped the book over so that its embossed title stood out.

"*Findings from The Church Senate Subcommittee on Intelligence,*" he read aloud. The book's title only added to the mystery.

"Wait," she said. "I studied this a few years ago in a poli-sci class." She drummed her fingers against her lip for a few seconds and then continued, "In 1973, Congress, led by Senator Church, held hearings on clandestine CIA activities in the 1950s and '60s."

"I think I remember something about that." Then a disturbing thought occurred to him. "Wasn't there some controversy caused by the participation of several renowned psychology academics in those operations?"

She nodded. "The Ivy League served as a top recruiting ground during the early days of the CIA."

Flipping the pages together, they skimmed over the details of a Top Secret operation known as MKULTRA. Beginning in 1953, the CIA had experimented with mind control techniques through the use of drugs, primarily LSD. The program examined ways in which Soviet defectors could be plied with psychoactive drugs to uncover what they knew. They also sought to control assassins with hypnosis and brainwashing, and even discussed whether entire populations could be made docile by putting hallucinogens in their water supply. The early experiments utilized willing subjects who ingested drugs or underwent total sensory deprivation to see the effects, but the CIA quickly came to understand that the only effective tests would be ones in which the participants had no idea that they were being drugged. They set up a safe house in San Francisco as a brothel where they administered drugs to the johns and the prostitutes and watched them on hidden cameras to test the effects. In one surreptitious test in Boston, a subject, thinking he was going insane, ran screaming down the hotel hallway and crashed through the glass window at the end, plummeting to his death.

Ethan shook his head. "I can't believe the extent of these experiments. How could an academic participate in this stuff?"

"I know. They were in violation of the Nuremberg Code."

He glanced at the graduate student, impressed with the breadth of her knowledge. After the Second World War, the judges at the Nuremberg trials had exposed the gruesome human experiments conducted by Nazi doctors and proposed ten points of research ethics that became known as the Nuremberg Code. The United States laws governing human experimentation followed these same principles. The most important points were that human subjects give their voluntary consent for any experimentation and that study participants never be in danger of real physical harm. For these reasons, his subjects—like Liz, his epilepsy patient, and Sister Terri—had to be informed and then sign off on all aspects of his studies.

Reading further, he learned that MKULTRA was disbanded not because of ethical concerns, but because the CIA realized that the drugs they were using were unpredictable at best in controlling behavior. When these experiments and other abuses at the Agency came to light in the 1970s, Congress enacted strict oversight of the CIA. Under President Carter, the covert operations capability of the Agency was essentially disbanded. Although its secret activities were renewed in the 1980s and again following 9/11, questions were raised in both of these cases because of abuses with the Iran-Contra scandal under Reagan and the torture of prisoners at Guantanamo under Bush.

All very interesting, he thought, *but why did Elijah send me to this book?* Turning another page, a paragraph jumped out at him that made his eyes widen.

Because of the covert nature of the experiments, the CIA went to great lengths to hide their involvement, even for the more innocuous research they funded at universities. They used the Josiah Macy Jr. Foundation and the Geschickter Fund for Medical Research to funnel money to numerous projects whose research was later adapted for CIA purposes.

He unbuttoned the next button down on his blue oxford shirt. He was sweating now. *Is it possible?* The memory of how odd Elijah had acted when talking about the Neurological Advancement Foundation that had funded their research blazed through his mind.

A distant clanging noise of metal caused both of them to look up.

The noise sounded like a door had just closed. He glanced at his watch: 11:35. "Probably the security guard coming to tell us our time is up."

He held his breath for a moment, listening again. *Nothing.*

"I'm sure that's it," Rachel said, but he heard an edge to her voice that hadn't been there earlier.

He turned his attention back to the book and then fished the Post-it note from his pocket. After the call number, he noticed a comma and the number 214. He flipped to page 214.

Rachel slapped his shoulder. "Good catch. I missed that."

A black-and-white picture stared back at them. The photograph showed six solemn figures standing in a lab. The team of Harvard psychologists was testing the effects of a combination of hypnosis, drugs, and sleep deprivation on memory and suggestibility. His breath caught in his chest when he noticed the two young graduate students on the far right side of the photo.

"Is that—" Rachel began.

"I can't believe it."

But what scared him was that he did believe it. The puzzle pieces were starting to fall into place. The first graduate student in the picture, tall with neat hair, was identified as Allen Wolfe. Next to Wolfe was his classmate, Elijah Schiff.

The squeaking of sneakers echoed through the stacks below them. "That doesn't sound like how that ancient guard would walk," she whispered.

She's right, he thought; the steps were quick and deliberate. "Maybe another student. I'll check." The image of his mentor and Wolfe working for the CIA burned in his mind. Careful not to scrape his chair against the floor, he stood and made his way to the staircase.

CHAPTER 25

THE MONASTERY

Mousa blinked rapidly. His eyes had been accustomed to the cloister's flickering candelabras when the intense light from the chapel hit him. As his pupils constricted, he realized that the light shone from a monumental stained glass window at the far end of the chapel opposite the doorway in which he stood. He felt the young priest's hand on his lower back, urging him into the room. He cast his eyes to the floor, whose polished white marble contrasted the textured, sand-colored stone of the rest of the monastery. His sandals slid across the smooth finish as he shuffled toward the light.

The stained glass was in the form of a cross over five meters in height. The glass was divided into various triangles of brilliant color, except for the center, which held no color and radiated a brilliant white light that seemed to pierce through to the innermost core of his brain.

"Welcome, Brother Mousa," a baritone voice called from the light.

Mousa shielded his eyes and walked the twenty paces to the far end of the chapel. The voice, he discovered, did not come from the light but from a regally appointed man sitting on an elevated golden throne underneath the stained glass.

The Bishop.

He had heard rumors of the Bishop. The priests spoke about him in reverent tones. He had the power of God within him, they said with a note of awe.

The Bishop beckoned to him. Mousa approached the throne, stepping onto a lush burgundy carpet that stretched out from the platform upon which the throne sat, raised above the marble floor. When they reached the base of the platform, the priest kneeled, bowing his head. Mousa followed his lead, kneeling also but looking up at the man on the throne. Embroidered silver silk robes hung from his shoulders to his feet, which were dressed in polished Italian wingtips. Adorning the man's head like a crown was a tall pointed hat made from the same silk as the robes.

The Bishop smiled in a fatherly way. "We are so happy to have you here with us, Mousa. Seeing you recover from such a great injustice brings joy to my heart."

"And I appreciate your hospitality"—he stood while the young priest remained kneeling—"but now that I am better, I'm ready to return to my family."

"That day is coming soon. We are working out the details with the local government. Because of the way you were treated, these things can take some time."

"All I want is to go home. I'm not looking to hold anyone responsible for my imprisonment."

"We know that, Son. Soon, very soon." The Bishop beamed a white smile at him. "But today we have something wonderful for you."

He raised his eyebrows but waited to hear what this "something" was.

"Have you ever truly experienced God?"

He glanced at the priest beside him, thinking of the conversation they'd just had. His understanding of Allah had deepened over the years, and he performed the *Salat*, praying five times a day while facing Mecca, but he was neither a Sufi nor a mullah.

"In what way?"

"When you accept that Jesus Christ is the one and only Son of God, you can experience through Him the power of the Holy Spirit." The Bishop's smile vanished, and his eyes narrowed. "Brother Mousa, I'm offering you the opportunity to accept Jesus into your life. Are you ready to confess your sins and give yourself to Christ in exchange for eternal life?"

The first thought that came to Mousa was to ask why it was necessary to accept Jesus as the *only* Son of God. Contrary to what the more radical members of his religion claimed, the Prophet Mohammad taught that Allah sent different prophets to speak to different peoples. Allah sent Moses to the Hebrews, Jesus to the Christians, and Mohammad to the Arabs. Mousa already understood that Jesus was the Son of God, but then again all of humanity were children of God. Since there was no truth but Allah, the spark of Allah was in everyone. Certain figures in history, however—Moses, Jesus, Mohammad, even the Buddha—lived a life more centered on this divine spark, lighting the way for others to follow their paths. The mistake Christians made, he thought, was in their deification of Jesus from a child of Allah and a great prophet into an idol rivaling Allah himself.

While these thoughts raced through his mind, he bowed his head and said in as heartfelt a tone as he could muster, "I accept Jesus as my Christ and Savior."

He had said these words many times before to the various priests who sat by his bed. They were just words, and they made his caring hosts happy. He figured that anything that made the priests happy brought him closer to his family.

The beaming smile returned to the Bishop's tanned face.

"Brother Mousa, our order here is unique. While we do have a simple hierarchy—Bishop, Fathers, Brothers—we recognize that in God's eyes we are all the same."

Mousa nodded. As different as their religions were, their teachings shared many similarities.

The Bishop rose from his throne. "In the Church, the *cathedra*, the bishop's chair, is a symbol of my authority and power, a power that comes from God through Jesus, passing to his apostles and then through a line of succession over history to me today."

The Bishop stepped aside and motioned to the chair. "Please, take a seat."

He glanced to the priest now standing beside him. The priest shared the same smile as the Bishop. Mousa stepped onto the platform and placed a hand on the smooth curved wood of the armrest. It felt luxurious. He turned and lowered himself onto the purple cushioned seat. Although the seatback was wood, it was contoured to his back and felt as comfortable as any recliner. The sides of the back were covered in gold leaf and swept up into a spiral decoration that swirled by his head.

"Close your eyes and relax," the Bishop said. "We will pray together for the Holy Spirit to come to you."

The baritone voice had a soothing effect. He'd enjoyed praying with the priests, and he admired their piety and their respect for Allah. He relaxed into the throne, resting his head on a cushion embedded in the wood. He closed his eyes. His lids felt heavy.

"Our Father, who art in heaven . . ." The baritone voice was joined by the blond-haired priest.

Mousa took up the prayer as well, his lips repeating the words he'd been taught during his stay in the monastery. His mind, however, began a different prayer: "In the name of Allah, the most beneficent, the most merciful, all appreciation, gratefulness, and thankfulness are to Allah alone, Lord of the World . . ." He didn't have anything against the Christian prayer, but the *Sura Al-Fatiha* felt more comfortable to him.

He didn't know how long he sat in the chair before he noticed the change. The rhythmic voices of the priests, along with the repetition of his prayer, obscured the passage of time. The change started as a subtle awareness. He felt or heard—he wasn't sure which—a slight hum. When he turned his attention to the sensation, he thought he detected a slight vibration. Maybe it was the powerful air conditioners that kept the monastery cool. Before he explored the sensation further, a new feeling arose. This feeling, however, didn't seem to come from outside of him but from a distant corner of his mind.

There is no god but Allah, and Mohammad is his messenger. The words rolled across the back of his eyelids. Then he felt as if a door opened in the dark recesses of his mind. The door didn't lead to any particular place, but rather it seemed to lead to space itself, as if the physical boundaries of his skull began to open. This space called to him like the distant light of an entrance to a cave beckoned to one lost inside. His prayer trailed off while the voices of the Bishop and priest faded into the darkness. He drifted toward the light. His body warmed as the cool air of the cave gave way to the heat of the sun. The desire to reach the light became irresistible, as if his very existence depended on it. The warmth spread from his skin inward, embracing his heart and eclipsing his fears and doubts about his future—even those about his family.

Suddenly the darkness vanished.

The feeling was overwhelming and indescribable. He surrendered to the warmth and the light that now bathed his body from the outside, and yet at the same time radiated outward from his very core. All words but one faded from his mind: *Islam*. For the first time in his life, he truly understood the teachings of his faith. The meaning of Allah went beyond doctrine, beyond history, beyond mythology, even beyond the prophets.

He experienced truth.

CHAPTER 26

STERLING MEMORIAL LIBRARY
YALE UNIVERSITY

Ethan stood at the top of the metal staircase listening to the sound of sneakers on the floor below him. The thought of Elijah's mysterious death popped into his head. He imagined that he could hear his heart beating louder as the steps seemed to get closer.

Stop it, he told himself.

He was being ridiculous—or rather, his limbic system was. He knew that from an evolutionary standpoint the body was wired to respond to danger. His brain was producing neurochemicals that dilated his vessels and increased his heart rate. His muscles were primed to react in an instant. That the danger was only imagined didn't matter. The same physiological response happened when one was watching a scary movie or being chased by a lion in the African savannah. For survival, it was better to be mistaken about the danger than to be eaten by a predator. The dark gothic library was playing with his mind.

Then another sound caught his attention. Every few seconds the footsteps below him paused, and he heard a click. His curiosity aroused, he descended the steps.

A librarian shelving books?

He reached the third step from the bottom and bent to peer around the metal banister. A movement to his left caught his eye. A man walked down the main aisle about five rows past the stairs. It wasn't the security guard but rather a man dressed in sweats. He paused at each row and flicked on the light switch before moving to the next one. He was methodically searching for something. *Or someone.* Although he couldn't be sure, he thought the man looked familiar. At the next row, he caught a glimpse of his profile.

I've seen him.

There was no mistaking the size of the man. Massive shoulders sloped away from a sunburned neck while his latissimus dorsi muscles formed a broad V shape down to a waist that seemed proportionately too small for the rest of the frame. Perched on top of the man's head was a pair of orange-tinted sunglasses.

My classroom.

This same hypertrophied man had been staring at him from the balcony during his lecture just over a week ago. Then he remembered seeing someone he thought was an athlete jogging on the sidewalk outside his office window earlier that evening. Next, an even more disturbing image flashed through his mind: Elijah strangled to death in their lab. The realization that this man was following him sent his limbic system into full fight-or-flight mode. He had no question as to which of these options he would take. But first he had to get Rachel. He inched back up the steps, careful not to strike his heels against the metal treads. In under a minute Muscleman would reach the end of the aisle, and then he would come up to the mezzanine.

When Ethan reached the mezzanine, he saw that Rachel had stepped out of the aisle and was looking at him with a quizzical expression. He put a finger to his lips, started toward her, and then had another idea. They had turned the lights on, which Muscleman would see as soon as he started climbing the stairs, but the stacks on the fourth floor above them were dark. Keeping his finger to his lips, he motioned with his free hand for her to join him at the steps. Her brow still scrunched, she walked on the balls of her feet toward him.

"Who?" she whispered. She handed him the book.

"We have to go now," he said into her ear. He tucked the book under his arm, took her hand, and led her up to the fourth floor. The aisle ahead of them was dark, as he expected, but he could see the line of light underneath the door about fifty feet ahead.

The squeaking of sneakers against metal sounded behind them. He turned his head, his breath coming quicker. Rachel's hand tightened around his. Muscleman was climbing the stairs. Ethan hoped he would take his time searching the mezzanine level, giving them the opportunity to sneak out the door and back down the elevator. He sped up the pace, remaining on his toes, his eyes focused on the thin line of light that was their destination.

The steel edge of a mobile shelving cart bit into his pelvic bone as he hit it hard. Although it was dark, he knew what the waist-high metal cart looked like: the librarians rolled the shelves that sat atop metal casters down the rows to replace books. He stumbled over his size thirteen feet, but Rachel's grip kept him from falling. The empty cart, however, shot forward and rammed into the nearest row of bookshelves. The noise couldn't have been louder if he'd taken a hammer to the metal shelf.

To make matters worse, his free arm flailed in front of him to steady his balance, causing the book tucked under it to fly out. He heard it hit the floor. He didn't waste time picking it up. Instead, he lunged for the door. Rachel didn't need encouragement either.

No longer trying to be stealthy, they let the door clang shut behind them just as the lights in the stacks flickered on. They broke into a sprint down the hallway, turned the corner, and skidded to a stop by the double elevators. His breath came in short deep gasps. Rachel's eyes were wide, her pupils dilated. He hit the down button and glanced up. Both elevators were on the third floor. Muscleman must have followed them by watching the indicator from the main floor. The hydraulic cables creaked as the old elevator started its ascent. He stabbed at the button three more times, willing it to move faster. *We're not going to make it*, he thought. His mind raced through the possibilities of what Muscleman had in store for them. Whatever it was, maybe he could delay the man long enough for Rachel to escape. Then he felt her tug on his arm.

"This way!" She pulled him toward a metal door to their left he hadn't noticed—the fire exit.

They disappeared into the faded pea-green stairwell as the sound of the door to the stacks opening echoed down the brick-lined hall.

CHAPTER 27

CIA HEADQUARTERS
LANGLEY, VIRGINIA

"**W**e have a slight problem."

"A problem?" Deputy Director Casey Richards massaged the top of his bald head as he paced around the oak desk in the center of his office. He took a sip of lukewarm coffee, black, and spoke into the headset. "But our last operation was a success, all because of this new technique of yours."

He wasn't sure whether the extended pause that came from the phone line was due to the signal traveling halfway across the globe or the doctor searching for the right words to say.

The cultured voice that came over the line displayed no uncertainty, however. "For most of the subjects, our new protocol has made life-altering changes, just as we demonstrated." He cleared his throat. "But we've recently experienced some anomalies."

"What kind of anomalies?"

"Psychotic breaks with reality."

"You mean your subjects have gone crazy?"

"That's a crude way of putting it."

"How many?"

"Two out of eighteen."

He threw his hands up in the air in a gesture of frustration. "Jericho has to graduate hundreds for it to work. We can't have dozens of psycho cases running around!" He thought of all of the Islamic prisoners being held in secret prisons around the globe, most of them low-level suspected terrorists.

"We're dealing with the problem." The doctor's voice remained confident. "The subjects who have not adapted to the protocol will be culled."

Richards gulped from his mug, placed it on the leather coaster on his desk, and sat in his chair. This project had the potential to alter the dynamics of the Middle East, halting millennia of religious violence, eliminating terrorism, and bringing stability to the world's largest source of oil. The first test on Youssef had proven that Jericho could be the mechanism that would allow them to infiltrate the terrorist cells they had never been able to penetrate before. They would finally be able to wipe out terrorism at the source, led there by double agents motivated by faith.

"I don't care how you do it"—he leaned forward on his desk as if the doctor were sitting opposite him—"but fix it now, or I'm shutting down Jericho." As important as the project was, every time he thought of the potential risks he questioned his decision to proceed.

"It won't come to that." The smooth voice cracked just a little. "We've already achieved what forty years ago was only a dream."

"You haven't achieved it yet. This program needs to be flawless."

"Psychological work is never flawless."

"You understand, Doctor, the dangers of exposure? Just one subject of yours not completely brainwashed could bring us down."

"I only need a few days. Our protocol requires a small tweak. We'll get to the bottom of this and be up and running with no problems by next week."

He massaged his scalp again. "You have until next Thursday."

He punched the button on his phone, disconnecting the line. Leaning to his right, he dialed a combination into the lock on the file cabinet under his desk. Thumbing through the green files, each marked "Eyes Only" with unique security code words assigned to them, he reached the J's and removed the Jericho file. He flipped through the pages until he reached the memo he prayed he'd never have to use. The memo detailed how to shut Jericho down quickly, with no trace left behind.

The doctor had one week.

CHAPTER 28

KOFFEE, NEW HAVEN

"I just don't see Elijah as the kind of man who would work for the CIA," Rachel said.

Ethan gazed at her across the wrought iron table at Koffee as they analyzed the events from the library the previous evening. After they had run out of the doors, they'd stopped at the front gate of Berkeley College, one of Yale's twelve residential colleges that housed its undergraduate students. Across an expansive lawn from the front entrance of the library, they'd debated whether or not to call the police. Once their heart rates settled, they realized that the police would never take them seriously: Ethan had merely seen a large man walking through the library stacks looking for something—a man who was dressed as a student athlete and who'd been in his lecture. Ethan was also sure that if he brought up his concerns of some kind of government covert operation involving his research and Elijah's death, the police would lock him up instead. After watching the front of the library for half an hour with no sign of Muscleman, he walked Rachel home. He declined her invitation to come in for a drink to continue their conversation, instead suggesting that they meet the following morning.

"And the man following us," she asked, "the bodybuilder dude you saw?"

"I know it sounds like some crazy plot from a thriller, but—"

She reached across the table and touched his arm. "Could you modify the Logos to read people's minds or maybe implant certain thoughts?"

"That's not the way it works; it's about producing an experience of what one already considers to be the divine."

"What does Chris think?"

"We haven't even spoken since Elijah's death." He drummed his fingers on the table. "This isn't something I can explain in a text message or leave on a voicemail." He shifted his gaze from her face to the window—another gray morning. "I just don't . . ." He took a deep breath. "Elijah was more than my partner; he was my friend, my confidant. But now that he's gone, I wonder how well I really knew him."

She placed her hand on top of his. Her touch was soft, smooth, and comforting. "Elijah cared deeply for you. I think he was trying to protect you from something, but he was killed before he could tell you what it was."

He glanced at her narrow fingers, whose short, manicured nails were without polish. As usual, the only jewelry she wore was the spark of a diamond in her nose. He imagined that long, colorful nails, dangling earrings, and watches would be too much a temptation for the monkeys. He rotated his hand so that their palms lightly touched. The sensation sent a current of electricity up his arm and into his chest.

What am I doing? he chastised himself. He quickly withdrew his hand and placed it in his lap. She smiled at him in the direct way she did that drew him in further. His phone began to vibrate in his pocket.

"Sorry," he said, happy for the distraction. He answered, "Dr. Lightman."

"Professor, how quickly can you get to my office?" Sam Houston's voice sounded almost giddy with excitement, a tone he'd never heard from the administrator before.

"What's going on?"

"I need you here now."

"I'm just around the block, but can—"

"Be here in five minutes." The line went dead.

He mirrored Rachel's quizzical expression.

"The head of the HRPP wants to see me."

"Houston?" Her expression morphed from questioning to concern.

"He sounded happy about something but was all business at the same time."

"Maybe the police got a break in the murder?"

He shrugged and then stood from the round table. "He demanded my presence now."

"That would be like him." She followed him out the door into the crisp morning air. "Let me know what you learn?" She placed her hand on his arm. This time he didn't move it.

"Want to grab a bite this evening?" He felt like he had to see her again soon, but then maybe he was just grasping at the company of the only person he could confide in.

"Got a birthday dinner for one of my roommates. Tomorrow?"

"Great. I'll text you."

He turned his body down the sidewalk, but his feet were rooted in place. He noticed that she didn't move away either, and that her hand remained on his arm. Their good-bye had already happened, but he felt as if a magnetic force kept them from separating.

The memory of the awkward good-byes that ended the few dates he'd had in high school flashed through his mind. Should he kiss the girl or give her a hug? Either option risked rejection. They would stare at each other for a moment in silence. He knew that once he started debating in his mind whether or not he should kiss the girl, the battle was lost. The girls always sensed his hesitation, his insecurity. They inevitably said, "See ya later, then." And then they closed the door as he continued to wait on the steps.

Standing outside the café's doorway, he knew that giving Rachel a hug, much less kissing her, was the wrong thing to do for many reasons. He was a professor, she a graduate student; his life was in upheaval. He glanced down the empty sidewalk, as if to will his body to move in that direction, but the glance was short. His eyes were drawn back to her.

Her smile lit up her face; her eyes sparkled. The strands of blond highlights embedded in her chestnut hair seemed to radiate energy. She tilted her face upward to him. The magnetic force drawing him closer to her was almost overpowering. He longed to kiss her.

Then the voice in his head intruded. *I can't do this.* He backed away.

"Um, I should go," he stammered.

"Okay." Her smile never dimmed. "I guess I'll see you tomorrow."

Before he could say anything else, she turned and walked away with a bounce in her step.

CHAPTER 29

SSS, YALE UNIVERSITY

Ethan was a scientist. He operated in the world of hypothesis followed by experimentation, observation, and then conclusion. As a psychology professor and a doctor, he knew that romantic attraction was a primitive emotion that was important to the survival of the species. But as much as he understood its biochemical source, triggered by hormones such as oxytocin, he didn't really know what to do about the emotion itself. A few minutes earlier, he'd almost kissed a student—out on the street and only a block away from his office, no less. He knew he had to stop his relationship with Rachel from heading down that path, but every cell in his body ached for just one kiss before he did so.

Approaching the door to Houston's office on the first floor of the SSS building, he shifted his focus to wondering why the administrator needed to see him. His research, his life's work, was at a standstill until Houston said otherwise. He hated not being in control of his own destiny. He wiped the sweat from his hands on his pants, hoping he didn't appear as uncomfortable as he felt, and knocked.

"Enter."

Houston's stern expression when Ethan opened the door presented a whole new layer of emotional confusion for him.

"I got here as fast as I could," Ethan said. "I was just around the corner having coffee with one of the CapLab techs." He didn't know why he felt the need to explain his whereabouts to Houston. His mouth seemed to be moving of its own accord.

"Yes, Rachel says that you two are spending quite a bit of time together."

The administrator's comment caused the hairs on his neck to prickle. *Rachel and Houston have been talking?* He was surprised that the elder professor even knew who the grad student was. Then a second thought occurred to him: *Why didn't she mention anything about this to me?*

Houston picked up a folder from a stack of similar folders off of his antique cherry desk. "Professor Lightman, describe for me the financial controls for the funding around the Logos Project."

"Financial controls?" He took a minute to process the unexpected question. "Elijah handled the relations with the foundation and Chris Sligh, our graduate student, was responsible for the paperwork. Since Elijah's death and your decision to suspend our experiments, we haven't done anything."

In fact, his repeated calls to the NAF had gone unanswered. He'd left numerous messages for Allen Wolfe, but each time he'd called the number on the business card the foundation president had given him, he'd received a message that Wolfe was traveling and would have limited phone access.

"The Neurological Advancement Foundation in Texas gave you a check"—Houston showed Ethan what appeared to be a copy of a bank statement—"for two hundred and fifty thousand dollars."

"Yes, that's right," he answered.

"Did you know that I receive monthly printouts of all of the university research accounts in our department?"

He's checking up on us, Ethan thought. He doubted whether the administrator was inspecting the activities of his colleagues with the same rigor. Then the previous night's events in the library replayed in his head. Was his fear about the NAF correct? Did Houston suspect where the true source of their project's funding came from? Did he know about Elijah's history?

"Two days ago, after I'd already suspended your project, twenty thousand dollars was wired out of the Logos account."

He felt his breath catch in his chest. He gripped his thighs so that his hands wouldn't fidget as he remembered the error in his own account. He'd meant to call the bank to check on the mistake that morning, but then the discovery of Elijah's note and the strange man in Sterling Library had caused him to forget about the deposit. The extra money in his account had been twenty thousand dollars.

"Where did that money go?"

"I have no idea what you're talking about." Technically, his reply wasn't a lie. He didn't know how the extra money ended up in his account, and until that moment, he hadn't known that the same amount was missing from the Logos account.

Houston eyed him over the top of the paper for a full minute of uncomfortable silence and then slapped the bank statement onto his desk.

"From the beginning of this project, I've been concerned about the corners you and Elijah have cut. Rest assured, I'll get to the bottom of this."

"I'm not sure that there's anything to get to the bottom of. The bank probably made a mistake."

And how did that mistake result in the money ending up in my account? He tried to control his breathing so as not to betray his racing pulse. If the university discovered that some of the project's money had ended up in his personal account, he would be through for good. Not only would he lose his job, the case would also be turned over to the police on charges of embezzlement.

But how did this happen? The question revolved in his head as he half-listened to Houston explaining the importance of controls, the reasons they had so many paperwork requirements, and the liability the university faced. The irony of the matter was that money wasn't important to him. Between the patients he saw and his university salary, he made more than enough to support his simple lifestyle. He did what he did not for money, but for the love of knowledge and the thrill that he and Elijah had been on the cutting edge of their field. They'd had the potential to change the way people viewed the brain and religious experience. But now his very freedom was in jeopardy.

He rose from the chair, causing it to screech against the wooden floor. Houston stopped mid-sentence.

"I'm sorry, Sam, I have to go. I swear I don't know how the money was transferred out of the account, but I can assure you that I will look into it and get it resolved." Without waiting for an answer, he turned and walked out the door.

CHAPTER 30

NEW HAVEN

Rachel stepped out of the shower, grabbed the towel resting on the toilet lid, and began to dry her hair. She was late. Her roommates had already left for the dinner. Normally she would have been excited to spend time with her friends, but at the moment she wished she were with Ethan, especially after the intimate moment they'd shared that morning. Thinking of him brought up a cocktail of emotions within her: an equal mixture of attraction, compassion, and frustration.

She knew that having a relationship with a professor was inappropriate, but from the first time she'd heard him lecture, she'd been intrigued by the tall doctor with the dark, shaggy locks. She'd sensed that he had no idea how many of his female students found him attractive, which just made him all the more desirable. In each class he exuded such passion for his work as he explained the inner workings of the mind. Too many people today lacked passion, she thought, and passion was sexy. Anyway, he was only in his early thirties—not terribly older than she was, and it wasn't like she was an undergraduate.

Her heart went out to him. His mentor had been murdered, his graduate student was out of town, and his research had been shut down. He was alone, and she wanted to comfort him. But this professor with the brilliant mind had the emotional openness of a stubborn child. How could she help him if he wouldn't let her in?

As she wrapped the towel around her body and turned on the hair dryer, she replayed the day she'd spent in CapLab after leaving the coffee shop. Since the experiment with the Logos, Anakin had grown increasingly erratic. Her frustration with Ethan extended to his dismissive attitude about her monkey. He was so invested in the outcome of his research that he was blind to the problem. He'd only been looking to see if the monkeys experienced an epileptic incident; they hadn't, but he refused to consider the possibility that his machine might have other negative psychological effects on the animals.

Most of the professors who dropped by to run experiments on the capuchins suffered from the same shortsighted perspective. They saw the creatures as glorified lab rats. But she understood each monkey's distinctive personality. With Anakin, she'd sensed immediately that his reaction to the Logos was different from the others'. What she couldn't put her finger on was why. Observing him take food from one of the larger males, something bothered her but she couldn't articulate what it was. The answer was there, just on the edge of her thoughts—she just couldn't quite reach it.

She clicked off the hair dryer and picked up a lipstick from the basket underneath the sink. On the rare occasions she wore makeup, she concentrated on her lips and eyes. She chose a dark hue.

Then she heard a noise.

She cracked the door. Cold air invaded the humid bathroom. Had she imagined the sound? She thought she'd heard the front door open—it was notoriously squeaky, but with the fan going it could have just been the old house creaking, as it did whenever the temperature changed. The four-bedroom, two-bath townhouse was small, and sound echoed across the hardwood finishes. She was on the second floor.

"Julie, Anneliese, Connie?" she called.

Nothing.

She shrugged and turned back to the mirror. She leaned in and examined her brows. When she reached in the basket for her tweezers, she heard the stairs creak. She froze.

Something wasn't right.

A feeling of unease descended over her. The old house could be spooky when she was alone—that was why she had three roommates. But this feeling was more intense than usual. Although the bathroom was warm, she shivered.

Stop it, she thought. Ethan had recently lectured on how powerful the mind was in creating realities that were not, in fact, real. She leaned closer to the mirror, blinked to focus, and raised the tweezers.

A movement from of the corner of her eye sucked the breath out of her chest.

She reacted on instinct. Without knowing what or who she saw, she dropped the tweezers and slammed the bathroom door closed. A howl of pain pierced through the wood panels. Four male fingers twitched inside the door-frame at the level of her nose. They blazed an angry red. The door shook violently. She shoved her shoulder against it, planting her feet by the tub.

Curses of pain and frustration came from the other side. She didn't know how long she could hold off the violence that seemed to shake the house. Then the door bucked inward with such a force that she was almost thrown into the tub. Somehow she managed to keep her weight against it. Then the door slammed shut completely. The man had jerked his fingers out.

She grasped for the lock, but her hand seemed to move in slow motion. She knew that in any moment the man would overpower her and be in the room. She found the silver knob and twisted it.

Panting, she slid to the floor. She kept her back to the door and her feet against the base of the tub.

"Get out of my house!" The words came out more forcefully than she expected. She'd never been more terrified in her life. Tears begin to sting her eyes. *Don't cry!* she scolded herself. *Think, if you want to get out of this.*

"Ms. Riley"—the deep voice with a note of pain in it came from the other side of the door.

He knows my name.

Before he could finish the sentence, she blurted out, "I'm calling the police right now." She searched the bathroom, her eyes darting from counter to floor. Her purse, with her cell phone in it, was sitting on her bed in the other room.

"Ms. Riley, I *am* the police. Officer Simms."

She hesitated. Could it be true, or just a ruse to have her open the door?

"If you're the police, why are you inside my house?"

She glanced over her shoulder at the small knob that was the old lock. It wouldn't withstand a hard kick. But he wasn't trying to force his way in anymore. Maybe he was telling the truth.

"Your door was unlocked. I came by because of your roommate. I called from the front door, but you must not have heard me. When I walked up the stairs to see if anyone was here, you slammed the door on my hand before I could say anything."

"My roommate? Is there a problem?"

The voice sounded reasonable, but her pulse still pounded in her ears.

"She's just been taken to Yale-New Haven Hospital. Hit and run on Park Street, just behind Davenport College."

Her heart sank—that was only a couple blocks away. *Please, not Julie*, she prayed. Not that she wished an injury on any of her roommates, but Julie was the closest friend she'd ever had.

"I need to get some information about how to contact her family," the official-sounding voice continued from the other side of the door. "If you would please unlock the door, I can show you my badge and write down her parents' phone numbers. The doctors have to speak to them."

She rose to her feet and reached for the lock, but stopped just short of turning it. The man sounded believable, but something still wasn't sitting right with her.

"Which roommate?"

"Huh?"

"I have three roommates. Which one was hit?"

"Let me see. I have to check my notebook." The silence that followed lasted too long.

Damn! Why don't I have my phone with me? She decided to bluff.

"Um, yes," she said as if she was talking on a phone, "I need the police to come to my house immediately. I have a man here who claims to be an Officer Simms."

When she paused, as if listening to the response from the nonexistent 911 operator, the door exploded inward. Splinters from the wood burst into the air. The force of the door followed by the man's body behind it tossed her like a ragdoll into the tub. A flash of pain shot through her legs when her shins collided with the porcelain. Shampoo bottles tumbled over her head as the wire tray hanging from the showerhead crashed to the floor. Scrambling to get her hands underneath her, she rose to her knees.

That's when she noticed she was naked. Her towel had fallen. A huge man with a crew cut and orange sunglasses stood in her bathroom, surrounded by the carnage that had been the door. Although she couldn't see his eyes, she knew they were roving her body.

Oh, God . . .

She crossed her arms in front of her chest and opened her mouth to scream. But before she could get a sound out, he lunged toward her, shot out a hand, and grabbed her throat. His fingers tightened, cutting off her air. As her lungs heaved in a vain attempt to breathe, a wave of panic coursed through her body. Both of her hands flew to his, her fear of suffocating outweighing her modesty. She tried to pry his fingers from her neck, but his grip was too strong. For the first time since she moved to Africa six years earlier, she wished she had longer nails. She tried to jerk her body away, but the man's strength was overpowering.

Just as her world began to darken, he eased his grip without releasing it. She sucked in a lungful of air that cleared her head.

"Stop struggling, don't scream, and I won't hurt you."

The man from the library! she realized. Finally able to breathe, she noted how the buttons on his striped shirt strained at the slabs of muscle across his chest and shoulders. He matched Ethan's description precisely.

"Please don't hurt me." The words came from her involuntarily. She hated to show weakness to a man, but her fear seemed to possess her body.

The corners of his mouth turned upwards, as if he was enjoying her terror. Then she saw something in his free hand, dangling by his side, which elevated her pounding pulse to a deafening level. *He's holding a syringe!* The thought sent a wave of nausea through her stomach. She didn't know if he was planning to rape her or kill her or do both, but she wasn't going to let either happen without a fight. She forced herself to release the breath she was holding. *Think, Rachel.* She couldn't overpower him, and she suspected she only had seconds left.

Then she noticed the razor. She kept it in the wire basket with her shampoo and conditioner, but when the basket's contents scattered into the tub, the razor had landed by her knee. A rudimentary plan formed in her head. She forced her body to relax by focusing on the physical sensation of the humid air flowing into her lungs. His grip in turn loosened more. Then she dropped her hands from his and crossed her left arm over her breasts. She sensed his gaze following her movement. Her right breast was completely obscured by her hand, but she allowed her left nipple to peak out just above her bicep. She had his attention. His nostrils flared outward like a horse preparing to breed. She would have only one chance.

Without taking her eyes off of his face, she felt by her knee with her right hand. *There!* The metal handle of the razor was cool. She moved without thinking, sweeping the razor up and across the tender skin on the underside of the wrist whose hand held her throat. The thickness of his forearms provided plenty of surface area to strike. A three-inch-long line of crimson opened across his tanned skin as if she'd drawn on it with a red sharpie.

"What the f—"

Before he finished the thought, she slashed the razor back across his forehead. Blood ran into his eyes. He rocked back on his heels, his hands flying to his face.

"You bitch!" His roar shook the bathroom.

Her strike hadn't done much real damage to the hulking man, but it had created the distraction she needed. He'd released her and dropped the syringe beside her. Free from his grasp, she snatched the syringe, hurdled out of the tub, and lunged for the splintered bathroom door.

The stairs!

Her attacker was much larger than she was, but she knew that if she could just reach the top of the stairs while he was preoccupied with the blood dripping in his eyes, she could escape. She ran three to five miles a day, and not at a leisurely pace.

When her bare feet hit the bathmat by the sink, she twisted her body to avoid touching the man holding his bloody forehead. The wooden banister that led to her freedom beckoned from just a few feet away. Her vision narrowed to the only thing important in her life at that moment: the path to her escape.

She leaped through the doorway.

Then her head snapped back, wrenching her neck as if she were an unruly dog whose leash had been jerked by its owner.

"You're not going anywhere!"

He dragged her back into the bathroom and turned her to face him. He gripped her long hair so tightly she worried he might tear it out by its roots. Tears welled in her eyes. His other hand grabbed her right wrist just above the hand that held the razor. His acne-covered face gleamed an angry red almost the same color of the blood that ran down his cheeks. His sunglasses had fallen from his face, revealing jaundiced eyes the color of urine. He pulled her down, forcing her to her knees.

Her breath came in short bursts. The fear in her chest threatened to explode outward. The grip on her wrist was so tight she couldn't feel her fingers. Whimpers of pain and frustration involuntarily escaped her.

He dropped his eyes down her body. A smirk spread across his tight lips. She felt her nakedness as if her skin radiated its own light. She knew what was going to happen. This man was going to rape her, possibly kill her afterward, and she was helpless to stop it.

"You're going to pay for this." His voice boomed off the white tile.

He twisted her wrist upward while digging his fingers into the tendons on the soft side of her forearm. Her hand opened as if he'd pressed a switch on her arm. She watched his eyes follow the razor's path as it bounced across the tile.

Then she remembered her other hand.

The syringe!

He'd been so focused on the razor he hadn't noticed she'd picked up the syringe.

She struck.

She'd given countless injections to the capuchins. She could jab and plunge the medicine into an arm or leg before they knew what was happening. Usually she distracted them for a moment with a piece of banana or slice of orange, but her attacker was already distracted. She had no idea what this syringe contained or what effect it would have on the man, but she had a suspicion it wouldn't be good for him. She aimed for his bicep, which was the size of both of her legs combined. The problem, however, was that all the injections she'd given were with her right hand. With it she could operate the plunger without looking. In her left hand, the syringe felt foreign.

"Ow! Shit!"

The needle pierced his shirt and sank into hard muscle. She willed her left thumb to manipulate the plunger, but it seemed to move in slow motion.

Suddenly, the revelation came to her. Engaged in a battle for her life, she was shocked that her mind went anywhere except for the task of escaping. The vision was brief. She was back in CapLab watching Anakin interact with the larger, more dominant capuchins, just as she was now fighting off a larger, more dominant attacker. Now she knew what made Anakin different. She understood what was wrong with Ethan's Logos machine.

She never saw the hand that released her wrist and struck her across the face. The blow lifted her off of her knees and knocked her head into the pedestal of the porcelain sink. Her vision blurred as she sank to the floor. The tile was cold against her back. Her head rang, and she felt the fight abandoning her body. She heard him mutter something unintelligible. Her eyes refocused in time to watch him pull the syringe from his arm. The plunger was still in the extended position.

In one smooth motion, he pushed down on her shoulder with a weight that threatened to crush her bones into the floor and injected the contents of the shot into the fleshy part of her arm.

She thrashed under his weight, but he just pushed harder. Seconds later, a warmth spread out from her arm to the rest of her body. Her mind raced through the possibilities—she was well versed in a number of drugs from her work with the capuchins, and none were appealing. The warmth in her body took on a weighty quality, as if her blood had turned to liquid lead. Her attacker's hand still pinned her to the cold floor, but she realized with a sickening in her gut that she was losing the ability to move. She glanced at her outstretched arm and tried to lift it. The lead flowing through her blood pinned it down. She saw the tips of her fingers quiver.

The man released her and sat back on his knees. She waited for the inevitable tunnel vision that would narrow down to complete darkness as she slipped into unconsciousness from whatever sedative he'd injected into her. Whatever this creature had in mind for her, she took some comfort that at least she wouldn't be aware of it.

But something was wrong.

The fluorescent bathroom fixture on the ceiling burned as bright as ever. The face leering at her exposed body stayed in focus. His chapped lips parted in a smile that revealed a gap between his front two teeth. He was enjoying her terror. Drops of blood rolled from his forehead and fell onto her cheek. She felt them crawl toward her mouth. She desperately wanted to wipe her face, but now she couldn't even move her head.

With a fear deeper than she thought it was possible to feel, a single realization shot through her mind: *I'm paralyzed!*

CHAPTER 31

NEW HAVEN

"Professor Lightman?" a deep voice asked from the other end of Ethan's cell phone.

"Allen Wolfe?" He collapsed into the worn leather sofa in his apartment's living room. He'd been trying to contact the director of the Neurological Advancement Foundation for the past week. He was relieved but also surprised that the foundation's director was calling him at ten o'clock at night.

"First, let me tell you how sorry I am for taking so long to get back to you. I've been traveling, and I just learned about Elijah's death this morning." He paused, his words catching in his throat. "As I'm sure Elijah told you, we've been friends since grad school. I just can't believe he's gone."

Ethan tilted his head back on the sofa's cushion. Wolfe sounded genuinely saddened. "Something strange is happening that I can't control and don't even understand." He should probably sound more confident, but he was out of options. Despite his disturbing discovery in the library of the true nature of Wolfe and Elijah's history together, he sensed that the director was the only one who would be able to help him.

"I spoke with Sam Houston earlier today," Wolfe said. "He is quite concerned about your program, and he mentioned an investigation into certain financial improprieties."

The words spilled out of Ethan as he explained his discovery about the money in his account. He'd spent most of the day on the phone with the bank and still had no explanation of who had authorized the transfer of the money from the project's account into his. He laid everything on the table for the director. He had no choice but to gain his trust.

"I really don't know how the transfer happened, but I swear to you I had nothing to do with it."

Then a thought ran through his mind that he didn't care to explore. Was Elijah responsible for the financial irregularities? Could his death have been related to money? He couldn't believe his mentor would be involved with anything so crass, but what other explanation was there? But then he replayed in his mind again the events in the library.

"Ethan, I think we should meet and discuss these events in person."

"Yes, I would appreciate that." A sense of relief passed over him.

"I'm tied up for the next few days and can't make it to New Haven. Would you mind flying to me?"

"Not at all." He remembered that the foundation's offices were in Dallas, and the idea of getting out of New Haven to someplace warm and sunny appealed to him, especially if it also provided the answers he desperately needed. "I can make reservations now."

"Don't trouble yourself. I'll have my assistant arrange a flight for you and send a car to pick you up first thing in the morning."

"Thank you."

"My pleasure, Son. Your work is truly visionary, and after this tragedy with Elijah, it's the least I can do."

Ethan stared out of the window from the backseat of the Lincoln Town Car and into the mist that was the early New Haven morning. The events of the past few days seemed surreal. He'd dedicated his career to helping people and to studying the human mind. So why did he feel as if someone was deliberately trying to ruin his life? He wanted to take some action to fix his predicament, just as he'd thrown himself into his research after Natalie's death. The long hours had paid off then; the Logos worked. But now he was being handcuffed from doing anything.

Turning the cell phone over in his hand, he dared to allow a glimmer of hope to pass into his thoughts. At least he'd get some answers from Wolfe. He pushed away the voice in his head that cautioned that maybe he wouldn't want to hear the truth. But he had to know. Then he would act.

The motion of the car turning right brought him out of his thoughts. The driver followed the signs into the New Haven airport, but instead of heading toward the departure terminal, he pulled down a smaller side street labeled with a green sign that read "FBO."

Never been this way before, he thought.

He dialed Rachel's number. He wanted to let her know about his call with Wolfe and his trip, but the call rolled straight to voicemail, just as it had last night. She and her roommates must have been out late. He needed to hear her voice, but if he was honest with himself, Houston's off-handed reference to speaking with her had also disturbed him. Could Rachel be playing a role in the bizarre events of late? He shook his head. He didn't think her involvement was any more plausible than Elijah's. He knew that if he closed his eyes he would be able to smell her hair and feel the way her skin felt next to his. *No.* He had to stop that line of thinking. He looked up to see the car pull around the side of a metal hangar building and stop at a gate.

He leaned over the leather seat toward the driver, a Middle Eastern man dressed in a dark suit. "Excuse me, but where are we going?"

"To your plane, Sir."

My plane?

The driver rolled down the window and punched a call button on the gate's security keypad. "I have Professor Lightman for his flight."

The chain-link gate rolled open and the car pulled through. They turned right, following a concrete road past three airplane hangars. When the driver approached the fourth, he slowed. The large rollup hangar door was open, revealing a sleek white jet. The car stopped a few feet from the metal staircase that led up to the plane's open door.

Wolfe sent a private plane to fly me to Dallas?

His confusion morphed into anticipation. He'd never been on a private plane before. He'd seen them parked along the runway, but usually they were much smaller than this—narrow metal tubes, low to the ground, with three or four windows. This one was the size of the commuter plane he and Natalie had taken to Maine one summer, but with jet engines rather than turboprops. Eight windows punctuated the flawless white paint on the fuselage, and the wingtips angled upward at right angles.

He grabbed his overnight duffel from the seat next to him. He hadn't asked Wolfe how many days he'd be in Dallas, so he'd packed for two. Without waiting for the driver, who was walking around the car, he opened his own door and hopped out. A figure appeared at the top of the stairs and waved him up.

"Welcome aboard our G-V EP, Professor." The man wore a cracked brown leather bomber jacket with patches that had various military and flight insignia on them, a white shirt and black tie, and gold-rimmed aviator sunglasses even though the morning was gray.

Ethan climbed the metal stairs, taking care not to slip on the aluminum treads, which were damp with the morning mist.

"Uh, hello." He stuck out his hand. "You're the pilot?"

"Captain Jason Hart." The pilot's handshake was firm and his smile warm.

"I wasn't really expecting this. I thought I was flying commercial."

"Dr. Wolfe wanted to make sure you arrived without delay. He's asked me to take good care of you." He ducked his head of short black hair and entered the plane. "Let me show you in."

After stooping to step inside, Ethan's eyes opened wide. Every inch of the cabin was covered in creamy leather or polished blond wood. To his left he caught a glimpse of the cockpit, where the copilot was checking over an array of multicolored digital displays that looked considerably more high-tech than the rows of switches and blinking lights he'd seen in commercial planes. He passed a bar/kitchenette whose wood surfaces beckoned him to reach out and feel the silkiness of the finish. The fixtures were all a shiny gold without any sign of a smudge or fingerprint.

"Sit wherever you like." The captain motioned to the various seats, which ranged from plush single recliners to sofas that were arranged to look more like a living room than a plane. "The lavatory is the door to the left there. The other door in the back leads to the bedroom, but it's being refurbished, so it's locked."

The plane has a bedroom!

He plopped down in a club chair whose supple leather seemed to caress his body. Although money had never much mattered to him, he realized that he could get used to traveling like this—no security to go through, no baggage claim, no parents with screaming kids.

The pilot bent over, pulled the stairs up, and swung the door closed. He called over his shoulder, "Once we're airborne and settled into our flight plan, I'll come back and check on you. We can go over the food options in the galley then."

"I'll be fine with just a water. How long's the flight—a couple hours?"

The whine of the plane's engines firing to life filled the cabin.

"Couple of hours?" The pilot chuckled. "The computer is showing twenty right now, but that depends how long we're on the ground in Paris. The French aren't the quickest at getting us refueled."

Twenty hours! Paris!

He sat up straighter. "We're not flying to Dallas?"

"Dr. Wolfe hasn't been in Dallas for some time," Hart laughed. "You're going to Egypt."

CHAPTER 32

EGYPTIAN AIRSPACE

"**P**rofessor Lightman, we'll be landing in ten minutes," the captain's voice crackled over the speakers.

Ethan yawned and pushed himself upright on the leather sofa. As luxurious as this plane was, traveling halfway across the world was still exhausting. He dropped his head first to the right and then the left, stretching his neck. Then he ran his fingers through his hair and rubbed his face. The day-old stubble scratched his palms. He imagined that the bedroom under renovation in the back had a shower in its lavatory. He stood and walked to the door to test the knob, but as the pilot had said, the door was locked.

The flight had been uneventful, but his mind still revolved over and over the question of why Wolfe was flying him to Egypt. His questions to the captain had resulted in a shrug and a quip that "I drive where I'm told." He'd considered getting off the plane as soon as he found out where he was headed—but other than Rachel, what was there to keep him in New Haven? He had been relieved of his teaching duties, and the Logos project had been suspended. But now more than ever, the book Elijah had pointed him to was taking on an ominous importance.

He glanced at his watch, but then he realized that he had no idea what time zone he was in. He lifted the shades covering the two windows behind the sofa and blinked his eyes against the piercing light that filled the cabin. The orange glow from the sun warmed his face.

The plane banked to the right. His only trips out of the country had been backpacking in Europe before starting med school and a couple of spring break trips to the Bahamas. When he thought of Egypt, he imagined pyramids, sphinxes, and tombs. The view out of the window, however, was of an endless beige desert that stretched as far as he could see. As the plane continued to bank and then descend, a break in the desert came into view. Blue fingers stretched into the undulating sand. Soon the source of the fingers appeared beneath the wing: an enormous lake.

As they passed over the lake, he saw that the northern edge was defined by an immense concrete dam, beyond which a wide river disappeared into the horizon. *The Nile.* He recalled some details about the river from his high school geography class. For thousands of years, the annual flooding of the Nile had deposited minerals for miles along the edges of the river, creating a rich soil that supported the cradle of ancient civilization. In the 1960s, the Egyptian government, under the leadership of President Nasser, had decided that the damage caused by the annual flooding outweighed the benefits for a society that had now developed cities along the banks. They'd dammed the river and created Lake Nasser, thus allowing the government to regulate the river's water flow.

After they passed over the lake, the topography returned to desert. The lush vegetation around the lake and the Nile transitioned to lifelessness as if a line had been drawn in the hot sand; life was permitted on one side, but on the other not even a single weed grew. They passed directly over a cluster of five or six warehouse-looking buildings that appeared abandoned. A dirt road led from the buildings back to the lake.

Minutes later, the plane touched down. When they taxied past the main terminal, the large white letters on the side of the small building announced Ethan's destination: Aswan. Although his knowledge of Egyptian geography was limited, he remembered that Aswan, along with Luxor, was one of the great Egyptian tourist destinations along the Nile because of its many ancient ruins. But when he caught a view of the far end of the runway, he felt a twinge of apprehension. A row of fighter jets was parked in front of two large bunkers built into the sand dunes at the end of the concrete. The small commercial airport also served as a military base.

"Hope you had a comfortable flight, Professor," Captain Hart said as he exited the cockpit and unlocked the cabin door. The copilot stayed seated, flipping switches and shutting down the engines.

A blast of dry heat rolled in as if the pilot had just opened an oven door.

"Do you know when you'll be taking me back?" He adjusted the bag on his shoulder.

Hart shrugged. "We'll hang around until Dr. Wolfe says we're needed again." He pointed to two black dots approaching through the wavy heat rising off of the concrete. "Your next ride is here."

As he stepped onto the runway, the two black SUVs continued toward them until they pulled up to the plane. The driver from the first one exited, walked around the car, and opened the rear door for him. He was an American with short hair, sunglasses, and a dark suit that seemed out of place in the desert. After Ethan climbed into the backseat, he turned to wave to Captain Hart. A movement from the rear of the plane behind the smiling pilot caught his eye.

Did the window shade just open?

He squinted against the reflection of the sun on the fuselage, but before he could confirm the vision, his driver closed the car door. The windows of the SUV were blacked out. His pulse quickened. The backseat was luxurious, limousine-like, with a divider between it and the front, but he suddenly felt trapped.

He buckled his seatbelt. He couldn't shake the feeling that someone was in the bedroom behind the locked door. Or were the sun and his jet-lagged mind just playing games with him?

CHAPTER 33

ASWAN, EGYPT

Twenty minutes later the SUV stopped. Where, Ethan had no idea. When the driver opened the door, a wave of dry heat hit clashed with the air-conditioned interior, just as it had when he'd exited the plane.

"Professor, if you would follow me."

He stepped onto a sandy gravel drive beside the black-suited driver. They weren't in the town of Aswan. His unease grew. They were in the middle of the desert, surrounded by a sea of sand and rock. Unlike the desert of Arizona, where he'd spent time visiting his aunt, there wasn't a single bush or cactus to break up the beige landscape. The only structure in sight was a rectangular warehouse with concrete walls the same color as the desert sand. The metal roof magnified the sun, whose intense rays were unobstructed by clouds in the indigo sky. He followed the driver toward a metal door in the center of the building's front wall.

The building was longer than a football field but had no windows. He recalled the warehouses he'd seen from the plane. He looked over his shoulder in the direction they'd just come from, but there was nothing more than compacted sand forming a road that disappeared over a dune on the horizon. He recalled that it led to the lake a couple of miles away.

"This way please, Sir." The driver held the thick metal door open for him.

Before he entered the building, he caught the sand-worn sign hanging above the door: "MDH Trading, Intl."

An import-export company in the middle of the desert?

The foyer was small—a fifteen-foot-square room with a speckled vinyl tile floor and white walls that were empty except for a single framed poster that read "Customers first! MDH Trading." A black leather sofa sat underneath the poster, and the glass coffee table held several issues of *Global Logistics & Supply Chain Strategies* and *World Trade Magazine*. In the upper left corner of the room, a security camera pointed at them.

"Professor Lightman, welcome! We've been expecting you." The voice came from behind a Plexiglas window to his right.

"Uh, where am I?" He turned toward a reception window that was almost two inches thick. Another metal door was located beside the window. The receptionist was another solidly built American, dressed, like his driver, in a dark suit.

"Is Dr. Allen Wolfe here? I'm supposed to be meeting him."

"Please, come in."

The receptionist reached under the desk. Ethan heard a buzzing noise, followed by the click of the metal door unlocking. His driver opened the door for him. As odd as the situation seemed, he took comfort in the politeness these men conveyed. He passed through the door, which, like the front door, appeared to be made of metal and was an inch or so thicker than a normal office door. Then the environment fell into place—the security, the solid men with short hair, their formality and efficient mannerisms. Everything struck him as military.

The door closed behind them with an authoritative clunk. The reception guard emerged from a door to the right and stood before him.

"If you don't mind, please raise your hands to the side. This is a secure facility."

He did as he was told—not that he had a choice—and received a pat down more intimate than any airport security search he'd ever experienced. He flinched when the man removed his wallet and cell phone from his pocket.

"These will be kept in a safe until your departure, Professor."

"My wallet too?"

"Everything will become clear soon."

Feeling naked without his cell phone and ID, he followed the driver down a corridor that could have belonged to any office building in the US. They passed closed doors on both sides of the hall. When they reached a door on the left that was slightly ajar, he hesitated, assuming that this was where he was going to meet Wolfe, but his driver closed the door instead of opening it.

Before his view was cut off, he glimpsed an unusual sight inside. The room behind the door was filled with electronics. He saw over a dozen flat-panel monitors on desks and along the walls. Three men sat in chairs studying them. The sight that surprised him was not the high-tech monitoring suite, but the way one of the men was dressed. Two of them wore black pants and white shirts, but the third was a priest.

After passing a single elevator door on their right, they stopped at the end of the corridor. The driver knocked on the final door. Another security camera watched him from the corner above. The sound of an electronic lock clicking open echoed in the bare hall. The driver opened the door but didn't go inside. He motioned for Ethan to enter and then closed the door behind him.

He now stood in a large office decorated in stark contrast to the plain surroundings of the rest of the building. The floor underneath his feet was a soft blue-gray carpet. The furniture was all of a sleek Scandinavian design, something one might expect to see in the office of an architect in a high-rise office tower, not in a warehouse in the middle of the desert.

Allen Wolfe, wearing a purple tie and matching pocket square, looked up from the papers he was reading behind the glass desk.

"Professor Ethan Lightman, welcome to the Monastery!"

Wolfe rose from his chair and extended a hand. Ethan shook it, hoping his palm wasn't too sweaty. His chest felt tight, as if a belt had been cinched around his rib cage and was allowing him to inflate his lungs only halfway.

"You must be full of questions." Wolfe's voice was deep and soothing.

"I don't even know where to begin."

He settled into a shiny black leather chair with polished stainless steel armrests opposite the desk. The chair looked fashionable but was uncomfortable, causing him to sit upright on the hard straps.

He inhaled as deeply as the imaginary belt around his torso would allow and jumped in. "Is the NAF a front for the CIA?"

He wasn't sure why he chose to suddenly articulate the suspicion he'd suppressed in the recesses of his mind since the night in Sterling Memorial Library three days ago.

"You got me." Wolfe smiled and spread his hands. "You put the pieces together after finding the book on MKULTRA?"

How does he know about the book?

Then the realization hit him: *Muscleman.* He'd dropped the book when being chased by the huge man.

"James Axelrod," Wolfe said, reading the expression on his face, "my head of security. But don't call him James when you run into him here. Goes by Axe." He chuckled. "I asked him to keep an eye on things in New Haven. We were making quite an investment in you and Elijah. I apologize if he gave you a start. He has a penchant for the dramatic at times."

Ethan thought about Axe's presence in his lecture a few weeks back. He felt only somewhat relieved at the knowledge that this guy had been sent to spy on him rather than accost him.

"So you and Elijah worked on MKULTRA as grad students."

"We were just a few years younger than you are now. We made a good team. He was the idealistic one, I the practical one. The government offered us a chance to take our research into the human psyche in directions that had never been explored." Wolfe pointed at him with a manicured finger. "Much in the way you've been doing with the Logos."

"I just don't see Elijah working for the CIA."

"It was an exciting time to be a psychiatrist."

"But the experiments—brainwashing, sensory deprivation, hallucinogenic drugs—were conducted on unsuspecting subjects without their consent."

"Times were different. We were in the midst of the Cold War. The Soviets were doing the same research we were."

"But the research never panned out."

"Our methods were too crude. The drugs unpredictable. We could extract information from our subjects, but we never could control them. The Manchurian Candidate was a myth."

"But you also rendered some catatonic, others had permanent amnesia, and at least one killed himself because he thought he was going insane." Elijah had been one of the most ethical and caring men he'd known. *How could he have been involved in such research?*

"As I said, our methods were crude then." Wolfe shrugged. "But we learned from our mistakes."

"Who killed Elijah?" The question came out before he had a chance to filter it. Since learning of his mentor's early involvement with the CIA, and in light of the way he'd been acting about the NAF and of the suspicious circumstances surrounding his death, Ethan had all but confirmed for himself that his friend's murder was related to the recent strange events.

An expression of genuine remorse passed over Wolfe's face as he shook his head. "Elijah was one of my oldest friends. We didn't always see eye-to-eye, but we had that bond you never lose from pulling all-nighters with your best friend in school." He opened a manila folder on his desk and flipped through the pages. "The police reports indicate that it was a robbery attempt that the murderer tried to disguise in an amateurish way by putting him into the Logos. New Haven can be a tough place." He paused as his voice cracked. "I just wish I had sent Axe there to protect him that night." Wolfe cast his steel gray eyes to the floor by his desk.

He's lost a friend, just as I have, Ethan realized, but a seed of doubt remained. He glanced around the office. Despite the expensive modern furniture, the walls were blank other than one that held a bookcase filled with various psychology texts.

"Why am I here?"

The CIA had funded his research, and now he was at some facility in the Middle East. With Wolfe's history of mind-control experiments, he felt sure that they had something in mind that had to do with the Logos. *But what?*

"What do you know about commercial tuna fishing?"

"I don't under—"

"Sometimes, when you cast a wide net, you catch dolphins when what you really want is tuna."

"What does that have to do with my machine?"

"In the war against Islamic fundamentalism that began after 9/11, our military and intelligence services, as well as those of friendly Arab nations, have rounded up suspected terrorists in an attempt to prevent future catastrophes. Our efforts have been largely effective. But sometimes, in addition to the hardcore terrorist leaders, we pick up lower-level operatives who we ultimately discover are not an immediate threat."

"We hold innocents in prison?"

"Innocent?" He chuckled. "In this world, I'm not sure if that word has any meaning. Suffice it to say that these prisoners are eventually released, but before they can be sent back to their homes, many need to be rehabilitated from their time in captivity. We are here to integrate the dolphins back into society after the harrowing experience of being caught in the net."

"You mean they've been tortured?"

"The things some of these men have been through." A shudder passed through his body. "And not by our people," he added quickly. "Our allies in this part of the world have different rules than we do."

"What about our use of waterboarding and sensory deprivation?"

"We may interrogate terrorists using various psychological means, but our methods don't cause real harm—nothing like the electricity to the genitals, the beatings, the pulling of fingernails that they do here. The atrocities these men have suffered are difficult to imagine." He shook his head. "What these governments don't understand is that physical torture is too blunt an instrument to use on a committed ideologue. The torture is often carried out by crude people who enjoy the barbarism."

The isolated location of the warehouse in the middle of the desert, the high security, and the American guards—it all started to make sense to him. "So this place is some kind of covert psychological rehab facility for suspected terrorists?"

"When they come to us they are no longer prisoners. They are on their way home—after we have counseled them and nursed them back to health both physically and mentally."

"So where are these men?" He guessed that he'd seen about a quarter of the warehouse building, but he had a hard time imagining that the rest would hold enough room for the type of operation Wolfe was describing.

A twinkle appeared in Wolfe's eyes. "I think you'll find this interesting." He stood from his desk. "Follow me."

Despite his unease, Ethan was curious. How was Wolfe rehabbing these prisoners, and what did the Logos have to do with it?

He followed the doctor out of the office to the elevator he'd passed earlier. Wolfe removed a lanyard from around his neck and swiped the attached card through a reader beside the elevator. The glass pad beside the reader came to life, glowing blue. When Wolfe pressed his palm against it, the light intensified around the edges of his hand, and the elevator door opened. The elevator was hospital spec, long enough to accommodate a stretcher. Inside, Ethan noted the lack of any buttons. They descended a short distance and stopped.

The knowledge that they were now underground increased his tension.

The door opened into a concrete tunnel that was only eight feet in height; he could reach up and almost touch the curved ceiling. He followed Wolfe to the left, ducking his head to avoid bumping into the various metal pipes and plastic conduits that crisscrossed the ceiling. When they turned a corner after walking about thirty feet, Wolfe stopped beside a glass window along the wall. All of the light in the corridor came from the window rather than the fluorescent fixtures suspended from the ceiling, which were powered off. Wolfe waited by the window.

The sight stopped Ethan in his tracks. He could sense the director grinning beside him.

"I don't understand," he said.

The scene before him was in stark contrast to everything else he'd seen in the building. The window looked into what appeared to be a replica of one of Yale's college dining halls. The room on the other side of the glass was rectangular in shape with three long rows of wooden tables with matching benches that could seat over a hundred people. The floor was a dark oak, as were the thick timbers that rose from the walls to support a cathedral ceiling. Even stranger than the dining hall were the groupings of people eating. At least twenty men, all Middle Eastern in appearance, were dressed in the brown cassocks of Franciscan monks, while about ten others, all Americans, were dressed in the flowing black robes and white collars of priests.

"The Monastery, or as we refer to it, Project Jericho," Wolfe said, as if that explained everything.

CHAPTER 34

THE MONASTERY

"I don't understand," Ethan said for what felt like the tenth time. "These former prisoners"—he motioned through the window—"are Muslims, but they're dressed as Christian monks."

"Precisely." Wolfe beamed.

"And the American priests?"

"Do you know why our intelligence services have failed so miserably in predicting, much less stopping, fundamentalist Islamic terrorist attacks?"

Ethan recalled the post-9/11 criticism of the American intelligence services missing the obvious signs of the impending attack. "Because we didn't put enough resources behind the task after the Cold War ended?"

Wolfe shook his head. "A popular but mistaken view." He paced in front of what Ethan assumed was a one-way window as the monks and priests dined on the other side. "During the Cold War we faced an enemy who ruled its population through coercion based on an economic ideology—communism—that ultimately proved unsustainable. In a country where you had to wait in line for toilet paper, bribing a government official to pass us secrets was easy. Our enemy today, however, is motivated by a drive stronger than money, sex, or even political power."

"Religion?"

"Exactly. Look at the populations of Saudi Arabia, Pakistan, Iran: you have a handful of elites in power and then masses of uneducated people with little hope for advancement or prosperity. The men in these societies are often at dead ends, barely scraping by. Multiple wives are permitted, but only the wealthy can afford a single one, much less more. This leaves little hope for these young men to earn more than a menial living, not enough to support a family. Then they go to a mosque and they hear the promise of the paradise that Allah will deliver to them. In these barren landscapes, paradise is depicted not only as overflowing with abundance, like an oasis in the desert, but as offering the promise of young virgins. How does one enter this paradise, the mullahs preach?"

"Through martyrdom."

Wolfe nodded. "These men are indoctrinated from a young age, when their futures look hopeless. They are brainwashed by a form of Islamic fundamentalism that we've found almost impossible to penetrate. When dying for your cause is believed to be the ultimate reward, there's little earthly persuasion we can use to change their minds."

Ethan looked through the window at the men dressed as Christian monks. "So you're trying to convert them?"

"What if we could take a religiously polluted mind and clean it as one might clean the bacteria from a kitchen counter after a piece of raw meat sat there?"

He saw where this was heading. An unease passed through his gut as the image of Sister Terri reclining in the Logos flashed through his head. "But Islam isn't the problem. It's illiteracy, poverty, dictatorships, and ego-driven mullahs who distort its teachings."

"We can never eliminate the inequality and poverty in these countries. But what if we can eliminate the religious reaction to it? What if we have a way to wipe the infected counter down and then serve healthy food there?"

The unease grew in his stomach like a widening gulf, but at the same time the scientific side of his mind was curious. He knew that deprogramming someone who had been brainwashed was a time-consuming and inexact process. He recalled the case studies he'd read in medical school of people who had been kidnapped and kept prisoner for extended periods of time. The victims often began to identify and even grow to love their captors, a condition known as Stockholm syndrome. Undoing the psychological damage could take years.

"How?"

Wolfe turned from the window and continued down the corridor. He stopped beside a row of metal lockers. He opened the first one and withdrew a long silken robe of silver and gold that he pulled over his head. Next he attached a white-banded collar around his neck. The rosaries that went last completed the picture.

"You look just like—"

"Inside they call me 'The Bishop.'" He winked.

Then he opened another locker door and removed a simple black cassock. "Put this over your head. The arms go here and here. And then tie the belt around your waist." After some fumbling with the material, Ethan did as instructed. Wolfe then retrieved a white collar from the locker. "Let me do this. These can be tricky."

When Wolfe snapped the collar into place, Ethan had to resist the instinct to tug on it. He felt the stiff material when he swallowed. When Wolfe stepped aside, he stared at the three-quarter-length mirror hanging on the inside of the locker door. The image reflected back at him was as foreign as this strange place. He'd never been comfortable in churches, and yet here he was, the image of a pious Catholic priest.

"Around the brothers—that's how we refer to our guests here—please do not ask questions. We must carefully control their experiences."

Wolfe moved to a door on the far side of the lockers. Rather than the electronic locks of the elevator, this had a simple numeric keypad. He pressed the numbers quickly, his body shielding the pad from Ethan's view.

Behind the door, the utilitarian concrete tunnel transformed in a way that rivaled what Disney Imagineers might have designed. They stepped into what appeared to be a centuries-old European monastery with stone floors, a plastered groin vaulted ceiling, and sconces of candles along the long wall. The soothing sound of chanting echoed through the hall. When Ethan inhaled incense, his body seemed to relax of its own accord. He couldn't guess what it had cost to construct such a space underneath the Egyptian desert. Then he thought about how quickly Wolfe had handed the check for two hundred and fifty thousand dollars to Elijah.

Wolfe's hand on his elbow guided him down the corridor. "When I first imagined the Monastery, I borrowed from some of the more effective techniques we experimented with forty-five years ago."

He paused by a heavy mahogany door and motioned for him to peer inside a square window with decorative iron bars crisscrossed over the opening. The small room contained a desk with a chair and a single twin bed. A man with a dark complexion lay sleeping. An IV bag hung next to the bed, the line snaking under the covers.

"We begin with two to four weeks of sleep and drug therapy, which allows the brothers to heal physically from their ordeals while also softening them up for the immersion stage."

Ethan knew that prolonged sleep could have profound psychological effects on a subject—they woke up disoriented and more pliable to suggestion. He glanced again at the IV bag and speculated at the drug cocktails given to the men: Thorazine, Ambien, Nembutal, Propofol, Seconal, Veronal, Phenergan.

"I thought MKULTRA failed because these techniques were too imprecise."

"That's why I created this." He gestured to the surroundings. "One of the lessons we learned from the use of psychoactive drugs was that the setting in which the subjects took them had almost as large an effect on the experience as the drugs themselves. Here in the Monastery, we immerse these men for months in an environment where we control everything they're exposed to."

Wolfe stopped in front of a second door, identical to the first, looked inside, and then gestured for Ethan to do the same. As he bent over, he thought he detected a smile on the director's face. This room was identical to the first, but the Arab man on the bed was awake, sitting up, and talking to another man. The other man had his back to the door, but Ethan noted his slicked-back blond hair, white collar, and black cassock.

"After we bring them out of sleep therapy, each is assigned one of my priests. Instruction consists of hours of Bible readings along with discussions of the benefits of Christianity."

"I take it they are no more priests than I am."

Wolfe's smile grew. He walked toward a set of double doors carved out of thick wood at the dead end of the corridor. "They're trained in psychology, all have a minimum of a master's degree, and some have their PhDs. Many are fluent in Arabic and Farsi. But each is also a committed Christian, well versed in scripture."

"But how is what you're doing any different than the indoctrination they received to Islam?" His voice came out louder than he intended.

"Isn't that obvious?" Wolfe scrunched up his brow as if mystified why Ethan would have asked the question. "They will now belong to us."

Ethan bit his tongue. Religious intolerance had been the cause of so many wars and so much suffering throughout history that he had a hard time imagining the Monastery would do anything other than perpetuate the misery. The audacity of what this man was attempting to do—in a Muslim country, no less—astounded him. *If this ever becomes public,* he thought.

Then a more disturbing question passed through his mind: *Why is he telling me this?* For what had to be a top secret project of the highest sensitivity, Wolfe was being loose with the details. The distinguished doctor seemed to relish in his creation, appeared almost eager to show it off. *What does he want from me?*

"These men have spent a lifetime being indoctrinated into their Islamic beliefs; how can you undo that in just a few months?"

Wolfe reached under his cassock and produced a long skeleton key. "Ah yes; you have now hit on the reason why you are here."

CHAPTER 35

THE MONASTERY

Ethan followed Wolfe across the marble floor of the chapel. Wood buttresses rose from the plaster walls to support the cathedral ceiling. He marveled at the detail that had gone into building the facility. Murals covered each of the walls. Although he hadn't been to church since his mother dragged him to Sunday school as a teenager, he recognized the depiction of the life of Jesus: the birth in Bethlehem, the baptism by John, the healing of cripples, the feeding of the masses, the crucifixion, and—the final scene, depicted in brilliant hues as if the paint were backlit—the resurrection.

Wolfe placed a hand on his shoulder. "When these men come to us, they've already been broken. They've been tortured to the brink of death, usually by their own people. We offer them hope, a chance to reclaim their lives." He dropped his hand and leaned on a baroque-looking throne set on a raised platform in front of the altar. "But we also offer them something one of their ayatollahs never could. We offer them a much more powerful experience." His grin widened. "We offer them the chance to experience God, in this lifetime, without having to martyr themselves first."

As if on cue, Ethan's eyes caught the inscription etched underneath the fifteen-foot-tall stained glass cross over the altar. The chill running across his skin seemed to penetrate to the depths of his marrow. He stepped around the throne and peered up at the inscription written in ancient Greek: Εν αρχη ην ο λογος, και ο λογος ην προς τον θεον, και θεος ην ο λογος.

He imagined that behind the stained glass were lights that would illuminate the cross and the inscription when turned on. Although he wasn't fluent in the language of the New Testament, he knew immediately the meaning of the phrase. A single word repeated three times in the inscription called out to him: λογος.

Logos.

He recited from memory, "In the beginning was the Word . . ."

"And the Word was with God, and the Word was God," Wolfe completed.

"The prologue to the Gospel of John."

Five years earlier, when Elijah first outlined to his graduate student his idea of converting a TMS machine into a device that could induce mystical experiences, he'd also explained why he would call the machine the Logos.

The first verses of John's Gospel, composed in Greek at the end of the first century, used the term *Logos* to describe the eternal nature of God as the source of all creation. Logos was usually translated as "word." Elijah had explained that the Hebrew Bible, what Christians called the Old Testament, frequently referred to the power of God's word as well. In the beginning of Genesis, for example, God spoke the universe into being: "And God *said*, let there be light."

"But the translation of *Logos* as 'word' misses the essence of the term," Elijah had said. "It's more like *language* or *discourse.*"

"So *Logos* doesn't refer to a specific word?" Ethan had asked.

"*Logos* is an organizing structure, like a language. This concept originated from Heraclitus in the fifth century BCE."

"The Greek philosopher?"

Elijah had nodded. "The universe, Heraclitus observed, is logical and ordered, obeying laws that can be divined through reason. He used the term *Logos* to refer to the organizing principle that lay beyond existence—a principle that gives rise to the physical laws that govern the universe."

"But you're Jewish. You agree with a New Testament description about God borrowed from a much older Greek philosopher?"

"While my view on the relationship of Jesus to the Logos is different from John's, I share his understanding of God as that which gives rise to existence.

And maybe this device"—he'd tapped a drawing sketched on a scrap of paper—"can give us a taste of this Logos."

"I assume you're curious about our plans for your Logos machine." Wolfe's voice brought Ethan out of his memory.

He turned to the man dressed as a bishop—the man who had funded his research when they were on the verge of going under; the man who he now knew wanted to replicate his machine to convert Muslims to Christianity.

"You take these men who've been broken physically and mentally by the torture they've endured, then you precondition them through sleep therapy. After they're shells of their former selves, you re-brainwash them with your fake priests, and now you want to use *my* machine to seal the deal by offering them a mystical experience that they will ascribe to their *conversion* to Christianity?"

"Precisely."

"But the Logos is about studying religion, about understanding its neurological sources." He struggled to keep his voice even. "Our purpose is exactly the opposite of what you plan on doing. The Logos can unlock the mystery of religious experience and expose the ideological baggage of the Church."

Wolfe patted his shoulder. "Do you think the military scientists who invented the Internet in the 1960s as a way for the government to remain in communication after a nuclear strike had any idea that today we'd be buying shoes or watching our favorite movies with it?" He paced around the throne. "Often it takes one kind of genius to invent something, but another to see its true value."

Ethan thought back to the origins of Elijah's vision for the Logos and their early experiments comparing SPECT analysis on the brains of Christian nuns like Sister Terri and Buddhist monks. "But the Logos isn't a Christian machine at all. If anything it shows the nonexclusivity of religious experience and emphasizes how religious doctrine is culturally conditioned. Our research shows that mystical experiences are common across faith traditions because they share the same neurological pathways regardless of beliefs."

"Hence the importance of context." Wolfe gestured to the chapel. "That is why we immerse the men in a Christian monastery, so that they attribute the experience from your Logos machine to the Christian faith."

"But you're increasing religious conflict here—substituting one form of fundamentalism for another."

"Actually, it's just the opposite. Your Logos has the potential to be a peace machine. Think of what we're doing as viral marketing. But before the viral message can spread, it needs to be seeded in the right communities."

"So these men here are supposed to be the Christian seeds you plan on returning into an Islamic society?"

Wolfe grinned.

"But you're dealing with nations of millions. You could never produce enough men to make a difference."

"A giant river starts somewhere as a tiny spring."

"But what if this becomes public? You could ignite a religious war and a wave of terrorism against the West that would make 9/11 seem like a warm-up."

Wolfe held up a hand. "That will not happen." The warmth in his voice turned icy. "We take our security very seriously."

He thought of the solid men he'd passed upstairs. Then he realized that as accommodating as Wolfe had seemed so far, the man was working for the CIA, and he was isolated in a secret facility in the middle of the Egyptian desert.

His stomach twisted at the thought of what was coming next. The missing piece in Wolfe's plan was the Logos. He would never go along with such a misuse of his research. But then his gaze was pulled toward the chapel's doors, and much like the irresistible urge to look at a horrible accident on the freeway, he wondered, *What does Wolfe's lab look like?* With all the money the CIA had spent on this place, he was curious where they planned to put the Logos. As much as he didn't want to admit it, a part of him was drawn, like a moth to a flame, to see where it would lead.

"Where is your lab?"

Wolfe ran his hand along the elaborately carved back of the throne. Ethan glanced at the purple velvet seat cushion. The pomposity with which church officials conducted themselves turned him off almost as much as their teachings of superstitions and myths as historical facts.

"You're standing in it."

"What?"

Rather than reply to the question, Wolfe moved away from the throne and gestured to it.

Could it be possible?

He stepped forward and looked more closely. The chair's back was constructed above the head level of the person who would sit in it. Near the top, where one's head would rest, it curved inward. The sides of the headrest were carved in a circular design and gilded in bronze. Then he remembered Wolfe's earlier comment about the importance of the setting in which the psychological programming took place. He ran his fingers along the curved design. What appeared to be wood felt like plastic.

"Incorporating your Logos into the *cathedra*, the traditional chair in which a bishop would sit, wasn't as hard as it might seem. The base is constructed out of steel for support with a mahogany veneer. We used a strong but lightweight composite for the headrest that conceals the solenoids while at the same time allowing the magnetic field to pass through undiluted."

"This is the Logos?"

"The mechanics of the machine are concealed in the base here." Wolfe knocked on the seat. "We've insulated it so the hum is not as noticeable. The wiring for the controls runs underneath the floor and then up the wall to our control room on the floor above us. That's where the processor sits that holds your programming."

My programming?

The spacious chapel seemed to close in around him. The only copy of that programming was on his laptop in New Haven. Studying the throne again, he realized that it would have taken them weeks to build it. They would have started construction well before the first test with Sister Terri in his lab. *They would have started the cathedra even before they started funding us! How did they get the design?*

Then he thought of Elijah's odd behavior in the days before his death. Had his mentor been feeding his old friend the design of the Logos from the beginning? He knew that Elijah had been under extreme pressure to finance their research, but he couldn't imagine him agreeing to what he'd seen here.

He chose his words carefully. "We only just tested the Logos a week ago. How did you get my algorithm?"

"Yes, your programming. That's what we need to talk about. Out of the twenty subjects we've tested it on—"

"You've tested it on twenty!"

"About three a day since your successful test on the nun. While you and Elijah were debating about retesting monkeys, we were moving your research forward." He lowered his voice to a conspiratorial whisper. "I share your frustration with the bureaucracy of academia." He shook his head. "Ethan, I brought you here to give you a unique opportunity." His tone deepened as his voice rose. "An opportunity to change the world. To bring peace to a region that hasn't seen it in centuries. To secure the future of our nation." He dropped his voice again. "And to conduct your research free from the oversight and restrictions that have prevented you from reaching your potential."

The image of Sam Houston's balding head popped into Ethan's mind. The chair of Yale's Human Research Protection Program had been trying to shut down his work from the beginning. Wolfe's offer tugged at his scientific curiosity, as well as his innate desire to see his and Elijah's work brought to fruition. But another voice in his head, a voice that sounded like Elijah's, blared an alarm. What the director was proposing was frightening, and the consequences if something went wrong were too terrible to even think about. *But,* he wondered, *what happens if I refuse his offer?* He had just been given a tour of one of the government's most top secret projects. Wolfe's words about the security of the project echoed in his head. The memory of finding Elijah's cold body in their lab sent another shiver across his skin.

"Why do you need me? You've been using the Logos more than I have."

Wolfe shifted to the side. For the first time his air of confidence deflated. "Well, you see"—he fidgeted with his white collar—"we've discovered a few anomalies in our tests."

"You've had complications with the subjects?" As soon as the words left his mouth, he recalled Rachel's concerns about one of her monkeys.

"In eighteen of the subjects, we've had varying degree of success. We've learned that it often takes a number of exposures to the Logos to achieve its full potential, in addition to the counseling with our priests."

"And the other two subjects?"

"They've had extreme negative reactions to your protocol."

"What kind of reactions?"

"It might be better if I showed you."

Wolfe spun on his Italian wingtips and led Ethan out of the chapel and down the cloistered hallway. Five minutes later he stopped outside the door of one of the monk's rooms.

Ethan peered inside the square window. The room appeared much like the ones he'd seen an hour earlier, but with an important difference: The man lying on the bed was neither sedated by IV drugs nor being read to by a priest. He was restrained by thick leather straps around his wrists and ankles. Even with the restraints, the man thrashed on the bed to such an extent that Ethan thought he might turn it over. He realized that the room must be sound-proofed because the Arab was shouting, yet he heard nothing.

At first, he worried that the man was having a seizure. The fear that his protocol had carried a greater risk of seizure than he'd predicted played through his head. But then he realized that the movements weren't uncontrolled as one would find in a grand mal. The Arab flailed about of his own accord.

Suddenly the man stopped moving and lifted his head to the extent allowed by his restraints. His jet-black hair was disheveled. His olive complexion glistened with sweat. But it was the eyes Ethan couldn't stop looking at. The Arab stared straight at him. Even though he suspected that the window in the door was one-way glass, he felt his own heart rate accelerate in his chest as his limbic system kicked into gear. He wanted to look away, but the Arab's eyes drew him into his tortured soul. He had heard the expression that someone *looked as if he'd seen the devil.* Now he knew what that expression looked like.

CHAPTER 36

THE MONASTERY

A t 3:16 in the morning the Monastery chapel was as quiet inside as it had appeared on the security monitor when James Axelrod had checked it ten minutes earlier. Although he was Jericho's head of security, Axe—the nickname he'd picked up when he enlisted in the Navy determined to become a SEAL—had volunteered to take the night watch that evening. He'd caught a few hours' sleep on the trip back from the States, but these days he rarely slept well anyway. The nightmares had been getting worse. He glanced at the shiny skin along his wrist where he'd sealed the gash caused by Rachel Riley's razor with surgical glue. Wolfe had chuckled when he'd recounted his difficulty with the monkey girl.

He lowered himself into the throne that held the Logos, feeling his glutes settle into the velvet cushion of the seat. His left ass cheek was still sore from the injection he'd given himself before his workout in the Monastery gym that afternoon. Being ambidextrous made shooting up easier—right hand for right cheek, left for left—just as it gave him an advantage in firing his H&K nine-millimeter with equal accuracy in either hand. He relished the power that came with starting a new cycle, stacking testosterone cypionate, deca, and HGH. He'd also popped a Nolvadex, an aromatase inhibitor that prevented the extra testosterone in his body from being converted into estrogen. The last thing he wanted was bitch tits.

Sitting in Wolfe's throne, he recalled his mother's voice from a decade ago, admonishing him as an eighteen-year-old, "Jimmy, don't get too big or you're going to look like a freak." What his mother didn't understand was that he wanted to be a freak; he wanted to be superhuman. He would never again suffer as he had when he'd spent his entire twelfth year in and out of hospitals. The kid who'd once been a robust Little League player had wasted away month after month while his doctors struggled to fight the infections that ravaged his young body. Between courses of antibiotics, they had performed multiple skin grafts on his severely burnt legs. His mother had prayed by his hospital bed every day. She'd begged God not to punish her foolish child by putting him through such a terrible ordeal.

Jimmy, as only his mother called him, had known why he was suffering. *But it wasn't my fault*, he'd told himself through tears. Bobby, his best friend since birth, had been the one to suggest spraying the stray cat with gasoline. Jimmy had just carried out the idea. And struck the match.

The doctors eventually rid his body of the infections, and the skin grafts on his legs left them fully functional but horribly scarred. To a child, the new skin the doctors were so proud of appeared to belong to an alien. His legs had also atrophied to sticks. He left the hospital a different boy: frail, but determined to rebuild himself into a new person. The emotional and financial strain of his treatment had worsened his father's alcoholism, and it wrecked his parents' marriage. They divorced six months after he healed.

He toyed with the LCD remote he'd swiped from the surveillance room. Wolfe had proudly explained that the protocol was automated. All he had to do was press the power button on the remote, wait for a short warm-up, and then click on the start icon. The machine would cycle through the programming, shutting off when it was finished.

He knew that he'd be disciplined if he got caught, but the temptation was too great. His main concern was whether the machine would work. Two men had gone crazy after using it, but he felt that the problem was most likely in the weak-minded men it had been used on. For the eighteen others, the results had been good.

Flexing his traps and then his delts, he felt blood pour into his shoulders. He liked the feeling of tightness in his muscles; it reminded him of his size. That afternoon he'd trained legs: seven sets each of squats, hack squats, leg presses, and leg extensions. Most people hated leg days, but he embraced the apprehension of staring down the squat rack, the bar bending from the 550 pounds of plates. It hurt like hell, but he'd attacked the weight. At the end of the first set, he'd run to a trashcan and vomited. Then he'd taken a swig of water and gone back for the next one. He was a legend in the gym for his pain tolerance. What his colleagues didn't know was that nothing he could do in the gym was worse than what he'd endured when he was twelve. He didn't mind the burning in his muscles; in fact, he relished it. Through punishment, he would grow stronger.

He shifted his weight in the throne and thought about the brilliance of Wolfe's dream of creating a new type of Christian soldier to battle the Islamic terrorists. *If this machine can create confident Christians from these broken-down Arabs, imagine what it will do to me.* Weeks earlier, he'd mentioned to Wolfe his idea of using the Logos on the Americans in the facility. They would strengthen their faith in doing God's work here, emboldening themselves further to serve their country and their Lord.

The Bishop had gotten a twinkle in his eye and said, "Patience, my boy."

But Axe wasn't patient. He'd built his body to superhuman proportions through his own determination and action, not by waiting around for others to help him. Tonight he would act. He would purge the remnants of the skinny, scared boy that still lurked in his mind. He would rid himself of the nightmares that still plagued his sleep.

The dream was always some variation of hell. His mother had described the horned devil many times in his childhood. After his parents' divorce, she had become bitter and had turned to the small church down the road for comfort. The stories the minister told and his mother repeated every night before his bedtime had frightened him. He couldn't remember when the nightmares began, but they woke him in a shivering sweat several nights a week. Beelzebub, whose face morphed between a man's and a lizard's, would tie him up and shoot flames at him from long, black fingernails. He would struggle against the ropes that held his ankles and wrists to a wooden cross, but he didn't have the strength to break the bonds. In the dream, Axe was missing his muscle—the muscle that acted both as a shield and a sword when he was awake.

If the professor's machine worked—if it really allowed him to speak with God—he would ask Him to banish Satan from his dreams. When he'd described his dreams to his mother, she'd explained that God was punishing him through Satan's fire because of his wickedness. Tonight he would explain to God how he'd redeemed himself. He'd built himself into a warrior in order to serve Him.

He stretched his head to the left and the right. The tendons in his neck strained with the effort. One drawback to his size was that it did limit his range of motion, but that was a small price to pay for the benefit of the fear that he saw in other men's eyes when they encountered him. He was powerful. Yet he knew that physical power wasn't enough. As he'd watched the Arab prisoners transform from broken men who believed in a false religion to committed Christians, he'd finally understood that salvation for him wouldn't come through his body, but through his soul.

He laid his head into the cushioned headrest and tapped the power button with his left thumb. A slight hum echoed through the cavernous room. He felt a gentle vibration through the seat. After sixty seconds of warm-up, a green light on the remote illuminated. Axe pressed the start icon. In a moment he would come face to face with God.

CHAPTER 37

THE MONASTERY

The sound came to Rachel from a distance. She struggled to awaken, but the melodic chant threatened to lull her back to sleep. With effort, she willed her eyes to open. She was in bed. What a strange dream she'd had. She stretched her arms over her head, but her limbs felt heavy. She pushed herself up on her elbows. The realization that she wasn't in her own bedroom jolted her out of her sluggishness.

The small room was dark and sparsely furnished. The only light came from a flickering candle on the small table by the narrow bed she lay on.

Then the memory flooded back: the attack in the bathroom, the huge man, the injection that paralyzed her. She touched her chest and glanced down. She was wearing a T-shirt and sweats.

Did he . . .

She ran her hands along her body. She didn't think she'd been raped, and she seemed to be uninjured. She swung her feet off the bed. Vertigo hit as soon as she tried to stand. She immediately sat back down. While she waited for the room to stop spinning, she closed her eyes.

The horror of the encounter in her bathroom replayed itself in slow motion. After she'd been paralyzed, she'd heard her attacker leave the bathroom. Her mind had screamed for help, but nothing had come from her mouth. The fear of being utterly helpless and at this man's mercy had threatened to overwhelm her. When he'd returned with her clothes, his rough hands had pawed at her naked body, grasping her breasts as he dressed her. She had never experienced pure terror like that before. She'd hoped that someone walking along the street might witness the spectacle of him carrying her out into the cold night, but her hope was dashed as soon as she felt herself shoved into the backseat of a car. Then he'd tied one of her scarves around her head, plunging her world into darkness. She wasn't sure how long she was in the car. It had felt like hours as her mind raced through the possibilities this man might have in store for her. She'd seen enough horror movies to know that she could end up shackled in some dungeon. When the car stopped, her attacker had carried her up a short flight of stairs and then lowered her onto what felt like a bed. Her last memory was of a sharp stinging on the inside of her elbow, followed by a warm feeling spreading up her arm. As she'd slipped into unconsciousness, she'd dreamed that the bed she lay on had levitated as if it were a magic carpet flying through the air.

She opened her eyes and shook her head. The man had brought her somewhere, but where? The room didn't have the appearance of a serial killer's dungeon. She stepped onto the cool tile floor and shuffled toward the heavy wood door, which looked like it had been carved by hand. She wasn't surprised that it was locked. That was when she became aware of the music again. The soft sound of monks chanting filled the air around her.

Axe didn't notice anything at first. He tried to relax into the throne with his eyes closed. The vibration from the Logos was almost pleasant. At some point he lost track of time. Even the hum faded into the distance. He wasn't sure when the sensation of falling began. It started slowly but soon began to pick up speed. Darkness engulfed him and then deepened as if he were plummeting down a mineshaft. An unease began to creep into the recesses of his thoughts. Where was the bright light he was supposed to see? He waited to hear from God. He desperately wanted the comfort of a voice that would call to him from the darkness, a voice that would reassure him that he had paid for his sins. But only silence pounded in his ears.

The unease in his gut grew into a feeling he'd despised in himself as a child, a feeling he saw in others as the ultimate weakness. He began to feel fear. The darkness surrounding him suddenly became part of him. He was no longer suspended in the chasm; the chasm seemed to originate within him. Each molecule that made up his body began to dissolve into the darkness. His breathing quickened as if he were in the middle of a set of squats. But rather than empowering him, each breath seemed to expel the essence of who he was out of his body and into the chasm. The fear gripped his heart, squeezing blood through the cord-like veins that fed his arms and legs. He knew that in seconds he would no longer exist. His entire essence would disappear into nothingness.

The scream came from deep in his belly as he launched himself out of the cathedra. He hit the cool stone floor, gasping for air.

He opened his eyes. Would he still have a body? What would it look like? As the room came into focus, he was surprised to see that nothing looked different. He rolled to his back and stared at the ceiling above his head. The candle flames from the altar cast sinister shadows along the wood beams. The throne beside him was empty. He could detect the slight vibration of the Logos, this time through the floor. He cast his eyes down his torso. His physique was intact, but he was trembling. The room wasn't cold, yet he couldn't stop shaking. He pushed himself to his knees. Bowing his head, he closed his eyes again. He inhaled deeply, expanding his ribcage to the point that he felt his lats stretch out the back of his shirt. He exhaled forcefully and rose to his feet.

He finally knew the truth. This new truth frightened him even more than the dream of being tortured by the devil. This truth spoke to him from his core.

God had abandoned him. He was alone.

CHAPTER 38

THE MONASTERY

"We can accomplish great things together." Wolfe's final words to Ethan the previous day echoed in his mind as he walked alone down one of the candelabra-lit corridors.

What have I gotten myself into?

Two days earlier he'd been in New Haven mourning the death of his friend and worrying about the future of his research. Now he was half a world away with the promise of unlimited resources for his work. But such freedom came at a price. He'd told Wolfe he would fix the Logos, but he struggled with the question, *What will I really do?* If he refused, he might just disappear. No one knew where he was. The uncertainties of how Wolfe was able to build the Logos and who killed Elijah swirled in his head like a tsunami, growing in power every second. Researching why two of the monks had experienced psychotic breaks would buy him time to figure out his next move. In truth, his curiosity about the flaw in the Logos was eating at him, but he was also more nervous than he'd ever been in his life. He was in over his head.

He reached into the pocket of the white lab coat he wore. Wolfe had decided that he should assume the mantle of a doctor rather than another priest—an easy role, since that's what he was. Wolfe had given him an electronic key that allowed access to the elevator and the lower monastery level of the facility, in addition to his room and the server area on the ground floor where the Logos machine was housed. He twirled the plastic card between his fingers. Wolfe had casually mentioned that it wouldn't grant him access to the outside of the building—"for your own safety." He wasn't quite a prisoner, but he wasn't free, either.

He glanced behind him at the monk's room he'd just left, one of the two who had been negatively affected by the Logos. The Arab man he'd just examined had babbled about visions. Even the interpreter, one of Wolfe's priests, could barely make sense of the ramblings. The man claimed he'd glimpsed hell and was convinced that dragons would consume him. The monk he'd seen prior to him was catatonic. He lay in his bed staring at the ceiling, unresponsive to questions. He reacted to physical stimuli, touch and light, but he refused to engage in conversation. Ethan had examined the men's files but couldn't find any prior conditions that would indicate that they were predisposed to psychosis.

What went wrong with my programming? Their negative reactions had started at the end of their sessions with the Logos. As suspected members of terrorist cells, both men had been treated harshly in their prior captivity, but no more harshly than the other eighteen men. *Could I have missed something in the algorithm?* He and Elijah had been concerned that the protocol might cause an epileptic event. *But visions of hell in an experiment meant to create a mystical experience of the divine?* That possibility had never occurred to them. He wondered whether an individual's belief system could cause the effect, but in his heart he doubted that a difference in belief would cause such a psychotic break. *The problem's in my code.* He'd decided to visit some of the other monks to see how the Logos had affected them. Although the CIA secret facility unnerved him, he couldn't help but feel a bit of anticipation. Wolfe had more experience using his creation than he had.

He stopped in front of the door to the room of a third monk, pulled the man's file from under his arm, and scanned the bio. Mousa bin Ibrahim Al-Mohammad was a Jordanian doctor who had been detained as a suspected accomplice to a bombing in Dubai. He recalled the bombing; it had decimated one of the largest malls in the Middle East. The file explained that the UAE's secret police had determined after intense questioning that he was probably innocent, but he'd been so badly tortured that they were reluctant to release him, fearing negative publicity. Wanting to be rid of a problem, they had turned him over to the Americans "for further debriefing," happy to wash their hands of what could have become a difficult diplomatic situation with Jordan. Curious about how the well-educated doctor would react to the program, Wolfe had accepted him into Jericho even though he didn't fit the profile of the other monks, who'd actually been involved in various terrorist cells.

When Ethan had reviewed the files early that morning, the notes from a new priest assigned to Mousa's case had caught his attention. "Father" Christopher wrote about his frustration with his charge's progress. The session with the Logos had gone well, but his handler was concerned that the Jordanian hadn't taken to his Christian indoctrination like the other subjects had. If anything, he'd become an even stronger Muslim, although he appeared to be cooperating with the program.

To understand the effects of the Logos, Ethan knew he needed to explore every anomaly, and Mousa was unlike the other nineteen men in the facility. While the others were illiterate and had been subjected to intense indoctrination in various religious camps as young men, the Jordanian doctor was educated and approached his faith from a different background. Ethan wanted to meet him.

He peered through the one-way glass window. The Jordanian doctor was alone, sitting on the edge of the bed with an open Bible on his lap. Ethan took a breath, knocked, and opened the door.

"Good morning, Brother Mousa." Wolfe had been clear that the patients should only be referred to as "Brother" followed by their first name. All aspects of communication should reinforce their conditioning. Ethan felt the form of address disrespectful, especially considering that this man was another doctor—a peer—but he played along with the protocol.

Mousa's eyebrows rose and then his eyes settled on the white lab coat.

"I'm Dr. Ethan Lightman." He approached the bed with an outstretched hand. "But please call me Ethan."

"Doctor?" Mousa's took the hand. His grip was strong. "MD, shrink, or PhD?" He spoke with a touch of a British accent.

Ethan smiled. "All three, actually."

"Are you here to determine whether I'm fit to return to my wife and children?" His voice held a note of hope.

Ethan was unsuccessful at suppressing the look of surprise that passed over his face. "I just arrived yesterday. Today I'm here to introduce myself and get to know the men."

"Where did you arrive?"

He caught himself just before the word "Aswan" came from his mouth. Wolfe had prepped him on how to answer. "Here at the monastery. Now"—he sat on the edge of the bed and removed the stethoscope from his neck—"let's have a look at you."

Mousa's eyes narrowed. *He's not buying it*, Ethan thought. He hoped the Jordanian wouldn't notice how sweaty his palms were. *I'm a doctor, not a spook*. He tried changing the conversation.

"What's your specialty?"

"Orthopedics."

"A couple of my friends from med school are too. While I'm stuck in my lab year-round, they're taking vacations to the Caribbean."

Mousa grinned for the first time. "In Jordan, our work doesn't pay quite the same as it does in the States, but we live comfortably too."

As he continued the physical exam, they shared stories about their favorite patients and more unusual colleagues. Mousa was the first doctor from a foreign country he'd talked shop with. Their practices weren't that different, he realized. The more they spoke, the more he felt a kinship to the man who exuded a warmth that he suspected won over his patients.

When he completed the exam, he pulled over the only chair in the room. "Well, physically you seem to be in good health—much better than was the case when you were brought here, I see from reading your chart."

"The priests have treated me well."

"How're you feeling? From a mental standpoint, I mean."

Mousa glanced at the closed door. A look of uncertainty passed over his face, as if he were contemplating how much to trust him. He lowered his voice. "I appreciate what these men have done for me. They've been kind, if somewhat persistent in their religious missionary work. But I don't fault them for that. I've seen far worse in my own country. I just want to get home to my family."

Missionary work. He wondered how to ask him about his experiences with the Logos.

"I'm sure you'll be heading home soon." He didn't know that to be the case, but he didn't see how or why Wolfe could hold the man much longer, even if the Logos wasn't as effective on him as it was on most of the others.

"There's something else, though." Mousa glanced again around the room as if to confirm they were alone.

"What's that?"

"Something strange is going on here. I think—"

Before he could finish his thoughts, a knock rang out from the door and then it sprang open.

"Good morning, Mousa. I've brought your tea."

Ethan stood and turned toward the oddly familiar voice behind him. The identity of the man dressed in the priest's robes took his breath away.

CHAPTER 39

THE MONASTERY

"**C**hris?" Ethan took a step backward at the sight of Christian Sligh, his graduate assistant.

"You know Father Christopher?" Mousa asked.

"We first met last year." Chris's wide grin never faltered. He carried a tray with a steaming cup of tea into the room. "I heard that the doctor just arrived, and I wanted to stop by and say hi."

Ethan stared at his student, unsure of which of the many questions racing through his head he should ask first. He sensed that Mousa was studying him.

Chris set the tea on the table by the bed. With his back to Mousa, his student shot a look to him that told him to hold his questions. He'd never seen such authority on his face before. He shifted his weight from one foot to another. He was usually the one giving the instructions.

"If you two are finished with your checkup, do you mind if I borrow Dr. Lightman for a minute?" Chris rested a hand on Ethan's shoulder.

Mousa glanced between the two of them. He held up the Bible in his lap. "I'll just get back to my reading. I was engrossed in the story of Job."

"A favorite of mine, too," Chris said. "Maybe we can chat about it later this afternoon."

"I'd enjoy that," Mousa said with a smile that looked forced.

"What in the hell is going on?" Ethan demanded as soon as the door closed behind them.

"Not here," Chris said under his breath. He hurried down the hall. Minutes later they sat across from one another at a long oak table, alone in the dining hall.

"I want some answers." Ethan brought his palm down on the hard surface. The slap echoed through the hall. "You work for Wolfe here at Jericho?"

"Beginning the summer after my sophomore year at Notre Dame, I started an unpaid internship at the CIA. It was a very competitive process to get selected. After all the interviews, the polygraph tests, they still took six months to do a background check. They interviewed my roommates, friends, and professors, trying to dig up dirt like whether I smoked pot and who I'd slept with." The student grinned, but Ethan didn't return the smile. "I returned the next two summers, and then the CIA offered to pay for grad school. I could pursue a PhD in psychology in exchange for working my vacations and summers during school, plus five years after I graduate. How could I refuse?"

Wolfe's use of the Logos in the Monastery fell into place for Ethan. He rocked back in his seat as if he'd been struck in the chest. "So you're the one who's been feeding our research—the design of the Logos, the software protocols, everything—to Wolfe?" The loose ends made sense to him now.

"Wolfe rescued the project!" Chris's voice rose an octave. "Without his financial help, Houston would have shut us down before we could have run the tests on Sister Terri."

He sensed that his student was trying to rationalize his actions to himself as much as to him.

"How much did Elijah know?" He wondered how far the conspiracy went.

Chris shook his head emphatically. "Wolfe followed Elijah's research from a distance for years. He pulled some strings to get me into Yale in order to place me with you guys. I was his eyes and ears. Wolfe didn't approach him directly until we ran out of money a couple months ago."

"When our original grant expired, I thought they refused to continue funding us because of our lack of results with the Logos, but now—"

"Wolfe made a few calls to that foundation. He knew Elijah wouldn't accept his help unless he was desperate."

Then the memory of Chris's actions immediately after Sister Terri's test came to him—he'd been texting someone on his phone. Then he'd left New Haven.

"Your father wasn't really sick?"

"I'm sorry I had to lie to you, but Wolfe required that I fly over the moment we had a successful test so I could supervise the Logos here."

He leaned across the table. "Do you know that Elijah was murdered?"

"I"—Chris's brow creased and his voice caught in his throat—"I can't believe he's gone. You and Elijah have been mentors to me ever since I arrived. You have to understand—although the CIA is paying my way through grad school, my passion is psychology. I've learned so much from you two." He wiped his reddening eyes with the sleeve of his robe. "Wolfe told me he was killed in a robbery?"

"That's what the police are saying, but—" Ethan glanced around the room, confirming they were alone, and then explained how he'd found Elijah sitting in the Logos, the cryptic note that had led him to the library, the chase by Wolfe's goon, and the mysterious transfer of the money into his bank account. Repeating the details for the first time aloud inside the multimillion-dollar secret prison whose success relied on his device raised the hairs on his arms. As much as he didn't want to believe it, he knew the strange events were not random. He noticed that his student's brow was scrunched in concern.

Does Chris know more than he's saying?

As disturbing as it was to find that his student was working for the CIA, he couldn't believe that he was involved in Elijah's death. He'd known Chris for over three years, but then, he'd also been lying to him all along.

"No way was Wolfe involved in Elijah's death. They were friends years ago."

He studied the pained expression on his student's face. "Why did you do it? I mean, beyond the funding for your education. You see what's happening here—the religious indoctrination, the brainwashing—it goes against everything our research is designed to explore."

"I was thirteen when the towers came down." Chris folded his arms across his chest and glanced up at the wood ceiling. "My Uncle Mark, my mom's older brother, had an office in Two World Trade. Mom got a call from him about ninety seconds before the tower collapsed. We were watching it on TV together. She was too hysterical to speak, so she handed the phone to me. Uncle Mark and I had always been close; he used to take me go-kart racing when I was younger. He'd tell the track that I was twelve so they'd let me on." His voice broke. "Mark was calm on the other line. He was standing at his office window. I yelled at him to run down the stairs. We'd already seen the first building collapse. 'It's too late for that, Chris,' he said, 'but I'm not afraid. God will take care of me.' The phone line went dead. I watched the second tower come down with the receiver in my hand."

"I'm so sorry. I never knew that." Ethan cleared his throat and paused for a moment. "But that doesn't excuse your betrayal of our work. We want to unlock the mystery of religion, not use it as a tool for continued violence."

"But what Wolfe is trying to do here has the potential to bring peace to this region."

"Bring peace? By introducing other religious zealots he's converted into the mix? That's a recipe for greater conflict, not less."

"We might not see the effects for decades, but we've got to start somewhere. Until now we've been unable to penetrate these terrorist networks. The Logos is our best chance to secure our country from future attacks."

He evaluated Chris for a moment. His assistant had fully bought into Wolfe's vision, a Machiavellian one in which peace was used as an excuse to justify immoral acts. But something about this place, something about Wolfe, disturbed him even more. He couldn't put his finger on the exact source of this unease, but he wondered how far Wolfe wanted to take this program.

"Why am I here, Chris? Wolfe opened up the whole facility to me."

"I told him that only you could fix the Logos. And he respects your work. He's been following you for years."

He found it strangely satisfying, yet unnerving, that the CIA was interested in his research. No one at the university respected what he was doing.

"What happens if I fix the Logos? Will Wolfe let me return to Yale to continue my research?"

Chris shifted in his seat. "I don't think you're going to be working on the Logos in public any more. The technology is just too incendiary. But I'm sure that Wolfe could make it financially rewarding for you to continue your research with him."

"He's never going to let me leave here, is he?"

Chris refused to meet his eyes.

CHAPTER 40

CIA HEADQUARTERS
LANGLEY, VIRGINIA

Deputy Director Casey Richards sat on the corner of his desk and massaged the top of his bald head with his free hand. The other held a file folder marked "Eyes Only: Jericho."

"How many are ready to go?" he asked into the cordless headset hooked around his ear.

After a brief delay as the signal bounced across the satellite and was processed by the descrambler, Allen Wolfe replied, "Ten, maybe a dozen if we stretch it."

"And the problems? We can't afford to have any of these guys flip out on us."

Richards massaged harder. The hostage exchange he'd authorized had been brokered by friends within the Saudi government. Officially, it wasn't even happening. The three journalists and two subcontractors, a combination of American and British nationals, had been held for fourteen months since they were kidnapped in Afghanistan the previous year. The intelligence had been embarrassingly sparse. They suspected the hostages were in Pakistan. On more than one occasion they'd scrambled Delta and SEAL teams to attempt a rescue. In each case the teams had arrived to find a couple of low-level Al Qaeda operatives but no hostages.

He flipped through the folder on his lap, scanning the bios of the men Dr. Wolfe planned to release. They'd been caught in various terrorist sweeps over the past few years and then held in secret prisons throughout Egypt, Jordan,

Saudi Arabia, and the UAE, where they'd been intensely interrogated. Each had gone through Project Jericho, and Wolfe assured him that these men were reliable converts. They would lead the CIA back to almost a dozen terrorist cells. Unlike the case with Youssef, drones wouldn't bomb these cells. The Jericho men would act as agents, feeding intel to their priest handlers, with whom they would meet every few months.

Richards planned to return the men the following week, with the simultaneous release of the Western hostages. The hostages would be met with worldwide media attention, and the White House would bask in the accolades. The release of the men from the Monastery, however, would happen below the radar screen of the press.

"Don't worry," Wolfe replied. "We're close to having the problem isolated and corrected. I've got the man who developed the Logos working on it now."

"I can't stress to you the critical nature of this project's success."

"I understand better than anyone."

He sensed a tone of annoyance in Wolfe's voice. "As much of an investment as I've made in Jericho, I will shut it down in a moment if its existence comes close to leaking out."

"In more exciting news, next month I'll be sending you a proposal for Phase II of Jericho. I have an idea that will make our terrorist infiltration plans look infantile."

He just ignored my threat, Richards thought. He shook his head.

The problem with many of the academic types he'd worked with over the years was that they lacked the vision of where their work could lead—the impact it could have on the country. That wasn't the case with Wolfe. He was, to put it mildly, ambitious. Ambition could change the world, but it could also destroy it. Jericho had the potential to do both.

"I need Jericho working flawlessly before we even begin to discuss any kind of Phase II."

Silence greeted his last instruction. Sometimes he wondered whether Wolfe understood that he was working for him and not the other way around.

CHAPTER 41

THE MONASTERY

E than sat on the floor, hunched over a laptop, shivering. The twelve-by-fifteen-foot server room on the ground floor was chilled to a meat-locker fifty-five degrees to keep the floor-to-ceiling racks of computer equipment from overheating. He guessed that most of the black boxes were either surveillance, communications, or computer servers. One piece of equipment—front and center on the bottom rack—he knew intimately: the control system for the Logos in the bishop's cathedra on the monastery level underneath him. A thick gray cable ran from the serial port on the back of the box and down the side of the rack, where it was neatly clipped together with other cables from the components above it. The cables disappeared into a hole in the white tile floor.

Two hours earlier, Chris had given him the laptop and left him in the room. His vision blurred from focusing on the lines of code that scrolled across the screen while a window in the corner displayed the binary code the computer translated the programming language into. He still couldn't figure out what had driven the two subjects to have psychotic breaks. If only one man had experienced a negative reaction, he might have dismissed it as an anomaly, but two? And why them? He was missing something, something right in front of him. *But what?*

Elijah and Rachel were right, he admitted. His confidence in his own work and zealousness to see it tested on humans had caused him to dismiss the potential problem with Anakin, the monkey who became disturbed after the test. The mental image of Elijah with his disheveled hair and warm grin brought an emptiness to his chest, but then the thought of Rachel and the spark in her eyes brought a different feeling to his stomach, one he found more difficult to ignore. She was the one person at Yale he'd felt comfortable confiding in when his life fell apart. He closed his eyes for a moment and recalled the touch of her hand, the way she smelled when they were close, the way she seemed to understand his struggles. He wondered if she'd tried to call him. Would she report him as a missing person to the police? No one in New Haven knew where he was. Then a disturbing thought crowded out the memory of the attractive and insightful grad student: she had been speaking to Houston about him behind his back. He shook his head.

As he clicked on the next page of code, another dilemma floated in his mind: what would he do if he discovered the flaw in his programming? If the US government was going to use his technology whether or not he approved, did he have an obligation to make sure they wouldn't create schizophrenic subjects in ten percent of the cases? Was it his responsibility to police how his invention was used? *That's exactly your responsibility*, said a voice in the back of his head that sounded a lot like Elijah.

He disconnected the USB cable from the Logos controller, closed the laptop, and stood. He wanted to examine the men again. Maybe he needed to get back to basics. He would start with routine physicals and then draw blood, followed by EEGs. Maybe the two men had a history of mental instability that their files didn't reveal. But then, all the men had been subjected to psychological extremes. Were any of them mentally stable?

As he turned to the door, a familiar sight caught his eye. Amid the racks of computer equipment, three boxes tucked away on the far right were instantly familiar. He hurried to the rack and ducked his head around the metal shelves to get a better look.

Three more Logos controllers?

Neither Wolfe nor Chris had mentioned any others. He followed the cables from the back of the machines. Rather than snaking down into the floor, the cables disappeared into the same two-inch plastic conduit. The conduit ran horizontally into the wall. Somewhere on the other side of that wall were three other Logos machines.

Thirty seconds later he stood in the fluorescent-lit hallway outside a metal door to the right of the server room. His heart thumped in his ears as he tried the handle.

Locked.

He turned and headed down the hall toward the elevator. The clicking of a door opening in the quiet corridor caused him to jump. He spun on his heels in time to see a man emerge from the locked door he'd just tried. He balanced two file boxes stacked in his arms. The boxes wobbled as the man walked in the opposite direction from him.

He didn't see me.

Ethan ran toward the door on the toes of his shoes. Even that seemed too loud, but the man didn't turn. The metal door was closing faster than he'd expected. He thrust his fingers into the narrow crack between the door and the frame. He winced when the door pinched his skin but resisted the urge to jerk out his hand.

With the exception of the breath expanding his chest, he didn't move. The man carrying the box disappeared around the corner at the end of the corridor without looking back. Ethan pushed open the door with his free hand and shook out the pain from the red crease across his fingers. He stepped into the dark room, closed the door behind him, and felt for the light switch.

The lights illuminated what appeared to be a storage and workroom about twenty by thirty feet in size. Several rows of file boxes were stacked to the right. To the left was a metal worktable where two dozen identical cell phones were plugged into several power strips. He thought back to his arrival and the guard who had taken his phone and wallet. He selected one on the end, where it would be least likely to be missed, and pocketed it. He wondered whether he could get a cell signal in this place. Then another thought occurred: *Who can I call for help?*

He walked deeper into the room, where he confronted an unusual sight. An intricately carved church pew faced him from the back wall. The curved back looked as if it was designed to cradle each occupant. Whereas a standard church pew might hit one in the mid-back, this was taller, with the wood extending to head height. Then he noticed the cables. He leaned over the pew. They entered the base at three locations. He then traced the cables along the floor where they disappeared into the wall. He knew where they led: into the three Logos controllers. He stepped back and studied the pew.

What is Wolfe up to?

Then he noticed the open door to his right. He approached the door and, after allowing a moment for his eyes to adjust to the darkness of the adjacent space, his mouth dropped open. He was staring into a warehouse with a high, unfinished ceiling and bare concrete floors. Stacked on pallets in the space were dozens of Logos machines, shrink-wrapped in plastic. Also stacked on the floor, one on top of the other, were rows of the modified church pews.

"Looking for something, Professor?"

The rough voice caused him to flinch in surprise. He turned to face a huge man. The man was a couple inches shorter than he was but weighed twice as much, and not an ounce was fat. His black T-shirt stretched over hypertrophied muscles. Even his black pants revealed the separation in his quadriceps.

The man's face told the complete story. From the acne scars, protruding brow, square jaw, and yellowed eyes, Ethan knew immediately that the man had been taking anabolic steroids for years. The acne and eyes were obvious symptoms of excess androgens, variations of the male hormone testosterone, while the overdeveloped brow and jaw could only result from abuse of HGH, human growth hormone. But something else in the jaundiced eyes disturbed him. The man looked nervous, as if he were struggling with a terrible thought that threatened to burst from his head. Then Ethan realized the source of his own unease. He imagined the man wearing reflective orange-lensed sunglasses.

"You must be James Axelrod—Axe, right?" The name of Wolfe's security goon came to him out of the blue. He struggled to keep his voice even.

"You are in a restricted area."

"What's going on here?" He gestured to the stacks of pews in the warehouse behind him. He was nervous, but his anger emboldened him. Maybe, he thought, he could deflect his presence in the locked room by taking the offensive.

"You will follow me." The look in Axe's eyes unnerved Ethan even more. "Now!"

Axe turned and headed for the door without looking back to see if he complied. Ethan knew he had no choice but to follow.

CHAPTER 42

THE MONASTERY

Mousa knocked out the twentieth pushup before his arms gave out. He collapsed on the floor, enjoying the cool feel of the tile against his stomach. His strength was returning. He'd already done thirty sit-ups—a far cry from the two hundred crunches and fifty pushups he began each morning with in Amman, but he was improving with each passing day. Many of his patients were elite athletes—football stars, tennis players—frustrated with the long recovery times from their surgeries. "Take each day as it comes," he counseled them, "and before you know it you'll be back to your old condition." He now understood that giving the advice was easier than taking it.

His right knee was doing better, but he was still missing the key ligament that would allow him to pivot the leg. He'd been doing squats and wall sits to strengthen his quadriceps muscles. He could probably even jog some now, but his knee wouldn't be able to sustain any cutting motions to the side. When he returned to Jordan, he'd have one of his colleagues do the surgery. He wished he could perform it on himself, he thought, smiling. He was the best.

The thought of home brought to mind images of his family. The hope of returning to them had sustained him through everything he'd suffered. The friendly priests had taken good care of him, but he was healthy now. Why was he still here?

A nagging thought played in the back of his mind. At first, he'd been ecstatic to leave the brutal hands of his fellow Arab torturers. But the more time he spent in the monastery, the more he felt that something wasn't right. The priests had a different demeanor than the imams at his mosque in Amman. They had an edge to them that didn't seem befitting of holy men, as if they lacked that certain sense of peace that religion brought.

Maybe that's the difference with their religion, he thought.

One of the central teachings of Islam was that complete surrender to Allah brought a lasting and deep internal peace. The literal meaning of the word *Islam* was just that: peace that comes through surrender. The fundamentalists of his faith had it wrong. They distorted the words of the Prophet to justify harm against civilians in the name of spreading their religion. Those men would do better to look within themselves, he thought, in search of the presence of Allah within. Doing so would quiet their blood-thirst and bring them real peace. The strange occurrence in the chapel had reinforced this knowledge. He'd glimpsed the power of Allah. He couldn't explain it, but now he better understood the mystics of his religion, the Sufis. Allah couldn't be described, only experienced.

He wiped off his forehead with the single towel hanging by his desk. His thoughts drifted from the priests who'd cared for him to the one person who didn't seem like the other Americans: the doctor. He was more inquisitive. He also was nervous, or maybe it was discomfort Mousa sensed.

He wondered whether he could trust Ethan Lightman. He was ready to leave this place, and his gut told him that Ethan would be the one to help him do so.

CHAPTER 43

THE MONASTERY

A xe burst through the doors of the dining hall. Ethan followed close behind, his mind scrambling for excuses as to why he had been in the locked room. The hall was deserted but for Wolfe and Chris, who were talking at the center table. Wolfe stopped mid-sentence when he saw them approaching.

"I found the doctor snooping around the warehouse," Axe said.

"I was working in the server room when I—"

Wolfe raised a hand, cutting off his explanation. "Axe, you may leave us now."

"But—"

Wolfe flicked the hand that was still raised, as if waving away an insect. "Thank you for bringing this to my attention."

Axe glowered at Ethan as he turned to leave. The expansive dining hall seemed to close in around him.

"So you have glimpsed the next phase of our project?"

"What are you planning on doing with my research?" He decided to forget the excuses.

"Doctor Lightman, what you don't understand is the true potential for your work. What we have created here"—he spread his arms—"is just a prototype. The first of many."

"You plan on building more monasteries?"

"We've spent billions of dollars on our military, but it remains ineffective at stopping suicide attacks. These lunatics line up to die for Allah; killing them isn't a deterrent. For every one we kill or capture, three more are behind him to take up the cause." He brought his fist down on the table. "The only way we can win this war is to destroy the enemy from the inside. Islam is like a virus— a virus that can only be eradicated with a Christian vaccine. We must begin a massive reeducation campaign."

"You'll start a world war." He glanced at Chris, who looked uncomfortable at Wolfe's words. "You can't keep all those facilities secret. Word will eventually get out, and every single Arab country will turn against us."

"That's the beauty of the plan." Wolfe grinned. "When we roll out Phase Two of Project Jericho, we'll hide in plain sight. We're going to establish new public churches—blend in with the existing Coptic Christians who have been here for centuries—but ours will have a kick."

"The pews?"

"Members of our congregations will have mystical experiences of God. They'll tell their friends and families how their lives have been changed by the gospel of Christ. We won't be able to build the churches fast enough."

"What you're planning is in direct violation of the Nuremberg Code."

Ethan couldn't believe what he was hearing. Everything about this plan violated the ethical principles he'd been taught since his first day of med school. What Wolfe envisioned was a massive violation of these protocols against hundreds, if not thousands, of unsuspecting subjects.

"The terrorists don't play by our rules."

"But our nation was founded on the principles of religious freedom and liberty. Isn't that what makes us different?"

"If we have the means to stop these madmen, wouldn't it be immoral not to use every method at our disposal?"

"At the expense of manipulating the brains of innocents? Over a billion people claim Islam as their religion—it's the fastest-growing religion in the world—but the fundamentalists who embrace terrorism are only a tiny percentage of this number. Judging all of Islam by a few is like judging all of Christianity because of the Crusades or the Inquisition."

"Sometimes we must sacrifice a few for the good of the many."

"Isn't that the same justification the terrorists use for exploding a bomb in a restaurant or train station where innocent women and children will be killed?"

"Those sound like Elijah's words." Wolfe shook his head. "He was holding you back, Ethan. My old friend was brilliant, yes"—he flashed his perfect teeth in a broad grin—"but you are more so. You can create things here with me that you never could have imagined at Yale."

Ethan had never considered himself an idealist. He was a scientist; everything he did was supported by research and careful thought. But what Wolfe proposed caused every alarm to ring in his body. He knew then that he had to make a decision. The comparison to Elijah made his decision all the more clear. He had to choose right from wrong.

"This project is bigger than a few men." Wolfe rose from his seat. "I have a flight to Cairo in an hour. When I return in two days, I expect the Logos to be working." He smoothed out the wrinkles on his silver bishop's robes. "We have a major operation coming up. I need to know whether I can count on your help." His eyes narrowed and his voice turned icy. "I would hate for anything unfortunate to happen to you like it did with Elijah. He was at the end of his career, but you have so much promise ahead of you."

Ethan's gut churned. Did Wolfe just confirm the suspicion he hadn't wanted to believe? He glanced at Chris, who refused to meet his eyes. The expression of dismay on his student's face seemed real. Then his mind became suddenly clear, as if the thoughts and questions that had swirled about for the past several days had settled down, allowing the light of pure reason to shine forth. Wolfe had killed Elijah and now threatened to do the same to him. He had to stop this madness, even if it meant risking his life. He had created the Logos, and now he had to prevent its use.

He took a deep breath, exhaled, and replied, "I have my reservations, but I'll fix the Logos." He managed a smile that he hoped didn't look forced.

"I thought so." The grin returned to Wolfe's face.

"I've already spent hours going over the programming, but I'm missing something. I'll run additional tests on the men this afternoon."

"Chris has a new resource that may help you." Wolfe opened the dining hall door. "Work quickly. You don't have the luxury of time."

The sound of the door closing echoed through the hall along with Wolfe's lingering admission of guilt in Elijah's death. Ethan knew that even if he fixed the Logos, Wolfe would never let him leave. He would disappear once he'd served his usefulness. He had two days to find a way out of there. His hand slipped into his pocket, where it closed around the hard shell of the cell phone.

CHAPTER 44

THE MONASTERY

Chris hurried Ethan down the corridor without speaking. He studied the creased brow of his student's face. Chris had seemed shocked at Wolfe's cryptic admission of the truth behind Elijah's death.

"I'll make him understand how important you are to the ongoing operation, but, Professor, you have to stop questioning the program."

"He had Elijah killed, Chris."

"I swear I didn't know." His voice cracked. "But what can I do?" He glanced over his shoulder. "I'm involved now too."

Ethan debated his next comment. Could he trust his student? His gut told him their prior relationship had been authentic. Anyway, he had no choice; he needed Chris's help. The electronic locks on the doors were programmed to each specific key card, and his wouldn't let him out of the facility. Then there was the matter of the desert that surrounded them for miles.

"Is this what you signed up for?"

The grad student glanced to the floor. "No," he whispered.

"I need your help getting out of here."

"Getting the two of you out of here without being noticed would be difficult." He stopped by the last door at the end of the corridor.

"Two?"

Chris turned the door handle and led Ethan into the room.

A woman sat on the bed, hunched over, with her face in her hands and her fingers entwined in her hair. The moment they entered, she jumped to her feet, produced a three-foot-long wooden stick from under the covers, and swung it at their heads. Ethan lurched backward. Chris, however, stepped toward the woman. He ducked the arc of the stick, caught the woman's wrist before she had a chance to bring it back into his face, and disarmed her.

Ethan locked eyes with Rachel. She stared at him with an open mouth and fiery eyes. Her hair was disheveled, as if she'd just woken up, but in a way he found alluring. In place of the form-fitting sweaters she wore around Yale, she sported a simple white T-shirt and black sweatpants. As his heart pounded from her sudden attack, a river of competing emotions washed over him: excitement at seeing her confronted an uneasy suspicion.

The questions he wanted to ask seemed to catch in his chest. *Why is she here? Is she a spook like Chris?* He'd longed to see her the past two days, but now he wasn't even sure who she was. He thought back to how she'd been flirty with him from the beginning of the semester. *Was that part of Wolfe's plan too?* He recalled Houston's comment about speaking with her. *Had she been undermining him all along?* His world had begun to unravel when she'd claimed that one of her monkeys was having problems. He felt an emptiness open in his stomach.

She struggled out of Chris's hold on her wrist and turned to face Ethan. "You are part of this?" she screamed.

"I . . ."

She turned her fury toward Chris. "And you too!" She glared at both men. "How could you?"

Chris stepped forward. "Professor Lightman didn't even know this place existed until yesterday."

"So you're responsible!"

Chris recoiled as if propelled by the force of her presence. "No, I just work for the Agency part time while I'm finishing up my degree."

"The Agency?" She looked between the men. "You mean the CIA?"

A flood of relief washed over Ethan. *She doesn't work for Wolfe.* He reached out and touched her arm. "I'm still figuring out the same questions."

She shrugged off his touch and, ignoring his comment, took a step toward Chris, backing him up to the wall. "The last thing I remember was getting ready to go out when this huge man—the same one who chased me and Ethan in the library—broke into my apartment and attacked me."

The hulking image of Wolfe's security chief caused Ethan's chest to tighten. "My God. Are you okay?"

"I was sure he was going to rape me." A shiver passed down her body. "Then he paralyzed me with some drug. I was conscious but completely unable to move." Her voice dripped with anger. "I can't begin to tell you the terror of being carried out of the house expecting to be taken to some cellar somewhere to await whatever sick torture . . ." Her voice trailed off and she stared past the two men at the blank wall. "My head was covered in some hood so I couldn't see anything, but I could tell that we'd arrived at the airport, and I figured he'd put me on a plane. But then he gave me another shot that knocked me out. The next thing I know I wake up in this room." She gestured to the walls. "Wherever the hell we are."

Ethan clenched his fists. Hearing her recount Axe's assault caused a surge of anger to flow through his veins. He recalled the locked door to the private jet's bedroom and realized that she'd been drugged there while he'd enjoyed the luxuries of the main cabin. The guilt of realizing that he'd been worrying about his career while she'd been in terror for her life only deepened the pit in his gut. *And to make matters worse*, he thought, *she's only here because of my research.* The desire to embrace her and hold her was overpowering. He wanted to protect Rachel with every cell in his body, yet he wasn't even sure how he was going to protect himself. Even if Chris agreed to help them escape, he struggled to think how they would elude the security of the place.

"We're in Aswan, Egypt," he said, trying to connect with her. "I was on the plane too. The pilot told me the bedroom in the back was being renovated. You must have been in there."

She turned her head toward him, the fire still in her eyes. "Egypt?"

Something about her wild-eyed look in that moment made her all the more beautiful. He motioned to the bed. "Maybe if we sit down for a moment, Chris can explain what's going on here."

"I'll stand." She whipped her head back to Chris. "Explain."

"First of all"—Chris swallowed—"I had no idea that you were here at the Monastery until last night; second, James Axelrod, the man who kidnapped you, went beyond his orders in his methods. Axe has a way about him." Chris turned the wooden stick he had taken from Rachel over in his hands. Then he went to the small table by the bed and stuck it back where it belonged—it was the rear leg closest to the bed.

Watching his student, a realization struck Ethan like a bat to the chest. Axe had been Wolfe's muscle in New Haven. The hulking man had followed them in the library and assaulted Rachel. He recalled Wolfe's veiled admission of involvement in Elijah's murder. A nauseous feeling rose from his stomach to his throat. *Axe killed Elijah.* He wanted to yell, but, seeing Rachel's expression, he held his breath to suppress the words that wanted to spill out.

Her eyes narrowed. "Monastery?"

Chris launched into the same description of the facility hidden under a warehouse in the Egyptian desert that Wolfe had given Ethan earlier. Rachel listened in silence. After Chris spoke about the importance of the project and the potential to bring a long-standing peace to the region through the introduction of a religion based on a mystical experience of the Christian God, Rachel began to fire off many of the same objections Ethan had posed earlier. Chris looked uncomfortable with his canned answers.

When it was obvious that she wasn't accepting his rationalizations, Chris whispered, "Look, when I was working with you two in New Haven, I didn't know the extent of Jericho either. I certainly had no idea Wolfe would bring either of you here."

"So why exactly am I here?" She crossed her arms.

"Wolfe was following all aspects of our research at Yale. When you raised a red flag about an anomaly in one of your monkeys, we ignored it at first. After all, monkeys aren't human, and it's not like they had epileptic attacks or anything."

Rachel's expression hardened. Chris continued, "But when we experienced two negative reactions to the Logos here, Wolfe took your claims seriously."

"Rachel, I—" Ethan began.

"Please leave." She flopped on the bed and put her face in her hands.

"I know it's a lot," Chris said. "Rest and we'll come back later."

As his student led him out of the room, the one nagging question in the back of Ethan's mind resurfaced. He knew from her reaction that she wasn't part of Jericho. He wanted to reach out to her, to convince her that he wasn't part of the conspiracy either, but he had to address his one remaining doubt. He stopped in the doorway.

"When Samuel Houston called me to his office when you and I were at Koffee together, he mentioned that you two had been speaking." Before he could articulate his question, Rachel lifted her head. Her expression was no longer steely. She seemed to be questioning him, as if she was trying to look deep inside his soul to uncover the truth of his involvement.

"Sam is my father."

CHAPTER 45

THE MONASTERY

Ethan watched Mousa through the one-way window in the doorway. Seeing the Jordanian doctor go through his exercise routine reminded him how much he missed his recent workouts at Yale's Payne Whitney Gymnasium. A hard workout on the rock-climbing wall would do him good now, especially with the tension he was feeling from his encounter with Rachel an hour ago. *Houston is her father?* Her admission had caused him to step back into her room, but Chris had pulled him out and closed the door. His student was right; she'd been traumatized. His questions could wait a couple of hours.

He returned his attention to the doctor, another innocent caught up in Wolfe's web. Mousa had been in the wrong place at the wrong time. He'd been torn from his family. He'd suffered physical and mental torture that Ethan couldn't even imagine enduring, and now Wolfe wanted to use his technology to destroy the man's faith. The doctor had healed physically from his unjust imprisonment; he should be headed home. But Wolfe planned to keep him there, continuing the brainwashing until he broke, just to prove the efficacy of Jericho. Thinking of his work being used on men like Mousa compounded the anger Ethan felt at learning of Elijah's murder and Rachael's kidnapping.

An escape plan began to form in his head, one in which Mousa would play a role. He felt a kindred connection with the orthopedic surgeon. Getting out of the Monastery was only part of the problem. They would have to navigate their way through a foreign country without being caught by Wolfe's henchmen. He'd seen enough movies to be wary of the technological capabilities of the CIA. Public transportation would be out of the question. Since neither he nor Rachel spoke any Arabic, the Jordanian would be critical once they were on the road. He knocked on the door, swiped his card key in front of the sensor, and entered the room.

Mousa looked up and smiled as he closed the door behind him. "Hello, Doctor."

"Doctor." He returned the smile.

Mousa's smile then vanished. "Why are you still keeping me here?"

Right to the point, he thought.

Before he could reply, Mousa continued, "These priests are determined in their efforts to convert me."

Ethan pulled the wooden chair to the side of the bed and sat. "Why haven't you just gone along with them? Humored them?"

Mousa's voice grew stronger. "That would be the easy thing to do, yes? I'm happy to read their scripture and even speak their prayers. The Prophet himself had deep respect for the Christian and Jewish writings—but I cannot betray my faith, just as they cannot betray theirs."

"But if it would get you out of here sooner?"

"Do you know the origins of the mistrust of the Arab world for the West?"

"Our support for Israel over the Palestinians."

Mousa shook his head. "A modern example of a much older trend. You're familiar with the Crusades, I assume?"

"Around the twelfth century, weren't they? I know a lot of atrocities were committed in an attempt to take the Holy Land from Muslim control."

"For over two hundred years, Christian crusaders came from Western Europe and slaughtered Islamic civilians, including women and children, for their faith. In the West today, your press writes about the *Jihads,* or Holy Wars, that a small minority of our fundamentalist sects declare, but during the Crusades, your various popes called it 'just war,' and they promised the forgiveness of sins to any Christians who traveled East as part of the campaigns. They were free from guilt or blame for any murder, torture, rape, or pillaging. For those who died in the battles for Jerusalem, the popes promised that they would be taken up immediately to Heaven, with no stopover in Purgatory."

"The fundamentalists in your tradition today use the same techniques to motivate martyrs into their terrorist acts."

"Religion is about love, peace, compassion, and meaning, but humans use religion as a tool to justify intolerance, violence, and war."

"We kill each other over whose God is the more loving."

Mousa chuckled at this. "But is religion the problem, or is it that fallible human beings are interpreting the infinite divine through a limited lens of finite perception?"

Ethan glanced at his hands. "You remind me of my mentor."

"Just look at our own profession. Doctors work to cure illness and save lives. But doctors have also been the ones who've created biological weapons. Physicists strive to understand the meaning behind the universe, yet they created nuclear weapons. Science has given us the tools both to understand the universe and to destroy the world in a way that religion never could."

Ethan studied Mousa's dark eyes, which were alive with energy. Then he removed the stethoscope from around his neck. He leaned in toward the Jordanian and feigned listening to his heart. He suspected from the time he'd spent in the server room that all of the cells were under surveillance. He wasn't sure if it was just video or whether it included audio as well, so he dropped his voice to a whisper.

"Are you ready to return to your family?"

"Now?" The surgeon's voice broke and his eyes welled up.

"Tell me what you know about the Egyptian city of Aswan," Ethan whispered.

One of the many problems in the nascent plan he was working out was that he knew little about this country.

A confused expression passed over Mousa's face. Then he seemed to catch on and spoke in similar hushed tones. "A tourist destination for people who want to cruise the Nile. I've done it twice. Boats travel between Aswan and Luxor, which, aside from the pyramids of Giza, contain the most visited of Egypt's ancient sites. It's a few days' trip, depending on the number of stops you make."

A major tourist destination means lots of people, especially Westerners, Ethan thought. They would be able to blend in, maybe even find someone willing to help them. He moved the stethoscope from Mousa's chest to his back. "Breathe deeply," he said loudly. Then he lowered his voice again and began to explain everything he knew to Mousa.

CHAPTER 46

THE MONASTERY

Ethan swiped his key card and turned the knob to Rachel's door. His heart beat out a loud rhythm in his chest. When he entered and closed the door behind him, she lifted her head of disheveled hair from where she sat on the edge of her bed and looked at him with red, puffy eyes.

"Rachel"—he shuffled from foot to foot—"I swear I had no idea that—"

"I know," she said softly. "Chris came back a few minutes ago and explained everything again. I just can't believe I'm here. I mean, I'm just a grad student studying monkeys."

He took a step closer to the bed and hesitated. "I'm so sorry. I can't help but think that this is my fault. If it weren't for my research—"

She stood, rushed to him, and threw her arms around his neck. Her body pressed into his while she buried her face into his chest. When he wrapped his arms around her, she squeezed him tight. "Stop it," she said. "That Allen Wolfe guy who runs this place had his ideas long before you and Elijah made the Logos work."

He knew that she was right, but he felt an urge that seemed to originate in the deepest level of his cellular structure to protect her. If he hadn't gotten close to her, she wouldn't be here now. But he also knew that his desire to escape with her went deeper than a mere sense of responsibility.

"I'm going to get you out of here," he whispered in her ear.

"How?"

"I'm working on it."

They held each for several minutes before she stepped back and looked up into his face. "I bet your mind has been spinning from my revelation too." She managed a smile.

"Samuel Houston is your dad?"

She ran her fingers through her hair, combing the wide strands from her face. "I should have told you sooner, but I was afraid it might change the way you saw me."

"But you have different last names."

"After my parents' divorce, Mom changed back to her maiden name, Riley. When I started at Yale, I registered under that instead of Houston. I wanted to succeed on my own merits, not because I was a senior faculty member's daughter."

He felt a twinge of discomfort at her keeping this information from him, but then he understood it too. He reported to Houston, and he probably would have distanced himself from her had he known about their relationship.

"But you followed in his footsteps?"

"Crazy, isn't it? If it weren't for CapLab, I would have gone somewhere else. But the strange thing is that we've gotten closer the last few years. I began to understand that behind his walled-off, controlling exterior lies the heart of a moral, good man dedicated to educating young people."

When Ethan thought back to his conversation with Houston, he recalled the rare warm tone the administrator had used when he'd mentioned her. "I think in his own way, he loves you deeply."

"He, like some other people I know"—she took his hand—"struggles to show how he truly feels. I tried to talk you up around him, though."

She spun around, dragged the chair from the table over to the bed, and plopped down on top of the covers, crossing her legs underneath her. When he sat in the chair, he noticed a small tattoo just above her delicate ankle. He was used to seeing her in boots, but now her feet were bare, and with her sweatpants pulled over her toned calves he could see what looked like the number three written in calligraphy.

"It's *Om*," she said. He felt his face redden at being caught checking out her legs, and he cut his eyes back to her face. She was smiling. "The Sanskrit symbol for the universal divine that is the ultimate reality beyond all existence."

Ultimate reality, he thought. His mind flickered to his core motivation for his research—a longing to understand. He pushed the thought away.

"I can barely touch my toes," he joked. "Not sure I could make it through a yoga class chanting an ancient Indian syllable."

She leaned toward him, placed her hands on his knees, and peered into his eyes. "I'm not buying the whole Mister Science act. You dedicated your career to studying and reproducing mystical experiences. I can't believe that you chose this path only because your mom dragged you to her fundamentalist church after your father died."

Her directness unsettled him. He considered deflecting the question, as he'd done many times in the past, but the expression on her face told him that she would know if he was holding back the truth. *Why did I join Elijah? Why did I become a doctor and a neurologist?* The memory from his youth that he'd never discussed with anyone but Natalie flashed into his consciousness: an experience that he could explain scientifically but had never understood in his heart. He gazed into Rachel's eyes and realized that for the first time in years, in spite of the frightening conditions they were under at Wolfe's secret facility, he felt safe.

"I was thirteen, and it was the day after my birthday," he began. "My doctor thought that my frequent headaches were just migraines. Later I learned that epilepsy is often misdiagnosed as migraines."

"You have epilepsy? Like your patients?"

"My best friend, Charlie, and I were jumping on the trampoline I'd gotten for my birthday. We took turns shooting each other with water guns as we bounced and then pretended to die dramatically. But one time I tried to shoot Charlie my hand froze. I couldn't pull the trigger. The next thing I knew I was lying on the damp grass. I don't remember falling, and I didn't feel any pain. Charlie was saying something, but I couldn't make out the words, like he was calling to me from a distance." He fidgeted with his hands. "Did you ever play the cloud game?"

"Yeah, my friends and I would try to spot bunnies, cats, and dogs in the sky."

"Charlie and I did too, but we searched for characters from *Lord of the Rings*: elves, hobbits, dwarves, and especially Gollum. But that day the clouds transfixed me in a weird way. I saw geometrical shapes. It was as if the clouds were revealing a secret substructure that wasn't normally visible to the naked eye. The longer I stared, the deeper the substructure seemed to go."

"You experienced a hidden vision of reality?"

He nodded. "Suddenly, Charlie's head came into view, blocking the clouds. He looked concerned, but I was focused only on the lines that connected his pupils to each other. Then another axis appeared to run from his forehead to his chin. I squinted, and his face disappeared into a superstructure of intersecting and connected vectors. Just as I'd seen a veiled structure behind the clouds moments before, I now saw the structure behind Charlie."

"So this geometry that made up your friend was part of the same geometry that made up the clouds?"

"But there was more. I couldn't help but wonder: was I part of the same structure? As I had that thought, my body began to tremble, and I fell unconscious."

"Your seizure became a grand mal?"

"I woke up in the ambulance with my parents cramped into the space beside my stretcher. Dad was really worried, and Mom cried as she held my hand. I remember trying to sit, but the straps across my chest held me down. After several days of tests, my doctors prescribed me Topiramate to prevent future seizures and to alleviate my headaches. I've taken it for the past twenty years."

She peered even deeper into his eyes. "Your education has been driven by a desire to understand neurologically what happened that day."

"Now I know. My seizure began in the left temporal lobe of my brain, where it fired neurons that sparked my vision, just like the cases of those who experience hyperreligiosity."

"Like your patient Liz you told me about? But your vision was so different."

He shrugged. "Maybe because my brain was wired for a scientific worldview—beginning at age ten I was addicted to *Discover Magazine* and science fiction—I saw geometric patterns rather than angels or Jesus."

He'd dedicated his career to understanding mystical experiences because, even after the years he'd spent studying, researching, experimenting—even after receiving an MD and a PhD—he still hadn't explained the singular conviction that had come from his core that day by the trampoline: *His vision of a structure underlying all of reality was real. A structure some ancient Greeks and early Christians had called the Logos.*

"Have you had other visions since then?"

"No, that was the only time." He examined his hands, turning them over in his lap. He felt his chest tighten.

"What aren't you telling me?" Her voice was compassionate yet firm.

Did he dare? He'd already just shared one of his most intimate secrets. Could he risk another—one more painful? For a reason he couldn't articulate, he trusted this woman he'd only known a short time. As much as he resisted the attraction, he was drawn to her. As he'd grown to know her better, the innate awkwardness he usually experienced with women had faded. He hadn't felt connected in that way to someone since . . . Natalie.

"I had one other epileptic event. It was brief, and I didn't have any visions." He swallowed the lump in his throat. "I hadn't taken my meds in a few weeks. I'd been happy and relaxed and hadn't had a headache in months. I'd become complacent."

She folded her hands in her lap and waited for him to continue.

"It was the night Natalie died"—he swallowed again—"when I was driving."

"A drunk driver hit you, right?" Her voice was soft.

"We were talking about something—I wish I could remember what—and she was laughing. Then I smelled something burning. We were in her car. I asked if she'd changed her oil recently. Those were the last words I ever said to her." He twisted his fingers into a knot. "I don't know whether or not she answered because my attention was drawn to a distant pair of lights that reflected off the raindrops on the windshield in a starburst pattern. As the lights got closer they multiplied, doubling every second until they almost eclipsed my field of vision." The knot with his fingers cinched tighter. "Natalie's scream must have shocked me out of the initial stages of the SPS, my simple partial seizure. The drunk's car was in our lane. I jerked the wheel, but it was too late."

Tears flowed from Rachel's eyes. She uncrossed her legs, scooted to the edge of the bed, and rested her hands on top of his.

"You hadn't had a seizure in almost two decades. You had no way of knowing it could happen that night."

"I'm a doctor. I knew better than to stop my Topiramate. My arrogance killed her."

"Ethan, you didn't kill Natalie. The drunk driver did."

"I wish I could convince myself of that." He felt his eyes well up. He wiped them on his shoulder. "Sorry, I didn't mean to get all emotional on you. I've only told this story once before—to Elijah."

"It's okay to feel the pain."

"I know it's the natural response of my amygdala—"

"Hey, Professor"—her voice rose—"enough of your biology lessons. You're using your intellect to deny the real feelings you've suppressed. You can lock up these memories in a box in your mind, but they'll always be there, festering, haunting you. At times when you think all is right, the cry of hurt will remind you that it isn't."

"I don't know how else to handle it."

"Why not allow the pain to be present? Feel it. Your love for Natalie and the tragedy of her death are part of who you are. Pain means that you're still alive. But pain doesn't have to define you either." She uncurled the knot that he'd made with his hands and interlaced her fingers in his. "I think that's the real purpose of your research. There exists something deeper within each of us, beyond our intellects and past our emotions, a true essence that we can experience as connection, as peace, and as love."

Her words resonated within him. He had avoided pain his whole life. He'd used his mind to seal away the hurt by defining his feelings in terms of biology and immersing himself in his work. But he'd never truly escaped his emotions. He looked into her eyes, which were moist with compassion, and he felt the vault around his heart unlock.

She stood, pulled him to his feet, and hugged him. Her body seemed to radiate an electricity that enlivened his very core. After a minute, she rose on her toes and kissed him on the cheek. "Thank you for sharing that."

As she started to lower, his hands seemed to move as if they had their own mind, sliding from her waist to the nape of her neck. This time the cautionary voice in his head was silent. He drew her face to his. Their lips brushed gently at first, but soon grew more urgent. The forcefulness of their kiss bordered between pleasure and pain, as if it might be the last one of their lives. With what he was planning, he thought, it just might be. At that moment, however, he only wanted to lose himself in her, feel her body melding into his, but the sound of the door opening caused both of them to jump backward.

CHAPTER 47

THE MONASTERY

"**H**ey, you two." Chris grinned at them as if he were a parent catching teenagers making out in the basement. He closed the door behind him, glanced upward at a smoke detector in the corner of the ceiling, and then positioned his back to it.

"Video?" Ethan guessed.

Chris nodded. "But no audio."

"What do you want?" Rachel asked.

"Look, I can't explain how horrible I feel about your harrowing experience, and"—he looked Ethan in the eyes—"how I betrayed your confidence. When I joined the Agency, I did it to protect Americans. My uncle didn't die in 9/11 so that I could bring harm to the people I care about, to those who've mentored me and taught me. I had no idea when I got sucked into this that Wolfe would go as far as he has."

"In Wolfe's mind, the future of Jericho is more important than the lives of a couple of scientists," Ethan said. "He'll justify disposing of us as sacrificing a few to save the many, just as he did with Elijah."

Chris cast his eyes to the floor. "I see that clearly now—which is why I'm going to get you guys out of here."

"How?" Rachel asked.

"I haven't figured that out yet."

Ethan heard the sincerity in his voice. "I've had a good look at the backbone of the electronics that run this place. I have an idea that will disable the monitoring systems while providing enough of a distraction to allow us to escape in the confusion." He pointed to the cardkey in Chris's hand. "We'll need help getting out of the building, as well as taking one of the cars."

"When?" Chris asked.

"We go tonight, before Wolfe returns." He outlined his plan in detail.

Chris shook his head. "It's crazy enough that it just might work."

Ethan turned to Rachel. "But we need an excuse to get you out of this room and into the chapel."

"That's easy," Chris said. "Wolfe thought her knowledge about the monkeys might help you fix the problem with the Logos—that's why she's here. All we have to do is pretend we need her assistance."

"You don't need to pretend," she said. The lines of worry that had been etched in her brow disappeared, and the spark Ethan was used to seeing radiated again from her eyes. "I know what's different about Anakin."

"You do?" He felt his heart rate accelerate. As dire as their situation was, the flaw in the Logos still ate at him.

She shuddered. "It came to me when I tried to escape that Axe guy who attacked me." She turned to Chris. "When you stopped by earlier, you said that two men out of twenty had negative reactions?"

"That's right."

"Can we see them?"

Chris removed a set of black robes from a hook on the door. "It's not exactly your tie-dye scrubs." A sly grin crept across his face. "You'll be Sister Rachel."

"Never imagined I'd hear those words," she said as she shrugged on the robes and covered her head with the habit. Then she walked over to the table by her bed and selected a red apple from a plate that also held grapes and figs. "Let's do it."

Ethan restrained himself from blurting out the questions that flew through his head. His detailed examinations of the men had revealed nothing that would explain why the Logos would affect them negatively. He recalled Elijah predicting that people would experience "the ultimate," as he called it, in different ways. Maybe the minds of the two men simply couldn't handle being exposed to something greater than their own limited realities. Maybe they interpreted the resulting ego dissolution that mystics found unifying and blissful as a terrifying loss of existence. But had Rachel discovered an anomaly that he'd missed? His curiosity ached to know.

When Chris led them down the cloistered hallway in silence, Ethan glanced at the faux-stained glass windows along the left wall opposite the doors to the monks' rooms. He immediately recognized the scene of a man lying on the desert sand beside his horse while the translucent figure of Jesus spoke to him from the sky. Less than two weeks previously, but half a world away, he'd shown Caravaggio's painting of this scene of the conversion of the Apostle Paul on the road to Damascus to his class—a class that included Rachel. Paul wrote cryptically about a physical ailment that plagued him, "a thorn of the flesh," as he referred to it. Could this ailment have been temporal lobe epilepsy, as some suggested—a neurological condition that led to his hyperreligiosity? Paul's vision altered his life and ultimately changed the religious landscape of the world. Seeing the stained glass, Ethan couldn't shake the realization that his own vision, though he knew the biological source of it, had done the same to him.

Chris stopped by the door of the monk who had been ranting about seeing the devil. "He's been sedated heavily, but he's awake."

When they gathered at the foot of his bed, the Arab's eyes fluttered open and wandered between them with a blurry expression. His fingers tapped lightly on the bed cover, but he was calm and silent. Ethan noted that his restraints had been removed. Rachel held the apple up in the air. The man's eyes followed the only color in the drab room. She tossed it to him.

The Arab caught the apple in his left hand.

Ethan looked from the man to Rachel. *What am I missing?*

"Anakin," she said, "is left-handed."

"Huh?"

"Like humans, capuchins and other primates show characteristics of handedness."

"How can you tell?"

"The way they dangle from a branch or feed themselves—they'll do it with their dominant hands. Of all of my capuchins, Anakin is the only one who is left-handed. He was also the only one to react negatively to having his temporal lobes stimulated by your machine."

Ethan's mind spun through the implications. "I can't believe I missed this."

"So being left-handed could make a difference with the way the Logos works?"

"Professor," Chris asked, "could it have something to do with the way the two brain hemispheres interact?"

He stared at his student. *He still thinks of me as his professor.*

"You're absolutely right. I just can't believe I overlooked it." He shook his head. He'd made the classic research mistake of seeing the world through a specific limited view—his own. He was right-handed, as were his initial subjects, and he'd neglected to account for the brain differences that occurred in the 8 to 10 percent of the population who were left-handed or ambidextrous.

He glanced at the Arab taking slow bites from the apple as if he were alone in the room. Ethan knew he spoke no English. "I programmed the Logos to stimulate the left temporal lobe, the dominant side of the brain in right-handed individuals, at more intense frequencies. I theorized, based on Liz's EEG and on the brain scans Elijah and I did on the monks and nuns, that the difference in the signals between the two temporal lobes of the brain created the feelings of spaciousness and the sense of otherworldliness that mystics describe. One half of the brain sensed something different than the other half." He grimaced. "I made the assumption that the relationships between the left and right temporal lobes would be similar for our future test subjects."

"But," Chris said, "in left-handed people, the left and right brain hemispheres often have reversed subspecialties."

"The overstimulation of the non-dominant hemisphere in these other subjects must have caused their feelings of panic, claustrophobia, and loss of control. In a religious setting, especially with someone preconditioned to see evil in a personalized form, they interpreted these feelings as being influenced by devils rather than God."

He turned to Rachel. "I should have taken your and Elijah's concerns more seriously. If only—"

She put her hand on his arm. "There will always be *ifs*. All that's important is what we do now. Anyway, I don't think anything you could have done would have changed Wolfe's actions here."

"She's right," Chris said.

The sight of the two students looking up at him opened a void of sadness in Ethan's heart. He missed Elijah. Not just for his brilliant mind, but for his counsel and his friendship. But now he was the one in charge. He wasn't at all sure about his plan. Too many contingencies could go wrong. But he knew two things with certainty: he had to stop the madness that was Project Jericho, and he refused to let anything happen to Rachel.

PART III

"Then a great and powerful wind tore the mountains apart and shattered the rocks . . .
but the Lord was not in the wind. After the wind there was an earthquake,
but the Lord was not in the earthquake. After the earthquake came a fire,
but the Lord was not in the fire. And after the fire came a gentle whisper.
When Elijah heard the whisper, he pulled his cloak over his face."

1 Kings 19:11-13

CHAPTER 48

THE MONASTERY

Ethan wiped the sweat from his eyes. Unlike the computer server room directly over his head, the utility room on the monastery level where he knelt had no air-conditioning. He'd discovered this room yesterday when inspecting the cable connections from the Logos server in the computer room that led to the machine in the chapel. He looked up. A gray conduit disappeared into the ceiling and the server room above it. He traced the conduit across the ceiling, down the far wall, and into the floor—where it ran into the chapel and then into the cathedra. Other than the conduit, the room contained two humming HVAC units that served the chapel and the dining hall. His attention, however, was focused on another piece of equipment.

He opened the tool bag he'd borrowed from one of Wolfe's goons. The tools were necessary, he'd explained, for the repairs to the Logos. Fortunately the guards had no idea whether the problems with the machine were mechanical or software-related. The one positive of his role here in the Monastery, he thought, was his access to off-limits areas.

The water heater was much larger than what he had in his New Haven apartment. This commercial model held one hundred and twenty gallons. It had been over a decade since he'd spent two of his undergraduate summers working for a local remodeling contractor to help pay his tuition. On one job where he'd helped to replace an old water heater, the foreman had regaled him with a tale of incredible destruction he'd seen years earlier when a heater had failed catastrophically. Ethan didn't buy the story until years later, when one of his favorite Discovery Channel shows confirmed the possibility of truth behind the foreman's urban myth. He hoped he remembered how the heater worked.

He selected wire cutters, pliers, and a Phillips-head screwdriver from the tool bag. His two concerns fell on opposite ends of the spectrum. On the one hand, what he was attempting might not work, and then they'd be stuck in the Monastery. On the other, it might work too well and kill him and the others he was trying to save.

He glanced at his watch and pushed both concerns from his mind. *Nine thirty.* The modifications should take no more than fifteen or twenty minutes. Chris would bring Rachel and Mousa to the chapel at ten. The other problem with his plan, though, was that its timing was unpredictable.

Ethan unscrewed the metal plate from the side of the water heater. Inside was the electronic thermostat that controlled the temperature in the heater, which was set for one hundred and ten degrees. He unscrewed the thermostat and followed the path of the wires leading from it. He stood and hit the electrical breaker on the wall that supplied power to the heater.

Checking that the LED light on the thermostat was no longer lit, he used the wire cutters to clip the black and red wires that led from the thermostat to the heating element of the tank. Once he'd disconnected the thermostat, he stripped the plastic coating from around the copper on the wires. He then twisted the wires together with the pliers. Now power would be fed to the tank's heating element continuously, regardless of the temperature of the water. He put the defunct thermostat into the cavity of the water heater and replaced the metal plate. On the off chance that one of the guards inspected the utility room in the next half an hour, he would find everything in place.

The thought of a guard doing an inspection sent a shiver down Ethan's spine that overrode the heat of the room. He glanced at the closed door. While he could explain his presence in the room—the wiring from the Logos ran through there—he couldn't explain why he was working on the heater. He had to move faster.

With the water heater wired to overheat, he turned his attention to the small pipe at the base of the heater. The pipe led to a floor drain. Between the pipe and the heater was a valve known as a TPR—a temperature-pressure relief valve. If the thermostat failed, the valve was designed to open and release the pressurized, overheated water.

He removed the soldering iron from the tool bag and began to disable the heater's secondary safety backup. Once he finished, he flipped the circuit breakers. The water heater began to vibrate subtly. It was heating again. He packed up his tools, hit the light switch, and left the room. He turned down the corridor toward the chapel, his rendezvous site with his friends.

"Working late, Professor?"

He jumped at the voice behind him. After inhaling sharply, he turned to face James Axelrod.

His mind raced. He'd thought through being discovered in the utility closet, and he'd rehearsed his explanation so it would sound natural. But with the hulking man dressed in the black robes of a priest glaring at him, the practiced justification vanished from his head and was replaced by a mixture of fear and rage at the man who had killed Elijah and kidnapped Rachel. He struggled to keep his face neutral.

"Um, I . . ."

"You're sweating." Axe moved closer, invading his personal space. "Do I make you nervous?"

"Of course not." He held up the bag of tools. "I was just double-checking the connections to the Logos."

Axe cut his gaze to the utility room door. His jaundiced eyes were blood-shot, as if he hadn't slept in days.

"I think I have the problem figured out," Ethan added, hoping to distract the spook from investigating the room. "I'm going to run some tests now."

He walked away from the utility room toward the end of the hall where the closed doors to the chapel beckoned him. "Director Wolfe is adamant that I have it working when he returns."

"The machine is working?" Axe's bloodshot eyes danced between him and the end of the corridor. Ethan thought he detected a note of apprehension in the man's voice.

"I'm making progress."

"Why was it broken?"

He hesitated. He had no plans to fix the Logos. Indeed, in a few minutes it would be destroyed and they would escape. Telling the truth, he decided, would come across as more genuine.

"The machine was tuned only for right-handed people. In left-handed individuals, like the two subjects who had psychotic breaks, the wiring of the temporal lobes is often different. I overlooked this when I was programming the Logos. All I had to do was design a separate protocol for left-handed people."

Axe's eyebrows peaked. "What about subjects who are ambidextrous?"

An insightful question, he thought, surprised. "Most ambidextrous people have left-handed brains. So yes, I would use the alternative programming on them as well."

"I'll watch your tests."

A pit formed in Ethan's stomach. "Maybe next time. Let me do some preliminary runs, and then I'll get you when I know it's working right."

He continued walking toward the chapel.

Heavy footsteps fell beside him. Axe walked so close he could feel the heat from his body.

"I'll watch now."

Ethan wiped his palms on his lab coat. The last thing he needed was Wolfe's chief of security hanging around during their escape attempt. He paused at the doors to the chapel.

"Actually, I could use your—"

Before he could get the word *help* out of his mouth, Axe brushed past him and flung open the doors. Rachel, Chris, and Mousa looked up at the abrupt entrance. Their eyes widened at the sight of the broad-shouldered man striding toward them.

"What's going on here?" Axe directed the question at Chris, who, like Axe, was dressed in his priest's robes and collar.

"I asked—" Ethan began, but stopped when Axe raised his hand.

Axe's eyes bored into the young grad student.

"Oh, hey, Father James," Chris answered in a casual tone. "Dr. Lightman asked to observe one of my prayer sessions with Brother Mousa this evening."

He motioned to Mousa, who stood next to the cathedra, dressed in his brown cassock. "I explained to our Brother that we are considering bringing nuns into the monastery to help with our work"—he nodded to Rachel—"and that Sister Rachel just arrived from the States to inspect our chapel."

He's smooth, Ethan thought. Then he caught sight of the expression on Rachel's face. She looked as if she might be sick. He imagined what the stress of seeing Axe was doing to her body. Her endocrine system had probably jumped into overdrive from the trigger of confronting her kidnapper. Then he chastised himself for the clinical direction of his mind, and he met her eyes. Although it was hard to tell in the dim light of the chapel, he thought her pupils were dilated more than normal. Her breath came in short, rapid bursts. He nodded imperceptibly. *You can do this*, he willed to her. She was strong, he knew. It was one of the qualities he admired most in her. Her eyes locked onto his and after a moment her shoulders dropped. She seemed to relax.

"Thank you, Father Christopher," Axe said. "Feel free to continue your services. Please don't let us intrude."

Chris led Mousa and Rachel to the altar, where he handed each of them long candles that they used to light the votives lining the stone table.

Axe lowered his voice so that Ethan had to lean in close to hear him. "What is she doing here?"

Ethan had to repress the urge to punch the man in the gut when he saw his eyes track Rachel's body as she bent over to light the candles. He matched the conspiratorial whisper. "She helped me figure out how to reprogram the Logos. I need her to observe the session with Mousa. But now that you're here"—he glanced at the three figures who were kneeling at the altar—"I could use your help."

"How?"

"There is always a possibility of an adverse reaction."

"Like the other guys who went crazy."

"A psychotic break from reality is a risk, as is a seizure." He opened the tool bag and removed the LCD remote that controlled the Logos. "I've programmed a switch here where I can toggle between settings for right-handed and left-handed individuals. I wanted to test a right-handed subject like

Mousa first to make sure that my new programming didn't corrupt the original settings. Then we'll try it on a left-handed subject." He leaned closer. Having to feign camaraderie with the man took every bit of his willpower. "Can you go upstairs to the medical supply room and bring me a syringe and a vial of Ativan?"

"To sedate the Arab if he has a bad reaction?"

"Exactly."

Axe looked toward the others and then back to him as if considering whether they could be trusted with only Chris. "I'll be right back."

Ethan exhaled when Axe left the chapel, and then he checked his watch. Twenty minutes had passed since he'd rigged the water heater. The anticipation of what would happen in the next few minutes made him feel nervous but alive at the same time.

He glanced at his watch again. Twenty-one minutes. Time was moving too slowly.

Axe swiped his card in front of the card reader by the elevator. As he waited, he squeezed and then released his calves. He usually started with his calves and then moved up his body, enjoying the feeling as the blood poured into his muscles. The scarring that covered his legs was a shame. His calves were the size of most large men's biceps. Though not as pleasurable as the pump he received when lifting, the feeling this exercise gave him would sustain him until he could hit the gym again in the morning, especially since he hadn't slept at all last night. After testing the machine on himself, he'd been afraid to close his eyes for too long. The silence, the abyss that had formed in his heart, beckoned to him as he lay in bed. A more terrifying suspicion had come to him in the darkness. Somewhere deep in the abyss waited a presence—a presence that made the nightmares of his youth seem like fairy tales. If he fell asleep, the abyss might pull him down into the horror.

How could he be afraid? His mere appearance instilled fear in others. He'd seen how the professor had started sweating the moment he'd walked up to him. But maybe the professor had the key to the answers he sought. Hearing that the machine needed to be programmed differently for ambidextrous people had sent a shot of adrenaline through him as powerful as a dose of testosterone cypionate. His ambidexterity had, until yesterday, always been a tactical advantage. He could shoot with either hand and take down a target with equal strength in both arms.

Once the professor confirmed the machine was fixed, he would try it on himself again. This time it had to work.

The elevator door opened, and he stepped inside. He thought about the professor and the girl whose naked body still burned in his mind. Again, Wolfe was right. They'd both been useful. But soon they would have served their purpose. Once the machine worked flawlessly, both would be terminated to protect the security of the operation. He would offer to carry out that assignment. The professor's death would be quick, but he would take his time with the girl.

CHAPTER 49

THE MONASTERY

Ethan glanced at his watch for what must be the tenth time in as many minutes. Axe would return soon. *What's taking so long with the water heater?* Had he missed something?

"The Suburbans are parked to the right of the entrance," Chris said.

Ethan looked up. "You're sure your key card can get us up the fire steps when the server room is taken out? Even if we lose power?"

"The card readers have lithium battery backups." Chris pointed to a green duffel bag on the floor behind the cathedra. "I have black cassocks in here for you two." He nodded to Mousa, who sat in the throne, and to Rachel, who kneeled beside it. "As soon as we go, throw those over your clothes and keep your heads down. I'm hoping that in the chaos no one will focus on your faces. Stay close behind me."

"How will we find our way to Luxor?" Rachel asked.

"I programmed the GPS in the second Suburban to take you there, but you'll travel into the desert first and stay on dirt roads for about thirty miles before you rejoin the main highway."

"What then?" Ethan asked.

"Last year," Mousa said, "I stayed at a large tourist hotel on the river—the Steigenberger Nile Palace. We can blend in there until we figure out how to get out of the country."

"I'll call in the morning and let them know to expect you," Chris said.

"Wait," Ethan said. "You're not coming with us?"

"If I'm missing, it'll be obvious I helped you escape. Plus, if I stay behind, I can misdirect any attempt to go after you."

"But if they suspect you—" Rachel began.

"Look, it's my fault you're here. I owe you this."

The door to the chapel banged open.

Chris, Mousa, and Rachel immediately bowed their heads and began to pray together. Ethan turned toward Axe, who strode into the room, his hands clasped behind him. Ethan motioned to him from behind the throne. They had prepared for the worst-case scenario—Axe returning before the explosion. Chris, Mousa, and Rachel appeared as if they were engaged in their worship practice, while he remained in position to start the machine. He held up the remote so that Axe could see it. Heat rose up the back of his neck, and he tried to control his breathing so he wouldn't appear as nervous he was. Their lives depended on him now. Seeing the outline of the man's physique straining the seams of his robes caused the heat to spread to Ethan's face. The problem with the sympathetic nervous system that was causing his blood vessels to dilate, he thought, was that it was automatic. But then, if there was ever a time for his fight-or-flight response to be activated, this was it. Unlike the night in the library, on this evening he would fight.

Axe rounded the cathedra and stopped next to him. From behind his back he produced a syringe and a small, clear vial. After handing them over, he moved to the side of the cathedra opposite Chris, bowed his head, and watched Ethan out of the corner of his eye while his lips moved in prayer.

Ethan pocketed the drug and then turned the remote over in his sweaty palm. He clicked on the green triangle. He felt the subtle vibration of the Logos through the floor. Mousa relaxed into the throne, his facial muscles softening. Axe stopped his pretense of praying and leaned forward expectantly.

I hope his acting is convincing, Ethan thought. As a doctor, Mousa would know the symptoms. The question was whether he could realistically reproduce them.

As if on cue, the left side of Mousa's face twitched. Then his hands opened and closed twice in succession. The doctor's legs began to tremble.

"Oh, no," Ethan said. He clicked off the Logos.

Mousa began a feigned myotonic seizure. His whole body straightened as if a current of electricity had shot through him. He slid from the throne to the floor. When he hit the cold tile, his limbs began to convulse. Rachel screamed and jumped backward.

"Grab him!" Ethan shouted, reaching into his pocket.

Chris and Axe dropped to their knees on either side of Mousa, but they had difficulty restraining his arms and legs, which jerked violently.

Ethan flicked off the plastic cap from the twenty-one-gauge needle and slid it into the top of the vial of the lorazepam, the generic name for the sedative Ativan. The usual dose for an intramuscular injection in the case of a patient experiencing a seizure was four milligrams, but Axe was a huge man, and he needed to incapacitate him. He didn't, however, want to overdose and kill him. He took his oath to preserve life seriously. He decided on six milligrams.

"Come on!" he yelled at the two men struggling to control the convulsing Mousa. "I need him steady!" He bent over and raised the syringe. He would have only one chance.

"Got him," Axe grunted. He had Mousa's left side pinned to the ground. Chris struggled more with his right. "Do it now!"

Ethan brought the needle down in a swift, continuous motion. It pierced the black robe and sunk into Axe's right deltoid. Ethan's thumb plunged the drug into his shoulder. Axe jerked his head toward him, a look of confusion on his face. Then his eyes focused on the needle pulling out of his arm. A roar escaped his lips.

He released Mousa, jumped to his feet, and swung an arm at Ethan. Axe moved faster than he expected for someone so large. He just avoided the reach of his paw-like hand by leaning backward. Axe lunged toward him, but he failed to notice Mousa going for his legs. The Jordanian tackled him, knocking him to the floor. Chris then leaped on top of them.

"Goddamn it!" Axe screamed as he thrashed beneath the men.

Ethan tossed the used syringe into the far corner and rushed toward Rachel. She grabbed his arm and pulled him close. He put his body between hers and the writhing mass on the floor. *The drug should have taken effect by now,* he thought. Had he misjudged the dose on such a muscular man? The adrenaline surge from the attack must be slowing its effect.

Axe was somehow gaining the upper hand in the wrestling match. He rolled to his side, twisted Chris's arm in a lock, and bent his wrist backward, eliciting a howl from the grad student. Then he head-butted Chris and rolled him away. He next grabbed Mousa, who still held his legs like a football player making a tackle, and tossed the surgeon to the side like a sack of fertilizer. He stood and faced Ethan.

Although Ethan was taller, Axe outweighed him by at least seventy pounds. *He can probably kill me with his bare hands.* The thought occurred with almost clinical detachment. He tensed his body, preparing for the attack he knew would come. He tried to deepen his breathing, but the air was caught in his throat, his lungs frozen. Rachel's grip on his arm threatened to cut off his circulation.

Chris and Mousa shook off the effects of being tossed aside and rose to wobbly feet. Axe ignored them. The fury in his eyes focused on Ethan.

If I can just keep him away from Rachel—

Axe lunged toward him. But the expected impact from the large man didn't happen. The chapel floor seemed to shift underneath them. Then a concussion of heat lifted them up off of their feet.

CHAPTER 50

THE MONASTERY

"**P**rofessor, can you hear me?"

Ethan felt a hand touch his shoulder. He opened his eyes to a pounding headache. Chris hovered above him. The student's hair was dripping wet. He touched his own shirt. He was soaking as well. He inhaled to clear his head. The air was heavy with moisture.

The water heater!

"It finally blew," Rachel said.

He pushed himself to a sitting position on the damp floor. "You okay?"

"That was more intense than I expected."

He glanced around the room. Halogen emergency lights over the exit cast spears of light across the floor where the heavy double doors lay—they'd been blown off their hinges by the explosion. A quiet had descended through the Monastery as well—no hum of HVAC units, no distant chanting of monks pumped through hidden speakers. The building had lost power.

Ignoring the throbbing behind his temples, Ethan stood and approached Axe, who lay motionless a few feet from him. He felt for a pulse on his carotid artery. Strong but slowed. Then the body below him stirred. The eyes remained closed.

"We have to get out of here," he said.

"The robes." Mousa sat by the throne, rubbing his temples.

Chris hurried behind the cathedra and produced the duffel bag. After they pulled on their black cassocks, they ran to the opening where the doors to the chapel used to hang. Another set of emergency lights shone through the heavy air that hung in the hallway like a mountain fog. The floor was littered with debris.

"Wow," Rachel said.

"Come on." Chris started down the corridor. "I don't know how long until they get their act together."

They raced down the hallway toward the emergency fire staircase, located at the opposite end. They passed the doors to the empty dining hall. One door lay inside the hall on the ground, while the other dangled from a single hinge. Just before they rounded the corner, they slowed to step around the door to the utility room, which now lay on the floor. They peered into the room.

"Praise Allah," Mousa muttered under his breath.

"I can't believe it." Rachel wiped the moisture from her eyes as she craned her head upward.

"It actually worked," Chris said.

Ethan stepped into the opening. The tank hadn't simply exploded like a bomb. With its electronic thermostat disabled, the heating element had heated the water past its safety cutoff, and since the pressure relief valve could no longer open, the pressure inside the tank had built as the temperature rose. The normal boiling point of water was two hundred and twelve degrees Fahrenheit, or one hundred Celsius, but those numbers assumed that the water was at sea level. The higher the pressure of the water, the higher the temperature it took to turn it into steam. Just what had happened to a number of unlucky homeowners across the US when their water heaters failed had happened here: the pressure building inside the tank hadn't affected the steel structure uniformly. The weakest link was the weld that joined the bottom of the tank to the sides. When the weld failed, the bottom blew off. As the pent-up pressure was released, the superheated water had instantly turned into steam, converting the one-hundred-and-twenty-gallon tank into a rocket.

Ethan gazed upward through the shredded drywall and the broken wood and steel supports that had formed the floor system. Beyond a tangled mass of wires that twisted through the empty space like red and black spaghetti, he saw stars. The water heater had blown through two stories and out the building's metal roof. He realized with satisfaction that the wires dangling above his head belonged to the server room that stored the security equipment and the brains of the Logos machines. The room was destroyed.

"We've got to keep moving," Chris called.

"What about the other monks?" Mousa asked.

"Their best chance is for you to get out of here safely."

Ethan felt Rachel at his side, but his attention was still transfixed by the sight above him. She took his hand and interlaced her fingers in his. He turned to her and met her eyes. She nodded, and they ran down the hall.

———————————

The desire to sleep was overwhelming. Axe wanted nothing more than to drift off into the warm comfort of unconsciousness. His senses felt dulled, like he was suspended in an endless ocean. The voices and footsteps had faded into the distance. He was alone.

Fighting the impulse to sleep, he blinked. His mind scrambled to piece together what had happened. With the effort required to push out the last rep of a final set, he rose to a seated position and surveyed the room.

An explosion.

The events began to return to him, as did the realization that the professor, the Arab, and the girl were attempting to escape. Angering him even more was the thought of Christian Sligh, one of Wolfe's favored operatives: *a traitor.* The professor had stuck him with the Ativan. That explained the vertigo causing the room to spin. Fortunately, he'd juiced earlier that day. His pulse and blood pressure were both running higher than normal.

He grabbed the leg of the cathedra and hoisted himself to his feet. He kept a hand on the chair as he waited for the room to stop spinning.

He would snap the professor's neck first. Then he would take great pleasure in killing the others one by one, especially the traitor Chris. He'd never liked the student; he thought he was so smart. Wolfe hadn't appreciated the dangers of sending someone undercover, especially someone of Sligh's young age and limited experience. The temptation to be seduced by those one was spying on was too great for most, and the longer one was embedded, the greater the chances of becoming loyal to the subjects over the mission itself.

He lurched toward the opening of the chapel, focusing his attention on his unsteady feet.

"Keep your heads down," Chris said as he reached for the doorknob at the top of the emergency staircase. "We're turning left. Don't look behind you. The heater blasted through the floor about forty feet back. The guards' quarters are at the end of the hall past there. They'll be spilling out, trying to figure out what happened. We'll go through two doors. The first leads to the reception room; the second leads outside. Nick Dawkins is on guard tonight." He reached under his robe and produced a semi-automatic pistol.

"Chris," Ethan said, surprised at the sight of his student handling a firearm with such ease, "I don't want you to use that unless you have to."

"Look, these guys play for keeps." He pulled the slide on the top of the gun backward, chambering a bullet from the gun's magazine, and then released it with a metallic clunk and replaced the gun under his robes. "But I don't want to shoot anyone either."

"How do we get past this Nick guy?" Rachel asked.

"I'll handle him. Just keep your faces averted," Chris replied. "Once outside, turn right and take the second SUV—that's the one whose GPS I programmed to take you to Luxor."

"And you?" Ethan asked. "Axe knows you're helping us now. You can't stay behind."

"I'll drive the first car into Aswan. That's where they'll expect you to go to catch the first plane or train in the morning. I'll try to lead them off your trail."

"If they find you?"

"I'll ditch the car on a side road and hide out until daylight. I know the town well. Then I'll hire a taxi to drive me to Luxor and I'll meet up with you there."

"How long's our drive?" Rachel asked.

"With your desert detour, about a hundred and forty miles. It'll be rough going at first, but you'll reach Luxor by morning. Get to the hotel and stay there until I arrive in the afternoon. Then we'll figure out how to get out of the country without passports."

The sound of a door opening echoed up from the stairwell below. Ethan shot a glance at his student, who mouthed the name *Axe*. He thought of the sedative he'd injected into the man. *How's he on his feet?*

Chris turned the knob and swung the door open. They rushed into the hallway, which was heavy with humidity and smelling of burning plastic. They raced to their left. Confused voices echoed through the hall from behind the walls.

Chris swiped his key in the reader at the end of the corridor, but the light on the lock remained a solid red. Ethan tried to swallow back the fluttering in his stomach, but his mouth had gone dry. Chris tried a second time and the lock still didn't open. Ethan glanced over his shoulder, even though he knew that he wasn't supposed to. Wolfe's head of security was less than a minute behind them, and they were trapped at a dead end if they couldn't open the door.

"Damn!" Chris said. He held up his card, examined the magnetic strip, and wiped it off on his cloak. On the third try the lock clicked green and opened. They pushed into the reception area.

"What the hell is going on?"

Chris turned toward the voice coming from behind the Plexiglas window. A man in a black suit with a dark crew cut stood on the other side of the window. Ethan moved beside Chris so that Nick Dawkins couldn't get a good look at either Rachel or Mousa.

"An explosion!" Chris shouted. "The gas stove in the kitchen."

Ethan jabbed a finger toward the outside door. "Get this open! We have to shut off the gas valve at the tank before the whole damn building blows."

Nick's eyes went wide, but he hesitated a moment, looking back and forth between the two men.

"Now, damn it!" Chris stepped toward the window. Ethan had never seen his student so in control before.

"Hurry," he added, "or we're all gonna die!"

The idea of dying must have motivated the guard because he hit a button on the desk. As soon as the click from the door lock sounded, Mousa pushed the door open. The cool, dry desert air beckoned to them.

When the door closed behind them, the silence of the still night calmed the pounding in Ethan's head. Without the footsteps of their pursuer behind him or the heavy air in his lungs, he felt his headache dissipating. They were almost free.

They ran across the drive, gravel crunching underneath their shoes. Rachel and Mousa rounded the side of the first black SUV.

That's when the gunshots rang out.

CHAPTER 51

THE MONASTERY

"**G**et down!" Chris shouted.

Ethan's brain took a moment to process what was occurring. Gunshots in real life were much louder than depicted in movies. Rather than drop to the ground, his instinct was to turn toward the explosions. Axe staggered out of the open door of the building thirty yards away. Somehow the security chief was still conscious, but judging from the way his body lurched with each step and how his arm—which was holding a short, black submachine gun—was wavering, the Ativan was having an effect on him. The vision of the gun pointed in Ethan's direction finally registered.

He's shooting at us!

"Take cover!" Chris reached underneath his black robe for his weapon.

Ethan hit the ground, grinding his knees and palms into the gravel. The first SUV was only a few feet in front of him. He wriggled on his belly toward it.

"Hurry!" Rachel called. She and Mousa had taken refuge on the other side of the car.

Crawling while remaining flat to the ground was difficult. Ethan's elbows scraped across the small pebbles; the taste of dust spread through his mouth.

As he reached the car's bumper, the shots exploded again. He cut his eyes toward Chris and saw him raise his weapon. The scene unfolded in slow motion. Axe had closed the gap by about a third and was standing with his feet shoulder-width apart, his body angled sideways toward them. The submachine gun's collapsible metal stock was extended and resting against his shoulder. Sparks of flame spat from the gun's barrel.

Chris seemed to take an eternity to sight his gun on his target. Ethan willed him to move faster. His own body convulsed as he watched Chris jerk backward twice. *Oh God!* But Chris didn't fall. Instead he began to return fire.

Axe dropped to the ground and rolled to his left. A small grouping of boulders outlined the walkway to the front door. Puffs of dirt and rock flew up from the ground as Chris continued shooting. Axe threw himself over the two-foot-tall rocks.

For a moment, the nighttime silence returned to the desert. Then he heard a metal clicking sound from the other side of the rocks. He guessed that Axe was swapping magazines in his gun. They had seconds left. Even in his drugged state, the trained killer would be able to pick them off from behind the cover of the rocks.

"Come on, Chris!" he yelled.

His student turned toward him. His face was pale. Ethan's stomach lurched when he saw the two red circles on his upper torso. Chris sank to his knees, turned his attention back to their adversary, and squeezed off two more shots, blasting chips off the top of the rocks. The top of Axe's head, which was just starting to poke above the cover, disappeared again. Chris's free hand swept his priestly robes aside and produced the keys to the SUV. He tossed the keys toward Ethan without taking his eyes off the boulders.

"Get out of here. I'll see how long I can delay him."

"You're coming with us!"

"There's no time. The others will be out here soon with more firepower. This is your only chance."

Ethan lunged for the keys in the dirt in front of him. Then, crouching, he ran around the side of the car.

How can I leave him here to die?

Chris had betrayed him and Elijah, but he was young and he had believed he was doing the right thing, serving their country. He'd had no idea the extremes to which Wolfe would take things. And now he'd risked his life to save them.

"Go now!" the grad student yelled.

He peered around the bumper. Chris still held the gun pointed in Axe's direction, but his other hand was now resting on the ground, supporting his weight. He was losing blood rapidly. Ethan knew what would happen if they didn't get him to a hospital soon. Chris was in hypovolemic shock. Soon his body would go into a baroreflex response as it detected a decrease in blood pressure from the loss of blood. His vascular system would restrict and his heart rate would increase in an attempt to maintain pressure. As the bleeding from the wounds continued, his heart would go tachycardic, sending his pulse over one hundred and twenty beats per minute. The pallor he saw in his student's face would increase even further then, and as the shock progressed he would start to lose consciousness.

But Ethan could save him. Surely Aswan had a hospital. One of the shots had struck him in the shoulder and the other in the chest—probably puncturing a lung, judging by the way he was struggling for breath. But neither wound was necessarily fatal.

"Doctor." He felt a hand on his arm. Mousa knelt beside him. "We have to leave."

Rachel crouched just behind the Jordanian. Her eyes were wide. Ethan realized that Chris was right. The others might come any second, and Axe still had the strategic advantage. He made his decision. The only true innocents there were Rachel and Mousa. He had to save them. He handed the keys—now damp with the sweat from his hand—to Mousa.

"Get her to Luxor."

Mousa nodded, moved to the second SUV, and opened the door. "Come with me, Ms. Riley."

She hesitated. "Ethan, you can't stay. You'll be killed. You have to come with us."

"I'll be a minute behind you. I can't leave Chris. I'm going to get him into the other car, drop him at the hospital, and then meet you in Luxor."

"But Axe has a machine gun."

"He's fighting the Ativan in his system as much as us now. We'll make it."

"But—"

"I grabbed a cell phone."

"You have a cell phone?"

"I'll leave you a message at the hotel in Luxor under the name"—he paused for a second—"Anakin Skywalker."

"Let me see the phone!"

He snatched it from his pocket and handed it to her. Her fingers flew over the keys. "I put my dad's cell phone number in it. He can help us."

"Ms. Riley!" Mousa called from the driver's seat. He cranked the engine. "Go!"

Rachel pressed the phone into Ethan's hand, threw her arms around his neck, and squeezed. Her damp priest's robes clung to his skin. She kissed him hard. Then she pulled away and jumped into the car.

"You better not die," she said before swinging the door closed.

Mousa gunned the engine. Gravel spat from the tires as they shot away.

Ethan crouched behind the rear tire well of the remaining SUV. "Chris, get over here," he whispered.

Chris glanced over his shoulder. His face fell when he saw Ethan peek around the car. He turned back to the boulders, fired three more shots, and then ran for the car. Machine gun fire followed him. Ethan ducked his head into his arms, hoping the car would protect him. The bullets sounded like metallic popcorn as they struck the SUV.

"Why didn't you go?"

Chris fell beside him. His breath came in rapid bursts.

"I'm not leaving you."

He opened Chris's robe and felt for the entry wounds. As he expected, one was in his right chest, missing his heart, but puncturing a lung. The other was just below his left clavicle. "You have to put pressure on these to stop the bleeding." He began to remove the cassock from Chris's shoulders, causing him to wince. "I'll tear this into sections that we can use as a compress."

"You don't have time. You have to go."

Another round of bullets rocked the SUV. "I'll drive us into Aswan while you hold the compresses. I'll drop you at a hospital and then disappear."

With his robe off, Chris reached into his pants pocket and produced a slender magazine. His right thumb depressed a lever on the side of the handgun that caused the spent magazine to drop to the ground. He slammed the fresh one in and chambered the first round.

"You shouldn't have done this."

Chris maneuvered himself so that he could see around the bumper of the car. Axe unleashed another volley of bullets.

Ethan reached up and opened the door. "Hand me the keys. I'll start the engine while you keep his head down."

They both noticed the hissing sound at the same time. Ethan felt his heart sink as he realized where the noise came from. The SUV listed to the side away from them. He felt the pressure of panic rise in his chest.

"He's shot the tires," Chris said without any emotion.

"We can still drive on the rims. Town's not that far away."

Chris stuck his gun around the car and fired off two rounds. Then he turned toward Ethan. His face had grown even more pallid, his breathing more labored. He stuck his hand into his pocket, but instead of pulling out the keys, he retrieved his wallet. Thrusting it into Ethan's chest, he said, "Use the cash, but be careful with the credit cards unless you absolutely need to use them. They can track you that way."

"But—"

"The car will never make it. They'll gun you down." He leaned into his professor. "Axe thinks you're in the car with the others." He pointed into the desert, where dunes rose and fell like waves on a dark ocean. "Run straight. The SUV will block you from view. When you've crested the dunes and are sure you can't be seen, turn southwest—that'll be to your left. We're two or three miles from Lake Nasser. These warehouses were built in the '60s to store supplies for the construction of the lake. Follow the shoreline west—away from Aswan. Eventually you'll come across some small fishing villages. You can pay someone there to drive you to Luxor."

"What about you?"

"If I can kill Axe before the others come outside, I'll tell them you guys shot both of us in your escape attempt."

He looked at his student. He knew the odds weren't good. But they were out of options, and the frequency of gunshots coming from Axe had decreased. The Ativan was winning the battle for his consciousness. He would pass out soon. Maybe Chris could finish him off. He took the wallet.

"Thank you."

Chris grabbed his shoulder. "Professor, I'm so sorry for what I've done here. I hope you can find it in your heart to forgive me one day."

"I already have. Just get the son of a bitch who killed Elijah."

He turned to the desert. Squatting, he hurried toward the top of the nearest dune. He was careful to keep the SUV between him and the boulders. When he crested the top of the dune, his hopes rose. The distinctive chatter of Axe's weapon had ceased. *Maybe he's unconscious.*

He started down the far side of the dune toward the emptiness of the desert. The moon was not yet up, and the myriad stars provided only faint illumination. He picked out the next series of dunes he would aim for. After he traversed them, he would head toward the lake as Chris suggested. He turned for one last look before his head disappeared behind the sand.

From his elevated angle at the top of the dune, he saw the danger before Chris did. The graduate student was leaning on the rear bumper of the car while he tracked the top of the boulders with his gun. Axe, however, was no longer popping up to shoot from the center of the rocks. He wasn't unconscious, either.

Ethan watched as the security chief crawled from around the far side of the boulders. The warning came to his lips a second too late. Axe fired a three-shot burst that caught Chris in the neck and head as his attention was focused on the top of the boulders.

"No!" Ethan screamed.

Chris dropped to the ground like a marionette whose strings had been cut. A surge of rage and sorrow welled up in Ethan. He should have ducked his head behind the sand and run, but the emotions that threatened to explode from his chest kept him anchored in place. Axe lifted his gaze from the fallen student to the dim horizon. He stood rooted in place, looking in Ethan's direction. Ethan had no idea if Axe could see him or not in the glare of the exterior lights of the warehouse.

As he slid down the opposite side of the dune, his last view of the Monastery was of Axe taking two steps forward and then falling face-down in the dirt.

CHAPTER 52

BETHESDA, MARYLAND

Casey Richards swirled his drink, Grey Goose on the rocks with lime, as he slouched in his leather armchair. The flames from the gas fireplace warmed the study of his townhome on the outskirts of Bethesda. After his divorce fifteen years ago, shortly after his fortieth birthday, the Deputy Director had given up dark alcohol. It no longer agreed with him. He used to be a bourbon man; now he stuck to vodka and gin. He glanced at the clock icon on his laptop. His General Tso's chicken—steamed, not fried—would arrive soon.

The phone on the side table chirped at him like a robotic bird. He looked up from his email browser and reached for the secure landline the Agency had installed.

"Hello," he said without identifying himself, a protocol that had been drilled into him from his training days.

The person on the other end asked him a code-worded question designed both to authenticate his identity and ensure he was alone and not under duress. He gave the appropriate answers.

"Sir, we have a priority message for you from Night Watch. An encrypted file has just been sent."

Richards scanned his email and saw the most recent file from the office. He entered his sixteen-digit password, pressed his finger on the print reader, and waited as the file downloaded. An image appeared on his screen.

"What am I looking at?"

He stared at a satellite picture of a warehouse building. The image was black-and-white, taken by one of their birds with thermal imaging capabilities—not as high-res as the daytime shots, but impressive for its ability to take pictures in pitch-black night.

"Project Jericho, Sir. We've lost contact."

"Lost contact?"

"There's been an explosion in the center of the building."

He hit the zoom button and looked closer. The middle of the building glowed white, a burning circle in the darkness.

"What the hell happened?"

"We have assets two hours out in Cairo that we're mobilizing to find out."

"Wolfe?"

"In Cairo too. No answer on his cell. We've sent someone to his hotel. A Black Hawk is standing by to bring him and our men to Jericho."

"I want to speak to him the moment you're in touch."

"Yes, Sir."

He glanced at the English antique clock on the mantel of his fireplace. 8:16. It wouldn't be daylight in Egypt for another three or four hours.

"We need real-time imagery."

"We've already tasked the satellite. You'll receive the data as soon as we do."

"Keep me posted."

"Will do, Sir."

The line went dead. He stared at the image on his screen again. *A gas leak or a problem with a furnace?* He zoomed in more, but the image pixelated too much to make out any helpful details. He shook his head. *Wishful thinking.* He'd been in the business long enough to know that accidents like that didn't happen on their own.

If the program is exposed . . .

He didn't want to think of the consequences. He'd trusted Wolfe. The doctor had worked miracles in the past, and the first test—the subject who'd led them to Abadi-Jabbar—had exceeded his expectations.

Now, he wondered whether he'd been too lenient with the doctor. In operations like this he knew better than to micromanage his field guys. Usually he didn't even want to know the details of what was taking place, as long as he got the results he was after. But Jericho had grown past the scope of a field op. He remembered the Agency's history: the Bay of Pigs, MKULTRA, Iran-Contra—all well-meaning covert operations that had gone wrong, and worse, become public. He wouldn't let that happen here.

He hated having to clean up a mess, but he'd done it many times before.

CHAPTER 53

SAHARA DESERT, EGYPT

Where am I? Ethan wondered.

He thought he'd followed Chris's instructions—travel straight until he was out of view of the Monastery and then turn left—but he'd been walking for almost two hours and the endless desert landscape hadn't changed. His eyes had adapted to the starlight, but all he could see around him were sand dunes—no sign of Lake Nasser.

He paused to catch his breath. The night air was cool, but he was warm from walking in the loose sand, which gave back some of his forward progress with every step up the side of a dune. His lips were chapped, and he was thirsty. The daytime sun would be brutal. With no water, he wasn't sure how long he would last before dehydration caused him to hallucinate and then collapse.

Surveying the dunes around him, he picked one to his right—the largest around him. He started up it in a jog. He'd learned early in his escape that walking up a dune was almost impossible. It was like trying to run up a down escalator; he had to move quickly or the loose, dry sand caused him to slip backward with each step. The sand was unlike that of any beach he'd experienced. The fine beige and red particles were each separate, with no moisture to clump them together or to provide a stable surface for his weight.

When he reached the top, he bent over, rested his hands on his knees, and breathed deeply. The only sign of life was a single thorny bush poking through the dune. He straightened and surveyed the landscape. He squinted to see if he could make out his path in the sand. His footsteps at the bottom of the dune were faint and he couldn't follow them far, but what he saw concerned him. Although he'd thought he was walking straight—his strategy had been to pick out a dune in the distance and head for it—his path definitively curved to the right.

How long have I been walking like that?

He sat on the top of the dune. The fear that he'd walked miles deeper into the desert began to settle over him. Indecision over his next move began to play in his mind. He could keep walking, but doing so might take him farther in the wrong direction—or worse, back toward the Monastery. He could wait for daylight on top of the dune. He might be able to make out the lake in the distance then. He sat up straighter. The thought of daylight brought a sudden realization: the rising sun would tell him which direction east was. If he traveled south, he would eventually hit the lake.

He lay back. The sand was soft and still radiated some of the heat absorbed from the previous day's sun. He was exhausted. He closed his eyes and replayed the escape in his mind.

The thought of Chris's death filled him with a sickly feeling. A hot, viscous sensation began to pour into his stomach and fill up his body until it reached his throat. Chris had betrayed him, but he'd saved their lives and sacrificed his own. Then his thoughts turned to Rachel and Mousa. Had they been able to escape? He held on to the hope that the guards were still disoriented from the explosion and that Axe was still incapacitated from the sedative. The image of Rachel's blue eyes and the memory of the touch of her full lips burned in his mind. The taste of their kiss still lingered in his mouth, and he imagined that with each breath he inhaled the floral scent of her hair. Neither Wolfe nor the brutish Axe would let her live if they caught her. His breathing became labored, as if his belt was cinched around his chest rather than his waist.

I can't lose her.

After Natalie's death, he hadn't thought he would ever again feel the intensity of connecting with another woman that way, yet now he knew he was falling for the insightful, feisty, and beautiful grad student.

But love carried with it the risk of loss—a pain so intense that he thought he would never be able to survive it again. With the adrenaline of the escape gone, the fear of that pain crept into his mind. He wished that praying for Rachel's safety would make it so. He opened his eyes and stared at the ocean of stars. He doubted that a superhuman grandfather figure was up there to intervene based on words he might mutter, a promise he might make, or a belief he might profess. In the dark night in the middle of the Sahara, he felt the loneliness in his bones as if the marrow had evaporated, leaving his skeleton hollow.

A particularly bright star close to the horizon caught his eye. The desert sky was wide open, like nothing he ever saw in New Haven. Staring at the broad brushstroke of stars that was the Milky Way stirred a memory. He remembered a Post-it note Elijah had once stuck to the back of his office chair: *Through the wonder and beauty of the natural world we can understand the nature of God.*

He'd pulled the note from his chair, crumpled it, and tossed it into the trash basket by his desk. "Two points," he'd said to Elijah, who watched him from behind reading glasses.

"One day, my friend, you will appreciate my bits of wisdom," Elijah had chuckled.

"Maybe that same day you'll reconcile for me your scientific world view with your spiritual one?"

Elijah had put down the journal article he was reading. "Ah, the tyranny of the logical mind." He'd swiveled his chair toward Ethan. "Reason is not our only way of perceiving the truth. Sometimes we must feel it, intuit it, and experience it."

"Sounds awfully fuzzy to me. Didn't we become scientists so that we could measure, test, and experiment in order to come to objective truths?"

"What if God doesn't operate from outside the universe, in violation of its physical laws, but from inside? What if God is not separate from us but part of us? We wouldn't be able to prove this kind of God scientifically because there would be no separate action outside of nature that we could point to."

"But then what's the point of even talking about, much less believing in and worshipping, such a God? Why not just worship nature or the universe?"

"Maybe we can experience God—not intellectually, but emotionally. We will never understand God, but maybe we can taste the presence of God. A two-dimensional creature can never truly understand what a three-dimensional world looks like. Its perception of reality is physically limited by its existence. Such a creature could only glimpse part of reality. Art, nature, beauty, love, peace, and the mystical states associated with religion may be our glimpses at this divine reality."

He'd always been respectfully dismissive of Elijah's views. His mentor, for all the brilliance of his research, had held on to quaint views from his upbringing. Now, for the first time, Ethan began to feel that his intellectual arrogance had been misplaced. His world had fallen apart around him—Elijah's murder, Rachel's kidnapping, his suspension from Yale, the perversion of his research, Chris's death. He was no longer sure of anything. Then he thought of the vision from his youth and the time he'd spent with Rachel.

He pushed himself up to a seated position. *All this introspection isn't going to get me out of the desert, nor will it help Rachel and Mousa.* He scanned the horizon, searching for any sign of dawn.

Then he saw it.

At first he thought his eyes were playing tricks on him. The light in the distance was closer than the horizon—it couldn't be the rising sun.

A CIA search party? The hairs on his arms stood on end.

He squinted, focusing on the light. It wasn't moving, nor was it the steady light of a car headlight or flashlight. This light was flickering.

A fire.

He was probably seeing the edge of one of the villages. He figured he must be close to the lake and freedom from the desert. He stood, noted the exact location of the fire in relation to the dunes around it, and took off running.

CHAPTER 54

SAHARA DESERT

Ethan approached a campsite of three tents. His initial hope that the camp marked the edge of a village was dispelled when he got closer. The fire that had led him there blazed in the middle of the same endless desert he'd been lost in for hours. But at least he'd found people. As he moved closer, he noticed that the long tents were hand-sewn from a quilt of various fabrics: hairy animal skins, colorful cloths, and recycled clothes.

A snorting sound to his right caused him to jump. He turned toward the noise and could just discern the outline of camels bedded down in the sand. He rounded the corner of a tent, wondering exactly what he was going to say to the people camped here.

A tented camp in the desert, he thought. *Must be Bedouins.* Nomadic tribes who wandered the desert, Bedouins lived by trading camels and goats the men raised and rugs the women wove in exchange for the supplies they needed. He remembered learning from a Discovery Channel documentary that they were known for showing hospitality to strangers. He hoped that to be true.

When he stepped into the clearing in front of the fire, he saw two men dressed in loose white robes with red scarves wrapped around their heads seated in plastic folding chairs. After a brief delay in which they stared at him as if trying to understand how a man could just appear out of the desert in the middle of the night, they jumped to their feet. His stomach lurched when each grabbed an antique rifle from beside their chair and pointed it at his chest. They yelled at him in Arabic.

"Help." He raised his hands in the air. "I need help. Do you speak English?"

The men waved their guns at him. He felt a trickle of sweat form on his brow in the cool air. His main concern was not further exciting the men with their fingers on the triggers of the guns pointed at him. Thoughts of how he might communicate his harmlessness to them raced through his head. Then he had an idea.

With his hands still up in the air, he pointed to himself and said, "Doctor. I'm a doctor."

The word had an immediate effect. They stopped yelling and began to speak between themselves. Ethan forced himself to release the breath he was holding. The more relaxed he was, the less tension the men with the guns would feel. At least he hoped that was the case.

One of the men said something in Arabic and then disappeared into the nearest tent. The other kept his gun trained on Ethan. After what felt like ten minutes, but was probably more like two, the man emerged from the tent. A third Bedouin followed him. Taller than the other two, he matched Ethan's height. Wisps of gray mixed with the long black hair that fell over his shoulders. Unlike the other two, who wore white robes, this man wore red; instead of the turbans the others covered their heads with, he had a blue scarf wrapped around his neck. The elder man rubbed his eyes as if he'd just been awoken.

He spoke in a gravelly voice. "Doctor?"

"You speak English?"

"I'm my tribe's sheikh." He raised his eyebrows, no doubt questioning why an American doctor had appeared in their camp in the middle of the night with no supplies.

"I'm lost." Ethan shrugged. "I have to get to Luxor quickly." Evaluating the skeptical expression on the tribal elder's face, he added, "And I can pay you for your troubles."

He hoped the last fact would motivate the Bedouin leader to help him without requesting details. As the elder continued to stare at him, he stuck out a hand. He didn't know the proper protocols for introduction here. "Dr. Ethan Lightman." He emphasized the word *doctor* again.

A smile spread across the sheikh's face. He grasped Ethan's hand in both of his. "You may call me Josef. Your money is not needed here. If a traveler in the desert is in need of a place to rest, he may always rely on our *diyafa*—our hospitality. You may stay with us for three days." His smile grew wider. "And we could use a doctor."

He turned and spoke in Arabic to the men behind him. They lowered their rifles. One went to the fire and placed a tarnished silver pot that had been sitting on a nearby blanket in the coals. The other disappeared into the far tent.

"Follow me to our *beit al-sha'ar*." The sheikh started toward the far tent.

Ethan wiped his palms on his pants and followed after him. "To your what?"

Josef parted what appeared to be goat hide, revealing the opening into the tent. "Our house of hair." He chuckled.

The tent was roomier and cozier than Ethan would have imagined. Lanterns on posts in three corners illuminated the interior with a soft, flickering glow. The floor was covered in colorful, hand-woven rugs, and groups of large red pillows defined seating areas. To his right a low table contained a hookah whose tentacle-like hoses snaked around a glass vase. Curtains at the rear separated the tent into other areas he couldn't see.

Two figures in the center of the room grabbed his attention. A woman dressed in a long black dress sat on the floor with a child of about ten resting his head in her lap. The guard who had preceded them into the tent stood behind them with a pained expression on his face. The woman's hair was hidden with a red veil but her face was uncovered. She gazed at Ethan, tears streaming from wide, dark eyes.

Josef exchanged words in Arabic with the woman and motioned to Ethan. She studied him a moment and then nodded.

"The boy, Muhammad, was showing off for the girls this afternoon. He tried to ride a camel while standing up." The sheikh crouched next to the boy and pulled down the goat-hide blanket covering his torso. The boy whimpered but kept his eyes closed. "He landed on his arm."

Ethan knelt beside the woman and tried to give her a reassuring smile, although he knew that bedside manner wasn't one of his strengths. The boy was curled in her lap on his left side. He cradled his right arm on his stomach.

"Okay, Muhammad," he said in a soothing tone. "Let's see what we have here."

The boy winced as Ethan pulled the sleeve of his robe up to his bicep. The cause of the boy's pain became immediately apparent. His right ulna—one of the two bones that, along with the radius, comprised the forearm—had sustained a fracture. A purple bruise covered an inch-high lump about halfway between the wrist and the elbow. He gently ran his fingers along the arm. When he palpated around the lump, the boy cried out.

"I know that hurts. I'm almost done."

At least the fracture's closed, he thought. The bone had clearly broken, but it hadn't sliced through the skin. Still, the arm had to be stabilized; a wrong movement could cause it to sever the nerves and blood vessels around it.

He turned to the sheikh. "He needs to go to a hospital. They'll x-ray and then set his arm in a cast."

"We were going to take him in the morning."

"How long is the drive?"

"Drive?" Josef laughed. "Two hours by camel, four by foot."

The boy stared at Ethan with curious eyes. Judging from his pallor, he was in a mild state of shock. Bouncing around on a camel would not work in the arm's current state, and he wouldn't be able to walk on his own either. The boy had only one option.

The thought of what he had to do made Ethan nervous. A simple procedure really, but one he'd done only as a resident in med school, years ago. He would have to set and then stabilize the arm.

He explained to Josef what he planned to do and then listed what he needed. The sheikh translated for the parents, who looked even more frightened but didn't protest. The boy's father left the tent, returning minutes later with two sticks two inches in diameter, probably from their supply of kindling for the fire. Ethan flexed each one. Both were strong enough. He broke off several knobs to smooth them out. Then he eyeballed the length of the boy's forearm and broke the branches so that they were about the same length. The splint would be rough, but it only needed to stabilize the arm until they could reach Aswan. Next he sorted through the strips of fabric the father had brought.

Now comes the unpleasant part, he thought.

"Josef, I could use your help."

The sheikh knelt beside him as the parents stared with furrowed brows. The boy's eyes went wide with fear.

"First, we need him on his back."

The sheikh translated for the mother. Together they shifted the boy so he lay flat on the rug; his head rested in his mother's lap. Tears fell from his eyes despite an obvious attempt to be brave. He bit his lip.

"Good." Ethan cradled the arm. "Now hold his shoulders firmly so he cannot move."

Josef placed his thick hands on the boy.

Ethan looked into Muhammad's eyes. "This is going to hurt a lot, but just for a second."

He waited for Josef to translate. The boy nodded, biting his lip. Ethan wrapped his hands around the boy's forearm, one on each side of the fracture. He then applied traction, pulling his hands apart in order to set the broken bone.

The boy's scream pierced through the nighttime quiet in the tent.

CHAPTER 55

SAHARA DESERT

Axe climbed into the Black Hawk as the engine began its start-up whine. *How did I fuck up so badly?* The evening's events still seemed blurry. One minute he was bent over, holding the Muslim in the chapel, and the next he'd been double-crossed by one of Wolfe's psychologist priests and attacked by the professor. His memory of the firefight was fuzzy. He hadn't realized he'd killed Chris Sligh until the others told him. His last memory was of firing his H&K from behind the boulders. He'd woken up in Wolfe's office with an IV in his arm.

After they'd pumped him full of stimulants, Wolfe, who'd just returned from Cairo in the Black Hawk, had chewed his ass out. "Do you understand the implications of this facility being made public!" Wolfe had paced his office floor like a caged jungle cat. "I'm barely holding off the Deputy Director from terminating the program with prejudice." Beads of sweat glistened on his forehead. Axe had never seen the boss sweat before. "And you know fucking well what that means!"

Axe let him rant. Nothing he could say would excuse what had happened. Excuses were for the weak. One either won or lost. Success or failure. Why didn't matter. He had only one option, and the orders that came from his boss next made that clear.

Wolfe stopped pacing, leaned over to bring himself eye-to-eye with him, and enunciated each word slowly. "Find them. And eliminate them."

The doctor, the girl, and the Muslim had a few hours' head start and had eluded detection so far. Unfortunately, the computer equipment that handled the Monastery's security had just been blown out the roof. A team was searching Aswan already, but Axe wasn't convinced they were headed in that direction. Driving toward the nearest town was too obvious a move. He would scour the desert, following the tire tracks, but he knew that as soon as they hit hard dirt, finding the car would require more luck than skill.

He flexed his triceps by locking out his arms and rotating his elbows inward. Most men made the mistaken assumption that to build huge arms they needed to do endless bicep curls, but he knew that the triceps made up three-quarters of the arm's muscle mass. Not that his biceps weren't huge also. He settled into the vinyl seat and buckled his shoulder strap. Next, he checked his M4 rifle and the thermal scope that would illuminate any living creature up to several hundred yards away by its heat signature. The helicopter rose vertically while moving forward at the same time.

Nick Dawkins sat across from him, adjusting the night-vision goggles on his head. Although Nick had made the boneheaded move of allowing the doctor, the Muslim, and the girl out the front door, he was a good operative—a new hire straight from his retirement as a member of SEAL Team Two. Although Axe had spent his teenage years dreaming of one day being a SEAL, motivating himself through brutal workouts with the image of the amount of ass he would kick, he'd never made it out of the Navy's two-week SEAL indoc program that preceded the seven-month-long BUD/S course.

When he'd arrived at Coronado Island, off the coast of San Diego, he was the largest guy in the barracks, and he'd relished the envious looks the other recruits gave him when he removed his shirt. Lieutenant Mills, however—a tanned and wiry New Yorker with a scratchy voice—had laughed at him. "You, Muscleman, will be the first to go," he'd said in a Jersey accent, jabbing a calloused finger at him.

Had they been anywhere else, Axe would have ripped the finger from his hand and then snapped his neck. *The first to go?* He would show all those pussies how powerful he was.

He'd lasted twelve days. He hadn't been the first to leave, but ultimately his greatest asset, his size, had been his downfall. He recalled how fucked up the

Navy's requirements were. Any program that would weed out someone of his stature was horribly flawed.

The O-course was the bane of the big men. Lieutenant Mills had explained that while strength was crucial for a SEAL, more important were speed, agility, and stealth. The fifteen sections of the obstacle course required the recruits to climb, crawl, jump, and run over, under, and through ropes, steel bars, and barbed wire. The problem for Axe occurred at the same point on each of his three attempts: the sixty-foot cargo net. About two-thirds of the way up, his muscles just tied up, refusing to cooperate, leaving him stranded with his arms and legs dangling, exhausted, from the thick rope. Lieutenant Mills sat at the top of the net on the round telephone pole that supported it after he'd scaled it with the speed of a spider.

"Get your steroid-inflated ass up here!"

Not only was Axe carrying an extra fifty to seventy pounds compared with most of the other men there, his muscles were composed predominantly of fast-twitch fibers. These fibers gave him explosive power during his lifting sessions, but once the energy from the fibers was depleted, they simply refused to fire.

On his third and last O-course attempt, the California sun had seemed magnified, causing sweat to pour from his head, stinging his eyes.

"You might be big, Axe, but you're just not strong enough, are you?" The voice jeered at him from the top. "Just give up and ring the bell."

He grunted and willed his hands to reach for the next higher rope. He was closer than he'd been on his previous attempts. Lieutenant Mills's foot dangled from the side of the pole just ten feet above him. Just a little farther and he would grab the foot and jerk the bastard down. But he had nothing left. His thighs quivered, causing the rope to shake. The burn in his forearms didn't bother him; it was nothing compared to the pain he'd suffered as a boy. The problem was that he couldn't get his fingers to move. They were frozen like those of an arthritic patient. He pried one hand loose while pushing up on the toes of the opposite foot.

He didn't remember the fall, only waking up moments later surrounded by men. He got over the concussion, but not the humiliation of washing out of SEAL training. He'd been relegated to a ship in the Gulf for the next two years. To make matters worse, the nightmares he'd suffered since the fire became more frequent. He awoke each night in the ship's narrow bunk, drenched in sweat after dreaming of the fires of hell melting the skin from his legs.

His temper on the ship had earned him numerous reprimands, but then the call had come. A quasi-governmental organization was looking for recruits. They had wanted Special Forces types, but with the ongoing operations in Afghanistan and Iraq, the military couldn't spare their most elite soldiers, so instead they were looking at men who had an interest in such things but had not quite made it. His commanders were happy to transfer him.

His new position as one of Wolfe's first hires had suited him perfectly. With everything off the books, he had even more flexibility than if he were a SEAL. He didn't have to worry about rules of engagement. He made his own rules. Plus, he believed in his mission. Wolfe was a genius, the smartest man he'd ever met, and he had more balls than his sorry excuse for a father could ever have hoped to have. All of the billions that the US had spent on military actions in the Middle East had done nothing to produce any lasting results. But Project Jericho would change the world.

He peered out the helicopter's window into the blackness of the night. Then he pulled on the pair of headphones hanging from a hook behind him and clicked on the microphone. "Hit the floods," he told the pilots.

His thermal scope wouldn't show the tire tracks. As the helicopter banked to the left, he felt his stomach lurch. He'd never had problems with motion sickness before; such a condition was only for the weak-minded.

Must be vertigo from the drugs, he thought.

It felt as if the sedative and the stimulant were battling each other inside of him, neither wanting to give in. He tried to stare at the horizon, but he could barely make out the outline of the dunes against the moonless sky. *Where are the damn lights?*

Suddenly, his perception changed. The rhythmic thumping of the rotors, the smell of oil and metal, and even the dim landscape outside the window disappeared as if a plug had been pulled and his sensations of the world had drained from him. He thought he was losing consciousness again, but soon realized he'd only lost his senses; his mind was still with him.

What's happening to me?

He willed himself to clear his head, but nothing shifted. An undefined fear began to crowd out his rational thought. The world around him began to dissolve. He was becoming part of the same dark void that was outside the chopper. Suddenly he was back in the chapel and sitting in the cathedra, his reality dissolving. Just as the sensation threatened to consume him, the helicopter's halogen lights lit up his world. The intensity hurt his eyes, causing him to blink rapidly, but he welcomed the pain that brought back his sense of sound and smell. He breathed in as deeply as his chest could inflate. His heart raced inside his ribcage.

He glanced toward Dawkins, who stared out his own window as if nothing were wrong. Then he understood what had happened. It wasn't the drugs, it was the damn Logos machine. He thought about the professor's explanation that the Logos could cause a negative reaction in ambidextrous people. A new feeling of dread began to spread through him, radiating out from his core, undeterred by the layers of muscle that usually protected him.

Am I losing my mind?

The coffee was thick, bitter, and hot, and was served in a small china cup that held no more than a single shot's worth. Ethan welcomed the jolt of caffeine. Between sips he tore into the plate of hummus with chunks of pita his hosts had placed in front of him.

The other six men sitting on the pillows around him took turns on the hookah. He politely declined when they passed it in his direction. Although it was after three in the morning, the sheikh and the two guards had been joined by three other Bedouins, who'd risen to see the American doctor who had walked out of the desert. The boy's father flashed an appreciative smile at him. The boy was sleeping in the rear section of the tent with his mother.

"You are free to take refuge with us for a few days," Josef said. "We have plenty of food and room in the tent for you to rest."

"Thank you, but I need to get to Luxor as quickly"—he paused for a moment —"and as discreetly as possible."

A knowing smile crept across the sheikh's face. Ethan suspected it wasn't unusual in their trading culture to encounter people who might not want attention drawn to their activities.

"If you could drop me at a village by Lake Nasser, maybe I can grab a ride."

Josef turned to his men, who debated how best to get him on the road to Luxor. All he could understand was that their idea had something to do with a camel and a *felucca*, though he didn't know what a *felucca* was.

As he ate and listened to the occasional translations from the sheikh, Ethan wondered about Rachel and Mousa. Had their journey into the desert rather than into the city eluded the men from the Monastery? Once he reunited with Rachel, he wouldn't let her out of his sight again.

Suddenly the boy's father raised a hand to silence the group. He rose to his feet, cocked his head, and spoke in Arabic. The sheikh stood.

"Stay in here and don't talk," Josef said before walking outside the tent.

The other men stared at him. Then Ethan heard the distinctive sound of a helicopter approaching.

───────────

"Fuck the rules of engagement!" Axe yelled to Dawkins as he opened the door to the Black Hawk. His M4 was locked and loaded.

If the hand that closed around his shoulder hadn't belonged to a fellow operative, he would have ripped it off at the wrist.

"Hey man," Dawkins said, "Wolfe will shit a brick if we rile up the locals. We've got to keep this low-key."

Axe glared at his partner, weighing his options. As if sensing his hesitation, Dawkins said, "I've got your back. You question the natives. I'll cover you from here."

"If you see one of them so much as flinch, smoke his ass."

He flicked the safety on his rifle with his thumb and swung it over his shoulder. They'd lost the tracks of the SUV forty-five minutes earlier, but at least they'd learned something. They'd briefly spotted footprints in the sand.

One of them, *probably the professor*, he thought based on his fuzzy memory of the firefight, was out on foot. They'd crisscrossed the desert in a radius he'd estimated a man could walk in the hours since the escape. The only sign of life, other than the villages of Lake Nasser, was the Bedouin tent camp they'd spotted from the air. Because the footprints led into the desert rather than to the lake, he decided to investigate the Bedouins first.

Ethan barely breathed as he listened to the harsh voices outside the tent. He couldn't make out the specifics through the roar of the still-spinning helicopter rotors, but he heard a mixture of English and Arabic. The sheikh seemed to be pretending not to understand anything being said to him. He wondered where the helicopter had come from. Then he caught the voice speaking in English: *James Axelrod.* His eyes darted around the tent, evaluating where he could hide if Axe decided to come inside. He felt the helplessness of having his life depend on men he'd only just met.

Then he heard the whine of the engine become higher pitched. The tent shook as the helicopter flew directly overhead. For a moment, he worried the fabric might fly apart, leaving him exposed in the night. But the sound of the aircraft faded into the distance. When he could no longer hear it, the opening to the tent parted. His breath caught in his chest.

Only the sheikh and the boy's father entered.

"We must leave before the sun," Josef said. "Your *friends*"—he emphasized the word—"are determined to find you."

A wave of relief passed through him. "Thank you. Those men are dangerous."

"Your kindness with the boy means much to us, and"—Josef shuddered—"the man asking for you had an evil look in his eyes. I've never seen a creature that size before."

Ethan allowed himself to feel a ray of hope. Axe was randomly searching the desert. Maybe he hadn't found Mousa and Rachel either.

CHAPTER 56

SAHARA DESERT

Ethan had finally adapted to the strange motion. He'd only been on a horse once in his life, on a trail ride in New Hampshire. The camel's rhythm was different: it rocked forward and back. He shifted in the saddle to relieve the chafing on his thighs. Because a camel's back was too wide to straddle like a horse's, he was sitting at the front of the saddle and crossing his ankles on the animal's neck. He yawned. More than once, he'd almost dozed off. The lack of sleep had caught up to him, especially now that his sympathetic system had stopped pumping hormones into his body.

The sheikh, the injured boy's father, and another Bedouin from the tribe had ridden with him for several hours. He squinted against the orange rays of light cresting the horizon. They were traveling east, into the dawn.

"The spark of Allah!" Josef exclaimed.

"Excuse me?" He turned toward the sheikh.

"The sun"—Josef pointed to the horizon—"warms us, lights our path, grows our food. The same way Allah is the essence of life itself."

"How do you know that to be true?"

"In my prayers, I feel it." He motioned his head to the boy's father. "And in our children, I see it."

Ethan adjusted the red-and-white-checkered headdress held in place by the braided cord around his forehead. The men had also given him an ankle-length white robe. His western clothes were rolled up in a cloth bag that was tied to his saddle alongside a one-liter bottle of water and several slices of pita.

"You almost look like one of us now," the sheikh had chuckled when he'd put on the attire.

A break in the endless sea of sand caught his attention. *A mirage?* He squinted and shielded his eyes with his hand. The land, which had been barren for hours, appeared green ahead. He sat up straighter. The color stretched across the horizon for as far as he could see.

"Is that—"

"The Nile."

The father of the injured boy turned to Ethan and gave him a thumbs-up sign. After he returned the gesture, the man yelled, "*Yulli Yulla!*"

Ethan had no idea what the phrase meant, but the camels did. They took off running. He struggled to hold on to the single rope attached to the harness around the camel's snout while also grabbing the horn on the front of the saddle. He squeezed his legs together until they began to cramp. The last thing he wanted was to be tossed off.

Ten minutes later, he could see the water across a field of waist-high, dark green crops. The Bedouins slowed the animals. He relaxed his grip and took a breath.

"Sugarcane," the sheikh said as he guided the group on a dirt path through the crops toward the riverbank.

The soil underneath them was almost black, manure-like, in contrast with the fine granules of beige and red sand they had abruptly left. Ethan guessed that the controlled flooding of the Nile from Lake Nasser hit the same spot every year. A few minutes later they arrived at a village of mud-brick huts. Smoke rose from two clay ovens on the edge of the village. Three sun-wrinkled women squatted on the ground as they worked dough on wooden trays. As they continued through the village, Ethan wrinkled his nose: the smell had transitioned from baking bread to the stench of decomposition. Garbage was piled outside the huts, and an open sewer ran to the riverbank.

His first close-up view of the Nile was different than he'd expected. He'd always pictured the world's most famous river as more untamed—rushing rapids with crocodiles lounging on the banks. Two hundred yards wide at this point, the water flowed almost without a ripple. Two old sailboats drifted across the water, while a third was tied to the shore in front of them.

They stopped at the top of the bank above the sailboat. Two villagers were readying the boat to leave. Judging from the nets they were loading into the hull, Ethan guessed they were fishermen. Each wore white, but their robes were tinted gray and needed a good washing. Their heads were uncovered. Unlike the olive-complected Bedouins, who had distinctly Arab features, these men were darker, with wider and flatter faces.

Josef called to the men and pointed to Ethan. After a discussion back and forth, with each side throwing their hands up in the air and gesturing to the American dressed as a Bedouin, the fishermen turned back to their work. Ethan looked at Josef.

"Nubians," the sheikh said. "They've agreed to take you to Luxor on their felucca. You'll be there tomorrow afternoon."

"How much?" He guessed that he only had a few hundred dollars in the wallet Chris had given him.

"Twenty American dollars." Josef grimaced. "I tried to talk them down, but they are busy fishing."

Ethan tried to suppress a smile. "I can make that work."

The sheik gave a command in Arabic, and the camels began to lower onto their stomachs. Ethan leaned backward. He'd learned his lesson when he first mounted the animal, almost falling off when it stood. The camel lowered its front legs, bending them underneath its body and pitching him forward. He jerked a second time as the creature's back legs folded down, and then he hopped off, thankful to be on the ground again.

He untied the bag containing his clothes and food from the saddle, slung it over his shoulder, and then walked over to the sheikh with his hand out. Instead of shaking it, Josef grasped him by his shoulders and kissed both his cheeks.

"*Ma'assalama*—go in peace, my friend."

Next, the boy's father approached. His embrace nearly squeezed the air out of Ethan's lungs.

"*Shukran*."

In response to his confused expression, the man grinned, exposing several missing teeth. He placed a hand on his chest, bowed his head, and said in a thick accent, "Thank you."

"Thank you." Ethan imitated the gesture. "Your hospitality saved my life."

The Nubian fishermen had finished their preparations and now stood by the wood boat. Ethan produced a twenty-dollar bill, which he handed to the first man before stepping over the side rail and into the open cockpit. He sat on a bench that had been painted blue at one time. The mast was set far forward, in front of a centerboard that was in the up position. Thick, frayed lines hung from the boom and single sail. The heavy scent of fish permeated the air.

After the Nubians pushed the boat off the shore, one took hold of the tiller while the other pulled in the sail. Ethan felt the boat glide across the flat water, a far more pleasant sensation than the camel ride. He ducked under the boom to wave good-bye to the men who had opened their tent to him and saved him from Axe, but they had already mounted their camels and were riding into the desert, where they would return to camp and take the injured boy to the hospital.

The boat seemed to drift more than sail down the great river. The serenity of the scenery struck him as surreal. Lush crops of sugar cane and alfalfa were interspersed with tall date palm trees along both banks; they contrasted the harsh desert two hundred yards farther out. Occasionally they passed laborers picking, digging, and carrying bundles of wheat balanced on their heads. The Nubians rarely spoke to each other: one tended to the tiller and sails, while the other untangled the fishing nets in the center of the cockpit.

Ethan tilted his face toward the warm morning sun. If he hadn't been running for his life, he would have found the trip relaxing. He couldn't shake the fear of not knowing whether Rachel and Mousa had been caught. As a scientist, his job was to know, to discover, to uncover the truth. Now he had to spend a day and a half on the river without any way to contact them and let them know he was okay and on his way.

Then he remembered—he did have a way to reach them. He opened the bag containing his clothes, pulled out his khakis, and searched the pockets until he felt the hard rectangular shape of the cell phone—the one he'd taken from the equipment storage room. His thumb hovered over the green power button, but then another doubt intruded.

He was dealing with the CIA. Tracking one of their missing cell phones would be simple for them. He knew enough from movies and TV shows that a cell phone could be located whenever the power was on since it sent out signals to the nearby towers. *But I destroyed their server room*, he thought. Then again, this was the CIA. He was pretty sure they could track him from their headquarters in Virginia too. The question was whether, in the chaos of the explosion and the escape, anyone had noticed that a phone was missing. He might get away with a couple of quick calls if he turned the phone off between them.

He passed the smooth plastic from hand to hand. He made his decision. More than anything he wanted to call the hotel in Luxor where he hoped to meet Rachel and Mousa. Had they checked in as planned? But he didn't know the phone number or even how to get directory help in this country, and he didn't want to waste valuable time trying to do so. Instead, he would contact the one person who might be able to help them—the same man who had made his last few years so difficult; the same man who had suspended him less than a week ago. He would contact Sam Houston, Rachel's father.

He carefully planned out his wording before powering on the phone and quickly typing several lengthy messages. He outlined the events of the past week: his discovery of the CIA as the funding source of the Logos, his trip to the Monastery in Aswan, Rachel's kidnapping, the innocent Jordanian doctor, and Chris's death. Since it was still the middle of the night in New Haven, he doubted Houston would see the messages until morning. It was fortunate that Rachel had programmed in his number.

The Yale administrator had never understood the Logos, and he now suspected Ethan of embezzling money from the project. But he couldn't ignore his daughter's peril. Houston also had the ear of the university's president, and they needed help from a powerful ally. The CIA was chasing them, and he didn't know how far up in the government the conspiracy went. Having a senior administrator from Yale contact a member of Congress, or maybe the *New York Times* or CNN, was their only hope of escaping the country.

But will he even believe me?

He pushed the thought aside. He had no choice. He hit the "send" button.

"You lost them!"

Axe refused to meet Wolfe's eyes as his boss paced around his office. He stood with perfect posture, his chest inflated, his rib cage expanded, his lats flexed so that his arms were held away from his sides, his legs apart to make room for his tree-trunk thighs. Mastering the art of appearing relaxed while displaying his superhuman physique had taken him years to perfect, but he wasn't feeling superhuman at the moment. The op was FUBAR. A black hole widened in his chest. Wolfe had rescued him from his dead-end Navy career. He'd believed in his abilities more than his own father had, and he'd given him the freedom to run security how he thought best. Now he'd lost his respect.

"I think they're traveling north to Luxor." His voice was unusually subdued. "We'll need to put in a ground team if we hope to find them among the thousands of tourists."

His boss shook his head in disgust.

"That's odd," Dawkins called out. The operative was hunched over two laptops on the conference table beside a young CIA tech who'd come with Wolfe from Cairo. Upon arriving, he'd set up a mobile workstation and established a satellite feed with Langley.

Wolfe faced them. "What now?"

"We just received a pop-up notification. One of our cell phones just logged onto the network."

"One of the prototypes?"

"It appears so."

"Here in the Monastery?"

Dawkins clicked several keys, then shook his head. "I'm trying to run a trace but"—his hands paused over the computer—"damn! It's gone. Whoever used the phone powered it off."

Wolfe rubbed his chin. "Axe, go take inventory of the prototypes."

Then Axe remembered. "I caught the professor in the supply room—that's when he saw the church pews. The phones are charged in there."

"Can you track it if he turns it back on?" Wolfe asked.

"I can pinpoint a general region within about forty seconds," the tech said, "but it will take longer to get a precise fix."

"Can you remotely activate the protocol?"

"Yes, sir," Dawkins said. "We just have to send the code to the number when the power is on. If the professor has the phone, he won't even know what's happening."

Wolfe leaned over the table. "Don't take your eyes off of that screen. Have the code ready the second he turns the phone back on. If it works like it's supposed to, we may buy ourselves enough time to trace it precisely." He paced back to the sofa and sat. "We may have a chance to test our latest device sooner than we expected."

CHAPTER 57

NILE RIVER, EGYPT

Ethan wished for his sunglasses as he reclined in the bow of the boat. The afternoon sunlight reflecting off the surface of the river seemed to pierce directly into his brain. At least he didn't feel a headache developing; he didn't have his meds with him. He drank warm water from the bottle given to him by the Bedouins while the two Nubians spoke in hushed tones in the stern, occasionally glancing in his direction.

He watched two other feluccas tack back and forth across the smooth water ahead. Further downriver he spied a much larger boat: a three-story-tall Nile cruise ship. He tugged the headdress over his ears to hide his American features. They'd passed another one of these tourist boats earlier in the morning, and he'd felt exposed on the small sailboat. It was only a matter of time before Wolfe's men started combing the river. The desert was expansive, but they'd soon realize that there was just one realistic destination that would work as an escape route.

Waiting was the hardest part. He wouldn't arrive in Luxor until the following day. He reached under his robe and produced the cell phone. He'd resisted the temptation to turn it back on since he'd sent the text hours earlier. *But Houston should have received it by now*, he thought. He flipped the hard case in his hand, opened it, and pressed the power button. *Just for a few seconds.* He wiped his brow, waiting for a signal. The air was still and dry.

The phone beeped. *A message!* He scanned Houston's brief reply. The administrator wanted to talk to him right away. The tone of the message was ambiguous, however. Did he want him to call because he believed the story and wanted to help, or did he want to admonish him for his far-fetched attempt at redemption?

He didn't have time to debate the possibilities. He clicked on the number. He'd give himself one minute. He pressed the phone to his ear and turned to face the water so the two men at the stern wouldn't be able to hear his conversation. They'd given him no indication that they spoke English, but he'd learned not to make assumptions about anything in this country.

As he waited for the call to connect, he studied yet another boat coming toward them. Unlike the feluccas, which were powered by the wind, this one moved through the water under the effort of two men, both pulling long wooden oars as sweat soaked through their blue shirts. The boat sat low in the water, weighed down by vegetables that threatened to spill over the sides at any time. Ethan marveled at the fertility of the Nile. The cauliflowers in the boat were the size of basketballs, the carrots an unusual color of Merlot.

A series of clicking sounds came from the phone as it went through the various relays to connect the call. He imagined the signal bouncing from satellite to satellite and then down to New Haven.

He wasn't sure when he first noticed the smell. *Burning rubber*, he thought. The tourist ship was still well ahead of them, but the exhaust from its engines must be drifting upriver, he guessed. His eyes caught the surface of the water. The ripples from the hull of the approaching rowboat spread outward in regular waves. They appeared to come toward him in a geometric pattern, as if in sync with the metronome of the oars. Sunlight danced across their crests. He stared without blinking.

A sudden thought popped into his head: *Each ripple is unique yet shares the river's water as its source and its connection with every other ripple.*

Then he noticed that embedded within each ripple were tiny bubbles. As he watched the bubbles surface and then pop, they seemed to form a pattern. *Binary code!* Just as he'd seen on his laptop when he'd been programming the Logos, each bubble appeared to him as a zero while the tiny splash made when they winked out of existence looked like a one. The binary pattern transfixed him:

0100100101101110001000000111010001101000011001010

1000000110001001100101011001110110100101101110011 0

1110011010010110111001100111001000000111011101100 0

0101110011001000000111010001101000011001010010000 0

011101110110111101110010011001000001011 10

He felt as if he was reading a hidden language describing the nature of the water. Then the river began to transform again. Like a photograph on a computer screen pixelating on high magnification, his vision telescoped. The ones and zeroes collapsed in on themselves: each bubble, he realized, was both a one and a zero. *There is no duality.* With that thought he no longer saw the bubble code, or even the water. Instead, he watched each water molecule spin and swirl around its neighbors. But like the binary code, even the molecules were not whole. Soon the hydrogen and oxygen atoms began to resolve into focus, but they remained only briefly. Then the subatomic particles that comprised each atom flitted about like sparks jumping off a campfire.

When he felt his own body begin to pixelate as well, he closed his eyes. He became aware that the cloud of particles that defined him was comprised of a single, vibrational energy. The essence of what made him was different in form, but not in kind, from the essence of what made the world. While new, the insight was also familiar. He'd glimpsed it lying on the grass by his trampoline two decades earlier. This Source of Existence—the Energy of Being itself—had always been present. The Source was manifested in the universe, just as it was manifested within him.

A feeling of warmth spread from the core of his body outward to his fingers and toes. The memories of those he'd lost in his life—his father, Natalie, Elijah, Chris—wove through this warmth like threads through a tapestry. Their deaths had brought him pain, but now he saw that these people were each part of a timeless reality, a reality still present. Their lives, while finite, were part of the Source he now saw so clearly. The essence that was each of his friends was still connected with the energy that made him who he was. The ripples in the river would die out, but the river remained.

For the first time in his life, he felt true peace.

"Hello." The voice seemed to come from inside his head.

"Is anyone there?"

There it is again, he thought.

He struggled to focus on the words, but his body longed to remain in its state of connectedness with being.

"Ethan, is that you?"

His eyes fluttered open. His vision flickered off, as if the plug had been pulled. The sunlight that replaced it was almost painful. He was still in the boat. His surroundings appeared normal. The river was just a river. He blinked again, feeling like he'd just woken from a long nap: sleepy yet relaxed.

Then he recognized the disembodied voice calling to him. "Professor Houston?"

"Where are you, Son?"

He pulled the phone from his ear and stared at it. The haze in his mind cleared instantly. He'd just had a mystical vision, similar in nature to the one he'd experienced as a teenager, only this time the vision had been deeper, more vivid.

Did I just have a seizure?

Then he noticed that the phone in his hand was vibrating.

Is it possible?

"Ethan?" Houston called.

He stared at the phone a second longer. Then he tossed it into the river.

"We got him!" Dawkins bent closer to his screen.

"Where?" Wolfe put the receiver to the scrambled satellite phone down on his desk. He was starting to dial Langley to report that he had nothing to report.

"On the Nile. Over a hundred clicks north of here."

"Can you pinpoint him?"

"The protocol worked?" Axe asked. Wolfe's idea was pure genius, he thought. Who else but Wolfe would have thought of inserting a tiny solenoid into a phone? The magnetic field wasn't very strong—nothing like the actual

Logos machine—but for someone who had already been conditioned in the cathedra, even a weak field might induce a feeling of being present with God. The Logos-phone was a way of keeping the subjects they sent out into the world in tune. They planned on giving each of the brothers a cell phone so their priests could keep in touch once a week. They would say a quiet prayer together over the phone while the Logos protocol was sent remotely to the handset. They'd already configured a dozen Logos-phones; they'd been planning on testing them that week on a few of the men.

Although the professor hadn't used his machine on himself—as far as they knew—they'd hoped that the phone would at least disorient him a bit so that they could track him. Earlier that morning the phone had powered on for just a few seconds; this time it stayed on for over a minute.

"Damn! We lost the signal."

"Was it long enough?" Wolfe asked.

"He's either on one of the roads bordering the river or on a boat. And he's heading north.

Luxor, Axe thought. He stood from the sofa. The drugs were finally out of his system. He would clean up his mess, just as he'd done with Chris Sligh. "Dawkins, inform the team in the Suburbans." He'd already scrambled the men based on his earlier hunch. "Then join me in the Black Hawk."

Wolfe turned to him. "We have one chance at this, James."

Axe met his boss's stare. The look of reproach fed the darkness within him.

CHAPTER 58

LUXOR, EGYPT

Ethan rubbed his neck. He was sore from the night on the boat's hard wooden bench, his second night in a row of little sleep. He hadn't been this tired since his residency. The Nubians had given him a mildew-infused blanket to ward off the cold, but he'd popped up his head to survey their surroundings at every unfamiliar noise.

A helicopter had passed overhead three times. He'd been careful to neither look up into the sky nor stare at the banks, where Wolfe's men might be scanning the river with binoculars. He kept the scarf covering his face while he pretended to work on the fishing nets with the Nubians. The principle thought that ran through his head, however, was not the danger of being caught on the river, but rather, *How did they do it?*

Somehow Wolfe had managed to miniaturize the Logos technology and conceal it in the cell phone. That was the only explanation for what had happened. Ethan's instinct to throw the phone away was probably the right one, but now he wished he'd just powered it off so that he could dismantle it.

He guessed that Wolfe had installed a small solenoid in the top of the phone and then triggered the Logos protocol remotely. *But how much of a magnetic field could be produced by such a small coil?* As impressed as Ethan was with the engineering feat, he was also curious about his response. He'd had a powerful dissociative experience, one even more powerful than his epileptic vision as a child. Had his earlier experience preconditioned him to react to the Logos protocol more readily, even at a weaker level?

Then another realization occurred to him: *I had a mystical vision but not a seizure.* Although he hadn't thought that his protocol would cause a seizure because of the way he'd targeted the magnetic pulses on the temporal lobes, his past history of epilepsy would have excluded him from his and Elijah's tests. After his failure to account for left-handed subjects in his programming, he had to admit a certain satisfaction at having gotten part of the protocol right.

What spoke to him most about the experience, however, was the reality of it. He knew that schizophrenics were often unable to distinguish their hallucinations from concrete reality, but something felt different about what he'd just seen. It wasn't the visual nature of his vision that struck him as real as much as his own intuition of the revelation. He felt in his core that he'd glimpsed an essence of reality that had always been there. *But what do I do with this knowledge?* As profound as the insight seemed, the more time that passed, the more difficult it was to remember the feeling of unity and connectedness the experience had inspired.

"Luxor!" One of the two Nubians pointed ahead and to the right, pulling Ethan out of his head.

He followed the man's finger. He could ponder the nature of existence at a time when his and Rachel's lives were not in danger. At the horizon, he saw, the landscape began to transform. The fields of crops transitioned into a city. He could just discern sand-colored concrete buildings and the tall minarets of mosques. As they sailed closer, he marveled at how tropical the famous city was: palm trees lined the streets and flowering plants of magenta grew everywhere.

In contrast to the city of Luxor, which was on the east bank of the Nile, the left bank was verdant cropland that became desert rising to mountains that were as barren as anything Ethan had seen. He imagined that the red, rough terrain was what the surface of Mars must look like. Although the air was dry, a haze hung over the mountains. *Maybe dust?* Then he noticed the traffic jam on the river. At least eight ferry-sized tourist boats were tied up at docks on the Luxor side of the river. Many spewed black exhaust.

As the Nubians readied their lines, he picked up the bag that contained his Western wear. He was grateful for the galabeya the Bedouins had given him—

the disguise had worked. But in a few minutes he would be stepping off into the middle of one of the largest tourist sites in the country. He began to change back into his own clothes. Looking like a tourist would be the best way to blend in.

Ten minutes later, they drifted toward a low dock just behind the tourist ships. Ethan slung his bag over his shoulder and shook hands with the Nubians. When they both continued to stare at him, he reached into his pocket and pulled out another twenty-dollar bill. Grins spread across their faces. They nodded and helped him off the boat. From the dock, he climbed stone stairs set into the concrete retaining wall that led to street level. As soon as he reached the sidewalk along the top of the wall, his heart rate accelerated.

Staring at him from no more than fifteen feet away were three Egyptian military officers. Dressed in black wool pants and button coats with black berets on their heads, each carried a Kalashnikov rifle with a collapsible stock. In addition to the curved ammunition magazine stuck in each rifle, they all had a second magazine taped with duct tape to the first, but upside down. Ethan had seen this in movies before. In the event of a firefight, all one had to do when the first clip ran out was to eject it and flip it around to start shooting again. These men were ready for a serious battle. He looked away, trying to appear casual despite the tightness in his chest.

One of the guards moved a hand to the butt of his rifle and strode toward him. He managed a smile he hoped wouldn't look forced. The guard stopped inches from him, eyeing him up and down. His eyes lingered on his hand-woven bag.

"Hello," Ethan managed.

"Why are you nervous?"

Do I look nervous?

"Not nervous at all. Just hot." He tugged at the collar of his oxford shirt. "Took a sail on a felucca." He pointed to the Nubians, who had already cast off. "But now I'm late to meet my group." He nodded toward the sea of people streaming from a line of waiting tour buses along the street. The words spilled out of his mouth faster than he wanted.

"British?"

"Me, uh, yeah."

As soon as he went along with the mistaken nationality, he wondered whether the Egyptians could distinguish an American from a British accent. If Wolfe had alerted the local authorities to keep an eye out for any Americans, appearing British might help him go undetected.

"You like Beatles?"

"The Beatles?" His father was an obsessive fan. He smiled. "*Abbey Road*—a classic."

The guard shook his head. "*Sergeant Pepper* is best." He laughed and turned back to the other officers.

Ethan tried to be subtle as he wiped his palms on his khakis. He didn't breathe again until he'd crossed the street and entered the maze of sidewalk stalls selling souvenirs. Tourists, mostly European, milled about the tables. The universal cry of "Good price, Mister!" rang out from the merchants selling tour books, postcards, T-shirts, and hats.

When a short man in a white galabeya stepped in front of him with a fistful of baseball caps, Ethan started to sidestep him but then paused. He selected a tan hat with the word "Luxor" stitched in gold across the front.

"How much?"

"Dollars or pounds?"

"US dollars."

"Five."

Not bothering to bargain, he produced a five and handed it to the man. He pulled the cap low across his forehead. Just as he started down the sidewalk, he spotted the man. He was perusing tour books about fifty feet to Ethan's right. He picked one up and flipped through it, then returned it and did the same with another. He never looked at Ethan, but his presence squeezed the air out of his lungs. He'd never seen the man before, but the creased black pants, the pressed white shirt, the sunglasses that hid his eyes, and the close-cropped haircut told him all he needed to know.

Ethan turned and walked in the opposite direction. After a few steps he stopped at a T-shirt vendor's stall and pretended to study the selection. He never even heard the sales pitch from the woman with a colorful scarf around her head; his entire attention was focused on his peripheral vision. The man hadn't moved.

He dropped the T-shirt he'd been pretending to admire and kept walking. He kept his pace brisk, but not so fast that he looked as if he was trying to avoid someone.

Maybe I'm just being paranoid, he thought.

"Hurry up, Durward," called a mid-sixties woman in a loud British accent. "The bus is leaving."

"They won't leave for Karnak without us, Dear," replied the man a step ahead of him. He wore a safari hat over pink skin and white hair.

When the two stopped at the next intersection, Ethan glanced across the street. Tourists were loading onto a bus. He had an idea. He vaguely recalled from his undergraduate days that the temple of Karnak was the largest archeological site in Egypt after the pyramids of Giza. He crossed the street with the British couple, resisting the temptation to look behind him to see if the man with the crew cut was following. A mid-thirties woman with her hair pulled into a bun on top of her head, a Burberry umbrella in one hand, and a clipboard in the other counted off the group as they boarded.

"Excuse me," he said to the guide after the English couple stepped on, "I'm John Stevens"—the fictitious name was the first that came to his mind—"and my tour group left without me. You wouldn't be heading to Karnak, would you?"

The woman looked him up and down; her eyes seemed to linger on his shoulders. "You Yanks have a history of independence, don't you? Always wandering off on your own as if everyone will wait around for you." Then she broke into a grin.

He shrugged and returned the smile. "I feel really stupid. If you have any room on your bus—"

"We have two extra seats. Take the one in the front row"—her eyes dropped down his torso again—"next to me." She reached out and touched his elbow. "I'm Robin."

He stepped onto the bus. "Thanks, Robin." As he ducked his head in the doorway, he caught a glimpse of the other side of the street. Standing on the sidewalk was the man, watching him.

CHAPTER 59

STEIGENBERGER NILE PALACE HOTEL
LUXOR, EGYPT

Rachel snatched the ringing phone from the bedside table.

"Hello."

"Rachel?"

"Ethan, is that you?"

She collapsed on the hotel bed at the sound of his voice. He and Chris should have been there yesterday. She'd been terrified that Axe had killed them. The last image she and Mousa had seen as they disappeared over the dune was Ethan hunkered behind the other SUV while sparks of gunfire exploded around him.

"Thank God you made it," he whispered over the sound of other voices in the background.

"Where are you?" She longed for his touch.

"Tour bus, heading to Karnak."

"The ancient temple site?"

"Long story. One of Wolfe's men may have spotted me. I'll try to lose him in the crowds there."

She turned to Mousa, who had just entered through the connecting door to his room. "They're at the temple of Karnak."

"That's close." The Jordanian sat on the twin bed opposite her. "We could be there in ten minutes."

"Mousa and I will come meet you guys!" She had a difficult time containing the enthusiasm in her voice.

When he didn't immediately respond, a disturbing thought crept into her head. "Ethan, Chris is with you, right?"

"Chris"—his voice faltered—"didn't make it."

"He didn't make it?" The phone trembled in her hand. "You mean—"

"I . . . I can't believe it either. Chris is dead."

Tears began to roll down Rachel's cheeks. At Yale she'd found the graduate student smart and funny, although she'd never felt romantic about him despite his open flirtation. After her initial shock at waking up in the Monastery, she'd believed his naivety about Wolfe's plans. He would never have knowingly put her or Ethan in harm's way. And now he'd given up his life to help them escape. She tried to speak, but the burning in her throat prevented the words from coming out.

Mousa rested a hand on her shoulder and took the phone. "Hello, Ethan."

"Mousa, I'm relieved to hear your voice."

"Likewise. We'll get a car and a driver from the hotel and pick you up at Karnak. That will be safer than you wandering around the open parking lot looking for a taxi."

"Where should we meet?"

"Go inside the main temple. You'll pass two giant statues of Ramses the Second. We'll meet you there. Hundreds of tourists will be milling around. You'll be safe in the crowds." He handed the phone back to Rachel.

"Hi again," she managed.

"I spoke to your dad."

"What did he say?" She wiped the tears from her face.

"I texted him a summary of what's happened, but"—he paused—"our conversation was cut off before I could explain more. Will you call him?"

"Yeah, I'll do it now, before we come meet you."

When they hung up, she sat on the bed and stared into Mousa's kind face. She struggled with the conflicting emotions flowing through her body. Her sadness at learning of Chris's death battled her joy at hearing Ethan's voice. More than anything she wanted to throw herself into his arms and feel his lips against hers.

For the first time in two days, Ethan felt hopeful. Talking to Rachel made him forget how tired he was. He passed the phone he'd borrowed back to Robin.

"Thanks. My friends are going to meet me at the temple."

"Well, you can tag along with us as long as you'd like." She leaned in close and whispered in his ear, "It's nice having someone my own age around."

She winked at him, picked up the microphone clipped to the back of the driver's seat, and stood to address the busload of seniors.

"I hope everyone enjoyed the last five days on the boat, but today is sure to be one of the highlights of your trip. In just a few minutes we'll be arriving at the temple of Karnak. The ancient Egyptians began construction on the temple complex approximately four thousand years ago in the heart of the city of Thebes."

"Thebes?" a loud voice called from several rows behind Ethan. He turned to see the woman he'd followed from the market poke her head into the aisle. "I thought we were in Luxor."

Robin seemed to catch herself beginning to roll her eyes. "Thebes is the Greek name for Luxor." She paused for a breath and continued, "As I explained on the boat, Thebes—or Luxor, if you wish—is one of the oldest cities on Earth. Its history dates back more than five thousand years. It was the capital of Egypt for centuries."

"Didn't Homer write about it?" a balding man with small, round glasses asked from the rear.

"In *The Iliad*," the guide said. "Now, the complex, as you'll see, is made up of a number of temples, courtyards—even a lake. It's expansive, so stay within eyeshot of me." She raised the Burberry umbrella. "We'll spend most of our time in the temple of Amun-Ra, considered to be the most important of the ancient Egyptian deities. As I'll explain in more detail when we arrive, he is a conglomeration of two earlier Gods: Amun, the distant creator god, and Ra, the sun god who brings warmth and light to our everyday lives."

Ethan listened with interest. *A god who is both distant and near*, he thought. Then an image flashed through his head. His vision on the river had shown him a view of a reality that was as intimate to his life as he was, yet hidden from ordinary view as well.

The bus veered to the left, pushing the British guide into his side. Her body lingered for a moment longer than necessary before she righted herself.

"Egyptian drivers," she said in his ear.

He glanced out the window. They pulled into a concrete parking lot so expansive they could have been entering Disney World. In a few minutes he would be reunited with Rachel. He ached to feel her touch, but the image of Wolfe's man staring at him from the sidewalk still blazed in his mind. Would he, a doctor and college professor, be able to avoid trained CIA spooks? He pushed the question away. He couldn't afford to have any doubt in his mind. His life, and more importantly Rachel's, depended on his thinking clearly.

CHAPTER 60

KARNAK TEMPLE COMPLEX

"**H**e's on a tourist bus," the voice in Axe's earpiece said, "heading to Karnak."

"What about the girl and the Arab?"

"No sign of them. Just the professor."

"On my way."

Axe relayed the intel to the driver of the black Suburban. They'd landed the Black Hawk in the desert just outside the city. His strategy of spreading his men around the small but crowded town while he coordinated their movements from the back of the SUV had paid off. He would now have all of his men converge on the tourist site. The professor would be trapped.

"We may have a problem," the voice in his ear continued. "I think he made me."

Axe shook his head. This entire operation had been characterized by sloppiness. When it was over, he was going to kick some ass.

"When you get to the temple, cover the entrance and any other escape routes. Recon only." He spoke the next words slower, emphasizing each syllable. "Don't make contact. I'm going after him myself."

He thought about the hidden compartment underneath the middle row seat that held several M4 rifles and a metal ammo box of loaded magazines. Unfortunately, with the tight security around the site and the Egyptians' fear of terrorism, he couldn't bring a gun inside the temple grounds, not even a compact sidearm. He recalled the shooting at Hatshepsut's temple that had left sixty-two tourists dead in 1997. The terrorists had dressed as Egyptian police, walked into the heart of the temple with submachine guns, and opened fire on the mass of tourists. Since the incident, security at the major architectural sites had been increased significantly.

He reached down, hiked up his pants leg, and ran his fingers inside the upper part of his calf-high black boots. He could feel the bumpy grip of the handle's composite plastic. The knife strapped just above his ankle only had a five-inch blade, but in the hands of a trained soldier, it was more than enough to do the job.

Ethan followed the British tour group down a stone ramp lined on both sides with dozens of ram-headed sphinxes, poised like an army of sentries guarding the main gate into the temple complex. The massive walls on either side of the gate towered at least seven stories over them. He walked through a world of beige: the sand, the stone pavers they walked upon, the blocks in the walls, even the sphinxes, were the same desert color.

"Stay together, now," Robin called with her umbrella held high above her head.

Ethan stuck to the rear of the group, close enough to appear to be part of them, but ready to separate the moment he saw Rachel and Mousa. He darted his eyes through the crowd, scanning every face. The anticipation of seeing Rachel again fueled him with an energy he hadn't had since their escape. The tour group had taken over fifteen minutes to disembark the bus, gathering cameras and passing out water bottles and tickets. He'd tried to look for his friends in the parking lot, but it was simply too big and crowded. He had no idea whether he was the first one to arrive or if they were waiting for him inside.

When Robin led them through the gate in the entrance wall, Ethan stopped and stared. The temple complex was larger than he'd imagined. Giant columns, monumental statues, obelisks that pierced the pure blue sky, and fallen blocks and rubble stretched for hundreds of yards in every direction as far as he could see.

"This way, please." Robin walked toward a stone statue of an Egyptian pharaoh so tall the top of her head only came up to its calf.

He craned his neck upward and admired the three-thousand-year-old craftsmanship. The male figure stood with his feet together, wearing a tunic of smooth stone over a long body; his arms were crossed on his chest. The face had round features with almond eyes and a wide nose. A smaller statue of a woman, carved out of the same giant block of stone, came up to the pharaoh's knees.

"Ramses the Second," Robin said when the group gathered in a semicircle around her in front. She had Ethan's full attention. This was where Mousa had said to wait for them. He searched the crowd again.

"As we discussed in Abu Simbel, Ramses's reign as Pharaoh over seven decades in the thirteenth century BC was the longest and one of the most spectacular in the history of Egypt."

"He certainly liked to build statues of himself," a man to Ethan's left said. "Was he compensating for something?"

Robin laughed. "He was one of the most prolific builders in ancient Egypt. The country also prospered under his reign. He was considered to be not just the ruler but an actual god." She pointed upward. "Who remembers the significance of the figure with crossed arms holding a crook and a flail in his hands?"

A stooped-over woman with a silk shawl draped over her head answered from the front row, "He's in the form of Osiris, god of the afterlife."

"Exactly. Note the difference to that one." She pointed to another monumental statue of Ramses on the opposite side of the walkway. "There he's standing with one foot in front of the other and his arms by his side. That's the depiction of Ramses in a living state."

"So we have the pharaoh pictured as a ruler both in this life and the next one," the stooped woman said.

"Wasn't Osiris resurrected from the dead, like Jesus?" said Durward, the man with the safari hat whom Ethan had followed onto the bus.

"The myth of Osiris is probably the oldest tale of resurrection we know of," Robin replied. "Evidence of Osiris worship dates back twenty-four-hundred years—two and a half millennia—before Christ. His brother, the evil god Set, kills Osiris and dismembers him in order to assume his throne. But the goddess Isis, Osiris's sister and wife, resurrects him by reassembling his parts. He then goes on to become the god of the underworld, the god who judges those deemed worthy of having eternal life by weighing their hearts on a scale. We'll see depictions of this scene from the Egyptian Book of the Dead when we visit the tombs in the Valley of the Kings tomorrow."

Ethan found the parallels to the story of Jesus fascinating: overcoming death, the battle of good versus evil, the moral judgment of human lives by a higher power. He'd taught in his classes how the religious myths common to ancient cultures arose from a human psychological need to make sense of the presence of evil in the world and to believe that justice ultimately prevails. These myths also helped to alleviate people's fear of their own mortality through belief in an idyllic afterlife that made the suffering of this world tolerable.

Staring at the imposing stone king silhouetted against the azure sky, Ethan wondered for the first time whether that explanation was complete. The memory of his vision the previous day flashed through his mind again. He didn't believe the miracle stories of people rising from the dead were historical events. Such things only happened in ancient times prior to the scientific worldview present today.

But what if the everyday physical reality in which he lived, a reality he knew to be finite, was not the entire story? As he pondered the possibility that his vision held truth, the sight of the person ahead of him in a maze of columns shocked him out of his thoughts.

———————

The security in the Karnak complex was much tighter than Axe would have liked. The Egyptians guarding the ancient site were not the rent-a-cops one might find at a monument in the US. These guys were military, and they were well armed. He would have to act quickly when he spotted the professor. Lightman's death would be seen as an unfortunate robbery. But first he had to find him amidst the hordes of tourists and the ruins.

He moved toward a set of giant columns seven stories tall that were part of an ancient temple whose roof had long since fallen and been replaced by a cloudless blue sky. He froze in place.

The Jordanian doctor!

Mousa walked among the columns at the opposite end of the temple. Axe's pulse quickened. Then he saw the girl with him. He couldn't suppress the smile that spread across his face. They must have come to rendezvous with Lightman. His job had just become much easier. Wolfe would be ecstatic.

"These columns are huge!" Rachel ran her fingers along the hieroglyphics carved into a stone column twenty feet in diameter and seventy feet tall.

"The Great Hypostyle Hall," Mousa said as they walked through the rows of columns in the fifty-thousand-square-foot temple. "The columns used to hold up a roof."

"You've been here before?"

"With my family two years ago."

He was so close to returning to his loved ones. He'd called his wife the moment they'd arrived at the hotel. When she'd put Amira on the phone, both father and daughter had cried so hard they'd had trouble understanding each other. The temptation to leave Luxor yesterday and race to the Jordanian embassy in Cairo had been intense. But he owed his life to the American doctor, and he had promised him he would take care of the delightful woman he had escaped with.

"So this is where you told Ethan to meet us?"

"Any minute."

"Any sign of the professor?" Axe spoke into his sleeve while he tracked his two targets.

"Negative," Dawkins voice came over his earpiece. "There's a shitload of tour buses here."

No matter. He would take care of these two first and then deal with Lightman.

He bent over, feigning scratching his calf, and slipped the five-inch K-bar knife out from his boot. He flipped the blade around, concealing it against his wrist and forearm. When they disappeared behind the next column, he advanced forward, keeping the maze of stone between him and his prey.

Other than the tour group he'd just passed outside the temple, he saw only a few others walking among the columns. Rachel and Mousa were isolated. It was the perfect time to strike.

———————

Ethan felt paralyzed. James Axelrod had just walked passed him. When the security man had swiveled his orange-tinted sunglasses in his direction, he'd ducked behind Durward's wide safari hat. Now the huge man bent over not thirty yards from him and removed something shiny from his boot.

"Does anyone recognize this?" Robin pointed to the hieroglyphics carved on an eight-foot-cubed block that had once been part of a larger wall.

"A Coptic cross," Durward replied.

The historical discussion barely registered for Ethan. The blood drained from his head the moment he saw what held Axe's attention. Walking amongst the giant columns were Rachel and Mousa. From their vantage point they couldn't see Axe. Then a realization sucked the air from his lungs: *He's stalking them with a knife!*

"Why would there be a Coptic cross in the middle of ancient Egyptian hieroglyphics?" the woman in the shawl asked loudly.

Ethan willed his feet to come unglued from the stone.

"Notice this scratched-out area at the top of the cross," Robin said

"It used to be something else."

"Exactly. Originally it was an ankh, the ancient Egyptian symbol for the key of eternal life. Tomorrow, when we visit the Valley of the Kings, you'll see ankhs depicted in every tomb painting, usually in the hands of a god leading the deceased emperor into the afterlife. Look here." She pointed to the top of the cross where the ankh had been defaced. "The loop at the top part of the ankh represents the delta of the Nile. The vertical line running down from the loop represents the Nile itself, the source of life in ancient Egypt, and"—she traced the horizontal section of the cross—"the horizontal line of the ankh signifies the unification of the eastern and western parts of Egypt."

"So why did they turn the ankh into a cross?" asked the woman wearing the shawl.

"As Christianity became the dominant religion of the Roman Empire in the fourth century, the Romans converted many of the ancient Egyptian temples into Christian churches. Tragically, they often destroyed the hieroglyphics; in some cases, like this one, they converted the Egyptian symbols into Christian ones."

As the lecture continued, Ethan looked around for the police he'd passed at the entrance into the temple complex. Of course they were omnipresent when he didn't need one, but now, in the heat of the afternoon, they were probably chatting in the shadow of the main entrance wall.

He was on his own. His skin tingled.

He scanned his surroundings for something he could use as a weapon. He wasn't sure how he was going to confront the huge man, but he had to protect Rachel. Then he saw it.

He left the British tour group and hurried toward a pile of rubble twenty yards to his right. He kept the baseball cap pulled low over his eyes in case Axe turned around. The moment Wolfe's man disappeared behind a column, Ethan sprinted. When he reached the rubble, he grabbed one of the waist-high metal rods attached to a rope that cordoned off the rubble from the tourists. He jerked upward, praying that it wasn't set in concrete. It pulled free of the sand. He worked frantically at the knot on the end. He only had seconds. When it came free, he spun on his heels and ran toward the columns. He could no longer see Axe or his friends.

Wolfe's head of security was well trained. He'd kidnapped Rachel and killed Elijah and Chris. What were Ethan's chances against a man like that? He tried to calm his rapid breathing, but his limbic system was on its own.

Fight or flight, he thought. *This time I'm going to fight.*

Axe ducked behind a column to his left as the girl stepped into an opening three rows ahead.

His only regret in taking her out was that he'd never have his way with her. The memory of her naked body quivering in fear the night he'd kidnapped her sent a wave of heat through his loins. He flexed and released his quads. When his mission was complete, he'd head into Cairo for a night of R&R. He'd always had good luck with the Eastern European prostitutes there. They had no one to go to if he was too rough.

When they passed in front of the next set of columns, he moved up two more rows. *This is too easy*, he thought.

"I'm taking them down now," he whispered into his mic. Dawkins had been shocked when he'd relayed the news of their sudden fortune.

"Roger. Get out quickly."

He glanced behind him. The tour group he'd passed outside hadn't entered the temple yet. He was alone with his targets.

He crept to the next column. Their voices came from the row ahead. He peeked around the edge of the stone. Their backs were to him. Both were gazing up at a section of roof still in place, a giant slab of stone seventy feet over their heads. The Muslim doctor was pointing out the remnants of the blue, red, and gold paint that remained, three thousand years later, on the underside of the ceiling.

The Arab had the greatest potential to put up a fight. Axe would dispatch him first. He flipped the knife in his hand, pointing the blade down. He would strike the kidney, a blow that would seize the man's body with pain. Then, with his prey unable to resist, he would draw the knife across the man's windpipe and carotid artery. The sight of blood spurting from his throat would paralyze the girl with fear and shock for a few seconds. He would be on her before she realized she needed to run.

He relaxed his grip on the knife and released his breath, just as he'd been trained. Then he attacked.

Often when Ethan was engrossed in his research, hours would pass without him even noticing. His focus would narrow so that he never heard the traffic on the street or the chatter of the students in the hallway. As he dashed from column to column, mirroring the path Axe took, he felt the same narrow focus. He was no longer aware of the tourists behind him, the heat from the desert sun, or the ancient artifacts around him. His senses were telescoped on the man a single row in front of him.

Axe paused and lifted his wrist to his mouth, radioing to Wolfe's other men. He couldn't hear Axe's words, but his friends' voices were clear.

What do I do now?

He was separated from the killer by only a few yards, but then that same distance separated Axe from his friends. If he yelled out, he'd lose the one advantage he had over the trained fighter: surprise.

He gripped the rough iron rod in his hand. For the first time, he noticed its weight. He began to doubt his initial plan of hurling it at Axe's head. He'd only get one shot. Should he throw it like a spear or fling it end over end? The truth was, his eye-hand coordination was abysmal. He wasn't at all confident he could hit Axe in the head, even from this short distance.

He had only one viable option. He readied himself to attack the muscular security man directly.

Suddenly Axe stepped from behind the column that blocked him from Rachel and Mousa. He didn't run, but somehow he moved much faster than Ethan expected.

He's starting his attack!

The realization sent Ethan's adrenal glands into hyperdrive. He broke into a sprint. But in his gut he had the empty feeling he would be too late.

CHAPTER 61

KARNAK TEMPLE COMPLEX

Axe rounded the column. His targets had their backs to him. The Jordanian was pointing at some carvings in the base of a column in front of them.

"—and the scarab here symbolizes rebirth and eternal life because—"

Just as he closed in on the final steps, a sensation unlike anything he'd ever experienced stopped him. His spine began to seize up. The image of a snake made of ice emerging from his skull and coiling itself around his vertebrae flashed through his mind. A black fear gripped him, just as it had on the helicopter ride over the desert.

"—the dung beetle, which is what the scarab is, hatches from an egg as larvae but stays in the ground until it emerges as a fully-formed beetle." Mousa moved to the left as he continued to explain the carving, his back still facing the immobile Axe. "So the seemingly miraculous emergence of a live beetle from the desert sand was seen as symbolic of the process of mummification and eternal life that would come to the pharaoh."

In seconds, he knew, he would be spotted. He willed his body to move, but the blackness threatened to overwhelm him. Then his training took over. His legs began to inch forward, and the strange vision and the cold dissipated. He reached the unarmed man in a few strides. The Jordanian would be dead in seconds.

Axe snaked his left hand out and around Mousa's head, clamping down on his mouth and jerking backward. But his gut told him that something was wrong with the tactical situation. An uncharacteristic hesitation of doubt entered his mind. Was his mind messing with him again? He shoved away the feeling and thrust his right hand, the one holding the knife, forward—toward the kidney.

As the knife sunk in to the hilt, a thunderclap went off inside his head.

The rod reverberated in Ethan's hand as it crunched against Axe's skull. The large man dropped to the ground as if the power had been cut from his body. But Ethan had been a second too late, even with the strange hesitation that had slowed Axe a moment before the attack. He'd seen the knife plunge into Mousa's back. The doctor collapsed on top of his attacker.

Please, let him be okay.

"What—" Rachel turned toward the men. When her eyes fell on Mousa lying on top of Axe, she screamed.

As much as he wanted to run to her, Ethan had to triage the knife wound first and then get his friends to safety. "He's been stabbed!"

"God, no!"

He dropped to his knees and glanced at the plastic hilt of the knife. The best course of action was to keep Mousa still, but he didn't know how much time they had before Wolfe's other men arrived.

"My back!" the Jordanian moaned.

"Mousa, we have to move you." In spite of the pounding in his chest, Ethan tried to use his best hospital tone. "This is going to hurt."

He grasped Mousa's forearm and his shoulder. "Rachel, his other arm!" Her eyes were wide and her hands shook, but she knelt and took Mousa's hand. Together they lifted him. He groaned as he stood on shaky legs.

They helped him walk several yards away from Axe, who lay unmoving on the dusty stone floor. "Can you support his weight for a minute?" Ethan asked her, placing Mousa's arm on her shoulder.

"Okay." Her voice quivered, but she widened her stance. "You can lean on me."

Ethan inspected the doctor's back. "The hilt of a small knife is protruding from your lower lumbar region." He touched the skin underneath the blue shirt just below the wound. His fingers became damp with blood. "It's embedded in the psoas major muscle, but it looks like it just missed your kidney." A wave of relief passed through him.

"Yes, that's what it feels like." A half-smile masked the grimace on Mousa's face.

Hearing that the Jordanian hadn't lost his macabre physician's humor encouraged Ethan. The wound would hurt like hell, but Mousa would live.

A quick look at Axe confirmed that he was unconscious. Ethan wondered if he would have brain damage. "Axe was stalking you. I got here a second too late."

"You were quick enough," Mousa said. "Thank you."

Rachel's eyes darted to Axe. "We've got to find the police." The panic in her voice was barely veiled.

Ethan glanced around the Hypostyle Hall. The columns hid them from the scores of other tourists, as well as the Egyptian police. "Axe was speaking on his radio; we should move somewhere more public."

"Surely you're going to pull that out?" Rachel pointed to the knife.

Mousa shook his head. "Extracting it might cause more damage—it will worsen the bleeding, too."

"I concur. They'll remove it at the hospital."

She stared at them with an incredulous expression as they calmly discussed the knife protruding from Mousa's back. Then a guttural groan escaped Axe's lips.

He's coming to already? The man was even stronger than he looked, which Ethan hadn't thought possible. Then he had an idea. He stepped over to Axe, kneeled, and grabbed a forearm the thickness and weight of a heavy tree branch. Clipped to his cuff was a black microphone. He dropped the arm and patted around a waist disproportionately small for the mass of muscle carried above it. Feeling a bulge, he jerked up Axe's shirt and pulled out a radio the size of a cell phone. He unplugged two wires from the radio, pocketed it, and stood.

Rachel stared at him with raised eyebrows when he returned to Mousa's side. "Saw him speaking into his sleeve. Now he can't call for backup when he wakes." He draped Mousa's arm over his shoulder. "Can you walk?"

"Not sure." The Jordanian exhaled sharply. "But I have to."

Axe noticed the taste of sand first. Dry and grainy, it stuck to his lips. Gradually the sounds returned, as if someone was slowly turning up the volume on a distant TV. The voices confused him. Snippets of German and Italian.

He forced his eyes open, then snapped them shut, praying for the hammering inside his head to clear so he could think. He rolled to his side and drew a deep breath. Bile rose to the back of his throat. He swallowed. The second time he opened his eyes, he cracked them open into a slit. A sandy stone floor came into focus. A few feet from him stood the base of an immense column. Then the memories flooded back.

He'd been finishing off the Arab doctor when someone attacked him from behind. He didn't see his assailant, but the thought that it must have been the lanky professor brought him out of his haze. He pushed himself to his hands and knees. His pounding headache brought with it a vertigo that tilted the ground at an unnatural angle. A few feet from him was an iron rod. He winced at the sight of it.

How had Lightman snuck up on him? His training had prepared him to be hyperaware of his surroundings. Then he remembered the strange sensation that had seized him before the attack. He grabbed the warm limestone of the column and hauled himself to his feet. He flexed his quads, his hams, and his calves in rapid succession. As the blood pumped into his muscles, the spinning subsided.

A quick survey revealed that a dozen tourists had wandered into the temple hall. His targets weren't among them. A door to his left led into another courtyard. How long had he been unconscious? The Jordanian wouldn't get far with that knife wound. He glanced at the droplets of blood on his right knuckles. Had he punctured the kidney? He'd flinched at the last second, just as he was plunging the blade forward. As much as he was hurting, however, the three of them would be slower. He willed his thighs to move, imagining that they were giant pistons pushing forward the powerful machine that was his body. On heavy lifting days, he would often visualize his body parts as indestructible mechanical devices made of titanium: levers, pulleys, and pistons.

As he headed toward the doorway, he brought his sleeve to his mouth. "Lost contact," he said. "The professor's here too. Anyone have a bead on them?"

He would have to think of a better way to explain what happened other than admitting the professor snuck up on him and hit him with a rod, but that could wait until after the mission was successful.

His earpiece was silent. "Dawkins, check in. Over."

He touched his ear. The earpiece was still in place. Then he noticed his shirt was untucked.

"Damn it!" They'd taken his radio.

He stepped through the doorway into a courtyard enclosed by stone walls. More tourists ambled about, but his targets weren't among them. In addition to the doorway he'd come through, two other openings led out to different areas of the complex. He picked the one straight ahead. Just outside the courtyard a monumental granite obelisk had fallen to the ground. Past it a lake stretched for several hundred yards. They would feel safer in the open.

When he reached the doorway, he saw a group gathered by the obelisk. He stopped. The tourists surrounded a man lying on the ground. *The Jordanian doctor.* Kneeling next to Mousa was an Egyptian security guard.

"Damn!" he muttered.

The operation was going to hell. He searched the tourists surrounding the man. Neither the girl nor the professor was there. He looked closer at Mousa, who lay on his side, facing away from him.

He grinned at seeing one good piece of news. The knife was still embedded to the hilt, and the Jordanian wasn't moving. He must have struck the kidney after all. Before the Egyptian guard could look in his direction, Axe turned and headed back through the enclosed courtyard toward the other doorway.

"I still don't feel right leaving him," Rachel said. Her tight grip on Ethan's hand threatened to cut off his circulation.

He led her through the maze of the Karnak Temple Complex. Two obelisks towered over them, piercing the pure blue sky as they were designed to do in honor of the sun god, Ra.

"I don't either, but he was right. We'll be safer if we split up. He needs to get to the hospital right away."

Mousa had told the tourists in the other courtyard that he'd been stabbed from behind in a robbery attempt. They'd agreed that revealing their involvement in a CIA conspiracy would not help matters.

"So how do we get out of here?" Rachel asked.

"Good question."

Ethan paused and surveyed their surroundings. On the far side of the two obelisks, he saw hundreds of stone blocks scattered around a courtyard. Some of the blocks were almost as tall as he was. About twenty yards into the piles of stone, the blocks began to take shape, forming walls. Farther in, one wall rose over seventy feet tall. Another ancient temple must have stood there, he guessed.

He would need to ask someone for directions. He'd become disoriented during the events of the past few minutes. He looked around. For the moment, they were alone.

"The bigger question is, what do we do when we leave here?"

Rachel grabbed his arm. "I called my father before we left the hotel."

"He got my text?"

"He's been totally freaked the past few days. My roommates called the New Haven police when they got home and saw that I was missing and the bathroom door was broken. Then after you texted him and your call disconnected, he assumed the worst. He's been in President Martin's office all day."

Ethan had only been in the Yale president's office once, for a cocktail reception when he was first hired as an assistant professor. The mahogany bookcase–lined suite had smelled of tradition.

"They've had some heated calls with Washington."

"Washington?" His doubt about whether he could trust Houston surfaced again. "Who?"

"If you would stop with the questions for a minute, I'll tell you everything I know."

"Sorry." He smiled, but before he could ask her to continue, a movement from his peripheral vision caught his attention. He swiveled his head. Jogging toward them from an adjacent courtyard was the hulking figure of James Axelrod.

"Oh, no!" Rachel cried.

Ethan took her hand and pulled her into the maze of the fallen stone blocks.

The pounding from the back of Axe's head had spread to behind his eyes, but he'd suffered worse pain during some of his tougher workouts. Sometimes the increase in blood pressure from a heavy set would cause a migraine, but he never stopped his workout. Besides, his targets were right in front of him. No way he was screwing up this time.

Fortunately for him, they'd just made a tactical mistake. They'd ducked into a bunch of rubble where they would be hidden from the Egyptians. The only exit to the temple complex was to his left, and his men had that covered. They might be able to avoid him among the rocks for a minute or so, but they were trapped. He'd seen the tall wall rising from the opposite side of the fallen stones.

His only weapon, the knife, was stuck in the Jordanian's back. But against these two he wouldn't need one. Their necks would snap like brittle branches. He picked up his pace as he passed the first block of granite. The officer who'd found the Jordanian would be calling for backup. He needed to get to the professor and the girl before the area was swarming with tourist police.

They dashed left and then right, trying to put as many rocks and turns between them and their pursuer as they could. Ethan heard Rachel's breath coming in short gasps. Her dilated pupils made her blue eyes seem black; sweat glistened on her neck, and her hand was cinched tight around his.

She slowed and looked behind them. "Not there," she panted. "Maybe we lost him?"

Ethan kept her moving forward, dodging another pile of rubble from the collapsed temple, this one taller than the others. "We need to make our way back to the entrance and the tourist police."

"I'm so turned around—which way is it?"

Ethan paused and surveyed the ruins. The two obelisks they'd passed a minute earlier cast sword-like shadows across their path. The various stacks of stone and the tall foundations obscured his view of the main temple complex.

"I have no idea."

Then he heard the sound of heavy footsteps falling on the stone path on the other side of the near rocks. He pulled her hand and continued forward. "Keep moving!" he whispered.

Somehow the man who had been lying unconscious from a blow to the head minutes ago was gaining on them.

They dodged around the foundation of another crumbling wall and then froze in their tracks. Ahead of them was the wall Ethan had seen earlier. It was as high as a six- or seven-story building. He flicked his head left and right. After twenty yards in each direction, the path was blocked off by fallen rubble. They'd reached the temple's rear wall—the only wall that still stood at its original height, a dead-end.

"We're trapped." The strain in Rachel's voice was evident.

Axe would be on top of them in seconds.

Ethan searched the ground for anything he could use as a weapon, but the rocks that comprised the temple rubble were all too large to move, much less pick up. Even if he found one, he feared he would be no match for the combat-trained man. Earlier he'd had surprise on his side. Now he had nothing.

His heart thumped in his chest like a bass drum at a rock concert. The wall obstructing their path was made of the same stone blocks they'd dodged around to end up where they were. The blocks were staggered, often with several inches overlapping the edges. He gazed upward. About three-quarters of the way up, the blocks were offset even more, creating several ledges wide enough to stand on. He had an idea.

He turned to Rachel. She was young, in shape, and had a petite frame. Their pursuer had to weigh over two-fifty. He grabbed her shoulders.

"Ever done the rock climbing wall at Payne Whitney?" If they could climb to one of those ledges, they could yell for the police above the maze of ruins. He didn't think Axe would attack them in full view of the authorities.

She shook her head. "Not a fan of heights." She cut her gaze to the wall. "You're not suggesting that—"

"It's our only escape."

Her eyes were wide in fear and her bangs were damp with perspiration. "Ethan, I—"

Axe would appear any second. They were out of time and options. He guided her hands to the stone.

"Climb like you're going up a ladder. Use your legs more than your arms, and don't look down."

She turned her head toward his, kissed him on the lips, and started to climb.

"Don't worry. I'll be right beside you."

"Damn!" Axe cursed under his breath. *Where are they?*

He rounded a corner. An elderly French couple approached him as they argued with each other, both waving their arms in the air. He stopped. He should have reached his targets already. Had he missed a turn? The possibility that they'd eluded him caused his pulse to accelerate further, which only served to worsen the pounding in his skull.

He pivoted and checked his flank. Then he pushed past the couple and jogged to the next intersection of rubble. He was close to the end of the temple. The seventy-foot wall he'd seen earlier was to his right, past a fallen column and another pile of boulders.

He sprinted to the wall. When he was about eight feet away, he could see down the length of it. *A dead end.*

Then a movement up on the wall caught his attention. He squinted against the blinding sun that seemed to amplify the pain in his head. The professor and the girl were about fifteen feet off the ground and climbing. They must have reached the wall and discovered they were trapped. Maybe they thought that they could yell for help once they reached a higher point. But he saw the flaw in that logic. Whether they screamed or not, he would reach them before any help did. Now he had an even better opportunity to finish them. He would toss both of them from the top of the wall to the stone ground. His cover story that they were terrorists the CIA had been tracking would require some finessing with the authorities, and Wolfe would throw a fit that their deaths had happened in public. But they would be gone, and Wolfe's problems solved.

He moved to the base of the wall, put his palms on the first block that came to his waist, and pressed his feet off the ground. But when he bent his knee, his foot didn't quite reach the top of the block. He dropped back to the ground and swore. He'd always thought the scrawny men with their yoga mats heading into the aerobics studio with the women were effeminate. Now, he wished for a little more flexibility.

No matter, he thought, *I'll just power myself up.* His upper body was stronger than that of his two targets combined. He pushed explosively with his hands as he jumped from the ground. His foot reached the edge of the block. A second later he balanced on the lip of the base block and reached for the next level. Then he encountered his second problem: the space where one block sat on top of the other was only about two inches wide. His tactical boots and thick fingers had difficulty finding holds, and he fought against slipping back to the ground. He plastered his body against the cool, smooth granite, turned his feet parallel to the wall, and dug his fingertips into the next ledge.

Then the memories flooded back. *Coronado. SEAL Indoc training. The cargo net.* The images that flashed through his mind reopened the black void in his chest. He fought back the nausea that rose into his throat. He closed his eyes and breathed deeply, focusing his attention on the cool stone underneath his fingers. He could do this. He was powerful. He was superhuman. He started to climb again. The climbing became easier with each block he ascended. Blood warmed his biceps and his quads.

In the weight room, he was famous for the primal screams he emitted as he pushed out squats or hauled up dead lifts. Now, he tried to make as little noise as possible; his prey was so focused on looking upward that they hadn't yet noticed him.

He closed the gap to ten feet. Rachel Riley was directly above his head; Professor Lightman was to the left, a few feet higher. He eyed the slim ankle exposed under the leg of Rachel's pants. In a moment he would jerk it hard enough to rip her fingers from their hold. The thought of wrapping his hand around her bare skin and then throwing her to her death caused a stirring in his loins. The anticipation even caused his headache to subside. He ignored the tightness that was beginning to develop in his fingers and forearms.

Then she looked down and met his eyes.

Ethan had developed a smooth flow to the climb. His limbs were loose; the wall felt familiar. He ascended slower than he did when he climbed at Yale because he didn't want to leave Rachel behind, and, he reminded himself, because he didn't have anyone belaying him. A slip to the stone below would be fatal.

"He's here!" Rachel's high-pitched scream startled him.

He cut his eyes to the right. She was one block below him, and Axe had appeared several blocks below her. The big man's face was red, and sweat poured from his temples as he lumbered upward. His climbing technique was counterproductive. Axe pulled with his upper body rather than pushing with his feet.

Ethan recalled his early climbing lessons. He'd had to overcome the mistake most men made when climbing: the tendency to overuse his arms. His instructor had explained that his legs were stronger and had more endurance. Climbing with one's arms might seem easier for the first twenty feet or so, but then the smaller muscles would tie up, refusing to fire and stranding one halfway up the wall.

Women were often more natural climbers. Rachel seemed to be proving the point. She climbed almost effortlessly, but too slowly. She took her time finding each hand- and foothold before moving to the next. At the rate she was ascending, Axe would catch her in less than thirty seconds.

"Keep moving." He tried to keep the panic out of his voice. "Look at me."

The fear in her face pained him. On the ground, he was no match for Axe, but on the wall he was confident he could elude the bulky man. *But how can I help Rachel?* The thought of what would happen if she didn't out-climb her pursuer was too horrifying to imagine.

"You've got it," he encouraged.

But then she made the mistake of looking down at her attacker again. She froze on the wall, her arms trembling. *Oh God*, he thought. *PTSD*. The trauma of being chased again by the man who'd kidnapped her in New Haven was paralyzing her.

"Rachel!" he screamed.

She glanced at him. The blood had drained from her face. She still didn't move.

"Rachel, I love you." She blinked at the words that came impulsively from his lips. "You're strong. You can do it. Just climb."

Her eyes narrowed. Her breath came in short bursts. She reached for the next higher block and pulled herself up despite the obvious terror she felt. *She's tough*, he thought. He prayed it would be enough.

Ethan moved up another block, still watching her. Then his hands groped a wide ledge—the one he'd seen from the ground. A plan began to form in his head.

———————

Axe had been so close he'd felt the heat from her body. But after the professor had yelled at her, she'd accelerated up the wall. She was petite—*probably not more than a buck-ten*—and she climbed with grace, like a dancer. Watching Lightman climb, though, caused the first seeds of doubt to enter his mind. The professor's long limbs moved easily, spider-like. *I've squashed plenty of spiders in my life*, he comforted himself. Even if they were faster, they would eventually run out of wall.

He paused, dug his toes into the rock, and shook out the fingers from his left hand. He breathed deeply, replaced his hand, and shook out his right. His forearms burned. He looked down for the first time since he'd started to climb. He fought off a wave of vertigo. He was twenty-five feet off the ground.

He was used to pain in the gym, but this was different. He knew what would follow the burning that was spreading to his biceps. The burn was caused by lactic acid building up in his muscles at the same time his cells were converting their glycogen stores into energy. At the point when the glycogen was depleted, the cells would simply stop firing. *Muscular failure.* He would be unable to move. The same process had caused him to seize up on the SEAL cargo net.

He pushed the fear from his mind, focused his attention back on his prey, and continued his climb. He paused again at the next level and took another deep breath, willing oxygen into his arms. His muscles—now engorged with blood—were starting to quiver. A normal heavy set for him was about twenty seconds in length, after which he'd rest several minutes to let his muscles recover before the next set—the perfect protocol to build mass. Climbing the wall had been the equivalent of four or five sets with no rest in between.

"Goddamn it!" he yelled. He stared at his arms, willing his muscles to recharge. The sun burned the back of his neck. Sweat stung his eyes. He squeezed his eyelids closed. He didn't dare release his hold to wipe them. The sprouting fear in his chest seemed to fill the abyss that had opened earlier. When he opened his eyes, the scene before him was blurry; sweat obscured his vision. The vertigo returned.

As his eyes refocused, the wall appeared to transform. He was no longer climbing a rock-faced wall in Egypt, but a cargo net high off the ground on Coronado Island. He was back in his last week of SEAL Indoc training. The cargo net had failed him several times before, and he had little energy left in the muscle fibers of his forearms, but this time he wouldn't give up. An ankle dangled just above his head.

Lieutenant Mills had taunted Axe from the day he'd arrived, delighting in how creatively he could insult the "ballooned-up roid head." The sinewy New Yorker sat on the telephone pole that ran across the top of the net, his legs dangling over each side. Axe was closer than he'd ever been. This time, he'd not only make it, he'd teach that son of a bitch a lesson.

With the last of his strength, Axe exploded up two rungs of the net faster than he'd ever climbed before. He grasped the net with his right hand, whose fingers now worked like an old woman's, and he thrust his left up toward the ankle. His cramped fingers tightened around the bare flesh. The lieutenant had narrow bones, not like the tree trunks Axe had for legs.

He pulled on the ankle, determined to toss the man who had taunted him the past weeks from the top of the mountain. He glanced at the lieutenant's face. He wanted to see his look of fear and shock. But instead of encountering the lieutenant's tanned cheekbones and salt-and-pepper crew cut, the vision before him almost caused him to fall backward off the net.

The face was long and thin, and it seemed to transform as he watched. The eyes narrowed and elongated, forming diamonds bursting with coal-black pupils. The nose grew to a point as horns appeared out of a mass of hair that wriggled like a nest of worms. He felt his heart catch in his chest. He was no longer looking at Lieutenant Mills; he was looking into the face of Satan, the same Satan who'd plagued his dreams. But now the devil was real, and he had grabbed ahold of him. Axe's fingers started to burn as if the skin of his hand were on fire.

Then the terrible creature opened its mouth, revealing sharp fangs and a fire-red throat. The scream that came next seemed to pierce Axe's very soul.

Ethan stood on a ledge forty feet off the ground. The height was unnerving, but he felt secure enough to shake his hands out by his side. He even had room to turn around. Several tourists had seen them and were pointing up from the ground. He didn't have time to pay attention to them. He had a bigger problem. Axe was only inches from Rachel.

He shuffled over until he was directly above her. She was only three feet below, a single block of stone away. He knelt and extended a hand.

"Almost there," he encouraged. "One more and then grab my hand."

Rachel's lips were pursed in determination and sweat trickled down her temple, but she no longer displayed the fear she had earlier.

Then he watched as Axe surged upward, propelled by an unseen force. The face of their pursuer was twisted in the expression of someone pushing through intense pain toward a goal he would stop at nothing to reach. With the metallic taste of fear on the back of his tongue, Ethan realized that Rachel wouldn't make it to the ledge in time. The dread in his chest was overwhelming. But he couldn't let fear prevent him from saving the woman he loved.

He dropped to his stomach. The smooth stone was warm, but the ledge wasn't wide enough for his torso. His right shoulder hung off the side; the sharp edge dug into his hipbone. He knew that a sudden movement to his right would cause him to plummet to the ground four stories below. He stretched his hand toward Rachel's extended fingers. When he closed around her delicate wrist, her fingers cinched around his arm.

The moment Ethan felt her weight, she was jerked downward. The force almost toppled him from his perch. He leaned with all of his strength into the wall. Whatever happened, he would never let go. *Even if I'm pulled off the wall too*, he decided.

They'd only needed another fifteen seconds. Then she would have reached the ledge, where he could have protected her better. His plan had been to put his body between hers and their pursuer. When Axe tried to climb onto the ledge, he would have stomped on his fingers. But now his worst fear was realized. Axe had grabbed her ankle. He watched Rachel turn her head toward her attacker and let loose a scream of pure terror.

He tightened his grip, feeling the strain from the tendons in his forearm to the muscles in his shoulder and neck. Then he noticed the headache that was starting in the back of his head.

Please, God, not now.

The fire from the devil's ankle that was burning Axe's hand was spreading down his arm and into his shoulder.

The cargo net had beaten him before, but this time was different. This time God Almighty Himself had forsaken him. All of the sacrifices he'd made over his life—the suffering as a child, the dissolution of his parents' marriage, the dedication to building his body into something that belonged on Olympus, the part he'd played in helping stamp out the misguided religion of the Middle East—had counted for nothing.

"Where are you, God?" The plea from his lips didn't even sound intelligible to him.

But God didn't answer; only Satan did, taunting him with his own terrible scream from above.

He experienced the sensation of the last of the glycogen in his muscle cells burning out as if his body were melting. The slabs of muscle that had instilled fear and awe in smaller men as he walked past them on the street evaporated from his skeleton. The cargo net had won again. He would fall to the sand pit below. In the depths of his soul he wanted nothing more than to pull the creature that the lieutenant had become down with him. If he fell, he would take the devil with him.

———————————

Just like on the night of Natalie's death, Ethan hadn't taken a Topiramate in some time. Environmental conditions—whether external, like the flashing lights of the drunk driver's car, or internal, like the stress he was now experiencing—could trigger his epilepsy. A seizure now would condemn Rachel to her death. His fear exacerbated the oncoming headache. He wanted to will away the terror, to fight against his body, just as he was fighting against gravity by holding on to Rachel. Then a memory flashed through his head that felt out of place in his desperate struggle. He was sitting with Rachel in her room at the Monastery. She was taking his hands and explaining how by suppressing his pain, he only magnified it.

He exhaled. *I am terrified*, he admitted to himself. He turned his attention to the physical sensations of fear in his body—not in the clinical way he'd done in the past, analyzing their biological origins, but instead by just feeling the physicality of them. He felt the pulse in his carotid artery expand and contract the skin on his neck. He noticed how each breath he took pressed his tight chest into the smooth stone of the wall that had stood for millennia. He felt the heat that radiated from every pore in his skin. The tension in his head began to ease. Then he focused on the sensation of his fingers wrapped around Rachel's wrist. Rachel was not Natalie, and that afternoon in Luxor was not the rainy night three years ago in New Haven. His mind cleared.

A roar from Axe snapped his attention to the bulky man, who was now teetering on the edge of the rock. If he fell while holding on to Rachel's ankle, he would pull both of them from the wall too. Without taking his eyes off her, Ethan reached with his left to the stone above him, searching for something to hold on to. The sweat from his right hand and Rachel's arm was loosening his grip.

There! His fingers found a reveal in the rock. He dug them in, leaned to his left, and pulled her upward with his right. Maybe if he pulled hard enough, Axe's grip would fail first. But the rock under his fingers must have been cracked, because it suddenly gave way. A chunk the size of a softball pulled off in his hand. *Damn!* He slid back closer to the edge. Rachel screamed again.

They weren't going to make it. The thought landed with cool detachment. He was past fear. Then a realization came to him.

The rock!

He now possessed a weapon. He would have one chance. The chunk of stone was heavy. His odds of hitting Rachel were about equal to those of hitting Axe, and he was using his left hand. But what other choice did he have? He held the rock over the side and lined it up with Axe's beet-red face. He wouldn't risk throwing it. Gravity should work for him.

Rachel's face was contorted with the effort of gripping his hand. They locked eyes.

"Duck," he said.

When she did, he dropped the stone.

———

The scene unfolded in slow motion. The devil's fire in his hand and arm was as excruciating as the fire that had burnt his legs years before. But this time Axe was older and stronger. He could endure the pain. But Satan had other weapons at his disposal as well. The brimstone fell from heaven, blackening the sun. He flinched when he saw it, but his only defense was to blink his eyes closed. The impact to his forehead sent a shock down his spine as if he'd been struck by a bolt of lightning. The shock caused his right hand, the one holding his two-hundred-and-seventy-pound frame to the cargo net, to open. The pull of gravity drew him backward, beckoning to him from the earth below. The fire had spread to his head and seemed to radiate outward from his mind. He opened his eyes to see that he no longer held the devil's ankle either; he'd released the beast.

He never felt the stomach-lurching sensation of his free fall to the ground. He seemed to float downward instead. The sensation was almost pleasant. As he dropped, the scene silhouetted by the blue sky transformed again. No longer was he falling from the cargo net on Coronado Island. He was dropping instead from a beige stone wall, part of the ruins of an ancient temple in Luxor, Egypt. The leg that dangled from the wall, the one that had belonged to the Dark One, was attached to the frightened but harmless-looking Rachel Riley. Professor Ethan Lightman was lying on a ledge above her, holding her arm.

When the impact came, he experienced no pain. He felt as if he'd been hit with a giant pillow, one that suddenly and permanently obscured the vision above him.

———————

Ethan winced at the crunching noise as Axe's head hit the stone forty feet below with a loud crack. He felt no pleasure in the violent man's death. But he felt safe.

The feeling of relief lasted for only a second, as the tendons connecting his arm to his shoulder were threatening to snap under Rachel's full weight. Axe's fall had pulled her other leg off the wall. If Ethan let go, she would meet the same fate Axe had. But he felt a strength like none he'd ever experienced before. His hand and Rachel's arm were no longer two separate appendages joined by the force of their respective grips. He sensed how his body, Rachel's, and the wall were connected with each other, just as the ripples of water he'd seen transform on the Nile had been connected to each other by the great river itself. The connection was as strong as the nuclear forces that bound the individual molecules within each of them. He knew intuitively that they would be okay.

"I've got you," he called to her.

He lifted her, allowing her toes to find the lip of the stone below them. Her free hand slapped the stone ledge by his face.

"Just one more," he said.

He pulled again. She pushed with her free hand, swung her legs up, and collapsed on the ledge in front of him, their faces inches apart. Tears streamed from her eyes.

"You saved my life." Her breath came in short gasps.

He brushed the tears from her cheek, moving the damp strands of hair from her face. He thought she'd never looked more beautiful. He kissed her. She eagerly returned the kiss, her mouth yielding to his.

Then she drew back and asked, "Did you mean what you said? You really love me?"

Peering into her eyes, he knew that words were inadequate to describe his true feelings. Any language he used would come from his head, not the energy vibrating in his heart.

"With all my soul," he said. For the first time, he truly understood what that word meant.

CHAPTER 62

THE MONASTERY

Wolfe stared at the secure phone on his desk. Silent. He ran his hands through his silver hair. His last conversation with Deputy Director Richards had been hours earlier. It hadn't gone well.

"Call off your men," Richards had instructed. "I'm terminating Jericho."

"Give me a half-hour, an hour tops." He'd rolled up his shirtsleeves as he cradled the phone on his shoulder. The AC in the building was not functioning well since the explosion. "My men are on top of them as we speak. They're trapped in the ruins of Karnak."

Richards had paused as if contemplating whether to trust his latest assessment.

"I guarantee I can contain this," he'd added, forcing a note of confidence into his baritone voice.

"Your guarantees so far have been worthless. I can't risk any further exposure of the operation. I'm taking control of Jericho as of this moment."

The matter-of-fact way that the Deputy Director delivered the news had caused Wolfe to flinch as if he'd been struck.

"But if we let them escape, our secrecy will be blown." His voice had gone up an octave against his wishes. "I can contain this!"

"They've already made contact with the outside." Richards's voice had turned soft, almost comforting. "Allen, I appreciate your passion. Your vision for Jericho was compelling. Look, it even sucked me in, but we overreached."

"It's not too late!" Wolfe had known he was pleading, something he despised when others did it. But his life's work was on the line: everything he'd desired since his graduate student days in the '60s. The CIA had abandoned him then, and now they were getting cold feet again.

Then he'd made a decision out of desperation, something he hated to do. He'd spilled his plans for Phase II of Jericho. He'd planned to present to Richards the idea of churches with the Logos pews after the current difficulties were resolved, but he'd had no choice but to put his cards on the table. He'd explained his vision of what Jericho could really be. They would expand it from a covert operation to infiltrate terrorist cells to a program that could convert masses of Muslims into Christians. They would change the balance of power in these countries, not through military or economic means, but religious ones.

Silence had greeted his explanation.

"Before you make any decisions, I'd like you to fly out here and let me show you what we've done. We've already constructed enough pews for a test church."

"You've already built them?"

"I used some of the money left over from the Monastery construction account. You really need to see how they work."

After another long pause, Richards had said, "Come back to Washington. We'll talk further here. Figure out our next steps. You'll be fine."

Wolfe stared again at the silent phone. The DD's assurances that he would "be fine" made him nervous. Why say that unless he had thoughts that indicated otherwise?

Despite his instructions to call off the hunt for the professor, the girl, and the Jordanian, he'd done no such thing. Axe and his well-trained men could handle the three amateurs. Silencing them was the best, really the only, solution to their predicament. He would ask forgiveness after the fact from Richards. The Deputy Director would yell at him for not following orders but would be secretly happy he'd solved the problem. Then he'd repair the Monastery, install stricter security measures, and kick Project Jericho into full gear.

The ringing of the phone caused him to jump in his seat. He snatched the receiver from the cradle.

"Wolfe here," he answered.

"Boss, it's Dawkins."

Finally, the update he'd been waiting for. "Do you have them?"

"Axe is dead," the operative said in an emotionless tone.

Before he could ask what happened, Dawkins continued, "Egyptian security is swarming. We can't reach the subjects."

"They're still free?"

"Sorry, Boss. We're clearing out."

He felt the blood drain from his head as if a stopper had been pulled where his skull joined his spine.

CHAPTER 63

CAIRO, EGYPT

"**H**ow can I take your money?" The Egyptian stepped in front of Ethan and Rachel, blocking their path between the crowded market stalls.

Rachel jumped backward and Ethan shielded her with his body. They were still jittery from the previous day's trauma in Luxor. The merchant thrust his hands toward them, displaying a plastic pyramid, a stuffed camel, and several colorful scarves.

"Not interested," Ethan said, pushing past the man. Rachel clasped his arm, hugging his side.

The man's face fell. "But I give best price in the Khan." When they continued to walk away, he called after them, "Guaranteed! You come back to Mohammad when ready for souvenir!"

"This place is a zoo," Rachel said.

"I'm not positive we're even heading in the right direction."

Ethan gazed at the hundreds of stalls wedged on the sidewalks in front of the three-story buildings. Merchants sold everything from spices to clothes and toys. The heavy scent of people and burning incense hung in the air. The Khan el-Khalili bazaar in the heart of Cairo had captured the essence of Egypt since it began in the fourteenth century. The swarms of people were just as diverse as the goods being sold. Egyptian men walked arm-in-arm with other men. Women dressed in Western fashion with silk scarves draped around their heads bargained with merchants over the rainbow of fabrics being sold, while others veiled in black burqas perused bins of silver bracelets.

European tourists weaved in and out of the stalls, speaking a smorgasbord of languages.

"The driver said it would be on the corner there." Rachel pointed ahead.

The car had taken them from their hotel overlooking the Nile through the bustling city of twelve million people down Al-Muski Street to the Khan. Traffic had been so heavy that an ambulance with its siren blazing had been stuck behind them for twenty minutes. No one, including their car, had made any attempt to move aside. Ethan had tried to ignore the chaos of Egyptian drivers, who paid no attention to lanes and came within inches of each other, and to focus instead on the European architecture of the city.

As they'd waited in the traffic, he'd thought back to their narrow escape the previous day in the temple of Karnak, and to the death of James Axelrod, which he'd confirmed after descending the wall.

He couldn't explain the burst of strength that had allowed him to hold on to Rachel's arm when the man intent on killing them grabbed her ankle. Nor could he make sense of the odd expression that had passed over the assassin's face before he released her leg and fell: a look of pure terror. Ethan knew that the combination of a hormonal surge from the adrenal gland and the heightened awareness one experienced in life-or-death circumstances would affect each person differently, but he couldn't help but think back to his experience on the river. The same interconnectedness he'd sensed then he felt with Rachel.

After searching for Axe's nonexistent pulse, they'd raced through the maze of rubble back to the central area of the temple complex by the Hypostyle Hall of columns. The people they'd passed who had seen them climbing the wall had given them strange looks, but they hadn't run into the Egyptian security forces. Ethan guessed that they'd gathered around Mousa. While they would have welcomed the authorities when Wolfe's man was chasing them, once they were safe, they weren't so sure. They didn't know what kind of influence the CIA could exert. They made their way back to the main entrance, ducking in and out of tourist groups to avoid any other men Wolfe might have deployed there.

They'd jumped into the first free taxi near the entrance to the temple complex. "Take us to the airport, please," Rachel had told the driver before turning to Ethan. Her face had been dusty from sand. She'd tucked a matted strand of hair behind her ear and grabbed his hands.

"We're going to Cairo now," she'd said.

"Your conversation with Houston?"

She'd nodded. "Flights leave Luxor every couple of hours. We'll have open tickets waiting for us at the airport."

"And then?"

"Tomorrow, we're supposed to go to meet him in a restaurant in some marketplace." She'd patted the pocket of her jeans. "Got the name written down."

"Your dad will be in Cairo tomorrow?"

"That's what he said."

"Why a restaurant and not the embassy or the Cairo airport?"

She'd shrugged. "Those were his instructions. He was in a hurry to get to JFK himself."

Ethan recalled her mentioning that Houston and the Yale president had been on the phone with someone in Washington. He didn't know whether to be comforted by or nervous about the vague plans. *Certainly Houston won't do anything to put his daughter in any greater risk*, he thought.

"I think it's to the left." Rachel's voice brought him out of the memory of the previous day.

She stopped at the intersection of a narrow street that bisected the market stalls. A stray dog with a wiry beige coat and a long, jackal-looking face sniffed around their feet. She turned onto the cobblestone road.

Then he saw the two men.

They were standing in front of a sandstone wall with brass lanterns on each side of a heavy wood door. The El-Fishawi Café—the restaurant where they were to meet Houston. A bronze plaque on the wall under the sign for the café bore the name Naguib Mahfouz, the Egyptian, Nobel Prize–winning author who frequented the restaurant.

Although both men sported sunglasses, Ethan felt their stares. They wore dark pants, white shirts, and blue windbreakers. *Americans.* He debated whether they should run back into the crowded market. Rachel's grip tightened on his arm. He was sure the men had weapons stashed under their jackets, but their open hands hung by their sides. Then the taller of the two nodded in the direction of the door.

"We can't run forever," Ethan said.

They had no passports and were running out of the cash Chris had given them. He squeezed Rachel's hand and started for the door.

CHAPTER 64

DAR AL FOUAD HOSPITAL
CAIRO, EGYPT

The first sensation that returned to Mousa was touch: soft sheets caressed his body. The second was smell: something clean, but in an antiseptic way. He opened his eyes. His environment was white: the bed, the walls, even the vinyl tile floor. The single window in the room even let in a white light from the midday sun. Although the intensity of the light hurt his eyes, he resisted the temptation to close them and drift back to sleep.

I'm alive!

He tried to shift his body, but had trouble moving. *Am I restrained?* A shot of fear went through him.

On his second attempt, he was able to raise his left arm. While heavy, it was free. He noted the IV taped to the back of his hand and the clear tube that ran to the bag hanging over his head. He shifted his body and felt a soft lump on his back. He was lying on a wad of gauze.

Then the fog lifted from his brain. He was in a hospital. The events from the day before replayed in his mind: the stabbing from behind, the pain that had paralyzed his body, Ethan and Rachel by his side, the crowd of people who had gathered after he'd sent them away, and then the fleeting image of a paramedic laying a hand on his neck to take his pulse before he slipped into unconsciousness.

As if on cue for the next question that came to mind—*Where am I?*—the door to the room opened and a doctor in a white coat approached the bed. He looked up from the clipboard he was reviewing and asked, "So Dr. Ibrahim, how are we feeling today?"

"Where am I?"

"Dar Al Fouad. A helicopter brought you here yesterday."

I'm in Cairo?

He'd been to the Dar Al Fouad Hospital several times for conferences with their renowned orthopedic department—the best in the Middle East. Then an uneasy feeling cut through the haze of the painkillers dripping through his IV.

This doctor is American, he realized. The man in the white coat approached his bed and checked the IV bag.

"Mousa, we need to talk."

With the doctor hovering over him, he got a closer look. The man's haircut was short and tidy, above the tops of his ears. Then he noticed that the white lab coat seemed to be too small for his frame, stretched over a broad physique. Mousa was now fully awake. This man had the look of one of the Bishop's priests in the Monastery. He was CIA.

CHAPTER 65

EL-FISHAWI CAFÉ
CAIRO, EGYPT

The dimly lit restaurant was paneled in dark cherrywood, and the mirrors on the walls gave it a maze-like appearance. The animated Arabic chatter from lunchtime patrons reclining in plushly upholstered chairs filled the space. The smell of cooked lamb, garlic, and assorted spices Ethan couldn't place filled his nostrils. A short, stout Egyptian in an immaculate charcoal suit led them to a doorway that opened into a private room containing two round tables.

He forgot about the smells and sounds when he saw the two men sitting at the table closest to the door. Neither spoke or ate. Only a solitary glass of water sat in front of each. Both were bulky Americans who could have been twins to the two stationed at the entrance to the restaurant. One stared at them with a penetrating gaze, while the other's attention stayed focused on the restaurant. The maître d' motioned for Ethan and Rachel to enter.

The second table in the corner of the room was larger and coated in a gold metallic finish. Multiple serving bowls and dishes overflowed with food: crispy broiled chicken, chunks of lamb in stew, warm flatbread, hummus drizzled with olive oil, dolmas, and steaming bowls of red, orange, and yellow vegetables.

"Ethan! Rachel!" Sam Houston stood from the table, while a second man remained seated.

A flood of emotions flowed through Ethan at the sight of the Yale administrator in his wire glasses, blue blazer, and gray slacks. On the one hand he was relieved to see a familiar face. On the other, he still didn't know if he could trust him.

Rachel dropped his hand and ran to the table. Houston embraced his daughter, lifting her off her feet. Ethan was shocked to see tears flowing from his face. He'd never seen this side of the professor before. He turned his attention to the second man, who appeared to be a few years younger than Houston. Where Houston was mostly bald, with a circle of gray hair around his crown, this man's head was shaved to a polish that reflected the light from the pair of iron sconces on the wall. Rather than Houston's thin neck and long limbs, the other man was short and thick—not over-muscled like the four men guarding him, but solid. The man leaned back in his chair. Smoke from a cigarette curled upward from his fingertips.

Finally, the man spoke. "Have a seat, Ms. Riley and Dr. Lightman." The tone of his voice indicated that they weren't being invited but ordered. Both sat.

"You have us at a disadvantage." Ethan attempted to keep his voice steady and confident. "You know us, but we've never met you."

"Ethan, Rachel," Houston said while fumbling with his own chair, "may I introduce you to Casey Richards." The administrator lowered his voice. "He's the Deputy Director of the NCS."

"NCS?" Rachel asked.

"The National Clandestine Services," Richards replied before taking a long drag.

Answering the confusion on her face, he explained, "The CIA. I'm in charge of the Agency's covert operations."

A sigh escaped Ethan's lips. "He's the one responsible for the Monastery. Wolfe works for him."

Wolfe scurried about his office. He hadn't heard from Nick Dawkins since the previous afternoon, when his operative had called back a few hours after he'd delivered the news from Karnak to tell him that he was going to the authorities to retrieve Axe's body and to clean up the mess. Dawkins and the others should have returned last night. Now they wouldn't answer his phone calls.

The skeletal staff that had remained to make repairs and watch over the confused prisoners—*monks*, he corrected himself—had heard nothing either.

He bent over the aluminum briefcase on his desk. It contained a laptop and two identical hard drives, each loaded with the Logos's programming. Although Professor Lightman hadn't fixed the flaw, it still worked perfectly in 90 percent of the subjects. That would have to do for now. He opened the left door on his credenza, revealing a safe that had been bolted into the ground and the wall. He spun the combination lock. Opening the door, he fished under the file folders stamped "TOP SECRET EYES ONLY" until he found what he was looking for. He removed the three bundles of cash secured by rubber bands, each valued at ten thousand dollars in denominations of Egyptian pounds, euros, and US dollars. He pulled several bills from each of the bundles and stuffed them into his wallet. Then he tossed the remaining cash into the briefcase.

The cash would get him out of the country and to his small house in the Guanacaste region of northwest Costa Rica. Once there, he would live off of the two million dollars he'd siphoned from the various projects he'd worked on over the years. After being laundering through banks on the Isle of Man, the funds now sat in a Cayman Islands account under the name of a Panamanian trust he controlled. Having access to off-the-books funding for black ops had its perks. In his line of work, you never knew when the political tides would turn against you.

He would just have to wait out this latest turn of events. His biggest fear was whether he would get another chance. He was seventy-one. Then he thought of the temperate weather, the exotic girls, and shrugged his shoulders. Living out his final years in paradise wasn't the worse thing that could happen. He reached into the rear of the safe and removed two passports: his US one under his real name and a Panamanian one under the identity of an international businessman—an alias he'd created five years earlier.

He would simply disappear.

Rachel leaned across the table like a lioness readying to pounce. "You had me kidnapped! You had Wolfe's goon shoot Chris, stab Mousa, and try to kill the two of us! You—"

Deputy Director Richards held up a hand, silencing her accusations. "Yes, Allen Wolfe reported to me, but you need to understand that he acted autonomously. The way my business works"—he took another drag from his cigarette and tilted his head upward to blow out the smoke—"sometimes it's better if we do not know the details of the operations."

"Bullshit," Ethan said, the anger rising within him in spite of his attempts to remain calm. "Building the Monastery must have cost millions of dollars, and what Wolfe is trying to do with my Logos machine is potentially destructive to our relations with the Arab world. You must have known what was going on here."

Richards evaluated him for a moment, stubbed out his cigarette in an ashtray, and said, "I'm glad you understand the sensitivity of this project and why it must be kept absolutely secret."

"Understand!" Ethan's face grew hot. "What I understand is that an agency of my government has tried to pervert my life's work, has murdered at least one of its innocent citizens, and is conducting human psychological brainwashing experiments that violate every ethical principal." He turned his attention to Houston with his final comment.

"The reason we came here—" Houston began, but stopped when Richards rested his free hand on his shoulder.

"Son, I don't need you to lecture me on ethics and morality from the top of your ivory tower. My job is to protect our country from dangerous men who have no sense of ethics, who are willing to murder innocent women and children indiscriminately to achieve their goals. War is not clean. War is not pretty."

"But if we want to win this war," Rachel said, "we can't stoop to their level. If we lose the moral high ground, then we will never defeat terrorism."

Richards tapped his fingers on the table. "Now, did Allen Wolfe overstep his authority? Certainly. Did Project Jericho get out of hand? No doubt. Wolfe, on numerous occasions, disobeyed my explicit instructions. He became a zealot for his own vision, and"—he took another drag on his cigarette—"actions may have been taken that were inappropriate. But sometimes, in my business, we have to give the operatives in the field leeway."

"Leeway?" Ethan said. "With his leeway, Wolfe planned to take Jericho from a program designed to indoctrinate low-level terrorism suspects to widespread population control." He faced Houston. "He had plans to build churches throughout the Middle East, incorporating the Logos into the pews in an attempt to indoctrinate the local civilian populations." Houston's eyes widened.

Richards raised his eyebrows as if he hadn't known the full extent of what was going on in the Monastery. When he spoke again, his voice grew softer. "Maybe in Wolfe's case I gave him too much freedom."

Houston straightened, took his daughter's hand, and cleared his throat. "What has happened here goes much further than an overstepping of authority." The commanding tone that came from the administrator was one Ethan had heard many times before, but this time he was thankful he'd found his voice.

"The entire design of Project Jericho," Houston continued, "and the significance of the name is not lost on me, is fundamentally anti-American. One of the founding premises of our nation is freedom of religion. The First Amendment protects us from the imposition of religious beliefs."

When Richards opened his mouth to interrupt him, Houston slapped the table with his free hand, silencing the CIA man for once. "Don't you dare tell me that the Constitution is only meant to protect Americans in our country. Forceful conversion of other populations runs contrary to the essence of the freedom we want to export to the rest of the world. The ends cannot justify the means in this case because the means and the ends are indistinguishable"—he locked eyes with Rachel and his voice turned icy—"especially when the means involves endangering innocent people."

Ethan sat back in his seat, moved by the words of the man who had caused him so many problems over the years. For the first time, he better understood Houston. Then Ethan added, "Plus, it never would have worked."

Richards raised an eyebrow. "I thought the anomalies in your programming that resulted in negative reactions in 10 percent of the subjects was something that could be solved."

Ethan resisted the urge to point out the obvious fact that the deputy director knew more about the details than he had first claimed, but Richards's comment also revealed another important piece of information: Axe must have taken his knowledge of the left-handed anomaly in the programming to his grave.

"I never figured out what was wrong with my programming. I think the problem is inherent in the nature of the whole project." Lying about his success with the Logos, especially in front of Houston, was painful, but he wanted to ensure that the CIA man didn't restart the project.

"Even if it *could* be perfected," he continued, "Wolfe never understood the Logos. In fact, until recently I didn't fully grasp Elijah's vision for the machine either. The Logos doesn't cause one to believe in a Christian God—or even any god, as we traditionally think of that word. It does the opposite: the Logos opens up the mind to the possibilities of the infinite, to seeing beyond our everyday reality to an ultimate reality that isn't exclusively Christian, Jewish, Muslim, Hindu, or Buddhist." A pang of sadness passed over him as he remembered his mentor. "Elijah Schiff, who dreamed up the Logos, explained to me once that these religions may point to this ultimate reality in ways that can be understood by their adherents, but that the reality itself is much greater, and it isn't something that can be put into words."

He sensed Rachel and Houston both staring at him. "The success Wolfe achieved with the Logos was only in a limited number of cases with uneducated terrorists who had already been subjected to brainwashing by the Islamic fundamentalists in their countries. As we learned in the case of a Jordanian doctor in the Monastery, the Logos could not convert an enlightened Muslim to Christianity; it instead made him a more devout, while also opening his mind to the truths and the limitations of all religions."

"All of this is moot now anyway," Richards grunted. "I'm shutting down Project Jericho."

"What exactly do you mean by shutting down?" Rachel asked.

"Professor Houston, the Yale President, your congresswoman from Connecticut who chairs the House Subcommittee on Intelligence, the CIA Director, and I spoke before I came here." He shifted in his seat. For the first time, he appeared uncomfortable. "We decided the risks of exposure are too great relative to the potential payoff. The Logos machines will be destroyed, the

Monastery dismantled. No one will ever know what happened in the desert of Egypt."

"I can't imagine Wolfe just giving up on his vision," Ethan said.

"We are used to cleaning up after ourselves. Allen Wolfe will not be a problem."

The ominous tone of the CIA's deputy director sent a shiver through him.

Richards slid two single sheets of paper across the table, one in front of each of them. Ethan glanced at the legal document. "Confidentiality agreements?"

"These contracts cover anything you two may have seen or learned while you were here. Project Jericho is classified as top secret, and this contract binds you to silence in the name of national security. You may not even mention the existence of the Monastery."

"Why would we even consider signing that?" Rachel asked, pushing her bangs out of her eyes. She glared at Richards and then her father.

"In exchange for your agreeing to stay quiet on these matters, Ms. Riley, you will be safely returned to the US, where you can continue your studies. And you'll be compensated for your traumatic experience."

"Compensated?"

"For the trauma you experienced from your detainment. By the time you arrive in New Haven, we will have deposited three hundred thousand dollars into your bank account, tax free, no questions asked." Richards cut his eyes to Houston. "And should you decide that you would like to stay at Yale next year and pursue your PhD, we have worked out an arrangement with the university that your tuition will be gratis."

Rachel picked up the paper, sat back in her chair, and studied the text.

Richards turned to Ethan. "Professor Lightman, we have cleared up the accounting irregularities from the NAF grant that funded the Logos project. I explained to Professor Houston and the university president that you're innocent of any wrongdoing."

"You mean how Wolfe made it seem like I was embezzling money from the project so I would have no choice but to work for him." Anger flushed Ethan's face at the memory of how his life had been turned upside down. "And how

Wolfe's man, your employee, James Axelrod, murdered Elijah Schiff, a tenured university professor, the most gentle and kind man I've ever known!"

Richards reached for another cigarette from the red-and-white pack in his shirt pocket and tapped it on the table. "Any suspicions the New Haven police had about your involvement in Professor Schiff's tragic death will also be resolved."

Ethan started to rise out of his seat but settled when Houston raised a hand. "Please, let him continue."

Richards clicked open a silver butane torch lighter and lit the cigarette. "In recognition of the groundbreaking research you and Professor Schiff accomplished, the university has agreed to offer you full tenure. The Agency will provide funding for your next project, whatever you choose to study, no questions asked."

"You want to buy me off!" He glanced over at Rachel, who looked up from her contract. "You expect us to stay silent about these abuses?"

The deputy director leaned forward on his elbows. "Do you want to be the cause of a religious war? A war that will bring terrorism to our country in a way that makes 9/11 look like a warm-up? A war that will cause tens if not hundreds of thousands of deaths?"

"No," Ethan whispered. He stared at the dishes of food on the table. He hadn't eaten yet that day, but he wasn't hungry. As much as it pained him to admit it, Richards was right. Nothing that had happened could become public. "So Wolfe and his men just get away with everything"—he glared at Richards—"with no consequences for their actions?"

"There are always consequences." Richards blew a cloud of smoke toward the ceiling. "First, I've lost millions from my budget that I'll never recover, James Axelrod has died, and Wolfe will be held accountable for his failures. This program has to disappear."

"So I'm supposed to return to Yale, pick up where I left off, as if none of this ever happened?"

"You're free to do as you wish." Richards rubbed his shiny head as if polishing it. "But you must give up on the Logos experiments. The machine in the hands of the police that contains your programming will be destroyed. The potential for abuse if your technology falls into the wrong hands is too great. Some frontiers are better off not being explored."

Ethan looked at Houston. The administrator had never respected his research, and that had always grated on him. *But,* he had to admit, *Houston was right.* Not about whether the technology would work. It had, and spectacularly so, but the head of Yale's Human Research Protection Program had been most concerned with his protocols regarding human experimentation. In his zeal to progress the research, to push the boundaries of psychological knowledge, he'd minimized the risks. *Risks that came to be realities.* Elijah had sensed the potential for abuse, too, since he'd experienced firsthand during his graduate school days how human psychological experimentation could be taken too far in the name of national security. But he'd chosen to blow off his mentor's concerns.

He looked at the two men waiting for his response. His first instinct had been to tell Richards where he could shove his money, but then a new idea came to him. *What if the suffering Wolfe caused could be turned to something good after all?* As he outlined the idea, the words spilling out of his mouth, he noticed Houston smiling at him.

When he finished, the CIA man nodded in agreement with his plan and then wiped his mouth with his napkin.

Rachel asked, "What will happen to the Arab men who are still in the facility when you close it down?"

"They will be treated on a case-by-case basis." Richards dropped the napkin on the table. "We'll move them to another facility, where they will be rehabilitated, and once we feel that they are no longer a threat they will be returned to their countries. Don't forget that these men belonged to terrorist organizations."

"Mousa was not a terrorist," Ethan said. "Axe tried to kill him in Luxor, and we haven't had any news of him."

Richards took a drink from his glass of water. "The Jordanian doctor was airlifted to a hospital here in Cairo where he is being treated. His injuries were serious but not life-threatening."

"He's here?" Rachel asked. "When can we see him?"

"We'll have to check with his doctors, but we'll see what we can arrange. He's scheduled to return home to his family in Amman in a few days."

Richards's mannerisms and vague responses made Ethan uncomfortable, especially since just moments earlier he'd been so confident when detailing his demands.

"I want to be perfectly clear on this." He leaned forward and pointed at the deputy director. "If anything happens to Mousa, I will go straight to *The New York Times* and CNN with this story. I don't give a damn what this agreement says or how much money you promise to put into our research. If I hear that Mousa has had a car accident, a mysterious fall while hiking, a drug mishap at the hospital"—he stabbed his finger at Richards to emphasize each point—"*anything at all*, then all of your shenanigans become public, regardless of the diplomatic consequences."

Richards visibly swallowed, nodded, and then said, "You have my word. Mousa will be safe."

CHAPTER 66

THE MONASTERY

Allen Wolfe snapped the locks closed on his briefcase and snatched the keys to one of the SUVs from the top of his desk. He would drive himself to Aswan Airport, where the chartered jet would pick him up in forty-five minutes.

"Hey, Boss."

He looked up. Nicholas Dawkins stood in his office doorway.

"Where've you been? I called you hours ago."

"Claiming Axe's body from the Luxor police took longer than expected. Had to call in some favors to get them to look the other way."

Wolfe tried not to show his surprise or concern. He should have been the one to place the call to the Agency, not his field operative.

"Yeah," Dawkins continued, "the big man caused quite a scene."

"He was acting strangely lately. Not himself." He started toward the door, but Dawkins blocked his exit. "The subjects?"

"Axe got to the Jordanian, but the girl and the professor . . ." Dawkins shrugged. "Once the authorities moved in, we had to back off. They vanished in the crowd."

Wolfe shook his head. *How did everything fall apart so quickly?* If only he hadn't been in Cairo during the escape. Without his direct supervision, these muscleheads were incapable of accomplishing anything.

"Where are your men now?" He used his most authoritative tone.

"Came back with me to regroup." Dawkins demeanor was relaxed, almost nonchalant.

"Well, I'm running late for a meeting with our assets in Cairo. We need to close in on Professor Lightman and Ms. Riley before they can get help. Without passports, they can't go far."

Dawkins stepped to the side, giving him room to pass. "We'll have this place back up and running in no time. Right, Boss?"

"Certainly." He grinned at his man. "We'll have to implement a stricter security protocol this time." He turned to walk down the hallway.

I'm free, he thought.

The stinging sensation in his neck caught him by surprise. He swatted at what he thought might be a mosquito biting him. Immediately, a rush of warmth spread like hot water from the veins in his neck down his torso. His limbs grew heavy and he slumped to the ground, his legs no longer able to support his weight.

"Dawkins, help me up." His speech was slurred. He tried to push to sitting, but even that required a strength he no longer had. "What's happening to—" Before he completed the question, he noticed the expression of curiosity on his deputy's face—an expression that should have been one of alarm.

Dawkins stood over him, silhouetted by the fluorescent lights in the ceiling. A syringe dangled in his hand. The lack of returned calls, the sketchy details he'd received about the operation to find Riley and Lightman, Dawkins's cavalier attitude: everything made sense now. He recalled Richards's warning about terminating Jericho with prejudice. Strangely, though, the reality of his impending demise didn't concern him. The fire in his blood had removed his desire to fight.

Allen Wolfe's breathing became labored. Fifteen seconds later, he slipped into a sleep from which he would never wake.

CHAPTER 67

DAR AL FOUAD HOSPITAL
CAIRO, EGYPT

"**M**ousa!" Rachel ran to the hospital bed and threw her arms around the Jordanian doctor's neck.

Ethan approached the bed with a grin plastered on his face. Seeing his friend safe released the tension that had been constricting his chest since they'd left the café an hour earlier. Despite Richards's assurances, he didn't trust the CIA, not after everything that had happened.

"You're okay?" Tears welled in Rachel's eyes.

"The knife just missed my kidney. I lost some blood, but I'll be fine." Mousa chuckled. "The food here—now that may kill me."

Ethan leaned over and embraced his new friend. "Everyone says we make the worst patients."

"Ah yes, I much prefer to be on the other side of the bed."

Ethan dragged two aqua blue plastic chairs from the corner of the room to the bed. "At least they gave you a private room. From what we saw, that's unusual in this facility."

"I imagine," Mousa lowered his voice, "they don't want me talking about my injuries to the other patients."

"Look—" Ethan fidgeted. "I can't begin to say how sorry I am for what happened to you. When I began my research, I never imagined that—"

Mousa held up a hand.

"I'll have none of your apologies."

"But if I had never developed the Logos—"

Mousa waved the hand he still held aloft.

"It was my own people, my Muslim brothers, who kidnapped and tortured me. Your CIA actually nursed me back to health."

"But what they were attempting to do . . ."

"Ah, but they didn't, did they? *Ma sa Allah*—God has willed it otherwise. You saved my life, Ethan. And that Logos machine of yours gave me an experience I'd only heard stories about—I experienced *fana*."

"*Fana*?" Rachel asked.

"Sufis, the mystical branch of Islam, practice various forms of meditation to become one with Allah."

"So *fana* is some sort of mystical state Sufis aspire to?" Ethan asked.

"The word translates literally as 'extinction,' a state in which the self disintegrates into the infinite being of Allah. Our earthly worries, the pain and suffering that is part of our human lives, all vanish in the glory of absorption into the reality of God."

"And you experienced this?" Ethan's vision on the Nile flashed through his mind. He'd been absorbed into the binary language that seemed to describe the fabric of the universe around him. For that brief time his personal identity had seemed both insignificant and also part of something eternal and infinite.

"Because of your Logos, I see now more than I ever did before that Allah truly is the center of all existence." Mousa smiled. "Allah is not only the source of my being, but Allah is also the source of yours, of the guards who tortured me in prison, and of the CIA priests who wanted to convert me. I am as intricately linked to my enemies as I am to my own children."

"And that is why you're not angry about what has happened to you?" Rachel asked.

"How could I not forgive these men? They live their lives in pain and suffering because they haven't looked deeply enough into existence. They haven't experienced true peace—*salaam*—a peace that comes from surrendering to Allah. That is the true nature of Islam, which I better understand now."

"I'm going to miss you, Doctor." Ethan squeezed his shoulder.

"I'll visit you in America." Mousa placed a warm hand on top of his. "Early next year I have a medical conference in Boston at Mass General."

"That's just a short train ride from New Haven!" Rachel said.

"Yes, I've always wanted to see the great university that is Yale, and now I have two tour guides to show me around."

"You are scheduled to travel back to Amman tomorrow?" Ethan wanted to confirm what Richards had told them.

The smile on Mousa's face became even wider. "A man from your government visited me earlier this morning. He gave me my passport and a ticket." He lowered his voice for the second time. "But you know we must never speak to anyone about what has happened here."

———————

Nick Dawkins placed the briefcase into the rear of the black SUV. He'd checked the contents after Wolfe died. His boss had been planning on running.

"Hey, where do you want this stuff to go?"

Two of his men approached. One held a black rectangular box—one of the Logos machines. In Wolfe's briefcase were two of the hard drives that ran the machine, but Deputy Director Richards had wanted a full, working machine returned to Langley as well. The second man carried a cardboard box in one arm and a set of rolled-up blueprints in the other.

"Are those the modified cell phones?" Nick asked.

"Yes, sir. The design plans, too."

"Stick them in the truck." Richards had called an hour earlier to ask him to bring these items as well. The Deputy Director had reached him just in time. Their work was almost done. "Where are the others?"

"Coming now."

He saw four other men hustle from the front door of the building. They didn't bother to lock the doors. "And the prisoners?" He'd dispensed with the fiction of calling them monks or brothers since he'd returned to clean up Wolfe's mess.

"In their cells."

He glanced at the timer counting down on his watch. "Let's get out of here. The plane is warming up on the tarmac." They would be airborne in less than fifteen minutes.

The men piled into the two SUVs with more haste than usual. Nick drove the lead car, correcting with a smooth input to the steering wheel as the car fishtailed on the dirt drive. He floored the accelerator as he pulled away from the isolated warehouse in the desert.

They were a half-mile away when the C4 detonated. Although the sun was high in the sky, the light from the explosion seemed to overtake the cars, which shook moments later as the concussion wave followed. He glanced in his rearview mirror. The warehouse—along with all evidence of the Monastery and its contents—existed no more.

CHAPTER 68

AMMAN, JORDAN

The wait in the customs line in the Amman airport brought a nervous sweat to Mousa's forehead. The last time he'd been in this position, his life had been ripped apart. He wiped his eyes with the sleeve of the white shirt that had been provided to him, along with a new pair of black slacks, before he left the hospital. His bloodstained clothes had been discarded after they'd been cut from his body. He passed his passport between his clammy hands.

The desk to the left opened up and the agent waved him over. He handed his passport to the portly man dressed in white, hoping he didn't appear as nervous as he felt. The man flipped through the passport, turned to his picture, and stared at him with dark, unblinking eyes. He managed a half-smile. The agent swiped it through a barcode reader and stared at his computer monitor for what seemed like too long a time. Just when Mousa began to fear that the agent could hear his heart thumping in his chest, the man flipped to a back page, stamped the passport, and returned it.

The walk through baggage claim was a blur to him. He had nothing to pick up. He passed through an automatic sliding door that opened to the noise of the arrival hall, which was crowded with families and drivers holding signs.

A high-pitched voice called to him from his right. "Baba!"

He turned to see his princess, Amira, waving to him from beside his wife. Bashirah's long hair flowed down her back underneath a colorful headscarf. She held their infant son in her arms, and tears streamed down her face. She had never looked so beautiful. Before Mousa could make his way through the crowd, Amira broke loose from her mother's hand and raced ahead, dodging the other passengers.

He wept as Amira leaped into his arms and threw her petite hands around his neck.

EPILOGUE

YALE UNIVERSITY

Ethan turned the key in the brass lock and pushed open the heavy wood door to his office in SSS. Feeling around the wall, he found the light switch. He blinked along with the flickering fluorescents, his eyes still accustomed to the New Haven night. When the door thudded closed behind him, he stood still for a moment, taking in the space that was his office and lab. The room felt too big without the Logos in the middle of the room. Elijah's and Chris's absences made it feel even more cavernous. The last time he'd been in the office, yellow police tape had cut across the door and the furniture had been in disarray. Now everything was clean and in its proper place. He missed his mentor's clutter.

Then he noticed the stack of mail on his desk. He'd been in New Haven for two days, but his time had been taken up first by sleep and then by meetings with Houston and the university president, who had been apoplectic when Ethan had retold the complete story over dinner while the three of them polished off two bottles of an earthy Bordeaux. Other than Rachel and Mousa, these men were the only ones he would ever be able to talk with about the events in Egypt and the deaths of his friends.

The most surprising change for him, however, was his new relationship with Houston. As different as their personalities were, they had bonded. The senior administrator had intervened with the CIA, saving his life, and now Houston was enthusiastic about both the possibilities of his new research and his relationship with Rachel.

Ethan rolled out the chair from his desk, turned on the Tiffany lamp, and began to shuffle through his mail. On top of the letters, scientific journals, and unpaid bills was a brown package a little smaller than a shoebox. Curious, he reached into his top desk drawer and grabbed his scissors. Then he noticed that although his name and office address were typed clearly on the mailing label, the package had neither postage nor a return label. He looked over his shoulder at the empty office and the closed door. Someone had hand-delivered the package.

Weighing the box in his hand, he poised to cut through the package tape that encircled it when he noticed the letter that had been under the box. This envelope had a return address: *St. Mary's Convent, Fairhaven, CT*. He set the box down and picked up the letter. *Sister Terri*, he thought. In the events after Elijah's death and then his journey to Egypt, he hadn't been able to speak to the kind nun who had been so integral to their research. He would have to visit her soon. He was sure she would have heard about Elijah's passing; he wished he'd been the one to tell her.

He tore into the envelope. In addition to a folded sheet of stationery, an index card with the convent's logo fell out. He turned over the card first. As he began to read the neat cursive writing, his throat constricted. Sister Terri had died in her sleep while he was in Egypt. One of the other nuns had found the enclosed letter next to her bed. She'd written it before turning off her light and falling asleep for the final time. He blinked back the tears burning his eyes, unfolded the stationery, and read her final words.

> *My dearest Ethan,*
>
> *When I heard of Elijah's tragic death this morning, I wanted to reach out and call you, but this thorn of the flesh that has plagued me for these many years has finally won. My voice is gone, but while I still have strength in my fingers, I am writing to thank you for the gift you gave me in my final days. I have spent a lifetime of contemplation searching for a connection to the Father. I tasted brief experiences of the Divine during times of quiet prayer or solitary walks through our gardens,*

but your Logos opened my mind in a way I'd never imagined possible.

I've listened politely as my sisters have come to my bedside and prayed for my health. I deeply appreciate their love and concern, but my experience in your lab merely confirmed what I had intuited many years before: God's role in the universe is not to interfere in specific cases such as mine. I've lived a complete life with no regrets. I've come to understand that prayer is not about asking God to do something but about listening to God.

Nothing external—disease, pain, doubt, sadness—no matter how terrible, can come between me and a God that is the center of my being. This is what Jesus discovered through his own lifetime of prayer and contemplation; this is why he urged his disciples to leave their possessions, even their families, to follow him.

As I lie here, knowing my last days on Earth are near, I look upon the suffering of my physical body almost with a curiosity. This process my body is going through as it shuts down is part of the larger process of life itself, a life behind which God is the energy and sustenance. I'm joyous that I can now see the infinite nature of God, a nature that encompasses all that I am and was, an infinite nature that I participate in—that is my reality now.

Thank you, Ethan.

Love and Peace, Terri

Ethan folded the letter, replaced it in the envelope, and wiped his eyes with his sleeve. As much as he'd needed to read this before he'd left for Egypt, he didn't think he would have understood it then the way he did now. While Terri had dedicated her life to faith, he'd dedicated his to science. He'd sought to explain experiences like Terri's—experiences like the ones he had as a teen and on the Nile. But now he understood a complexity he hadn't before. He and Elijah had recreated the mechanics behind mystical visions, but his science missed part of the picture. He knew that Elijah had tried to impress on him this limitation, but he hadn't seen it. Science excelled at explaining *mechanics*, but it struggled with giving *meaning*.

He thought back to the vision he'd had on the Nile, a vision induced mechanically by the cell phone programmed with his Logos protocol. He then recalled the vision he'd had as a teenager, a vision brought on by the neurons in his temporal lobes misfiring—his epilepsy. He understood what had caused these visions, but he still couldn't shake a deep-seated feeling, a feeling that was more instinctual than logical: *the meaning behind these experiences was real.* Yet how could he reconcile this intuitive understanding with his logical mind? Math, physics, biology, and chemistry ruled supreme in his twenty-first-century universe, but then their elegance was also awe-inspiring in an almost religious way. Could these scientific laws be reflections of the creative power of God?

For so much of his life Ethan had resisted the image of God as a father figure living somewhere in the sky: a king or a judge ruling over his subjects, capriciously deciding who suffers and who doesn't, who is saved and who is condemned, like a cosmic puppeteer playing with humanity for his amusement. But now he realized that the image of God he had rejected was nothing more than a straw man, a finite and weak idea of God. The God that Terri, a Christian nun, had described in her letter, the God that Elijah, a Jew, had tried to get him to understand, and the God that Mousa, a Muslim, had experienced, was much greater. Theirs was a God that was the fabric of universe itself, the fabric at the core of who we are as living beings. But this was not the common view of God taught in churches and temples; this was not the view of God used by fanatics and fundamentalists to justify their own closed-mindedness.

But if scientific theories evolve over time as we learn more, he wondered, *why not our views of religion?*

The creaking of the door opening snapped him out of his thoughts. He swiveled his chair around.

"Hi, Stranger." Rachel strode into the room wearing jeans and a thick black sweater that clung to her curves.

Ethan smiled and felt a rush of joy at seeing her. "How are things at Cap-Lab?"

"Crazy." She pulled the chair from Elijah's desk over toward his and plopped down in it. She then scooted it closer so that her knees slipped on either side of his. "Professor Sanchez was worried sick about me when I disappeared. Dad spoke to her and conveyed the message that I was involved in an important government project I couldn't discuss. I could tell it was killing her not to ask me specifics about it." She pointed to the box sitting in his lap. "Hey, what's that?"

"Not sure. Must have been hand-delivered this morning."

"Well, are you gonna open it?"

Using the scissors, he sliced into the cardboard. Styrofoam peanuts spilled out like confetti. Digging around, he pulled out three shiny black cell phones and a flash drive.

"Deputy Director Richards lived up to his agreement," Rachel said.

Ethan stared at the Logos-programmed phones, identical to the one he'd used on the Nile. Sitting across the table from Houston and Richards in Cairo and faced with the loss of his research, an inspiration had come to him. He'd delved far into understanding the complex electrical misfirings that caused epileptic seizures, and he'd wondered, *What if I could reverse engineer these misfirings and induce an electrical current in the brain that would halt a seizure the moment it began?* What if he could take Wolfe's modified cell phone and create a portable device that could stop an epileptic attack—a pacemaker for the brain?

Then he'd thought of other neurological conditions that the TMS technology they'd based the Logos on was used to treat: depression, schizophrenia, and chronic pain. He turned the shiny black plastic case around in his hand. Could all of these diseases be treated with electromagnetic devices that a patient could use as easily as their phones? In exchange for his signing the CIA's non-disclosure agreement, he'd demanded access to Wolfe's design of the Logos cell phones, as well as the money to support the research that could change the lives of millions of people. He twirled the flash drive through his fingers. He guessed it contained the miniaturization technology schematics he'd requested.

"So they gave you the funding too?" she asked.

"I met with Houston and President Martin last night. They confirmed the government grant for a five-year longitudinal study."

"Don't you worry about staying involved with Richards and his people?"

"That's the great part. The funding is coming through the NSF, the National Science Foundation, not from CIA sources."

"And they agreed that once you reengineer Wolfe's phone, you'll hold the patents? That could be worth millions if it works."

"Oh, yeah, that too." He smiled. "Wolfe's design was based on my protocol, after all." He replaced two of the phones in the box. "Of course, I'll have to wipe any of my original Logos programming from these before we start to tinker with them, but first"—he toyed with the third phone—"how's Anakin doing?"

Rachel cast her eyes to the ground. "Professor Sanchez said that his behavior became even more erratic while I was gone. She thinks we're going to have to put him down."

"I have an idea." He held up the phone. "Let me stop by tomorrow. I'll reprogram this phone with a Logos protocol to handle left-handed brains. We can try it on Anakin."

Her face brightened. "Will it help?"

He nodded. "It should reverse the effects of the first test." He set the phone on his desk. "Then I'll erase the Logos program completely, just as I promised Richards." A smile crept across his face.

She stood, pushed her chair back, and straddled his legs. "Thank you." She lowered herself onto his lap, grabbed his neck, and kissed him.

The weight of her body sent a jolt of electricity through him. The softness of her lips gave way to the urgency of the kiss. Her arms tightened around his neck while he entwined his fingers in her hair. They kissed as if trying to make up for time lost. After several minutes, he was startled when the memory of Natalie flashed through his mind. For the first time, however, he felt neither the pain of loss nor the emptiness of regret. Their time together would always be part of him, but it no longer blocked him from moving forward. His sadness over Elijah's and Chris's deaths seemed to dissolve as well. He felt liberated, like the shackles he'd never realized were binding him had been removed.

Rachel leaned back and brushed her bangs from her eyes. "Oh, when Sanchez heard the university offered me a place in the PhD program, she practically begged me to stay. Said she couldn't see running the lab without me."

"Well, I will need help with animal trials when I develop my new protocol."

"Exactly." A smile started at her mouth and spread to her eyes. "And I certainly don't trust you around my monkeys without me there."

The depth in Rachel's eyes that Ethan had first noticed when she sat in the front row of his class drew him in, but now he no longer resisted the feeling. He felt connected to her in a way he sensed but could not describe. The connection possessed the same quality that his two visions revealing a hidden dimension and structure to reality had.

Love, he thought. Ethan now understood in his very soul that a depth to being existed that neither science nor religion could fully encompass or explain. The everyday realities of matter and energy, the joy and the suffering of humanity, and the finitude of life itself were not the end of the story.

ACKNOWLEDGEMENTS

Although *The Jericho Deception* is completely fictional, the genesis of my novel came from the fascinating research of three scientists I have never met. First, over a decade ago, Dr. Michael Persinger, a neuropsychologist at Laurentian University in Ontario, experimented with a device that came to be known as the "God helmet." Persinger claimed that, like the Logos, his device, which stimulated the temporal lobes of the brain with electromagnetic waves, produced mystical sensations in his subjects. Subsequent research by other scientists with this technology, however, yielded inconsistent results. I am also indebted to the research of University of Pennsylvania's Professor Andrew Newberg, one of the pioneers in the field of neurotheology, the study of the interrelation of the mind and religious experience. The experiments exploring the neurological similarities of Buddhist meditation and Christian contemplative prayer that Ethan and Elijah discuss in my novel are real studies performed on monks and nuns by Dr. Newberg, which he describes in his excellent books. Finally, my interest in the psychology of mystical experiences was first piqued by the grandfather of this field, Harvard Professor William James. His 1902 masterpiece, *The Varieties of Religious Experience*, which describes the commonalities of mystical experiences across religious traditions, is still one of the most important treatises in this field.

I am also deeply grateful for the interview Yale Professor and Director of CapLab Laurie Santos allowed me to conduct with her in New Haven over a cup of coffee at Koffee (Ethan and Rachel's hangout), as well as the medical advice and background provided by neurologist and good friend Dr. Art Schiff. All inaccuracies in the novel relating to their fields are either my own mistakes or the purposeful result of my creative license as a fiction writer!

My greatest inspiration, however, comes from the two most important women in my life. My brilliant and beautiful wife, Alison, has an uncanny knack of handing me an article or pointing me to a documentary and saying, "This could make an interesting book." A *Wired Magazine* piece on Dr. Persinger that she gave me sparked my idea for this novel, while a Discovery Channel show on the mystery of the missing years in the life of Jesus led me to the plot of *The Breath of God*. My insightful and talented daughter, Ella, has a voracious appetite for thrillers that makes me wish I could write faster. For their love and infinite patience, I am forever grateful.

I'm also thankful for the unlimited understanding and support of my parents, Jeff and Eileen, and my forum friends—Malon, John, Reed, Jim, Greg, Rob, and Jay—all of whom have encouraged me to pursue my passion of writing.

Once again, I would like to thank Mark Bernstein, my publisher, and the folks at West Hills/Hundreds of Heads and PGW for making my dream a reality. My novel would also be vastly inferior without the guidance and prodding of my editors—Brooke Warner and Caitlin Alexander—both of whom challenge me to become a better writer.

Finally, to the wonderful fans of my first novel, *The Breath of God*, who have been eagerly awaiting this book: I cannot express how touched I have been by your enthusiasm. Thank you!

ABOUT THE AUTHOR

Jeffrey Small is the author of the critically acclaimed novel, *The Breath of God*, which won the Nautilus Book Award Gold Medal for Best Fiction and was hailed as a "thought-provoking masterpiece" by RT Book Reviews, "visionary fiction" by Library Journal, and "a fast-paced adventure" by Kirkus. Jeffrey is also a popular speaker on religion and spirituality in the 21st century. He graduated *summa cum laude* from Yale University, *magna cum laude* from Harvard Law School, and he holds a Masters in the Study of Religions from Oxford University in England. Active in the Episcopal Church, Jeffrey has also studied Yoga in India, practiced Buddhist meditation in Bhutan, explored the ancient temples in Egypt, and journeyed throughout the Holy Land. He lives in Atlanta with his wife, daughter, and a lovable Newfoundland that looks like a giant black bear. For more information or to contact Jeffrey, please visit www.JeffreySmall.com

ALSO FROM JEFFREY SMALL

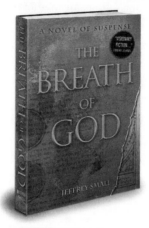

"This meticulously researched, thought-provoking masterpiece is filled with high adventure and intrigue. Based on an actual document from 1887, Small's stunning debut reveals the impact of such a find. RT Rating: 4 1/2 stars TOP PICK!"

—*RT Book Reviews*

"This tale is for fans of Dan Brown's thrillers as well as readers who enjoy visionary fiction."

—*Library Journal*

"A fast-paced adventure with a deep backdrop of religious scholarship."

—*Kirkus*

"Jeffrey Small, a Harvard/Yale/Oxford-educated speaker on religion and spirituality, makes an impressive literary debut with a thriller . . . Small's themes, such as the common ground of the world's religions, are timely."

—*Atlanta Magazine*

"Winner of the 2012 Gold Medal for Best Fiction"

—Nautilus Book Awards

"Winner of the 2012 Gold Medal for Best Adventure Fiction"
—Living Now Book Awards

"Silver Medal for Best Regional Fiction (Southeast) 2012"
—Independent Publisher Book Awards

"There is nothing better than reading a novel that exceeds expectation. *The Breath of God* is a spectacular thriller that spans the world, history, and the limits of imagination; an epic adventure that left me yearning for more."
—Richard Doetsch, author of *The Thieves of Darkness* and *The 13th Hour*

"Jeffrey Small explodes on the writing scene with his first novel and this book has Best Seller written all over it! *The Breath of God* is a riveting novel that grips the reader from the first chapter and does not let go until the last paragraph."
—*FeatureMe2 Reviews*

"In this gripping tale—played out against an intriguing international setting— East meets West, mystery meets romance, the human spirit meets the divine spirit, and the reader meets a novelist of the first caliber."
—The Honorable Raymond Seitz, Former US Ambassador to Great Britain

"A spellbinding novel, full of suspense as well as the thrills of a lifetime. Very hard to put down. It also brings religion to the forefront of the reader's mind, no matter what faith he or she follows, raising questions that have not been asked before, as well as bringing other parts of the world into the living room. Not to be missed."
—Bookloons.com

"*The Breath of God* is sure to create controversy while exploring the plausibility of an ancient legend that could tie the world's religions to each other. Mr. Small paints a colorful and realistic depiction of India that reflects the multi-faceted environment of daily existence in that country. A must-read for those that love suspense and mystery; also for those who wish to expand their knowledge of the world's religions, check out this novel."
—*The Universal Learning Series Radio Show*